Carla Cassidy is an award-winning, *New York Times* bestselling author who has written over 150 novels for Mills & Boon. In 1995, she won Best Silhouette Romance from *RT Book Reviews* for *Anything for Danny*.

In 1998, she won a Career Achievement Award for Best Innovative Series from *RT Book Reviews*. Carla believes the only thing better than curling up with a good book to read is sitting down at the computer with a good story to write.

USA TODAY bestselling author **Rita Herron** wrote her first book when she was twelve but didn't think real people grew up to be writers. Now she writes so she doesn't have to get a real job. A former kindergarten teacher and workshop leader, she traded storytelling to kids for writing romance, and now she writes romantic comedies and romantic suspense. Rita lives in Georgia with her family. She loves to hear from readers, so please visit her website, ritaherron.com

D1633939

LIVE

Also by Carla Cassidy

Desperate Strangers
Desperate Intentions
Desperate Measures
Scene of the Crime: Bridgewater, Texas
Scene of the Crime: Bachelor Moon
Scene of the Crime: Widow Creek
Scene of the Crime: Mystic Lake
Scene of the Crime: Black Creek
Scene of the Crime: Deadman's Bluff
Scene of the Crime: Return to Bachelor

Also by Rita Herron

Mysterious Abduction
Badge of Justice
Redemption at Hawk's Landing
Safe at Hawk's Landing
Hideaway at Hawk's Landing
Hostage at Hawk's Landing
Lock, Stock and McCullen
McCullen's Secret Son
Roping Ray McCullen
Warrior Son

Discover more at millsandboon.co.uk

48 HOUR LOCKDOWN

CARLA CASSIDY

LEFT TO DIE

RITA HERRON

MILLS & BOON

All rights reserved including the right of reproduction in whole or in part in any form. This edition is published by arrangement with Harlequin Books S.A.

This is a work of fiction. Names, characters, places, locations and incidents are purely fictional and bear no relationship to any real life individuals, living or dead, or to any actual places, business establishments, locations, events or incidents. Any resemblance is entirely coincidental.

This book is sold subject to the condition that it shall not, by way of trade or otherwise, be lent, resold, hired out or otherwise circulated without the prior consent of the publisher in any form of binding or cover other than that in which it is published and without a similar condition including this condition being imposed on the subsequent purchaser.

® and ™ are trademarks owned and used by the trademark owner and/or its licensee. Trademarks marked with ® are registered with the United Kingdom Patent Office and/or the Office for Harmonisation in the Internal Market and in other countries.

First Published in Great Britain 2020
by Mills & Boon, an imprint of HarperCollins*Publishers*
1 London Bridge Street, London, SE1 9GF

48 Hour Lockdown © 2020 Harlequin Books S.A.
Left to Die © 2020 Rita B. Herron

Special thanks and acknowledgement are given to Carla Cassidy for her contribution to the *Tactical Crime Division* series.

ISBN: 978-0-263-28025-8

0420

MIX
Paper from
responsible sources
FSC® C007454

FSC
www.fsc.org

This book is produced from independently certified FSC™ paper to ensure responsible forest management.

For more information visit: www.harpercollins.co.uk/green

Printed and bound in Spain
by CPI, Barcelona

48 HOUR LOCKDOWN

CARLA CASSIDY

Prologue

"I've written a short essay on the board. Why don't you all rewrite it using our secret code?" Annalise Taylor said, and watched as the three girls seated before her focused on the computers in front of them.

Tanya Walton was thirteen years old, Emily Clariton was ten and Sadie Brubaker was nine. All of them wore blue trousers and white blouses with the Sandhurst School emblem embroidered in blue and green on the breast pocket.

The girls came from different areas of the United States, but they all shared a background of abject poverty, some abuse and a lack of opportunities. Until their bright minds brought them to this unusual private school built specifically for children like them, this place where their intelligence was both celebrated and nurtured.

As the girls continued to work, Annalise walked over to the window next to her desk and gazed outside. The school was located on fifteen acres on the outskirts of the charming town of Pearson, North Carolina.

From this vantage point, the view was absolutely

breathtaking. The Blue Ridge Mountains surrounded the city. With more than a million acres of protected wilderness, there were plenty of hiking trails, secluded back roads and streams and waterfalls to explore. Right now the leaves on the trees were beginning to display the reds and oranges of autumn.

Annalise turned away from the vista and sat at her desk. She released a deep, weary sigh. It had been a long day. This class was not officially part of the curriculum, rather it was a sort of after-school club to feed the passions of these particular girls, who always looked forward to a little extra time to work and play on their computers.

A loud boom jolted her out of her mental haze, followed by another and another one. Annalise straightened. Was that…was that gunfire? What was going on? Gunfire! For a moment her brain froze in horror as the three girls screamed.

Lock the door! Push desks against it! The orders sounded in her head. That's what she was supposed to do. That's what she'd been trained to do in a situation like this.

Heart pounding, she jumped up from her seat and ran toward her classroom door. But before she could reach it, the door exploded inward and a large, burly man with a long gun stood on the threshold.

"Get down, get down," he screamed, and pointed to a wall with his automatic weapon. "All of you, sit down with your backs against the wall. Now."

"What's going on? What do you want?" Annalise asked the questions as she gathered her students close to her.

"Shut up and sit down," he demanded.

Terror ripped through Annalise as she moved the

girls to the wall where they all slid down to sit on the floor. The girls were crying and she tried to comfort them…to shush them. The last thing she wanted was for their cries to irritate the man with the gun.

What did he want? Why was he here? Just then a tall, thin man came into the room. "I thought you told us nobody else would be here except these four," he said, and gestured toward Annalise and the girls.

"That was the information I had," the burly man replied.

"Well, now there's a dead security guard in the lobby, and two dead women in the main office." He shifted from one foot to the other. "Let's go. This has all gone sideways. We need to get the hell out of here."

Dear God. Annalise's heart beat so fast her stomach churned with nausea and an icy chill filled her veins. Bert was dead? The security guard with the great smile who loved to tell silly knock-knock jokes was gone? And which two women had been killed? Who had been in the office at the time of this…this attack?

What were these killers doing here? What did they want?

The sound of distant sirens pierced the air. The big man cursed loudly.

"We were supposed to get in and out of here before the cops showed up," the tall, thin man said with barely suppressed desperation in his voice.

"Too late for that now," the big man replied. He turned and pointed his gun at Annalise. She stiffened. Was he going to kill her, as well? Was he going to shoot her right now? Kill the girls? She put her arms around her students and tried to pull them all behind her.

More sirens whirred and whooped, coming closer and closer.

"Don't move," he snarled at them. He took the butt of his gun and busted out one of the windows. The sound of the shattering glass followed by a rapid burst of gunfire out the window made her realize just how dangerous this situation was.

The police were outside. She and her students were inside with murderous gunmen, and she couldn't imagine how this all was going to end.

Chapter One

Evan Duran sat at his kitchen table, dividing his attention between his television and his phone while he sipped his second cup of coffee. It was just a few minutes before ten on a Wednesday, his day off, and he'd slept later than usual.

Normally he would be already finished with his daily five-mile run, and in the office rather than waiting this late in the morning to even get started on his run.

He paused with his mug halfway between his mouth and the table when a news alert broke into the talk show that had been on.

HOSTAGE SITUATION IN NORTH CAROLINA. The bold words scrolled across the bottom of the screen. Evan grabbed his remote and turned up the sound as the female newscaster began the story.

"Breaking news out of the small town of Pearson, North Carolina, this morning. Last night at approximately five o'clock armed men burst into the Sandhurst School. According to the latest reports, there has already been confirmed fatalities and the hostages include teachers and students. The names of the children are being withheld, but the staff inside include Annalise Taylor and Belinda Baker..."

Evan stared at the television as he slowly put down

his mug. Annalise? A hostage in a school in Pearson, North Carolina? Last he knew, she was working at an elite private college in Missouri.

It wasn't necessarily his personal history with Annalise that pulled him up from his chair and set him in motion. If there was an ongoing hostage situation, Evan needed to get there to help.

He went into his master bedroom, quickly changing out of his running clothes and into a white button-down shirt and a pair of black pants. He grabbed his jacket with TCD—Tactical Crime Division—stenciled on the back and headed for the front door.

Annalise. A vision of her exploded in his head. For two years they'd been a couple. He'd just assumed eventually they'd marry. Instead, almost three years ago she had left him. She'd broken it off with him in a text message.

He couldn't think about all the emotions thoughts of her threatened to evoke. Right now there was a hostage situation.

When it came to hostage negotiation, nobody was better than him. A fact. Not conceit.

Adrenaline rocked through Evan minutes later as he drove toward Knoxville, Tennessee, to Old City, where the TCD offices were located. While the FBI's headquarters were in DC, there were field offices all over the country.

The Tactical Crime Division was a specialized tech and tactical unit combining skilled professionals from several active divisions. Because they were smaller units they were more nimble for rapid deployment and could quickly proffer assistance to address various situations—especially in more rural areas without a large police force.

As he drove he made a few phone calls, and he finally pulled up in front of the nondescript brick building where TCD's offices were located. He parked, got out of his car and hurried inside. As he strode down the hallway toward the main meeting room, he could hear Director Jill Pembrook apparently still conducting the morning meeting.

The main conference room was the heart of the office. It was where assignments were handed out and situations were brainstormed. The agents sat at a long, highly glossed wooden table. On one wall was an oversize FBI logo, and opposite that was the TCD emblem. A large, digital flat screen was mounted on the far side of the room, and a tablet lay at the head of the table.

Evan burst through the door. Director Jill Pembrook looked at him in surprise. "Agent Duran, how nice of you to join us on your day off."

The director was an attractive, stylish woman of substance with cropped steel gray hair and a penchant for dark, custom-tailored suits.

She'd been with the FBI for over forty years, and she was definitely a force to be reckoned with. Her blue eyes could be warm and friendly or they could frost a puddle of water into a sheet of ice.

"I just saw the news out of Pearson," he stated. "I need to get there... It's Annalise."

There was a collective groan from some of the other agents. Evan ignored it. "I'll need you to arrange a plane to be ready for takeoff. Also, I'll need Hendrick's help on this. And I'm taking Agents Brennan and Lathrop with me."

"Call off the SEAL team, Duran is on the case, everyone," "Agent at Large" Kane Bradshaw murmured as the three men headed for the door.

Evan ignored him. While he liked Kane okay, there were times in the past they had butted heads when Kane could sometimes be a bit of an arrogant jerk. Director Pembrook though tolerated his glib attitude. And while Kane had no official rank as an agent with the bureau, he had an extensive background with deep black ops.

Hendrick Maynard, the tech guru nodded. "You got it," he answered without hesitation. "Heading to my desk now. I'll send you any relevant info ASAP."

The director narrowed her eyes, and Evan felt the frost radiating from her. "Agent Duran, you are way out of line." She paused and continued to hold his gaze. "Ten minutes ago North Carolina state officials called for federal help…" She paused and he was wondering if he should offer to submit his resignation. "You will also take Special Agent Rogers along with the others. This is an all hands on deck situation. Rowan as usual will accompany you and provide team support."

Rowan Cooper, an attractive woman with long dark hair who worked as a liaison between the local police departments and the TCD team members, also rose and followed the men out the door. She accompanied any crew that deployed to a different location. Her specialty was smoothing over any personality difference or turf wars among different law enforcement units on scene. But her main responsibility was arranging overnight accommodations and making sure the agents had what they needed in order to remain focused on the task at hand.

"Yes, ma'am," he replied to the director. He knew he'd overstepped boundaries by barging in, but he'd felt the need to act immediately when he'd heard about the situation… About Annalise…

"Plane leaves in twenty minutes. Now go," Director

Pembrook said. To him she added, "Duran...don't pull this kind of stunt again."

Evan would have offered to quit *after* the assignment if he met any resistance from the director to him heading up the detail due to his personal connection to Annalise. Nothing was going to keep him from negotiating this hostage situation.

"Never," Evan replied before turning to leave.

The team headed for the locker rooms where the agents had go bags of clothing and personal items since they often headed out on a moment's notice. Rowan was equally prepared for the mission. Usually she would precede the agents to any given location when assignments were handed out, but in this case there was no time.

He knew he was working with the best team and that they would resolve the hostage situation no matter what. Special Agent Davis Rogers was a former army ranger and had been with TCD for only three years, but he was a good fit. He excelled at tricky reconnaissance, among other things.

Agents Nick Brennan and Daniel Lathrop were both not only easy to get along with, but they also possessed specific skills that would make them assets.

The four of them, along with the local law enforcement officials, had to work together to end the standoff with nobody else getting hurt—or worse.

By the time he and the other agents boarded the plane, Hendrick had already sent them all an email with information about the school, along with blueprints of the building.

The school had been established five years earlier by Regina Sandhurst, the CEO of a large tech company who had grown up in the area and wanted to give back.

She believed the youth of the nation was a resource to nurture and foster.

She also believed children from disadvantaged communities needed to be fostered, and therefore the year-round school offered full scholarships to under-privileged girls who made up the student body.

The twenty-six students lived on the stately campus, and most were between the ages of nine and fourteen. Dr. Olivia Wright was the principal, and six teachers provided the daily curriculum. There was also a cleaning and cooking staff and six women who were live-in residents and looked after the students.

Evan read carefully over the information. High risk negotiation was what he did, but the stakes were always higher when children were involved. And Annalise...

Her name whispered through his head, but he shoved any thoughts of her away. He had a job to do, and it didn't matter who was being held in the school; he intended to get everyone out alive and well.

"According to Hendrick, nobody has learned what the hostage takers want." Evan broke the silence that had overtaken everyone in the plane.

"What would these people want to achieve by invading a school?" Nick asked.

"I don't have a clue," Evan replied. "According to Hendrick's notes, the school doesn't hold large amounts of cash on-site."

"Maybe they are planning to ransom off the kids," Daniel said.

"To who?" Evan countered as he continued to read the brief. "It seems most of these kids come from impoverished households." He looked up. "Let's hope by the time we touch down the local authorities will have more information for us. This situation has already gone on for a full night."

They all fell silent once again. With each minute that ticked by, the tension in the plane increased. He knew all the agents were feeling the pressure of getting this right, but ultimately as the negotiator, the weight of this situation was on his shoulders.

While there were a lot of tried and true ways to deal with a hostage taker, much of his strategy would ultimately come down to instinct as each situation was different. There was no way to prepare for what was ahead of him. He just had to be ready for anything and rely on his extensive training.

By the time the plane landed, he was pumped and ready to get to the scene as quickly as possible. They loaded into a waiting van and took off for the scene of the crime.

"Hendrick sent me some information about the Pearson chief of police," Rowan said from the front seat.

She was young for an agent, only in her early twenties. Rowan was skilled in dealing with all levels of police personnel. She was a real asset when it came to coordinating the team with local law enforcement and also skilled at clearing red tape for the agents.

"Walter Cummings has been chief of police here for the past seven years. According to the locals, he's a bit of a blowhard and showman but runs his department with an iron fist," Rowan said.

"I'm sure you'll manage him just fine," Evan said. "We're going to need the support of all the local police."

He sat up straighter in his seat as he saw the two brick buildings in the distance. The larger one housed dorms for the residents. The smaller one held the classrooms the students attended every day—even on week-ends for half days—and that was where the armed men had burst in and taken hostages.

In front of the school was a wide paved driveway. The relatively small parking lot was filled with a fleet of first responder vehicles and personnel as well as what appeared to be a large onlooker presence. Too many civilians for Evan's comfort level.

"It looks like a cluster—" Davis started to say.

The van came to a halt. "Let's get this under control," Evan said as they all exited the unmarked vehicle.

It took Evan and Rowan several minutes to work their way through the crowd and finally locate Chief Walter Cummings. He was a squat, barrel-chested man with salt-and-pepper hair and broken blood vessels across his nose and cheeks.

"Chief Cummings?" Rowan said, and held out her hand. "Rowan Cooper with the TCD. This is Special Agent Evan Duran, TCD's top hostage negotiator."

He shook Rowan's hand first, then Evan's, using a hard, viselike grip that Evan assumed was meant to be intimidating. It didn't work. "I'd say I'm glad to see you folks here, but I'll be honest. This is a matter I thought we could handle. But you know the state boys were worried about regulations—"

"The last thing we want to do is step on anyone's toes," Rowan replied smoothly. "We all have one goal in mind, right? We need to get the hostages out safe and sound and put the hostage takers behind bars."

"I'll need details about the hostages inside the building," Evan said, cutting to the chase.

The chief rocked back on his heels. "The principal, two teachers and four students, along with a security guard."

"Do you know how many hostage takers are in there?" Evan asked.

"No, I don't," he replied. "We've tried to call the main office, but nobody from the inside is talking to let us know what's going on in there. We know the security guard is dead, but we aren't sure who else might be." The chief grimaced. "Bert Epstein was a personal friend of mine. His body is there in the front doorway."

"I'm sorry you lost your friend," Evan replied, but did not have time for more than the cursory condolence. "You have a number for a phone inside the school?" Evan didn't remember whether Hendrick had sent a phone number or not.

Walter nodded and gave it to him. "It's the only number I have. It rings in the office."

"And you have no idea who the armed men are or what they want?" Evan asked. This situation had already been going on for almost twenty-four hours, and Chief Cummings didn't know anything? Was the man just that incompetent?

Walter shrugged. "No clue."

Evan looked toward the other building on the property. "I understand that is where all the students live. I'm assuming you have armed guards at the door and the place is on lockdown?"

"Affirmative," the chief replied.

"Who are all these people?" Evan asked, and swept one of his arms toward the onlookers. "There seems to be a lot of civilians just standing around." They were people who not only contributed to the chaos of the active scene but also stood a chance of taking a bullet if things went sideways. They needed to be moved out of the area immediately.

"Some of them are teachers who work at the school

and are concerned for the people who are inside. They're also townsfolk interested in what's going on. We don't usually have a situation like this," Chief Cummings explained.

"We need to move them all out of here as quickly as possible," Evan said. He looked at Rowan. "Maybe you could help the chief get some of his men together to get any civilians safely off the premises."

"Are you sure you don't need any of my input right now on how you're going to handle this?" the chief asked.

"Not at this moment," Evan replied. Right now more than anything he hoped to make contact with somebody inside. He wouldn't know how to negotiate the release of the hostages without gaining some kind of information about the people who were holding them. The most important thing was to find out why they were in the school and what they wanted in order to release the hostages unharmed.

He stared at the school. How many people were actually dead inside? Was it possible Annalise was one of the them? He could see a man's body lying prone in the front doorway. That would be the security guard Chief Cummings had mentioned.

His chest tightened. The stakes were high. If these men had already killed people, then they had nothing to lose and there was no assurance they wouldn't kill more.

IT HAD BEEN a night of hell. Throughout the long hours of darkness, men had been in and out of the room, peeking out the window and cursing. The girls had whimpered and cried, and Annalise had also heard the cries and moans of fellow teacher Belinda Baker and another student coming from the room across the hall.

Finally the girls had all fallen into an exhausted sleep, and even Annalise had managed to catch an hour or two of dreamless sleep.

But the day was upon them, a day of fear and uncertainty. "The girls need to use the restroom again," she said to the burly man who seemed to be in charge of everything. She'd heard several of the other men call him Jacob.

He whirled around from his position on a chair just to the side of the broken window and scowled at her, as if she were personally responsible for nature's call.

"Gretchen," he bellowed.

Annalise sat up straighter. Gretchen? There was a woman here with all the men? A tiny bit of hope surged inside her. Maybe she could talk a woman into letting the children go.

A woman with grayish hair fashioned into two long braids strode into the room. She carried a pistol and smiled at Jacob. "Hey, baby, did you call for me?"

"Yeah, they have to go to the bathroom. You want to take them?"

"Sure," she replied. She turned to Annalise and the children. "Up," she said curtly. "Let's go."

Gretchen was a thin older woman with light blue eyes and a careworn face. Whether she could reason with this woman was an unknown. Nonetheless, right now it felt good to get up and stretch after sitting for so long, but the situation also still felt volatile and dangerous.

The restroom was right outside the classroom and to the left. Annalise wanted to check in on Belinda and whoever might be with the fellow teacher in the room across the way, but she got no opportunity as Gretchen led them directly to the girls' restroom.

She stood just outside the door as Annalise and the

girls went inside. Alone with the girls, she wiped away tears and told them she would do whatever possible to keep them safe. "We all just have to be brave," she said.

As the girls were washing their hands, Annalise stepped out where Gretchen awaited. "Is there any way I can appeal to you to let the children go?" she said. "You'll all still have me as a hostage, but this is no place for children."

Gretchen shrugged. "Sorry. My husband is in charge of this operation and he makes the rules."

"Your husband?"

"Jacob." Gretchen's chin shot up in obvious pride. "He's the leader of the Brotherhood of Jacob, and all of us who are here believe in the path he has us on."

"A path of crime and murder?" The words snapped out of Annalise with a hint of the anger that had been festering inside her since this all began.

Gretchen stepped closer to Annalise and without warning slapped her hard. Annalise immediately raised her hand to her burning cheek as her eyes began to water. "Have some respect," Gretchen snarled.

Anger swelled up in Annalise, but she had to swallow hard against it as at that moment the girls came out of the bathroom. Besides, Gretchen had a gun and Annalise had no idea if the woman would actually use it or not. As they once again took their positions against the wall, Annalise's cheek still burned.

"Everything all right?" Jacob asked.

"Everything is fine. I just had to give the teacher a lesson in respect," Gretchen replied. The woman looked at Annalise with narrowed eyes. "Let's hope she's a fast study."

Moments later when Gretchen had left the room, Annalise glanced at the girls. Although Tanya and Emily continued to cry, it was Sadie who worried Annalise the most.

Sadie's background not only included poverty, she had also been physically and emotionally abused by her mother, a young drug addict hooked on heroin and bad men.

When Sadie had first come to the school, she had been a solemn, closed-off child who flinched each time she made a mistake. Over the past few months, Sadie had shared a lot of feelings and emotions with Annalise, creating a special bond between teacher and student.

It had been Annalise's greatest joy to watch the little girl blossom and become a precocious, giggling nine-year-old who loved hugs and reveled in her own accomplishments. Despite being the youngest, she was the brightest of the three, but at the moment none of that beautiful light shone from her eyes.

Now, she was stone-faced, her big blue eyes holding a blankness that broke Annalise's heart. What damage was this doing to her? To all the girls?

"Please let the children go," she said to Jacob. "You'll still have me as a hostage. Just let the children go."

"That's not going to happen so just shut up about it," he replied, and raked a hand through his black hair.

"What's the Brotherhood of Jacob?" she asked. She was aware that her cell phone was plugged into an outlet behind the desk and on a shelf half-hidden by puzzle books. Thankfully the ringer and notifications were turned off. So far she hadn't had a chance to get to it, but if she did get a chance she would call out and at least be able to tell the police who these people were and what they wanted. All she needed was to find out exactly why they were here and what they did want.

"We are the Brotherhood of Jacob," Jacob replied.

"We have a plan, and we intend to see it through to the end."

"Surely your plan didn't include being trapped inside this building that by now is surrounded by squads of law enforcement officers. What is it you want? Why did you come here in the first place?"

"You don't need to know anything, so just shut your trap and don't bother me." He turned back toward the window.

In the relative quiet of the building, she could hear low moans coming from across the hallway and a phone ringing. The phone had to be the one in the main office as that was the only phone in the building.

The moans worried her. She was sure it had to be Belinda, and she had to be hurt to be moaning so much. Was anything being done to help her? Who else was in that classroom with her?

Jacob turned to look at her once again. "Is there any food in this place?"

"The only thing is a snack closet in the hallway. Would you please see to it that these girls get something to eat? I'm sure they're all hungry."

The snack closet was supplied with relatively healthy food like fruit chews and prepackaged apple slices and baked goods. Granola bars were usually replenished daily. There were also some juice packs, bags of chips and candy bars.

In this situation if the girls had pretzels for breakfast, she didn't care, as long as they got something to eat.

"I thought this was all a really bad dream," Tanya whispered.

"Me, too," Emily replied.

"We're all okay. Mr. Jacob has said he'll give you

something to eat in just a little while," Annalise said softly. "What about you, Sadie? Are you hungry?"

Sadie grabbed the ends of her long blond hair and began to twirl them, a gesture Annalise recognized as an old, self-soothing action. Her blue eyes stared at Annalise as she shook her head negatively.

"Jacob, won't you please let the girls go?"

"They aren't going anywhere. What do you think is keeping the cops from storming this building right now? These girls are our golden ticket out of here."

Gretchen came back into the room. "People are complaining about being hungry."

Jacob told her about the food closet. "See to it that you throw something to these girls, too."

"Thank you, Mr. Jacob," Sadie said, surprising Annalise. Apparently Sadie was paying far more attention to what was going on around her than Annalise had initially believed.

Jacob grunted. Minutes later Gretchen returned with three packages of minimuffins. She tossed one to each of the girls. "What about Miss Annalise?" Sadie asked.

"She'll be fine," Gretchen said, her blue eyes cold as she gazed at Annalise.

Sadie frowned and looked at Annalise. "I'll share with you, Miss Annalise."

"It's okay, honey. You go ahead and eat it. I'm not hungry right now." Annalise only wanted these sweet, wonderful girls out of here. She'd do anything to get them to safety.

The morning hours crept by slowly. What did these people, these Brotherhood of Jacob members, want and how did they believe they would ever be able to somehow walk away from all this? According to what she'd heard, there were already three dead people. All she could hope for was that the girls who depended on her would get out of this safely.

The tall, thin man, named Thomas, came into the room. He'd been in and out several times throughout the night. "Jacob, some of our people are still complaining about that ringing phone," he said.

Jacob released a breath that was clearly exasperation. "Sounds like I've got a lot of whiners and complainers with me. Next thing you know you'll all be screaming like a bunch of pathetic women, and you know how much I hate pathetic women."

"Jacob, we all agreed to your original plan, but none of us signed up to get trapped inside this building for an endless amount of time," Thomas replied.

"Do you doubt our mission?" Jacob's voice thundered, and his eyes filled with a fiery glint. "Do you doubt that we are the chosen ones to follow through on this mission? Do you all doubt me?"

"Of course not." Thomas took a couple of steps backward, as if moved there by the sheer force of Jacob's voice and fierceness. "We all believe in this…we believe in you, but how long before you start negotiating our way out of this mess?"

Jacob rose from his chair, his features twisted with anger. "I'll negotiate when I think the time is right." He turned around and shot off his gun through the window. The three short blasts caused Annalise to jump and the girls to scream.

He turned and faced them. "Shut up! Stop that screaming."

Annalise pulled the girls closer to her and tried to shush them. Fear torched through her. The man was obviously volatile and unpredictable. Thankfully no return fire came from the outside.

"Stop calling that phone," Jacob yelled out the window. "If you don't stop, I'm going to start throwing out the bodies of dead little girls."

An icy chill filled Annalise. Would he really follow through on the threat? It was obvious the phone had been ringing because somebody on the outside was trying to make contact. The ringing stopped.

"How are you going to get out of here if you don't talk to anyone from the outside?" Annalise asked in frustration. "And why are you here? What do you want?"

"Nobody is talking to you, so you need to shut up and mind your own business," Jacob growled at her. "Besides, the longer they get nervous out there, the more apt they are to bargain with me."

"You know no money is kept here and most of the students come from impoverished families." There was no way the students could be exchanged for a large sum of money.

"Don't you worry about what I know," Jacob retorted.

"I'm speaking to the people in the school building. I'm Special Agent Evan Duran with the Tactical Crimes Division of the FBI," a deep voice said from a bullhorn outside.

Annalise's heart seemed to stop beating for a wild moment. *Evan...?* Evan was here? Suddenly her head was filled with sweeping memories...memories of passion and laughter, of love and of loss.

There had been a time when he'd been the love of her life—her endgame, she thought. He now held her life in his hands. She just hoped he took better care of it than she had with his heart.

Chapter Two

The gunfire coming out of the school window definitely had everyone on the outside scrambling for cover, but the good news was somebody had yelled out the window and hopefully that meant the people inside were ready to engage.

The other good news was all the civilians had been moved away from the scene, and Evan had everything in place that he needed.

He now held the bullhorn in his hand, although he stood behind a patrol car in case more bullets flew out the window and he needed to take cover.

He had considered turning off the electricity to the building to make things more uncomfortable for the hostage takers, but ultimately had decided against it considering there were children involved. They had kept the water on for the same reason.

Right now he was angry—beyond angry—that apparently somebody had been calling the school's office over and over again and that somebody had not been him, nor had they been working under his direct orders. He had a sneaking suspicion who it had been.

He turned to Nick, who was standing beside him. "Do me a favor. Find the chief of police and bring him to me."

"On it." Nick left and Evan turned his attention back at the school. The first thing he wanted to address with the hostage takers was the wounded and dead. But he hadn't had a chance to do anything before shots had been fired out of the window, along with the dire warning about throwing out bodies.

Regina Sandhurst had been out of town when this all went down, but she was expected to arrive sometime late this afternoon. Hopefully she would have some useful information for them.

"You wanted to see me?" The police chief's voice boomed from behind Evan.

He turned to face him. The chief was definitely beginning to look worse for wear. Lines of exhaustion were etched across his broad forehead, and his uniform was a wrinkled mess. He had a stain on the front of his shirt and what appeared to be crumbs from a pastry on his fingers. Rowan stood just behind him, obviously ready to smooth any ruffled feathers that might—would—occur.

Rowan knew Evan very well. He didn't suffer fools gladly and he often didn't mince words, especially when lives were on the line.

"Have you been the one calling the school phone over and over again?" Evan asked.

"Yes. I was hoping to open up a line of conversation," he replied.

"They just threatened to throw out a dead child if the ringing doesn't stop," Evan replied, and tried to tamp down his anger. "You were working at cross-purposes with me. We can't do that. Do not interfere without talking to my team first. There can only be one lead in this situation, and right now I'm it."

The chief frowned, and it was obvious he didn't

like what Evan had to say. "I'm still the chief of police around here," he began.

Rowan placed a hand on the chief's shoulder. "We certainly respect your position," she said smoothly. "Our goal is like yours…to get the hostages out safe and sound and the killers behind bars. Agent Duran is highly trained in negotiation, and we need to give him a chance to do his job."

The chief grunted and then raked a hand through his hair. "If you're sure you've got this for now, I believe I'll take off. I'll go home. It was a long night."

It was the man's way of acquiescing to Evan without losing face. "Hopefully when you get back this will all be over and the hostages will be safe," Evan replied. Things would definitely go smoother if the chief was off-site and Evan didn't have to worry about him mucking things up.

To that end Evan raised the bullhorn to his mouth once again. "I'm talking to the men in the school. Will you tell me who I'm speaking with?"

"You're speaking to the man in charge." A deep voice boomed out one of the broken windows.

Evan squinted in an effort to get a visual of the person speaking, but the man kept his body just out of sight. Daniel was a skilled sniper, and Evan knew he was already looking for a place to set up where he would have a kill shot if necessary.

"Give me your name," Evan yelled back.

"I'll tell you when you need to know who I am," the man yelled back.

"Okay. Look, I'm sure you didn't plan on or want to be in the situation you're in right now. I'd like to understand your position better. Could you tell me why you're here?"

"I'm not ready to have a conversation right now."

"I'm sure we can work something out here as long as none of the hostages are harmed. Right now I'd like for you to release anyone who needs medical help." Evan not only wanted anyone who was hurt to be released, but once that was done he needed to get the deceased out of that building.

"Why don't you back up all your officers as a show of good faith?" the gruff voice yelled from the window.

"I'd like to do that for you, but before I do could you let us get to the wounded?" Evan asked.

"We have nothing to talk about." Gunfire punctuated the man's sentence.

Evan cursed and ducked back behind the patrol car. "At least you got somebody talking to you," Davis said as he crouched next to Evan.

"It didn't do much to move things forward, but it did break the ice." Evan sighed in frustration. "I really wish we could get a name of the leader inside. With a little information on him, I might know what buttons to push. As it is, I'm working completely blind."

Davis clapped him on the back. "You'll get this right, Evan. You've gotten it right a hundred times before."

Evan nodded even as his frustration grew. There just wasn't enough information. The FBI had five negotiation techniques that had more often than not worked for Evan in past situations.

The first step was to listen to their side of things and make them aware he was listening. Unfortunately, so far they weren't really talking to Evan.

The next step was to show empathy, to let them know Evan had an understanding of where they were coming from and how they felt.

Then it was important to establish a rapport that

would get them to start to trust him. Once he'd established that trust, then they could work on the problem together and he'd recommend a course of action.

Finally, if all those steps were followed, the last step was a behavioral change on their part, a change that would hopefully have them surrender.

Unfortunately, the process didn't work well if any of the steps were skipped, and right now he couldn't even get past the first step.

"Agent Duran?" He turned at the sound of an unfamiliar female voice. Two older women approached him. "I'm Susan DeKalb and this is Lydia McGraw," the older of the two began.

"You shouldn't be here," Evan said. Taking Susan's elbow, he walked her back behind the line of fire. "Now, what can I do for you?" He frowned, not liking the fact that the two had gotten past the police officers who were supposed to be keeping unauthorized people out of this area.

"We're both teachers and we're here with another teacher, Candice Winsky. We were wondering what, if anything, we can do to help."

"Do you have any idea who the people are who stormed the school?" he asked.

"None of us have a clue," Susan said. "We were wondering what you know about this." She grabbed Evan's forearm, desperation in her light brown eyes. "Do you know who is inside? Has anyone told you what this is all about?" She dropped her hold on his arm.

"Not at this point. Has anyone interviewed you all yet?"

"No, nobody has talked to us about any of this," Susan replied.

Once again Evan was struck by how little had been

done before his arrival to secure the scene and gather information. "The best thing you can all do right now is stay behind the lines." He gestured to Nick. "This is Agent Brennan. I'd like him to interview you all. Nick, will you take care of this for me?"

"Absolutely."

As Nick led the women to a van set up specifically for interviews, Evan returned to his position by the patrol car. Not only should all of the teachers be interviewed, but also everyone who worked at the school. He'd just assumed that Chief Cummings had already begun that process, but it was obvious Evan needed to set that up with his own people. He also needed to find out who made deliveries to the school and have those people interviewed. Given that the local law officers probably did little more than handle traffic violations, the current situation was likely more extreme than they had ever handled, and they were understandably in over their heads.

He turned and stared at the building, gathering his thoughts. He had to get this right. If he screwed this up, people would die. Children were in danger.

The name of another little girl flew through his head. Maria. A deep, familiar pain ripped through him. She had been his younger sister, and he somehow felt that in saving the children in the school, it might assuage some of the guilt he carried for not being able to save Maria.

HENDRICK MAYNARD SAT in his office at TCD headquarters with his feet up on his desk and his chair reared back. Mounted on the wall straight ahead were half a dozen monitors, and three state-of-the-art computers sat on the desk before him.

The wall to his left held two large posters, despite

being against regulations, of his favorite bands frozen in performance. This little office was his space—his world—and he had to confess he liked to color outside the lines.

He'd been waiting for something…anything he could get that would help the situation in Pearson. But despite surfing the web all night long, he'd found absolutely nothing useful. Now it was up to Evan to get him something to sink his teeth into, something he could do to help the victims.

He hated that children were involved. He hated any crimes that were perpetrated against innocent kids. He personally knew what it was like to be a kid and to be helpless in a bad situation. He knew what it was like to look to adults for help and for none to be forthcoming.

He grabbed the energy drink can on the desk and took a drink. The last thing he wanted to do was fall back into old and painful memories that would help nobody.

Shifting positions in his chair, he continued to check the monitors for any sign of Evan or any of the other agents in Pearson. He knew they had a mobile van set up there with a computer directly linked to him.

Unfortunately, the four security cameras on the campus had been destroyed and now weren't recording anything. He'd checked the images right before they had stopped working, and three of them had shown nothing amiss until they'd malfunctioned. He assumed those cameras had probably been shot out from a distance.

The fourth camera had shown a black panel van approaching the school's back door. Before anyone got out of the van, that camera had been shot out, as well.

During the night another agent had come into the

office to spell him, but Hendrick had refused to relinquish his position at the computers. Evan couldn't take a break, and so neither would Hendrick. He was Evan's ride or die agent on this particular case.

Hendrick looked at Evan like the big brother he'd never had. The two men had shared many conversations, deep conversations that had touched on personal things. Evan was the only person with whom Hendrick had shared the true horror of the first ten years of his life. Evan was definitely more like family to him.

"Hey, how about some lunch? For some reason Director Pembrook thinks you might need to eat," Will Simpson said as he came into the office. Will worked as a civilian employee for TCD. He carried a tray from the cafeteria with him. "Today's special is baked pasta with garlic toast and an apple."

"Ah, ziti...the food of the gods," Hendrick replied.

Will laughed. Hendrick took the tray from him. "Thanks, man."

"Anything breaking?" Will asked, and gestured toward the computers.

"Not a damned thing. I'm thinking about doing my 'catch a perp' dance around the room except it requires a good deal of nudity and incense."

Will laughed again and shook his head. "Nothing you could do would ever surprise me, Hendrick."

"Whatever is good for the cause, man...right?"

"Right," Will replied with a wide grin. "I'll just get out of here and let you eat."

Minutes later, as Hendrick ate his meal and kept his eyes on the monitors, he marveled at where his life had taken him. He'd never really thought about being an FBI agent. He'd never thought of being any kind of law enforcement official while growing up.

When he'd been attending Harvard on a full scholarship, he'd just assumed he'd graduate with a degree in computer sciences and then maybe start his own business.

But halfway through his junior year, exceeding his teachers' expectations but bored to death with the curriculum, he'd dropped out.

He'd had no idea what he was going to do. He'd considered backpacking in Europe for a while, but that felt way too clichéd. He'd finally settled for a job with an IT company.

For the next three months, he was once again bored out of his mind. He spent his days doing his job and collecting a sizable paycheck, then at night he wrote code for all kinds of programs just to challenge himself.

When a couple of FBI agents had shown up at his front door late one evening, his first thought was that he was going to be arrested. He sometimes broke through firewalls on the internet. The bigger the company the larger the thrill. He did this just to see if he could, and he'd believed he was busted.

Instead of arresting him, to his surprise, the FBI had offered him a job. He'd landed at the TCD five years ago when he'd turned twenty-one years old. He'd never looked back.

He'd immediately felt at home here. He liked and admired the men and women who were his coworkers, but more important he felt like he'd finally found a real purpose in life. He liked using his brain and his skills for all the right reasons. He liked helping the other agents catch the criminals.

"Come on, Evan," he whispered toward the blank monitor. "Get me something."

ONE HOUR BLENDED into another and another as the girls and Annalise remained seated against the wall. Tanya and Emily napped off and on, but Sadie remained wide-awake.

"Are we going to die?" she whispered to Annalise.

"No, honey, we're going to be fine. We just need to be strong right now. Have you heard the man on the loudspeaker outside?" Sadie nodded. "He'll make sure we're all okay."

Sadie finally settled against Annalise's side and dozed off. Annalise wished she felt as confident as she hoped her words had sounded to Sadie.

Evan was a skilled negotiator, but he couldn't talk rationally and work out some sort of compromise with a madman. Evan was good, but Jacob definitely looked and acted like a crazy person, and his wife Gretchen was even worse.

Evan had been talking to Jacob over the bullhorn about every fifteen minutes, but Jacob wasn't responding. He just sat in the chair to the side of the broken window and stared out. Occasionally one of the other men or Gretchen would come in to whisper with Jacob.

It was after one man left the room that Jacob stood and stretched. "I'm going to leave you alone right now, but if you try to do anything to get away or help the girls escape, I'll shoot you without hesitation. Got it?" His dark eyes burned into hers.

She held his cold gaze and nodded. A shudder threatened to work through her as he stared at her for another long terrifying moment before he finally left the classroom.

What did he expect her to do? Stuff each of the traumatized girls out of the broken window? That would be far too dangerous. It was possible the children might be mistaken for the killers and hurt or even shot by the phalanx of armed police outside. Besides, she had no idea who might be watching out other school windows and could possibly shoot them all in the back as they tried to run for safety. No, it was far too risky.

However, with nobody watching them there were two things she needed to do. She wanted to get her phone and try to reach police or someone on the outside, and she needed to check on Belinda.

The minute Jacob left, she sprang into action. She raced across the room, grabbed her cell phone and hit 911. "I'm a hostage in the Sandhurst School in North Carolina," she said when the call connected, speaking as quickly and as quietly as she could. "My name is Annalise Taylor, and I'm here with three students in room 106 at the Sandhurst School. We're being held by a group called the Brotherhood of Jacob. They've killed three people and wounded at least one more." She then gave her phone number and hung up.

She quickly hung up, replaced her phone, then ran across the room to the doorway. She peeked out. Seeing nobody, and hearing Jacob's voice coming from another room up the hallway, she raced across to the classroom.

Belinda Baker, the math teacher, was slumped against the wall, her bloody hands holding a wound in her stomach. Next to her was ten-year-old Amanda Ingraham, another student who looked positively terrified.

"Belinda—" Annalise fell to the floor next to her fellow teacher "—how bad is it?"

"I'm not sure, but it's definitely painful." The words came in short gasps. "Annalise, you need to take care of Amanda…promise me."

"I promise, but I'm going to try to get you out of here so you can get some medical attention."

Belinda released a small laugh that transformed into a deep sob. "Good luck with that. They left me in here to die. Do they know you're in here talking to me?"

"No. Jacob left the room, so I sneaked over here."

Belinda's brown eyes widened. "Annalise, go before you get caught. You need to stay safe so you can take care of the children. Please…just go."

Annalise knew she was right, but she hated to leave the wounded woman without being able to help her in some way. She got up and ran to the closet where most teachers kept a first-aid kit. She found the metal box on the top shelf, pulled it down and then quickly ran back to Belinda's side.

Tears blurred her vision as she opened it and stared down at the contents. Bandages, antibacterial ointment, adhesive tape…things for small wounds and scrapes. There was absolutely nothing in there that could help a woman who had been shot in the stomach.

"Go, Annalise," Belinda said. "Go before you get caught."

Reluctantly she rose and shot back across the hall and slid back into her place against the wall just moments before Jacob walked back in.

Her heart pounded a million beats a minute, making her feel half-nauseous. Had her phone message been received? She'd been so frantic to get the information out she hadn't given the 911 operator a chance to say anything. Would the message find its way to Evan?

And what about Belinda? She had to do something to get the woman help. "Jacob, I know there's somebody wounded across the hall. We can hear her moans. Won't you please let her go so she can get medical treatment?"

"You need to mind your own business," he replied

tersely. "I'm not letting anyone go, and I don't want you talking to me about it again."

Annalise sighed in frustration. She sat up a little straighter as two men she hadn't seen before came into the room. How many of them were there?

The men spoke in low tones, and she couldn't hear any of the conversation. Were they plotting something? Her blood chilled as one of the men turned and looked at the girls.

Were they planning on using the girls as human shields to escape from here? Worse, were they here to take the girls for some sort of human trafficking?

No, surely not. Unfortunate as it was, there were much easier ways to grab little children off the streets. This was far too big a scheme. They were after something else, but what?

She tried to stop her imagination from running wild with horrible scenarios, but it was difficult not to think of terrible things in the position they were in and considering the man who was in charge.

One of the men left the room while the second man remained. Sadie awakened, and before Annalise could stop her, she jumped to her feet and walked over to Jacob. "Did I say that you could get up?" he half snarled at her.

"No, but I wanted to ask you if you would please get us something else to eat. My belly has been growling and growling because I'm so hungry. And what about Miss Annalise? She needs to eat, too."

"You're Sadie, aren't you?"

"I'm Sadie Louise Brubaker. What's your name besides Jacob?" she asked, her blue eyes big and wide.

"Jacob Joseph Noble. Now, Sadie, go back and sit

and don't get up again unless I tell you that you can get up. Understand?"

Sadie nodded vigorously and quickly returned to her place. Annalise wrapped her arm around Sadie, shocked by the little girl's actions.

Jacob turned to the man standing next to him. "Mick, get something for Sadie from the food closet."

"And the others, too," Sadie said. "All of us need something to eat, not just me. I'm not going to eat if everyone doesn't get to eat."

Jacob looked at her for a long moment. "Okay, Sadie, since we want to keep you happy, then Mick will get everyone something to eat."

By that time Tanya and Emily had awakened from their naps. The man named Mick left and returned a few minutes later. He had carrot sticks and apples for all of them. It was hardly a real meal, but at least it was something.

Would they all still be in here when the food closet ran out of snacks? How many men were eating those snacks beside these girls? Were Belinda and Amanda getting something to eat?

She'd hated leaving Amanda there instead of bringing her over here with the rest of the girls, but she'd been afraid of Jacob's wrath if he knew she'd gone to the other classroom.

"Do you have lots of friends here with you, Mr. Jacob?" Sadie asked.

"I got enough, and you talk too much," Jacob replied.

Annalise pulled Sadie tighter against her side. "You need not to bother Mr. Jacob anymore," Annalise said to her.

"Maybe if we're all really nice to him, then he won't kill us," Sadie replied. The matter-of-fact way the child said it made Annalise wonder how many times in the past Sadie had thought she'd be killed by the monster mother who beat her regularly.

Annalise hugged her close. "Honey, I think the best way to be nice to Mr. Jacob is if we don't talk to him unless he talks to us first."

"You think about what your teacher just told you," Jacob said gruffly.

"People in the school." Evan's deep voice sounded from outside. "We would be glad to work with you all to get the deceased removed from the premises. Just let me know how we can get that done."

Annalise tensed as Gretchen came into the room. "Hey, baby, you need to arrange for them to get the bodies out of here."

Jacob frowned. "Yeah, yeah."

"Be careful in making the arrangements. Those cops out there will kill any of us if they get half a chance."

"I know they'd like to put a bullet in my head."

She smiled at him. "We definitely don't want that. Figure out a plan that gets the dead out and still keeps us all safe." Gretchen placed a hand on his big shoulder. "Figure it out, baby. Take the trash out for me."

Annalise gasped at the woman's callous statements. Dear heaven, what had happened in these people's lives that had made them all so broken?

"Get those bodies into the school lobby as close to the main door as possible," Jacob said. "Then I want everyone in the lobby with their guns ready. If the men who come in to get those bodies try anything, we shoot them on the spot. Tell everyone to be ready and to be in position in fifteen minutes."

"Got it," Gretchen replied, and then left the room.

"Agent Duran," Jacob yelled through the broken window. "In fifteen minutes I'll allow you and two of your men to come to the front door and get the dead. I need to see that you're all unarmed. If I see a gun, we'll shoot. You start walking toward the building on my command. Got it?"

"Can we bring hospital gurneys with us?" Evan asked.

"As long as they are completely bare. I want them stripped down to the metal so there's no place to hide a gun. I'll let you know when it's time to walk." Jacob got up and left the room.

Fifteen minutes. Somehow, someway Annalise needed to make sure Belinda got out with the dead. Otherwise she feared Belinda would become one of the dead, and this might be the only opportunity she got.

"No matter what happens, you girls stay here," Annalise instructed. She had no idea what repercussions there might be for her trying to help Belinda. For all she knew she could be killed. No matter what happened, she needed to know the girls would stay in place whatever went down.

The minutes ticked by with agonizing slowness. Dusk was beginning to fall, with violet shadows seeping into the room through the window.

"Raise up your pants legs so I can see you don't have any ankle holsters," she finally heard Jacob yell out another window. Annalise got up and looked down the hallway that led to the door. Although there were several men standing there, they all had their backs to her, their attention obviously riveted to the front door in the lobby.

It was about to happen. Within minutes FBI agents would be at the front door, and it might be the only way to get Belinda out of here.

She ran across the hallway. "Belinda, you have to get up."

"I can't, Annalise." Tears fell down her cheeks. "I'm too weak and I'm in too much pain."

"You have to try. Amanda, go across the hall and sit with the other girls. You've been very brave so far, and you have to keep being brave."

Amanda got up, tears racing down her cheeks. "Is Miss Belinda going to be okay?"

"I'm going to try to help her. Now go on, honey. Go across the hall," Annalise replied.

Once Amanda was gone, Annalise reached down to Belinda. "Come on, we've got to get you up and on your feet." With Annalise's help, Belinda managed to get to her feet, although she remained crouched forward with her hands over her wound.

"What are we doing? Where are we going?" Belinda asked, and then released a deep moan.

"We're going to try to get you out of here," Annalise said.

She heard Jacob instruct the men outside to start walking toward the building. "Lean on me," she said to Belinda. "I'll help you. We need to get to the front door."

"I can't," Belinda replied.

"You have to. Now, lean on me and let's go." The woman felt fevered, making Annalise even more concerned for her.

Belinda leaned heavily on Annalise as they made their way out of the room and into the hallway. Belinda gasped as she saw the armed men with their backs to them. She stopped walking, her eyes widened with fear.

"Come on, Belinda. This is your only chance." She urged her forward once again. Annalise's heart raced.

She had no idea what was going to happen when Jacob saw them. Would he order them both shot?

It didn't matter. They had to take this chance; it might be the only one they had to get Belinda the medical assistance she needed. "Just try to be quiet," Annalise whispered.

The timing had to be perfect. The FBI agents had to be in the school lobby when Annalise shoved Belinda toward them. She stopped walking and listened to Jacob, who was yelling at the agents.

"The bodies are right inside. If you make a move to do anything but get them, then we'll shoot you," he said. "Come in slowly."

With those words, a wave of adrenaline shot through Annalise. She grabbed Belinda firmly by the arm and surged forward. She was half blinded with her need to get Belinda out of the school.

"Hey, what's going on!" one of the men exclaimed as Annalise shoved past him and into the lobby.

She got a brief glimpse of Evan, who held her gaze for only a moment, and two other men with him. She shoved Belinda toward them. "Take her, she needs medical help," she yelled.

A relieved sigh escaped her as Evan took Belinda's arm and pulled her out of the school lobby. At the same time, somebody grabbed Annalise by her hair and yanked her backward.

Pain ripped through her scalp and then shot through her back as she fell to the floor. Gretchen stood over her. She drew back a booted foot and then kicked her in the ribs. Once…twice…three times. The breath whooshed out of Annalise even as she struggled to get to her feet. She glanced back and saw no sign of Belinda.

Despite the pain that racked her, a sweet feeling of

success rushed through her. At least Belinda would get the medical treatment she needed and hopefully it would save her life.

Gretchen grabbed her up by the arm and slammed her into the wall. She placed the barrel of her gun under Annalise's chin. Annalise didn't move. She scarcely breathed.

"I should pull this trigger right now," Gretchen said. Her eyes flamed with rage.

"Gretchen," Jacob yelled from the lobby. "Take her back to the classroom. I'll deal with her later."

The woman held the gun on Annalise for another long moment, then lowered it and once again jerked Annalise by the arm. She propelled her down the hallway and shoved her into the classroom.

"Sit down, bitch, and don't move from the wall," Gretchen said.

Annalise slid down the wall next to the girls, who were all crying. "It's okay," she said to them as Gretchen left the room. "We're all okay."

She closed her eyes. Her scalp hurt where her hair had been pulled, and her body ached from the kick she'd received. She didn't know what was going to happen when Jacob came back, but no matter what she knew she'd done the right thing in getting Belinda out so she could receive medical help.

For now, all she could do was gather her strength and wait for the full consequences of her actions. She just hoped she would continue to be here for the sake of the four girls until they were freed from this hell.

ROWAN COOPER HAD dealt with a lot of egotistical, bull-headed small-town cops in her career. She'd also had to try to get along with FBI agents who could be arrogant and rigid and difficult to work with.

Evan was an agent that she not only respected, but also liked to work with. He didn't have an egotistical bone in his body, and he never made any unnecessary drama. The only negative thing she could say about Evan was his tendency for being a bit of a control freak.

He often wasn't great at delegating tasks to his fellow agents and sometimes advice fell on deaf ears, but she certainly couldn't argue with his success rate.

She didn't know how this particular trait might affect his personal life, but when he was in the field working a scene, it was generally an asset.

On this particular case, the problem wasn't Evan, but rather Police Chief Walter Cummings. He was definitely having issues when it came to relinquishing control of the situation to Evan and the other TCD agents.

She'd breathed a little easier when earlier in the day Chief Cummings had left the scene to go home and freshen up. He'd returned just in time to see Evan, Agent Rogers and Agent Brennen getting the dead and one wounded woman out of the school building. Belinda Baker had been rushed to the hospital, and sadly, the bodies of the security guard, the school principal and one other teacher had gone to the morgue.

Since she'd arrived, Rowan had set up hotel rooms for the agents and had spoken to someone from a local café about catering meals to the scene.

She had worked with Evan long enough that she knew he wouldn't take a break until this situation was resolved with the hostages free. He'd remain single-minded and focused no matter how many hours, no matter how many days passed. Then when this was all over, he would go to his hotel room and crash before returning to headquarters in Knoxville.

Her job was to do whatever was in her power to make sure the agents on the scene were well taken care of and left without any outside stress. That meant dealing with the locals. Her biggest job right now was to make sure Chief Cummings didn't do anything to interfere in the operation or undermine Evan.

She now ducked down and carried a sandwich and a bag of chips from the catering truck to where Evan sat in the passenger side of a patrol car. "Evan, you haven't had anything to eat all day long."

"I'm really not hungry," he replied.

"But you know you need to eat," she chided him softly.

He took the food from her. "Thanks, Mom," he replied. His teasing smile lasted only a moment before it was gone and he once again focused on the school building.

Complete darkness had fallen, but the entire area was lit up like daytime thanks to dozens of powerful floodlights. The school was dark except for the occasional glow of a flashlight inside.

"This one is tough, Ro," he said softly. "We're this far into it, and I still don't know what they want. At least if they were making demands I'd have something to work with."

"Thankfully, you managed to get the injured teacher out of there, along with the deceased," Rowan said.

Evan frowned and was silent for a long minute.

"You'll get this right, Evan. You always do," she said with confidence. "Let me know if you need anything else, and I'll see you later."

She remained ducked down and moved away from

the scene. She mentally groaned as she spied Chief Cummings beelining for Evan. *What now*, she wondered.

"Chief Cummings," she shouted, hoping to intercept the man before he got to Evan. She ran over to him.

He held up a hand as if to ward her off. "I've got important information to give to Agent Duran."

Rowan bristled at his dismissive gesture but kept her cool. "What kind of information?"

"A 911 call that came in earlier." He held a piece of paper clutched tight against his chest, and in his other hand he held something wrapped in foil. "I have the transcript of the call right here, and it's something Agent Duran needs to see right away."

Rowan followed behind the chief, hoping that whatever he had in his hand was worth bothering Evan. "Agent Duran, Chief Cummings has some information for you," she said.

Evan frowned at the lawman. "What is it?"

Chief Cumming's chest puffed up with obvious self-importance. "Earlier in the day 911 received a call from a hostage inside the school. She said she and three students are in room 106, and the group who are holding them are called the Brotherhood of Jacob. The call was made by Annalise Taylor and she gave us her number. She said her ringer and notifications are turned off."

Evan took the paper from Chief Cummings and frowned. "Why are we just now getting this information? This call came in much earlier."

"To be honest, I don't know what the holdup was in getting this to us. I'm investigating that now," Chief Cummings replied. "Oh, and this is for you." He held out the aluminum-foil-wrapped item. "A little peace offering. My wife is a hell of a baker. She always says that talent was what kept her from being beaten when she was in foster care. Anyway, it's cranberry and orange bread and she loves giving her baked goods to people I work with."

Rowan held her breath, waiting to see if Evan was going to lose his temper. Thankfully, he murmured a thank-you to the chief, took the bread and then he headed for the mobile van which had arrived early that morning from a nearby FBI office. The van was equipped with all the communication equipment necessary to stay in touch with Hendrick and anyone else they might need to bring this to an end. Rowan was even more grateful that the chief didn't follow Evan, but instead headed back to his squad car.

Chapter Three

Evan had managed to keep his emotions in check and off the fact that Annalise, the woman he had once been deeply in love with, was one of the hostages.

When they had gone in to get the deceased and she'd suddenly appeared, pushing the injured Belinda Baker into their arms, he'd wanted to reach in and grab her out of there, as well.

Then she'd been yanked backward by her hair and out of sight, and Evan had fought against a blinding rage and fear for her. He'd been surprised by the bravery she'd shown to get a fellow teacher help, but he could only hope she was okay now.

In that instant of seeing her again, with her long blond hair loose around her face and her piercing green eyes holding a desperate appeal, he'd wanted to scream to her to run to the safety of his arms.

Annalise had been the second most devastating loss in his life. The first one had forever changed who he was at his core. Losing Annalise, though, had left deep scars on his heart, scars that even after all this time had yet to completely heal.

His mind snapped into sharper focus. He couldn't think about the past right now. He had a job to do that would need his careful attention if the hostages had any hope of walking out unharmed from the horrible situation they were in.

The Brotherhood of Jacob…the name rang a vague bell in his head, but he couldn't access why. At least he finally might gain some information to help him negotiate a way out for those inside.

He hurried to the mobile van, and once inside he tapped on the keys of one of the computers and Hendrick appeared on the screen.

"Evan, talk to me, man," Hendrick said.

"I need you to drop all the other searches you're doing right now and find out everything you can on the Brotherhood of Jacob," Evan replied.

"On it," Hendrick replied, and Evan could hear the immediate clacking of computer keys. He left the van, knowing Hendrick would text him to let him know when he had the information to share.

When they'd gone in to get the deceased, he'd tried to gather as much information as he could. He'd counted six men—maybe seven—and one woman in the lobby, more than enough to guard the two doors in the building. Each one had been armed with either long guns or pistols. They definitely had plenty of firepower.

He returned to his position next to the patrol car and pulled out his phone. At least with Annalise's number, they now had a way to communicate with somebody on the inside. He punched in the number Annalise had given to the authorities and then texted.

Annalise this is Evan. I know you can't answer your phone. Whatever information you can get out to us will be helpful. Let us know you are all ok. We have a whole team working to get you all out safely.

He hesitated a moment and then added, Remember the moon.

He hit the send button and then cursed himself. Why had he felt the need to add that last line? He told himself it was because he wanted her to think of something happy, if only for a moment, while being held hostage.

He believed she had been happy on the night they had shared a midnight picnic in his backyard beneath a full moon. He frowned as another image filled his head and he remembered that moment when she'd been pulled by her hair out of the school lobby.

Was she okay? Had she been badly beaten or worse? Before he could continue with these dark thoughts, he picked up the bullhorn. "People in the school…will you tell me why you're here and what you want so we can bring this situation to a successful end for all of us?"

"People are trying to sleep. I don't want to hear you yapping all night long," the familiar deep voice yelled out the window. "We had to listen to the damned phone ringing all last night. I don't want to hear anything tonight."

"If you walk out of there right now, we can offer you comfortable beds for the remainder of the night," Evan replied. Of course those beds would be in a jail cell.

"Nobody is walking out."

"Can you tell me what you want? I'd really like to work with you," Evan said.

"If you want to work with me, then leave the area. Get all the police out of here."

"You know I can't do that," Evan replied. "Maybe if you release a hostage or two—or at least the children—we could see about moving some people back."

"I'm done talking to you for the night." Gunfire punctuated the words.

Evan cursed. The man was so unpredictable and so uncooperative. He turned and smiled grimly at Daniel as the FBI sniper approached him.

"I've got a spot behind that tree over there where I have a perfect visual of the window where the boss man is located. But he's been very good at staying out of the line of fire," Daniel said. "He's obviously savvy enough to expect a sniper."

"Right now I'm not ready for you to deliver a kill shot," Evan replied. "I'm still hoping I can negotiate everyone out of there. I now have some information that might move things forward."

"I just wanted to let you know I'm set up and ready. Sooner or later he'll make a mistake and I'll get my shot. All I need from you is the go-ahead."

Evan clapped Daniel on the back. "Right now I'm waiting to get more information about this group. I'll let you know if and when I'm ready for you to act."

When Daniel left, Nick walked over to Evan. "Maybe we should go over the blueprints of the school that Hendrick sent us again. Maybe we missed something… some way for us to get inside and get the hostages out."

Evan frowned. "I've already looked at them half a dozen times. They're pretty simple…one door in the front and one door in the back, which makes it pretty easy for just a couple of men to guard from the inside. There's no basement, and right now there is no way to get close enough to the building to get any of our men on the roof. I am thinking that maybe under the cover of night, I might try to get to the van parked by the back door and move it away from the school."

"That would take away any form of transportation they have out of here, although they'd be stupid to attempt to drive it away with the heavy police presence surrounding the area."

"Yeah, but desperate people do desperate things," Evan replied. His phone buzzed with an incoming text message and he read it. "I've got to go," he said to Nick and then hurried toward the mobile van. Hendrick had information.

HENDRICK LEANED FORWARD in his chair, his hand going to a squishy plastic ball he sometimes used for stress relief. And discovering what he had about the Brotherhood of Jacob had sent his stress level through the ceiling.

He now looked at Evan on his computer screen. "The Brotherhood of Jacob was founded eight years ago by a man named Jacob Noble."

"What kind of organization are they?"

Hendrick frowned at his fellow agent. "It has all the markings of a cult masquerading as some sort of church and charity." Old memories slashed through Hendrick's mind, memories of pain, of endless hunger and never-ending fear.

He shook his head to dispel them and released his grip on the squishy ball. Right now more than anything he needed to stay focused and get as much information to Evan as possible.

"They have a membership of about thirty men, fifteen women and ten children. They all live on an off-the-grid compound in the mountains just outside of Pearson. Several of the men have been arrested for a variety of crimes that include bank robbery, stolen firearms, domestic terrorism and murder. But Jacob Noble has no criminal record to date."

Hendrick drew a deep breath and then continued.

"Their mission statement is to end world hunger and return power to the righteous."

"And let me guess…this Jacob gets to pick who is righteous," Evan replied dryly. "What can you tell me about Jacob Noble's background?"

"Not much," Hendrick replied. "He was born to poor and modest parents on a farm outside of Raleigh. He married Gretchen Owens three years ago, and I haven't been able to find out much about her. Most of the information I've gained is from Jacob speaking in his official capacity as leader of the group. It looks like they recruit new members by taking to the streets to reach out to people."

"Do you have any more names of the members for me?"

"Only a couple." He told Evan the few names he'd been able to dig up. "For the most part, there seems to be a lot of secrecy surrounding the members, the group and the compound itself. I'm just now starting to dig into the financials to see what might be there, and I'll continue to try to dig into Jacob's background. If I find any other information that will help, I'll be back in touch."

"Thanks, Hendrick."

"Evan, if this man is truly the leader of a cult, then he's a complete narcissist. He'll have made many wonderful promises to the members, and he's probably very charismatic."

"He's definitely not showing much of that particular personality trait right now," Evan replied dryly.

"He's probably angry that he's not in control right now and he's only going to get angrier. Evan, whatever it takes…get those children out of there," Hendrick said fervently.

"I'm working on it. This info will hopefully help." With a murmured goodbye, Evan disappeared from view.

Hendrick continued to stare at the screen as the memories he'd fought off earlier washed over him again. He had been born into a cult and for the first ten years of his life had lived in a compound just outside of Little Rock, Arkansas.

His first memory was of the hunger. The rules of the cult were that the men ate first, women second and then the children were fed whatever was left. And there was never enough food.

There had also been very little love. Children lived separately from their parents, the boys in one house and the girls in another. While his father had occasionally sneaked hugs to Hendrick, his mother had followed the strict guidelines set by the leader, Father Timothy, of no personal interaction.

Hendrick would see his mother out working in the gardens, and as a young boy he'd yearn for her. He wanted her to wrap her arms around him and tell him he was loved. He desperately wanted her to smile at him with love in her eyes, but she remained distant and true to the discipline of the cult.

There were rules for every minute of every day. You woke, you worshipped and you worked long hours. There was not supposed to be any idle chatting among the members, and a punishment always involved physical and emotional pain. Rules changed on a whim, and often even the adults were disciplined for breaking the rules. It was a terrifying way to live.

He was also shocked when he was eight to learn that he had a six-year-old little sister named Elizabeth. He'd immediately gotten close to her. They would whisper together whenever they found themselves working side by side. He tried to protect her from the harsh existence that was everyday life. He sneaked her extra food and hugs. He'd loved her, and he'd believed she loved him back.

She'd been so sweet and in trying to protect and take care of her, Hendrick had taken many beatings. It was after a particularly vicious beating when he'd been ten that his father had come to him in the middle of the night with a plan to escape.

Even though Father Timothy assured them all that the armed guards surrounding the compound were to keep people out, in truth they were there to keep people inside. But Hendrick's father had found a weakness in the security, and that night he intended to exploit it to get his family out.

However, Hendrick's mother and sister had refused to leave. They had chosen the cult over their family. His mother had chosen the cult over him. Hendrick still had plenty of emotional baggage where his mother's total abandonment was concerned.

He sucked in a deep breath, realizing he'd been holding it as his dark memories had raced through his mind. He swiped his hands down the sides of his face, shocked by the light sheen of sweat there.

Remembering his childhood always unsettled him. He was twenty-six-years old, and he'd spent much of the past sixteen years not allowing anyone to dictate much of anything about his life. He'd had enough rigid rules and pain in his first ten years of life.

It had taken a long time for his father and him to figure out how to live out in the real world. It had also taken a long time for Hendrick to forgive his father for being in the abusive cult and the two to develop a good relationship.

If the Brotherhood of Jacob was anything like the cult he had endured, then he knew the lives of the hostages weren't worth anything. They could easily be sacrificed on the altar of the madness that drove the people who held them.

EVAN STOOD IN the wooded area in the back of the school where dozens of local police officers were stationed. He stared at the black van parked by the back door. Even though Davis and Nick had both volunteered to attempt to move it, Evan knew it was dangerous, and he wasn't going to let anyone do it but himself.

The lights surrounding the building suddenly went dark, just as Evan had arranged. However, he didn't intend to make a move for at least another hour or two.

He was making a calculated guess that nothing would happen with the group in the school during the unexpected lights out. He was hoping they were all tired and hungry and not as alert as they had been earlier in the day.

Moving the van away from the building wasn't an absolute necessity, but with it taken out of the equation it would be one less thing for him to worry about.

From his left he could hear a couple of the police officers talking softly. The clicking and whirring of night insects surrounded him, and a rustle in the brush behind him indicated the presence of a rabbit or other small animal.

Thankfully the moon overhead was mostly hidden by cloud cover, and he'd exchanged his white shirt for a black pullover that Rowan had obtained for him. Even in the dark, Evan could hot-wire a vehicle within minutes.

As he waited for the darkness to deepen, he once again thought about Annalise. It had been almost three years since she'd left him. A job offer took her to a different state, and while he wanted to make the long-distance relationship work, she didn't. He hadn't expected to ever see her again. He certainly hadn't expected to see her being dragged by her long beautiful hair by hostage takers in a school under siege.

The last thing he needed was to let his emotions get hold of him. One of his strengths had always been his complete control over his emotions.

He once again focused on the task at hand. He'd been afraid to raise the bullhorn again after he'd been warned not to, but first thing in the morning he would begin a new approach in an effort to get this situation to a satisfying end. The conversations would be different now that Evan had a little knowledge about the group. Hopefully he would be able to connect better with Jacob Noble and the members of his group.

It was about 2:00 a.m. when he decided to make his move on the van. He used his radio to alert everyone that he was going in, and then drew a slow deep breath that turned him into a machine with a job to do.

He crouched and raced as fast as he could toward a tree that was halfway between the police line at the edge of a wooded area and the van. When he reached it, he slammed his body to the ground and waited and watched.

He saw no movement from the back of the school where there were six broken-out windows. Maybe nobody was manning this back side of the building during the night.

There was no cover between the tree and the van. Once he left the safety of the tree trunk, he would be completely exposed and vulnerable. He drew another deep breath, resumed a low crouch and then slowly moved toward the van.

He hadn't gone far when shots rang out. Bullets whizzed by him, and once again he hit the ground. More shots came from the school building, and the police presence behind him returned fire in an attempt to provide him cover.

Hoping he wouldn't be shot by the hostage takers or friendly fire, he slithered like a snake back behind the police line at the edge of the woods where Davis waited for him.

The broad-shouldered African American frowned at him. "You shouldn't have taken on that job yourself, man," he said. "I know you like to control your scene, but if you get hurt, those hostages are screwed. We don't have another hostage negotiator just hanging around."

"Right now I'm just frustrated that it was an epic fail," Evan replied with frustration. "They're more alert in there than I thought they would be after all this time."

"Maybe you should see about getting some sleep while you have a chance," Davis said.

"Yeah, you're probably right." Minutes later the lights were back shining on the building, and Evan was back in the passenger seat of the patrol car. He leaned his head back and closed his eyes, fighting off not only weariness, but also a deep frustration.

When they had arrived here earlier in the day, he'd hoped to get the hostages out by nightfall. He was disturbed that hadn't happened.

He could only hope that when morning came Jacob would be more agreeable to having a conversation that would see the safe release of the hostages.

If that didn't happen, Evan would need to consider other, more dangerous options. That thought kept him awake for a very long time.

Chapter Four

The gunfire coming from the back of the building jolted Annalise. Thankfully the noise hadn't awakened the girls, who were likely too emotionally and physically exhausted.

She raised her hand and touched her swollen lower lip. When Jacob had come back in the room after she'd gotten Belinda to safety, he'd backhanded her hard enough to rattle her brain. She'd just been grateful that he hadn't killed her.

She had a feeling the only reason that she was still alive was to deal with the girls and keep them as quiet as possible.

Once the gunfire began, Jacob cursed and ran out of the room, and Annalise took the opportunity to run to her phone and snatch it off the charger. She returned to her place against the wall, her heart banging unsteadily as she held the phone tightly in her hand.

When the gunfire stopped, Jacob didn't return and she could hear him yelling in a room down the hallway. She pulled her phone up so the screen was visible.

She had one message. She opened it and read the note from Evan. Thank goodness the 911 call she'd made had gotten through to him. It gave her some solace knowing that of all the people in the world, her life and the lives of the girls were in his hands. She knew just how good he was at what he did, how utterly devoted he was to the job.

Remember the moon.

Tears blurred her vision as she read those words. They were tears of exhaustion and the sweet memory of tremendous love. *Remember the moon.* She wondered why he had texted that to her. Even as she thought about it, she realized the answer was probably that he wanted her to have a happy thought to help her through this horrible ordeal.

And the memory of that night under a full moon in his backyard was more than just a happy place in her heart, it was a place of warmth and love with the man who, at that time, she'd believed would be her partner through life.

She looked toward the doorway, wondering how much time she had before Jacob came back into the room. Maybe he wouldn't return for the rest of the night. She'd seen a weight of exhaustion riding his big shoulders. She suspected there weren't enough men with him to rotate the guard duty at all the doors and windows and also get enough sleep. Maybe this was the night the leader of this group would find someplace in the building to hole up and sleep until morning.

The phone burned in her hand. Her need to reach out to Evan and hear his voice was nearly overwhelming, but so was her fear of somehow getting caught.

Jacob was already angry with her about Belinda. If he caught her with the phone talking to the outside authorities, she wasn't convinced that Jacob wouldn't kill her, or get his wife to do the dirty work. If that happened, then who would be here to protect the girls? Who would soothe them when they cried?

She began to softly hum, her gaze going once again to the doorway. She looked back at the phone and Evan's message, and her fingers hit the phone icon.

He answered before the first ring had completely finished. "Annalise."

She squeezed her eyes tightly shut at the sound of his familiar deep voice. "Evan," she whispered into the phone, and once again kept her gaze on the doorway.

"Are you all right? Are you safe to talk?" His voice held the same kind of urgency that sizzled through her body.

"I'm okay…and I'm safe for now. There are four students with me and we're all okay. We're hungry and tired and just want to get out of here." Tears blurred her vision. "Is Belinda okay? Have you heard anything about her condition?"

"I'm sorry, I haven't, but I know she's in the hospital where she belongs."

"They didn't even want to release her, but I was afraid if I didn't get her out of here, she would have died."

"I saw somebody grab you by your hair…were you hurt?"

"No, I'm okay," she said, and then ran her tongue over her swollen lip. "Jacob is crazy, but his wife, Gretchen, is pure evil."

"Annalise, do you know what these people want? Have you heard a reason why they burst into the school in the first place?"

"I don't know what they want. I've asked and asked, but I don't know what they want or why they're here," she replied helplessly. She wished she had the answers so Evan would have the information he needed to do his job.

"I'm using every resource I have to get you all out of there safely," he said. "You just need to be patient and stay safe."

"I know. I just want these girls out of here. If you can get them to release any hostages, it's got to be the girls who get out."

"I want you all out safely," he replied. He asked her several more logistical questions. Then, "I couldn't believe it when I heard you were in there. I thought you were teaching at a college in Missouri."

"I was, but I got this offer to work here and I needed a change. These kids…oh Evan, they are wonderful. They are so bright and so loving."

"Uh… I have to ask this next question… Do you have a spouse we need to contact for you?"

"No significant other." She looked toward the doorway to assure that she was still safe to talk. There were so many questions she wanted to ask him. They were personal questions that had no place in what was happening right now.

"Evan, are we going to get out of here?"

"We'll do whatever it takes to make that happen." She could hear the determination in his voice.

She pressed the phone more closely to her ear and made sure the girls were sleeping. "Evan, I'm scared." The words fell from her lips before she'd fully realized they were in her head. "I'm trying to act so brave for the children, but inside I'm just as terrified as they are."

"Annalise, I want you to stay afraid. It might be that fear that keeps you on your toes and alive," he said.

"I always hated it when you were blunt with me," she

replied with a panic-stricken laugh. A short, awkward moment of silence ensued.

In that moment flashes of the times they'd shared together swept through her mind. He'd always made her feel like a sexy, passionate woman whenever he'd gazed at her with a hunger in his dark brown eyes.

Their backgrounds couldn't have been more different. He had grown up poor and on the streets of the Bronx while she came from wealthy, nurturing parents in Knoxville. A chance meeting in a coffee shop in Knoxville had been the beginning of a two-year relationship that had ended with her making the difficult, but necessary decision to leave him, and ultimately she'd taken the job offer in Missouri to make the break a clean one.

"Are you still there?" His voice broke through the memories.

"For now, but if Jacob comes back I'll need to disconnect quickly. He has no idea I have the phone, and he's got a nasty temper. His wife's is even worse."

"For God's sake, Annalise, don't take any unnecessary chances."

"I know it's been a long time, but maybe you could give me a big hug when I get out of here?" Tears once again burned at her eyes. "I'm sorry, I sound so pathetic."

"You don't. You just need to stay strong until that can happen."

"I'm working on it."

"Can you tell me if there are any weaknesses in the guards, anyplace or anything we can exploit to get you all out of there?"

"I know they didn't plan for this. They wanted to get in and out for whatever reason before any police arrived. They're eating snacks we keep in here for the students, but that isn't going to last long. I also think there's some in-fighting among the group."

"That's all helpful to know. Anything else?"

She frowned thoughtfully. "I can't think of anything."

"That's okay. You're doing a great job," he said encouragingly.

She leaned her head back against the wall. "Evan... I'm sorry about how things ended between us."

"I have a lot of regrets, too," he replied softly. "I..."

She heard footsteps approaching from the hall and hit the disconnect button on the phone. She slid it under her thigh just before Jacob walked into the room.

He turned and stared at her with narrowed eyes. Although there were no lights on in the classroom, he was visible from the bright lights shining in from the outside. "I thought I heard talking in here."

Her heart banged against her ribs beneath his suspicious glare. "I was humming to myself. It's how I self-soothe in a stressful situation."

Dear God, she hoped he bought it. If he didn't, and for some reason he made her stand up, then he would find the phone. She held eye contact with him as her heart continued to race and finally he grunted. "Don't do it again," he warned, and then headed to his chair near the window.

She released a shuddery sigh of relief and felt the burn of the phone beneath her leg. It was her lifeline to the outside...to Evan.

Once again she leaned her head back and closed her eyes. Images of Evan chased through her mind, images of happy times they had spent together.

She'd known the very first time she'd seen him that

he was going to be somebody special in her life. It had been a Saturday morning, and she'd been getting a coffee in her favorite café. The shop was crowded, but she'd managed to claim one of the small, round tables near the front window.

The minute she'd seen him walk in, her heart had jolted. She couldn't help but notice how good-looking he was. When he'd approached her and asked to share her table, she'd readily agreed. That day they had spent two hours talking together.

She finally drifted off to sleep and dreamed of the midnight picnic under the full moon. He'd surprised her that night. He'd picked her up at her apartment at dusk and then had taken her to his backyard, where he had a blanket spread out on the close-cropped lawn. He'd had chicken salad sandwiches and fresh strawberries, chunks of her favorite cheese and champagne.

In her dream she was in his big, strong arms and he was kissing her with all the passion of a man in love. She'd believed he loved her as she did him. She had believed on that night they would eventually get married.

She awoke suddenly, unsure what had roused her. Darkness still filled the room and she heard the heavy, deep breathing of Jacob. She released a deep sigh. Not only had love not been enough to keep her and Evan together, but now she had to face the real possibility that she'd have no future…the possibility that she wouldn't get out of here alive.

HEARING ANNALISE'S VOICE filled with such fear had shot arrows of pain through Evan. Hearing her voice had also renewed the deep ache he'd felt when she had left him. It had taken him a very long time to get over her. If he was honest with himself, there were days and nights he still didn't think he was quite over her.

But he couldn't focus on the past. Still, for the past nearly three years he'd been haunted by the what-ifs. Regrets? Hell yes he had regrets. He spent the rest of the night thinking about those regrets as he also processed the information she'd given him…information that might help bring this situation to an end.

It was good that there was a limited food source, and it was definitely good if the hostage takers were fighting among themselves.

While he waited for the darkness of night to pass, he gathered his thoughts for the emotional assault he intended to launch at daybreak.

He could have used the bullhorn and bellowed at them all night long, but he hadn't trusted Jacob not to lose it completely. He'd threatened to toss out dead little girls when a phone had rung all night. Evan didn't want to give him a reason to go off about being shouted at all night long.

Meanwhile, Chief Cummings was badgering him for an all-out attack on the building, something Evan feared might result in the injury or death of the hostages if not also official personnel. He finally had a name and some information about the group to use, and he also believed the hunger issue might bring this all to an end before force needed to be used.

Was his hesitancy with the option of using force to go in because he knew Annalise was inside? Was he allowing that fact to influence the decisions he needed to make? No, it didn't matter who was in that building; force was always the very last option used in any hostage case.

Evan could be very patient. He knew that was one of

his strengths as a negotiator. He'd rather get this done right than get it done fast. Chief Cummings was just going to have to live with the decisions made. If he tried to do anything behind Evan's back, Evan would see the man brought up on charges.

He hoped Annalise would get an opportunity to speak to him again, but the rest of the night passed without any more contact. As always, one of his fears was that she had or would get caught with the phone.

The standoff had begun on a Tuesday with the locals, and within hours it was going to be Thursday morning. That meant the armed men had been in the building for two nights and days with only snack food to eat. Surely that food was running out. It wouldn't feed grown men for an indefinite amount of time.

Regina Sandhurst had arrived at the scene earlier in the evening. She was a petite brunette whose main residence was in New York, but she also had a condo in Pearson and had assured them that she would remain here until the hostages were free.

She had tried to be as helpful as possible, but she had no clue what the people in the school might be after. She brought with her a list of all the deliveries that were made on a regular basis to the school, along with a list of everyone on staff. She'd left for her condo at dusk with the promise to be back this morning.

He heard from Hendrick once again with information about some of the financials of the group. So far everything appeared to be aboveboard, but the tech guru was still chasing down a few things. Evan knew if anything was hidden, Hendrick would find it. The man matched Evan in his passion and commitment to his job.

It was just after dawn when he picked up the bullhorn once again. "Jacob Noble and men in the school. I understand the goal of the Brotherhood of Jacob is to end world hunger. That's a wonderful goal to be pursuing."

"Is this the part where you try to be my friend so I'll give up?" Jacob yelled out the window. "Sorry, Agent Duran, I'm not buying what you're selling. I don't want to be your friend."

In another circumstance Evan might have unarmed himself as a show of good faith, and he would attempt to walk to the building for an up close and personal meeting with Jacob.

But the fact that he was so quick to fire his weapon indiscriminately with no provocation at all kept Evan from attempting it. As Davis had reminded him earlier, a dead hostage negotiator certainly wouldn't help matters.

"I want you to scale down and back up the police presence, and I need a bulletproof van for our use," Jacob yelled.

"It would take me some time to arrange something like that," Evan replied. "How about you let all the hostages go, and I'll see what I can do to accommodate you."

"You accommodate me, and then we'll talk about letting the hostages go. This conversation is now over." He fired a burst of bullets out the window.

"Big surprise that he wants a bulletproof van to get out of here," Nick said. He was a good man with a family of his own. Evan had worked with him several times before and admired the man's dedication to his wife and kids and the job.

"Don't they all," Evan replied dryly. "But sooner or later they're going to get hungry. According to Annalise, they've been eating snacks that were there for the students, but they won't last long."

"At least you have some leverage there," Nick replied.

"Yeah, I just hate the idea of those kids being hungry." And Annalise—he couldn't imagine what she was going through. He also couldn't allow his thoughts to dwell on her. He had to keep all his emotions in check to do the best job possible. Thoughts of Annalise and his relationship with her would only be distracting.

As Nick moved away, Evan raised the bullhorn once again. "People in the school, I'm sure you all must be getting hungry. If you want some food brought to you, then all you need to do is release the hostages."

There was a long silence, and then Jacob's gun came out the window. "I'm not releasing any of the hostages, and we're doing just fine in here. All you need to do is move back your men and get me an armored van."

"I told you I'm not working on that for you until the hostages are released," Evan replied.

"You've got this all backward. I'm the one in charge here," Jacob yelled. "Do what I ask, and I'll let the hostages go."

"Maybe some of your men would like some egg sandwiches," Evan replied. "I'm sure that teacher and the four little girls you have in there are getting hungry. Maybe your wife would like a hot breakfast sandwich, too."

This time there was a longer pause. Evan imagined Jacob was wondering just how much information the authorities knew about what was happening inside the school. He probably figured Belinda would have given Evan information about who was inside and that Jacob's wife was one of the hostage takers.

"Jacob, I'd like to understand what your goal is. Could you tell me why you went into the school? How were you looking to advance your goal by forcefully entering the school? If I understand your position better, then maybe we can agree on some things."

"You don't need to understand anything," Jacob replied.

"The offer for food still stands," Evan yelled. "Release the hostages, and a hot breakfast will be delivered to the doorstep."

Suddenly Jacob fired out the window. "Shut up about the food. I'm not interested in anything but you getting me an armored van and promising me and my people safe passage out of here, and that's all I got to say to you."

"We're talking in circles, Jacob. The only way I can even think about doing that is when the hostages have all been released," Evan replied. "Maybe you could release a couple of hostages to show your good faith. After that happens we can talk about how you and your men can get out of the school."

Silence.

The silence wasn't necessarily a bad thing. What he hoped was happening was that some of the men were trying to talk some sense into Jacob. Annalise had suspected some in-fighting, and Evan definitely wanted to exploit that. He was hoping that hunger was what would ultimately drive a wedge between Jacob and his followers.

His phone rang. Annalise was on a video call. He answered it. He'd only had a quick glimpse of her before, but now he was rendered speechless as he drank in the sight of her.

Her blond hair was longer than it had been the last time he'd seen her, but her eyes were just as green. His chest tightened as he saw her red, swollen lower lip.

She wore a pink blouse that looked rumpled, but he

couldn't dwell on how she looked. Instead, he focused on her surroundings.

Behind her was a plain white wall that gave no clue as to exactly where she and the children were in the room. Thankfully she'd already told him they were seated against the south wall in the classroom. The school faced north.

"Evan…" she said softly, and her eyes filled with tears.

"What happened to your lip?" he asked as a small knot of anger tightened his chest.

She shook her head. "It was the price I paid for getting Belinda help. It's no big deal."

It was a very big deal to him. It let him know that Jacob not only had the ability to kill when he thought necessary, but he'd also rough up the hostages as he saw fit. "Are you sure you're safe to talk?"

She nodded. "For now it's okay. They're all in another room, and I can hear them arguing. Some of the men want to give up. They're hungry and afraid."

"That's a good thing," he replied. "How are you and the girls doing?"

"We're all hungry and tired of being here, but we're hanging in."

He could see the deep exhaustion in her eyes, and he ached for her and the children he knew she was comforting to the best of her ability. "I'm doing everything possible on my end."

She smiled. "I know. It gives me great comfort to know that the best hostage negotiator in the world is on the case."

He'd believed he'd moved on from her, from what had been them, but that smile of hers shot a rivulet of unexpected heat through him. God, he wanted her, he wanted all of them out of there.

"I just want you to stay safe until I get you out of there," he said. "Whatever you do, don't get caught with the phone, Annalise. Jacob will get more and more desperate and angry as he continues to lose control of everything."

"We're being smart," she replied. "Sadie has been helping me by acting as a lookout so I can get the phone off and on the charger. Right now I can still hear the men yelling and arguing with each other. I just… I just needed to see your face."

"It's good to see you, too." He swallowed against a rise of emotions and reminded himself that emotions had no place in this environment.

"I like the beard. It looks good on you," she commented.

"Thanks."

Her smile was so soft, he wanted to reach right through the phone and pull her into his arms. But just that quickly her features registered alarm, and her face disappeared and the line disconnected. Damn. His heart thundered loudly in his ears. He hoped she hadn't just got caught.

He drew a deep breath and turned to look at the scene behind him, where news trucks had begun to gather the evening before. This morning more had joined the rigs already parked. It was not only local reporters; national news organizations had also arrived.

Rowan had been busy with the ever-growing crowd, and so far had done a terrific job of using some of the local police to keep the press far away from the immediate scene.

She'd even set up a podium so that throughout the

day Chief Cummings could do news updates. Hopefully that would keep him busy and feeling important while Evan did all the hard negotiating behind the scenes and not get any of the credit for the eventual release of the hostages. Not that he cared about credit…he just cared about the ultimate results.

"Nick—" he turned to the man who had just approached "—why don't you get Davis and Daniel and meet me at the mobile van," he said. "I need some updates." He also needed to refocus on the task at hand and not on his past with Annalise.

Within minutes the four men were huddled by the side of the mobile van. "Daniel, tell me what's going on at the compound where these people live." The agent was not only a skilled sniper, he'd also been working with the local police and Hendrick per Evan's instructions.

"According to what Hendrick could find out, there's only one way in and one way out of the place. The entire compound is surrounded by a high fence and guarded, but we now have a heavy presence at the gates. We're checking out any vehicles that go in and come out. If any of these scumbags manage to get out of here, they won't be able to go home to roost."

"Good. Anything to report, Davis?"

Davis frowned. He'd been working with the local police to make sure the back of the building was being guarded, and that men were on call for a potential entry into the school.

"The men are complaining about working so many hours, but I think the gunfire out the back windows when you tried to get to the van woke them up as to just how serious the situation is," he said.

"As if armed men holding five hostages wasn't serious enough?" Evan replied with disgust.

"With all the action happening at the front of the building, I think they forgot that they needed to stay on their toes. Besides, I have a feeling the toughest crime scene those men have seen is in a convenience store where a lollipop was stolen," Davis said with equal disgust.

"Chief Cummings is constantly crowing about how good his men are," Daniel said.

"Let's hope his men are good," Evan said. "We need them to be good. What about the interviews, Nick. How are they coming?"

"We've now interviewed all the teachers who work here, but none of them had any information about what's going on. I know Hendrick is checking into their backgrounds. We're also working off the list Regina Sandhurst gave us of the other staff and delivery services, and will be conducting interviews with them throughout the afternoon. I also spoke to Director Pembrook earlier," Nick continued. "She didn't want to bother you, but she told me to tell you to take your time and don't feel pressured by either the locals or the news reports."

"Hell, you all know me well enough to know I don't give a damn about what any of the reporters say about me," Evan replied. "And Chief Cummings isn't about to push me to do anything I'm not ready to do."

"You know we all trust your judgment," Nick replied. "We're all behind you."

Evan clapped him on the back. "Thanks, man. Let's all check back in with each other in about two hours. I know we're all tired, but stay on your toes. I intend to start really putting on some pressure, and you all know that things can change in the blink of an eye."

Evan returned to his position at the patrol car, his head swirling with thoughts and information. Under different circumstances, he would have seriously considered telling Daniel to get into position and shoot Jacob.

There was really only one reason holding him back from doing that, and that was Annalise's assessment that Jacob's wife was even more evil than her husband. If Jacob was taken out by a sniper's bullet, he worried about what Gretchen might do. So, right now killing Jacob wasn't an option.

This would also usually be the time he'd tell the people inside that he needed proof that the hostages were still alive.

But the last thing he wanted was for Jacob to drag Annalise and the girls up to a window knowing that she was hiding her phone. Besides, he knew the hostages were still alive thanks to Annalise keeping him informed.

He raised the bullhorn. "Brotherhood of Jacob members, if you tell me what you want and why you are in the school, we might be able to work something out. We need to have an open dialogue."

There was no response from Jacob. Evan waited fifteen minutes and then delivered the same message. Again there was no reply.

Evan hoped Jacob's men were becoming mutinous. He hoped like hell that hunger, discomfort and isolation were making the men rebellious against the leader who had put them in this situation in the first place. And for what? What on earth had drawn them to the school building where there was nothing but a closet full of snack food?

The school office had no money. They still hadn't asked for any kind of a ransom. They'd made no contact with Regina Sandhurst, so what in the hell were they doing here? What had been their initial plan?

Damn it, what had they been looking for when they'd barged into the school with guns blazing? It was the one question, despite all the resources at his fingertips, he'd been unable to answer.

He raised the bullhorn to his mouth once again. "Jacob Noble, tell me what you and your men want. Why are you inside the school and what is it you were after? Talk to me about your mission. Help me understand."

There was still no response. This had now become an ominous silence. He had a gut feeling this hostage situation was coming to a head. He also had a bad feeling because he couldn't see exactly how it would end.

HENDRICK HAD A bad feeling. This whole standoff situation at the school was going on for too long, and according to Evan, there had been absolutely no give at all from the hostage takers. The man in charge was not having any real dialogue with Evan.

Unfortunately, Hendrick hadn't been able to figure out what the group had wanted when they'd stormed the school. He'd searched every avenue he had to try to find the answer without any success.

Even though he had 100 percent faith in Evan, Hendrick knew the man had been thrown for a loop when he'd learned Annalise Taylor was one of the hostages.

Hendrick remembered just how crazy Evan had been over her. He'd talked about her all the time while the two had been dating. Hendrick also remembered how utterly devastated his friend had been when Annalise had left Knoxville to go teach at a private college in Missouri. He couldn't imagine what kind of conflict had to be swirling inside Evan's head knowing that she was one of the hostages in the school. He'd always suspected Evan hadn't really gotten over her.

Even though the minute she'd left town he had stopped talking about her, Hendrick believed Evan had brooded about her far more often than he'd ever admit.

None of your business, he told himself. Still, their love for each other had seemed so strong, so real to Hendrick.

He was definitely a skeptic when it came to love. He was smart enough to know that his mother's abandonment and the lack of love earlier in his life had certainly fed into his beliefs. He rarely dated, preferring time on a computer to putting himself out into the dating scene.

At least his computers never rejected him. The computers understood his quirkiness and his need to sometimes control his environment.

He frowned. The last thing he needed to be thinking about was his own particular list of dysfunctions. He reminded himself that his only job here was to provide support and research that might give Evan more tools in his toolbox.

To that end Hendrick had been digging up anything and everything he could about Jacob Noble and his group of followers. He now leaned back in his chair and scrubbed at his burning, tired eyes with his fists.

He'd managed to chase down all the financials of the Brotherhood of Jacob and everything appeared aboveboard, but in digging into Jacob Noble's personal finances, he was running into some interesting discrepancies.

Jacob Noble and his followers might lead a simple, back to the earth kind of lifestyle on the compound, but Jacob and his wife owned some property in the Caymen

Islands, and Hendrick suspected they were also hiding a sizable amount of funds there.

Hendrick was still trying to confirm it. He'd given this information to Evan in their last face-to-face, and he hoped like hell his friend could use it to finally bring this all to an end. Surely Jacob's followers would be interested to hear that their leader wasn't being aboveboard with them and instead was lining his own pockets.

One thing Hendrick knew for sure—if Evan wasn't successful in getting Annalise out of that building alive and well, then Evan would never, ever be the same again.

As THE DAY wore on, Evan was on the bullhorn every fifteen minutes trying to get a dialogue going with Jacob. The only communication happening was the cult leader screaming and cursing and shooting at him.

There was no question Evan was getting frustrated. Jacob was forcing his hand by not being willing to communicate in a meaningful way.

It was as if the man was so far gone in his own head and into his need for control, he didn't recognize that he and his followers were in a lose-lose situation. They had no food and no way out. So, how long would it take for them to finally break? Were they going to break, or was Evan going to have to go in forcefully when and if he had an opportunity that would hopefully not endanger the hostages.

The weather had gotten cooler and the sky overhead had become cloudy and gray, reflecting Evan's current mood. Thankfully Rowan had kept Chief Cummings busy giving regular updates to the press. It was obvious the chief was loving the limelight and his time in front of the cameras. That worked just fine with Evan.

It was late afternoon when he decided to use another tactic. "If any of you men want to just walk out of there, all you have to do is put your weapons down and come out the front door with your hands up over your head."

If what Annalise had told him about the in-fighting was true, then hopefully he could turn a couple of the men inside and get them to walk out. Eventually, surely that would make Jacob surrender the hostages and come out before anyone else got hurt.

"We will not fire on you if you put your hands up and come out peacefully," he said.

"It would be nice if they'd all just walk out of there," Nick said. "I can't believe that none of the men inside have grown weary of this whole thing."

"If we can get a couple of them to surrender, then I'm hoping Jacob will give up, too," Evan replied. "He's definitely in a delusional state of mind if he thinks he's going to outlast us or that I'm going to provide an armored van and just let them all drive away from this."

"At least if one man walks out maybe he'd be able to give us some information, like how many men are really in there and what in the hell they were after when they forced their way into the school," Nick replied.

Davis appeared at Evan's side. "Just wanted to let you know Regina Sandhurst is back on scene. Right now she's over by the food truck."

"Thanks. I think I'll go check in with her." Evan headed toward the food truck in the distance.

"Agent Duran," Regina greeted him with a grim smile. "Any progress being made?"

"Unfortunately not much. I was wondering if any of

the hostage takers have contacted you yet to pay a ransom? We were wondering if that's a possible motive."

"Nobody has contacted me," she replied. "I almost wish somebody had so we'd know that was what they're after."

"It was just a long shot," Evan replied in frustration.

"You know I'll do anything I can to help bring this all to an end," she said. "I just feel so helpless, and I fear this bad publicity is going to affect the donations that keep the school running."

"Hopefully that won't happen," Evan replied. She obviously didn't realize that she sounded a little cold worrying about donations while there were lives on the line.

"You'll keep me updated on any information you get? I want to know absolutely everything that's going on," she replied. "I don't want to get my information from that pompous ass we call a police chief."

"I'll be sure and keep you informed," he replied, although he didn't remark about her assessment of Chief Cummings.

The two spoke for a few more minutes and then Evan returned to his position. The breeze had picked up a bit and tossed around the leaves on the nearby trees.

Under different circumstances the scene before them would have been quite pretty and peaceful. The two blond brick buildings sat on manicured, lush green grass with the tall, mature trees and bushes adding to the attractive landscape.

But there was nothing pretty about the scene as far as Evan was concerned. He saw each tree trunk as a potential place for a shooter from the school to hide behind. The colorful blowing leaves were nothing more than a distraction.

In all his years of hostage negotiation, he'd never had

a hostage taker who didn't want to talk about themselves and what they wanted. Most hostage takers couldn't wait to tell the world what was going on in their life and what had brought them to the situation they were in.

Jacob was definitely an anomaly in that he had no apparent desire to talk about himself or what he and his followers were doing. His unwillingness to do so made Evan's training pretty much go out the window in this situation.

He now groaned at the sight of Chief Cummings approaching with Rowan hurrying just behind him. "Agent Duran, a word," the chief said.

"About what?" Evan asked.

"My men are tired, and I'm running out of funds for all the extra personnel we're using. It's past time to end all this."

"We're all tired," Evan replied curtly. "I'm sure you can work something out with the local council concerning the funding for the extra personnel."

"We need to coordinate going in with force and bringing this to an end right now," Chief Cummings continued. "My men are all ready to go."

"We're not going in with force at this point," Evan replied firmly. "I have information that the men inside are now arguing. I don't think it will be long before some of the men walk out of there. We just need to sit tight and wait for that to happen."

"I disagree with you. My men and I are tired of sitting tight." The man took a step closer to Evan. "This should have already been over. We have enough men to take the building by storm, and that's what we need to do. Besides, having all these men here is leaving the streets of my city unsafe."

"You have the right to reassign some of your men to

wherever you need them. We've got this situation covered." Evan drew in a deep breath as he felt his patience slipping and his anger with the man rising.

"The community is pressing me to act!" Chief Cummings exclaimed.

"I don't give a damn what anyone says. I don't take advice from a mob."

Chief Cummings's nose flared in obvious frustration. "You don't care about the local attention because once this is all done and over, you all will just pack your bags and leave. My men and I have to still live and work here."

"I'll take the next presser on your behalf," Rowan said, and stepped between the two men. "Chief Cummings, I'll make sure they know how much we appreciate your support and how helpful you and your officers have been."

The chief grunted, but he didn't step back from Evan. "I still think you're making a big mistake not ending this right now."

"Why in the hell would I risk the hostages' lives by going in with force? Have you forgotten that there are four children inside the building? Right now they're alive, and I want to make sure I keep them that way." Evan's anger rose higher as he glared at the man before him. "Eventually fatigue and hunger will drive them out, and we won't need to use force."

Rowan placed her hand on the chief's shoulder. "Come on, Chief, let's go over the progress so far. I'm sure reporters are eager to hear from you again."

God bless Rowan, for if Evan had to continue to face off with the man, he might have wound up punching him in his pugnacious face. Thankfully, as it was, the potential of getting in front of the cameras again and his reputation lifted by Rowan's words of praise appealed to him more than standing his ground with Evan.

"That man is a complete and total joke," Nick said once Rowan and the chief walked away. "He's also a big jerk."

"He's definitely getting on my last nerve," Evan replied. "I'm just not ready to do something drastic right now to bring this to an end. We've only been working this for the last twenty-four hours."

"You're definitely right that holding out is the way to go, especially with the kids in there."

Evan nodded. "I really believe at this point it's just a matter of us outwaiting them."

He stared at the school building. At least for now the hostages were alive. He could only hope they remained that way and he was making the right choice.

Chapter Five

"Mr. Jacob, could we have something else to eat?" Sadie asked.

Jacob was once again in his position in a chair to the side of the window. He turned to look at Sadie. "There's nothing left," he replied. "And I don't want any of you whining or crying that you're hungry. I don't like whiners almost as much as I hate screamers."

Annalise tightened her arm around Sadie. "What does the Brotherhood of Jacob do?" Annalise asked. "Why did you form this group in the first place?" She held her breath, wondering what his response would be to her questions and if somehow she might be able to make sense of what was going on.

"Society has got no place for people like me. I've got no formal education, and I grew up dirt-poor with a mother who screamed at me and beat me half to death every other day of my life."

"I'm sorry you had to endure that," Annalise said.

He frowned. "Everyone today is out for themselves, and nobody is tending to the poor and hungry. We've got homeless and starving people on the streets of our cities, and nobody is interested in helping them. The Brotherhood of Jacob brought together people who want to help."

"So what does the Brotherhood of Jacob do to help?" Annalise asked. Any information she could glean might help Evan.

"We grow vegetables and take boxes to the homeless on the streets. We also sell them and send money to charities we deem are appropriate." A scowl stretched across his forehead. "Nobody ever gave me a helping hand. Now I've got the power in the Brotherhood of Jacob, and I decide who we help and when."

"So what about your wife? I guess she has the same views you do?"

An unexpected grin lifted his lips. "Gretchen hates almost everyone but me. She grew up in the foster care system where she was abused nearly every single day of her life. She learned young that nobody was on her side. But she's found her place with me and within the arms of the Brotherhood."

"So how does being here in the school help anyone?"

Before he could reply, Gretchen walked in. "Everything okay in here?" she asked with a smile at Jacob.

"Yeah, except the teacher has a lot of questions," he replied.

Gretchen turned and stared at Annalise and then looked back at her husband. "Let me know if you need me to shut her up. I'll be glad to knock her teeth in."

Jacob laughed. "That's my girl…always willing to go the extra mile for her man."

My God, who were these people? Annalise wondered when Gretchen had left the room again. What had life done to them to twist them so badly?

Despite Jacob's brief laughter, there was no question there was a new tension in the man in charge. He'd screamed at his men throughout the day, and even as he now sat silently at the window she could feel a deranged kind of tension radiating from him.

She was concerned for the girls, who were lethargic and sleeping too much of the time. Now, knowing there was no more food for them made her even more worried.

How long could this go on? How long would these men go without food and being exhausted? What was the endgame? Was Jacob crazy enough to commit mass murder and then kill himself? Far too often these kinds of situations ended that way.

No, she had to stop thinking so negatively. She shouldn't go to such dark places in her mind. Surely after all this time, one way or another, these precious girls would be saved. She would do all she could to make sure of it. She had to keep believing that. She absolutely couldn't lose all hope.

Dusk had fallen once again, and Jacob stood and stretched. Annalise's heart beat a little bit faster in anticipation of him leaving the room.

She quickly closed her eyes and pretended to be asleep. Her heart still thudded rapidly in her chest. The minute she heard his heavy footsteps leaving the room, she sprang into action.

She rushed to her phone, grabbed it and returned to her position. With Jacob still gone, she hit the button that brought up Evan's ruggedly handsome face on the screen. "Evan," she whispered, for a moment overcome with so many emotions she could say nothing more.

"Annalise, are you and the kids still okay?"

She nodded. "We're okay, but the snack food is gone."

"I know it's tough, but that's a good thing. It will make

the men more apt to walk out of there. I'm sorry that you and the kids have to do without until that happens."

She nodded again, knowing there was nothing that could be done to change the situation right now. "Talk to me, Evan. I need to have something else in my mind besides fear." She quickly glanced to the doorway and then relaxed as she heard Jacob yelling someplace else in the building.

His smile was soft. "We had a lot of good times together," he said.

"Yes, we did." How she wished she could have those wonderful times again with him. "I've thought about those good times a lot during the past three years."

"Yeah, me, too," he replied.

"I wish—"

"You all stop your bitching and stick with me." Jacob's voice boomed from just outside the doorway.

Annalise hung up and hid the phone beneath her thigh, then closed her eyes and once again pretended to be asleep. She sensed him staring at her for a couple of long moments and then heard his heavy footsteps as he walked across the room. The chair near the window creaked beneath his weight.

As the night wore on, he left the room one more time and she managed to get her phone back on the charger. Finally she fell into an exhausted sleep without dreams.

When she awakened again, it was morning. Once the girls were up, Jacob escorted them to the bathroom. "Listen, girls," Annalise said. "There is no more food for anybody. Drink as much water as you can since that is all you're getting." They drank using their hands as cups.

"Can't we get out of here?" Tanya asked. "I want to be back in my own room."

"Me, too." Emily broke down in tears. "I'm tired of being here. I'm so tired of being scared."

Annalise hugged the little girl close and then released her. "We need to stay strong. You all know by now that Jacob doesn't like crying. I know it's hard, but we've all got to keep our emotions in check until somebody gets us out of here."

It was going to be a difficult day. The girls were fussy, and Annalise did her best to give them a pep talk, not only to keep them strong, but also to keep them alive.

When they returned to the classroom, the girls once again took their positions against the wall, but Annalise remained standing.

"Jacob, I want the girls to sit at the desks and work today," she said.

One of his bushy black eyebrows shot up. "Who made you boss today?" he sputtered with a laugh of disbelief. "I don't give a damn what you want."

A faint fear trembled through her as she faced off with her captor. "I know you're calling the shots, Jacob, but I have to think about the well-being of my students. It would be better for their mental health to focus on some work."

"I think it's best if you shut up and sit down," he replied.

Annalise remained standing. "The girls need to do something besides just sit against the wall for another day." It suddenly seemed vitally important that she stand her ground.

He gazed at her for a long moment. She boldly maintained eye contact with him. He finally looked away and frowned. "Can they work and be quiet? I don't want any damned noise."

"They can be very quiet," Annalise replied. She quickly turned to the girls. "Go to your computers," she said.

Thankfully they all moved quietly, eagerly to their desks. Jacob watched them. "Hey, Sadie, a little bird told me you're the smartest girl in this room."

"I am smart," Sadie replied. There was no pride in her voice, rather it was just a statement of fact.

"I heard you really know your way around computers," he said.

"Sometimes I think I might be smarter in computer arts than Miss Annalise," Sadie replied with pride, and flashed a small smile to her teacher.

"Yep, that's what the little bird told me," Jacob said.

"What's the name of your little bird?" Annalise asked. Had somebody on the inside told him how smart Sadie was? Was there somebody else involved in all this? Who from inside the school would have anything to do with this madness?

"The name is none of your business," he snapped. "I gave into them working at their desks, now stop asking me questions."

"Why don't you all build your own web page," Annalise said to the girls. "I want it to be a happy page with links to your favorite foods and animals and anything else that you love."

As the girls got to work, Annalise sat at her desk. Even though she knew in the grand scheme of things nothing had really changed, this felt like another success to her.

She wondered if Jacob had really had inside information on how bright Sadie was, or if he'd merely picked her out because she'd interacted with him and the other girls hadn't.

She didn't know, and at the moment it didn't matter. All that really mattered was that the girls were engaged in their work instead of sitting against a wall with nothing to think about but their own fear. At least now, hopefully, they were thinking about their skills and creativity.

As the girls continued to work, she heard Evan on the bullhorn. He was attempting to build a relationship with Jacob, but the cult leader was having nothing to do with it. He would curse and demand Evan move the police presence away. He would then fire his gun out the window.

Meanwhile, as the girls worked, Gretchen walked between the desks, apparently checking to make sure the girls did nothing to contact anyone from the outside world. She occasionally asked questions to different girls, and it was obvious when they answered that the students were all terrified of her.

By noon Evan wasn't talking to Jacob anymore, but rather directed his comments to the men in the building. He told them that he understood and supported their mission of feeding the hungry and that he wanted a peaceful resolve to all of this.

Annalise knew Evan was using all the tools in his box to get to the men with Jacob. Unfortunately some of the attributes that make him a great hostage negotiator were also the traits that had eventually torn apart their relationship.

He'd been controlling and often emotionally unavailable to her during the time they had been together. She'd loved him desperately…still had deep feelings for him, but she hadn't been able to live with his control of her. She believed he'd seen her as too weak and too inadequate to run her own life. Not that any of that mattered now.

The standoff continued. Annalise knew at some point Evan was going to have to make a decision as far as ending this. If they used force to enter the building, she prayed that Jacob and his men would just put their hands up and surrender.

But there was no way to predict exactly what Jacob might do. There was no question that he appeared to grow more and more angry and agitated and quick to fire his gun as the minutes ticked by.

The girls seemed to have grown accustomed to Jacob firing his gun. When it happened, they no longer screamed or cried.

Jacob left the room often, and she could hear him yelling at his men. She had a feeling Evan's tactics were definitely getting to them.

She was more than ready to get out of here with her students. She just didn't know if Jacob and his deranged wife, Gretchen, would allow this to come to a peaceful end.

ANOTHER DAY WAS slowly drawing to an end. Evan was not only frustrated, but also his throat was sore and slightly husky from all the talking he'd done that day.

He lifted the bullhorn to his mouth once again. "Jacob, how about you let me come in there and have a one-on-one conversation with you. I'll come in unarmed and we can talk face-to-face."

"Just you?" Jacob yelled back.

Hope filled Evan. "Just me," he replied. If he could get inside and talk to the man face-to-face, he was sure he could convince Jacob to give up.

"Step out where I can see you," Jacob said.

This certainly wouldn't be the first time Evan had entered a building to talk to a hostage taker, but he'd never gone in to speak to one who was so volatile and unpredictable. He stepped out from behind the patrol car and walked forward.

He took only a couple of steps when Jacob told him to halt.

"I'm going to lay down my gun," Evan said. With one hand up in the air, he used his other hand to unfasten the shoulder holster holding his gun. When he was finished, he laid it on the ground in front of him and then raised both hands above his head. "I'm unarmed and I'm coming in."

He took two steps forward and was about to take another when Jacob fired. Thankfully, the bullets kicked up the ground to the left and didn't hit him. Evan cursed, grabbed his gun and then scurried back behind the patrol car.

Jacob laughed. "Sorry, I changed my mind. I got nothing to say to you."

"Are you okay?" Nick asked Evan once he was back to safety.

"I'm fine." He released a deep breath. "If he'd wanted to kill me, he could have. I was an easy target."

"He's crazy," Nick replied.

"Crazy like a fox."

"Too bad Dr. Larsen couldn't identify what the trigger was for all this," Nick said.

Dr. Melinda Larsen was a criminal profiler. She was an attractive woman who was a specialist in reading body language for the FBI. Evan had contacted her to get a more thorough profile on Jacob Noble.

Her assessment was that Jacob was a narcissist who thrived on chaos. One of his teachings was that in the coming years food sources would dry up and only the wealthy would be able to feed themselves, thus building an "us versus them" mind-set in his followers.

He had set himself up as a godlike leader who would keep his followers safe and fed as things crumbled in society.

According to the information Hendrick had been able to give Dr. Larsen, she also believed Jacob used a combination of fear and unpredictability to control cult members.

It had been that unpredictability that he'd just shown, only in this case it was to prove to his followers that he was still in control and could make the FBI jump.

He raised the bullhorn. "I'm talking to the men inside the school. You have no way out of here. Jacob has led you into a corner where there is no escape. It's time to give up. This is a dead end, and if you don't surrender, then this will not end well."

He paused a moment and then spoke again. "At least let the hostages go."

The sun was dipping lower in the horizon, casting everything in shadows. He started to raise the bullhorn once again but paused as a tall man stood in the entrance of the school.

"Everyone hold your fire…hold your fire," he yelled to his men.

"If you're coming out, put your hands up over your head," he said to the man. "Get your hands up and walk out slowly."

The man hesitated for a long moment and then took one tentative step out of the building and raised his hands toward the sky. "Don't shoot," he said. "I'm unarmed. Please don't shoot me."

"Just walk forward slowly and keep your hands up

over your head," Evan instructed. The air snapped with tension, and nobody else in the area spoke a word. For the first time since he'd arrived on scene, hope buoyed up in Evan. If this man walked out, then maybe the others would follow.

"Keep walking," Evan said. "You're doing fine. Just come straight forward, walk toward the sound of my voice."

The man took baby steps, and it was obvious he was afraid. He kept his arms over his head, but they shook with nerves. "Please don't shoot," he said again. "Please…please don't shoot me."

"Nobody is going to shoot you," Evan assured him. "Identify yourself."

"My name is Tim… Timothy Summers."

"Okay, Tim. You're doing great."

The man continued to move forward tiny step by tiny step. He got halfway between the school building and the TCD team when gunfire filled the air.

Evan muttered a curse. "Hold your fire. Hold your damn fire," he yelled even as Tim screamed out in pain and then fell face-first to the ground.

It was then Evan realized it wasn't his men shooting, but rather Jacob or somebody from inside the school. "Cover me, cover me," Evan yelled.

As his men began to return fire, Evan grabbed a helmet, and crouching, he raced for the injured man, unmindful of any personal danger. All he saw was a human being who desperately needed help.

As he ran, a steady barrage of gunfire came from his men, providing him the cover he needed. The air filled with the acrid smoke from the blazing guns.

When Evan reached Tim, he wasn't conscious and his legs and back were riddled with gunshot wounds.

He was bleeding badly. Evan grabbed him beneath his shoulders and began to pull him back toward safety.

Davis rushed to them and helped get the man behind the police line. The gunshots stopped and an eerie silence fell over the site.

"We need to get him into the ambulance right away," Davis said.

Evan motioned for the EMTs who were standing by with an ambulance, and they got the wounded man loaded on a gurney. Minutes later the emergency vehicle pulled away with sirens screaming.

"I doubt he's going to make it," Davis said grimly. "He took a lot of bullets."

"Damn it!" Evan exclaimed. He stared toward the brick building as an icy chill filled him. Jacob—or somebody in there—had just shot one of their own. The odds just got worse that Annalise and those girls were going to get out of there alive.

ANNALISE'S HEART BEAT so fast she thought she was going to pass out. The amount of gunfire…the sound of a man screaming from outside and Jacob cursing and firing his weapon out the window had scared not only the children, but also her.

Something had happened…something bad, but she didn't know what it was or what it might mean for these precious girls and herself.

They were all back against the wall for the night after spending the day working at their desks. When Jacob stormed out of the room, Annalise raced for her phone. Her fingers trembled as she texted Evan, asking what had just happened.

Annalise tried to keep it together for the girls, but

tears raced down her cheeks. She was frightened, and she wanted her students to be anywhere but here.

After several minutes she received a text back from Evan, telling her that everything was okay. He said that there had been an exchange of gunfire, and one of Jacob's men was shot. He once again told her to stay strong and that he was doing all he could to get them out.

She quickly wiped away her tears, not only for herself, but also for the four girls holed up next to her and terrified. She had to stay strong for herself, but more so she had to stay strong for her students.

She heard Jacob's voice getting closer to the room, and she quickly disconnected from the phone and slid it beneath her thigh.

"They're either with me or against me," Jacob yelled as he and Gretchen stormed back into the room. "And if they're against me, then they will all pay the price."

He paced back and forth in front of the girls. "I won't stand for traitors. I won't stand for it."

"Calm down, Jacob. You're still the man in control," Gretchen said.

Jacob stopped in front of Annalise. "What's that?"

Annalise looked down and to her horror saw that the last rays of light coming in through the window shone off the edge of her cell phone that hadn't been tucked completely under her thigh. She froze, her heart beating fast and furiously.

"Yeah, what is that?" Gretchen leaned over and grabbed the cell phone. "What have we here?" She backhanded Annalise, the blow causing Annalise's head to hit the wall behind her. Her ears rang and her face stung from the blow.

"Stop it!" Sadie exclaimed. "Don't hurt her. Please Mr. Jacob, don't let her hurt Miss Annalise."

"Hush, Sadie," Annalise said, not wanting their anger turned on the child.

"I should shoot you," Gretchen said, her pale blue eyes cold as ice.

"Give me the phone," Jacob said. "Let's see who she's been talking to."

Annalise's heart continued to pound as Jacob thumbed through her messages. Thankfully most of her interaction with Evan had been by phone and Face-Time, and there was no recording of those.

Jacob dropped the phone to the floor and then ground it beneath the heel of his boot. All the while his dark eyes remained locked on Annalise.

Her breath caught in her chest, and every muscle in her body tensed. The girls were crying on either side of her, and she felt like throwing up as she waited for her consequences.

"I just shot a traitor," Jacob said with eyes narrowed.

"Let me take her out," Gretchen said. "I don't like her."

"You don't even know me," Annalise replied, pleased by the strength in her voice.

"I don't want to know you." She turned to her husband. "She's just another one of those girls who looked down on me all my life."

Jacob frowned. "We got more important things to do. Go check in with the men. And you," he said to Annalise. "Shut those girls up."

Annalise breathed a sigh of relief as Gretchen left the room. She quickly shushed the girls as her heartbeat resumed a more normal pace.

Within minutes complete darkness claimed the room.

Jacob left the classroom and could be heard down the hallway talking loudly with his men.

Something was going to happen. Annalise could feel it in her bones, but she couldn't guess what it might be. Were they all finally going to give up?

She desperately wanted that to happen. She wanted them to give up peacefully. She wanted the girls to be out of here. She wished she had her phone. Evan had stopped talking on the bullhorn, and she wondered if he was planning to storm the building.

Being cut off from the outside world—from Evan—was terrifying as the night deepened and the tension inside of the school grew more intense. Jacob returned to his chair, and men came in and out of the room and whispered feverishly with him.

The girls finally fell asleep and Annalise closed her eyes, as well. Her thoughts went to the girls on either side of her. Emily was a sweet girl who was always the first to give a hug or offer encouragement to others. Tanya was a jokester and loved to make her friends giggle. Amanda was quiet and thoughtful. Then, of course, there was Sadie, who was not only sweet and giving, but also wise beyond her age.

How traumatized were they going to be by this event? Would they get out of here unscathed only to suffer from anxiety and or PTSD for the rest of their lives? Would Tanya lose her sense of humor forever? Would Emily withdraw from everyone? And what about Sadie, who had already been through so much in her short life?

Hopefully Regina Sandhurst would be willing to spend whatever money necessary on some therapy for her star students. These girls not only needed to survive the night, but also they needed to thrive in their lives going forward in spite of this horrifying event.

She had almost fallen asleep when gunfire snapped her eyes wide open and sent her heart racing. It wasn't just Jacob firing out the window in their room, it sounded like everyone in the building was shooting all at the same time. The girls screaming added to the cacophony of noise.

Within minutes smoke began to fill the air, coming in from the hallway. What was happening? Was the Brotherhood trying to kill all the police officers outside? Her heartbeat banged so erratically she wondered if she was about to have a heart attack. What was going on?

Gretchen ran into the room. "Let's go," she screamed at Jacob. "We have a chance if we move right now. It's time to go." To Annalise's horror, she yanked Sadie up by her arm.

"Leave her alone," Annalise yelled. She struggled to her feet and tried to get Sadie away from Gretchen. "Let go of her," she screamed as she held tight to Sadie's other arm.

"Let her go," Gretchen yelled as she tugged Sadie closer to her. "I swear before this is all over I'm going to kill you."

"I'm not letting go," Annalise replied feverishly. She couldn't let Gretchen take Sadie. She tried to pull the little girl closer to her.

Gretchen punched Annalise in the stomach hard. Her breath whooshed out of her, and pain weakened her knees. Still, she reached out and grabbed one of Gretchen's braids and held tight.

The woman screamed and grabbed Annalise's wrist. As long as Gretchen had one hand holding Sadie and the other holding Annalise, she couldn't get to the gun in her waistband.

Annalise yanked as hard as she could on the woman's hair. Gretchen screamed again in outrage. Jacob rushed them both, and shoved Annalise so hard her back smashed against the wall and she lost her grip on Sadie and Gretchen. "No," she screamed. Jacob swung the child up over his broad shoulder, and then he and his wife ran out of the room.

Chapter Six

Annalise struggled to her feet, half breathless and nauseous from the blow she had taken to the stomach and the force of her back slamming into the wall. She had no idea what was going on. All she knew was she desperately needed to get Sadie back.

She ran out into the hallway, but she saw no sign of them. *Oh, God, where had they gone?* The smoke grew thicker, and she narrowed her eyes against it. She coughed as it burned the back of her throat.

Was the building on fire? She felt no heat radiating from anywhere. She didn't believe there was a fire threat. She suspected it came from a smoke bomb. And that meant the people outside were taking the building by storm.

It all seemed surreal…the smoke, the gunshots…the terror. When she heard the cries of the other three girls, she ran back into the classroom.

"Come on, girls. You need to get up. I want you to get beneath the desks. Duck and cover." Unsure what to expect, she only hoped the desks would provide the girls some measure of safety against whatever was happening.

It felt like the apocalypse, like the entire world was exploding all around them. The sound of shattering glass added to the chaos. The girls continued to cry as they huddled beneath the desks.

Again Annalise looked out into the hallway. Where was Sadie? Where had they taken her and for what reason? Would they be back to take the other girls? Maybe she should move the girls out of here.

She stepped back into the classroom, intending to do just that when the gunfire suddenly halted. The only sound was that of men yelling for help.

"Annalise!" Evan's voice rose above the pandemonium. It came from somewhere just outside the room.

"In here," she cried desperately. "Evan, we're in here."

Then he was there, standing right in front of her, and she was in his arms. "They took Sadie," she cried. "You have to find her. Evan, they took her and then ran out of the room."

"Gretchen hit Miss Annalise in the stomach," Emily said.

"And Jacob pushed her real hard and she fell back," Amanda added.

Evan looked at her in alarm. "I'm okay. You just need to find Sadie," she replied.

He released her and got on his radio, which was attached to the top of his shoulder. Annalise gathered the girls close to her side and prayed that the good guys outside had Jacob and Gretchen in custody and Sadie was safe somewhere out of the school building.

Evan got off his radio and drew all of them closer to him. "We're going to get the girls to go out through the window."

As he said the words, another man appeared outside the window. He knocked out what was left of the jagged glass, and Evan hunched down in front of the girls.

"That man at the window is Davis and he's with Nick, another agent. They are going to carry you all to safety."

Annalise hurried the girls to the window, where Evan raised Tanya and passed her out the window. He did the same with the other two girls.

"Is Sadie safe?" Annalise asked worriedly. "Do they have her someplace safe outside?"

"Let's get you out of here," he replied. He grabbed her hand, and she squeezed his tightly.

They left the classroom and immediately she understood why he had taken the girls out the window. Chaos reigned in the hallway. Several wounded men cried out as paramedics and other emergency personnel attended to them.

Evan dropped her hand and instead threw his arm around her shoulders and pulled her closer as they maneuvered their way around the wounded and then stepped out of the building.

Free. She was finally free. She breathed in the cool night air, but her relief in being out of the school only lasted a moment. "Evan, where is Sadie? Jacob and Gretchen grabbed her and took off with her. Did somebody catch them? Is she okay?"

Evan took her by the arm and led her toward an awaiting ambulance. "I don't need any medical care," she protested. She stopped walking and faced him. "I just need to know if Sadie is safe." Worry flooded her veins. Why wasn't he telling her anything about Sadie?

"Annalise, look, we still have a situation here." A pulse throbbed in his strong jawline. "Jacob and Gretchen managed to get away, and they have Sadie with them."

"My God." Annalise nearly fell to the ground in horror. How on earth had they gotten away and why had they taken Sadie with them? Despite the chaos of the scene surrounding them, her brain now whirled with all the things that had happened between Sadie and Jacob.

Before she could speak, an attractive woman with long dark hair approached them. "This is Rowan. She'll see to it that you get the medical attention you need and get home safely," Evan said. "Somebody will be in contact with you to arrange to take your statement at a later time."

"I'm not going home," Annalise protested vehemently. "I... I think he took Sadie because, despite her age, she is a computer genius. I know if she gets anywhere near a computer she'll contact me. We...we have a secret page set up and a secret language." She grabbed Evan's forearm. "I know she'll try to contact me, and she'll help us rescue her."

He stared at her. "What makes you think he took her for her computer skills?" he asked.

"He knew she was the smartest on the computer. I... I think he had some inside information about her." Evan looked at her sharply as she continued. "I think they came into the school specifically to take Sadie, but the police arrived too quickly for them to get out. If I'm right about all this, then I can help. Evan, I'm not going home."

He hesitated, frowned and rubbed the back of his neck. "Okay," he finally relented. He then looked at Rowan once again. "Let the paramedics take a look at her wounds and then bring her to the hotel and arrange a room for her and a meal, and make sure she has a computer. I have to go." Without another word he turned away and headed into the center of the chaos.

"Annalise, let's go," Rowan said gently, and she touched the teacher's shoulder.

On the short drive to the hotel, all Annalise could think of was Sadie with her big blue eyes and happy smile. What exactly did Jacob want from her? There was little doubt in Annalise's mind that Sadie had been taken because of her computer skills, so what did they want her to do? And if she did what was asked of her, would she be killed afterward?

"I'm sure you're exhausted," Rowan said minutes later as she opened the door to room 110 of a hotel close to the school.

"I just want Sadie to be found and returned safe and sound," Annalise replied. "I… I was supposed to protect her. It was my job to protect her and I failed." Tears blurred her vision.

To her surprise Rowan put her arms around Annalise and hugged her. "You did everything in your power, Annalise. You did an amazing job in keeping those girls safe in a dangerous situation. Don't beat yourself up."

Rowan finally released her and then stepped away. "I'll be right back with a computer for you to use."

When she left the room, Annalise stared around her. The hotel room was serviceable, with a king-size bed covered by a light blue spread, and a dresser and a television. A desk and a small round table sat in a corner.

Rowan returned with a laptop and carried it to the desk. "This should work for you," she said, taking a moment to power it up. "I'll go get you something to eat. I know you've been existing on next to nothing for the last couple of days. Is there anything special you'd like?"

"I'm not really hungry," Annalise replied. She didn't

want to even think about food when Sadie was missing, kidnapped by a deranged man and his sadistic wife.

She sat in the desk chair and opened up the laptop. She quickly connected to the internet and went to the page she'd set up just for her and her students to use.

Tears once again blurred her vision. Sadie had been so incredibly brave throughout the entire ordeal, and she had stayed strong throughout the passing days and nights. Annalise prayed she would continue to be brave and strong wherever she was at the moment.

Was Sadie going to get a meal? Would Jacob and Gretchen make sure she had food? When the two adults fed their own faces, would they remember to feed Sadie?

She hadn't expected to see anything from Sadie so soon on the page, and there wasn't anything there yet. She drew in a deep breath and released it slowly.

Evan. Seeing him again, even for only a few moments, had stirred something deep inside her. But there were so many other crazy emotions racing through her right now it was difficult to sort it all out.

Had she been so happy to see him simply because he represented safety and her freedom? Or was there still something there, something that yearned for what might have been with him.

She released another deep breath. Hopefully Evan and his men would find Jacob and Gretchen soon and bring Sadie back to safety.

"I should have fought harder," she murmured to herself as she thought about that moment when Gretchen had grabbed Sadie. It had been so unexpected. However, somehow, someway she should have fought much harder and never let them take her.

It was difficult for her to realize it was Friday night. Thankfully Evan had gotten them out of there in just a little over forty-eight hours. If Chief Cummings had continued to be in charge of the situation, who knew when they might have gotten out. Who knew if they would have even survived?

She hadn't realized Rowan had gone to get her food until she returned with several sacks from the local diner. "I wasn't sure what you'd like," Rowan said as she began to unload the items onto the table. "There's a salad and some chicken noodle soup. I also brought you a few personal items like a new hairbrush and a toothbrush and toothpaste and a change of clothing."

Despite Annalise's worry, the scent of the food was heavenly. "Thank you for everything, and I guess I am hungry after all. That soup smells really good."

"Eat and then try to get some rest. You've been through a terrible ordeal," Rowan said.

"It's not over yet," Annalise replied darkly. "It won't be over until Sadie is safe and sound. Where are the other girls now?"

"They are currently in the hospital being treated for dehydration and getting other medical treatment they might require. Their resident attendants are with them, and they're all doing just fine," Rowan assured her.

"What about Belinda? Do you know how she is?"

"She immediately went in for emergency surgery and is now in serious, but stable condition. She should be just fine, thanks to you. It's a good thing you got her out when you did. Now, I need to get back to the school. Are you going to be okay here alone?"

"I'm good," Annalise replied. "All I really want is for Sadie to be found."

"I'm sure the team is working very hard to find her and the two fugitives," Rowan replied. "Do you need anything else?"

"No, you've been more than kind," Annalise replied.

"Then let's hope the next time I talk with you will be when Sadie is safe and the bad guys are behind bars." Then with a quick goodbye Rowan left.

At least Annalise could rest assured that the other three girls were being well taken care of. All of the girls at the school were very close to their resident attendants and looked to them for emotional support. The resident attendants were good at loving and supporting their young charges.

She stared at the computer screen even as she moved from the chair at the desk to a chair at the table. From there she could still see if anything popped up on the internet page while she ate.

The salad tasted fresh and good, and then she dove into the hearty delicious soup. Once she was full and her mind had finally slowed down from the chaos of the past couple of days, her thoughts once again filled with Evan.

Did she want to see him again so badly because she hoped he had news about Sadie? Absolutely. But, there was also a small part of her that wanted to reconnect with him after the ordeal.

Still, what she wanted more than anything was for him to tell her that Jacob and Gretchen were behind bars and Sadie was safe and with her resident attendant.

"DAMN IT, HOW did this happen?" Evan yelled in a rage as he glared at Chief Cummings. "How in the hell did your men allow this to happen?"

When the dust had settled, Evan was told that the black van that had been parked behind the school was gone. Jacob had apparently driven it right through the police line and had gotten away.

"My men did what they could, but somebody was shooting through one of the van windows," Chief Cummings replied defensively.

"What did they do? Did they just run into the woods and hide instead of returning fire? If nothing else, why in the hell didn't somebody think to shoot out the tires so they couldn't drive away?"

"I'm sure they tried," Chief Cummings replied. "I pulled a lot of my men off the guard duty at the back of the school. Some of them needed a break, and others I reassigned to regular patrol duty."

"Right, because it was more important to ticket jaywalkers?" Evan asked incredulously.

"You said I had the right to reassign some of my men," Chief Cummings protested.

"Nevertheless, nobody from inside the school should have had a chance to get into that van, let alone drive it off." Evan didn't wait for an answer. If he looked at Chief Cummings for one more minute, he was going to completely lose it.

Instead, he turned and headed toward the mobile vehicle. He couldn't believe the lack of professionalism that Chief Cummings had shown, or the lack of training the force had since they appeared to allow Jacob to just drive away, apparently with his wife and Sadie, as well.

Still, he'd known something was going down when the men in the school had all begun firing out the front school windows at the same time. It had been a coordinated assault, and Evan had known immediately that it had been a ruse for something else that might be happening.

Evan had already made the decision to go in, not trusting that Jacob was going to hold it together for another night. He'd instructed his men to prepare to move in so they were immediately ready to respond.

Flash-bang grenades and smoke bombs had disoriented the men inside enough to force them to surrender and make the assault on the school successful. Evan now realized Jacob had ordered all of his men to shoot through the front windows and provide the distraction so that he and his wife could make their escape out of the back of the school.

Evan's anger was rich and thick and filled his chest with an uncomfortable tightness. They now had two criminals on the run with a little girl as a hostage. Things had gone from bad to worse.

Was Annalise right? Had Sadie been taken because she was so gifted with her ability regarding computer science? Had Jacob had inside information about the students? Or had they taken her to use as a human shield if needed when they had escaped? If the latter was true, then they would probably dump Sadie the first chance they got. The real question was if they'd dump her dead or alive. The pressure in his chest increased.

"Hendrick," he said once he'd connected with the tech. "What have you got for me?"

"Not much. They must be traveling on back roads, and there are a hell of a lot of mountain roads without cameras in that area," Hendrick replied. "Since we don't know what direction they fled, I'm watching the available traffic cameras within a twenty-five-mile radius in each direction. But so far I've got nothing. I'll let you know the minute I do."

"I need you to also be on the lookout for any report of a child found," Evan said. "It's possible Sadie will be dumped on the side of the road somewhere if she's no longer useful to them." Hopefully, if that happened, they would dump her alive.

"Got it," Hendrick replied.

"Also, Annalise had a feeling Jacob had some inside information on the girls. I need you to do thorough background checks on all the employees and see what you find."

"I'm on it."

As Evan disconnected, Nick stuck his head in the doorway. "Hey, man, we've got a live one out here. He's not hurt and he's singing like a bird."

Maybe they would finally get some answers that had eluded them so far. Evan followed Nick to the back of a patrol car where a tall, blond-haired, handcuffed man stood. "I'm Special Agent Evan Duran," he said to the prisoner. "What's your name?"

"Ben… Ben Hanson. This…this all wasn't supposed to be like this." He looked utterly shell-shocked. "This is the very last thing we all wanted."

"So, what exactly did you want when you came into the school?" Evan asked. "Why are you here?"

"We were supposed to get in, grab one of the genius students and then get out. We didn't intend to fire a shot. There wasn't supposed to be a standoff. Nobody was ever supposed to get hurt."

"So, what made it go south?" Evan asked.

"First of all Jacob told us nobody would be in the school except a teacher and a few of her students. Somebody panicked and started shooting. Then I guess the security guard managed to ring the alarm and the cops started showing up way before we expected."

"What did you want with the student?" Evan asked.

Ben frowned. "Jacob said the kids in the school were smart enough to break into the World Bank. He said when that happened there would be all kinds of financial chaos, and during that pandemonium he'd transfer enough money to distribute to the poor and hungry. We all knew it was illegal, but we believed it was for the greater good. He said we would help to stop hunger all over the world."

"Did you all know that Jacob and his wife own some property in the Caymen Islands along with a healthy bank account in their names only?"

Ben stared at him for a long moment and then slowly shook his head and released a deep, bitter laugh. "I don't know why that should surprise me now. In the end they only saved their own skins and left the rest of us here to die. He even fired at Tim. He shot him in the back when he was giving himself up."

Ben's eyes filled with tears. "I saw the ambulance pull away after he got shot. Is…is he okay?"

"He didn't make it," Nick said curtly. Evan knew Nick had gotten the information from the hospital. Despite Evan's and Davis's best efforts to save the man, he had been DOA.

Ben's eyes glazed over with emotion. "Damn Jacob for killing him. We thought Jacob was a great leader for change in society, but he turned out to be nothing more than a greedy monster."

"What was the plan? Where was Jacob planning on taking the child?" Evan asked.

"The plan was for all of us to return to the compound, but now I have no idea where they might have gone."

"Has Jacob or Gretchen ever talked about any other property they own?" Evan asked. "Does anyone close to them own someplace where they might go?"

Ben shook his head. "As far as I know, neither of

them had any family. None of us own any property. If anyone had any, we all sold it and donated the proceeds to the group before we moved into the compound with Jacob. I've never heard either of them talk about any property they might own, especially a place in the Caymen Islands," he finished bitterly.

Evan sighed in frustration and turned to Nick. "Go ahead and get him processed and out of here."

Everything that could be done was being done. His men were processing the crime scene, and Jacob's thugs had been rounded up. The wounded were being attended to, and officials all over the area were looking for the black panel van. Law enforcement at all the nearby airports was also on the lookout for the fugitives.

Maybe Annalise was right and somehow Sadie would manage to contact them and be able to tell them where she was. With this thought in mind, he decided to head to the hotel.

As Rowan drove him to the room his head filled with thoughts of Annalise. Seeing her again, even so briefly, had been surprisingly good and difficult at the same time.

He was relieved she was safe, but he couldn't be content until Sadie was also safe. Right now, Annalise was a means to that end.

"Try to get some rest," Rowan said as she pulled up in front of the hotel. "I know things aren't resolved yet, but you can't keep pushing yourself like you've been doing since you got here. You need to take time to sleep and recharge, otherwise you'll end up being no good to anyone."

"I know," he replied. Just that quickly a thick blanket of exhaustion fell over him. He tried to shrug it off as he got out of the car, but he was only half-successful.

She handed him a room key. "You're in room 108 and Annalise is in room 110."

"Got it," he replied.

"I'll be back with some food for you," Rowan said. "And I'll arrange for a rental car, too."

"Sounds good," he replied, and then braced himself for seeing Annalise again. He knocked on her hotel room door.

"Come in."

He was surprised to find her door unlocked. He pushed open the door and stepped inside. She stood from the chair at the desk and faced him. There was a charged stillness between them for a long moment.

She moved forward and into his waiting arms. She'd just been through a horrendous event. Who knew what she'd had to do to survive her time in that classroom.

He held her as she buried her face in the crook of his neck and cried. He knew her tears were a combination of exhaustion and stress, and fear for the little girl who was still missing.

He caressed a hand up and down her back and murmured soothing sounds as he waited for her to stop crying. He wanted to be here for her, but he also needed her to move away from him.

Holding her was bringing up old memories he shouldn't entertain. Besides, he still had an active crime to resolve, and that's where all his thoughts and the last of his energy needed to go.

Finally she gathered her emotions, and after drawing several deep, shuddery breaths, she stepped back from him and sat on the edge of the bed. "Any news on Sadie?"

He turned to close and lock her door, then faced her once again. "Not yet. We're doing everything possible to find them, but so far we have nothing." He gestured toward the computer. "You said Sadie might try to get you a message, and let's hope that happens soon. One of Jacob's men confirmed that was their plan all along, to take one of the girls and break into a banking system. I'd send you home, but you also mentioned a secret language you all have."

She tucked a strand of her long hair behind her ear, an old nervous habit he remembered from years past. "It was mostly just for fun. The girls loved learning it and using it to communicate with me and each other. For me it was just another tool to keep their minds engaged and challenged."

"So, do you really think Sadie will try to contact you on this page?"

"Absolutely. If she gets an opportunity to get on a computer, then I believe she'll make contact. She's very smart, Evan." Tears glistened in her beautiful green eyes once again. "She's very special, and she's already been through a lot in her short life."

"We'll get her back, Annalise," he said. There was no question that Jacob and his wife were dangerous criminals, but at the moment they needed Sadie to go through with their insane plan.

"You mentioned something about thinking Jacob had inside information?"

She frowned thoughtfully. "I can't be absolutely sure, but all my instincts say yes. Jacob knew Sadie was the smartest of the girls. He told her that a little bird had told him she was the smartest. At one point he offered her something to eat and not the others. He also said something about having information that the only people who would be in the school when they burst in would be me and a few students."

"That definitely sounds like there was an insider working with them." He grimaced. "I've got Hendrick checking into the backgrounds of everyone who works at the school. Is there anyone you can think of who might be a part of this?"

Her frown deepened. "I can't imagine anyone I work with helping those monsters. I truly believe all the teachers love their jobs and the students, and would never have anything to do with what happened."

"I know you must be exhausted. Why don't you take a shower and then sleep for a couple of hours? I'll stay here and keep an eye on the web page, and I'll wake you if anything shows up there," he suggested.

She looked down at herself and frowned and nodded in agreement. He knew Rowan had provided fresh clothing for her as well as some toiletries.

"A hot shower sounds wonderful. Maybe I can wash off some of the filth I feel after being around those horrible people."

She picked up the things Rowan had gotten for her and then headed for the bathroom. Once she was gone and the door had closed behind her, he sank down on the edge of the bed and drew in several deep breaths.

The sound of the shower running instantly evoked a vision of her beautiful naked body beneath the water. He closed his eyes. They used to love to shower together.

He opened his eyes and released another deep sigh. He'd worked many difficult cases in his years with TCD, but to save a little girl in danger by working with the ex-lover who had walked out on him promised to be one of his most challenging ever.

Chapter Seven

The long hot shower refreshed Annalise more than she wanted to admit under the circumstances, but it didn't completely wash away the trauma of the entire event. Her lower lip was still slightly swollen from the slaps she'd received, and her body ached from the various bouts of physical abuse she'd endured from Gretchen.

Still, she'd take the aches and pain. At least she was alive, and she prayed that Sadie would be recovered alive and well.

She pulled on the jeans and TCD tee Rowan had provided, and then stood in front of the vanity mirror and dried her long hair, trying not to think about Evan and their past relationship. That was over and done, and there was absolutely nothing between them now but the shared desire to save a little girl.

She mentally thanked Rowan for the personal items as she brushed her teeth, and by the time she was finished with the simple task, a deep weariness filled her.

The energy she'd expended over the ordeal had been both mental and physical. She'd gotten very little sleep during the days and nights in captivity, and the continuous stream of adrenaline she'd endured while in that classroom resulted in a bone weariness she could no longer fight off.

"Anything?" she asked as she stepped out of the bathroom.

"Nothing so far," Evan replied. He was seated at the table eating a large sandwich. "The only thing that happened while you were showering is that Rowan got me some food."

She sat on the edge of the bed. "Rowan's an angel."

"She is, and she's really smart, too. She handles all aspects of the ground game. I swear if she hadn't gotten between me and the chief of police several times, I might have shot him."

He explained some of the issues he'd had with the chief, and as he spoke she found her eyelids growing heavier and heavier. "Get some sleep, Annalise," he finally said. "You're too tired to even pretend to be listening to me."

"I'm listening," she protested sleepily.

He got up and turned off the light over the table, leaving only a small desk lamp illuminating the room. "I promise I'll wake you if something breaks," he told her.

"Okay." She stretched out on the bed without turning down the spread. It was so amazing to rest and know she was safe. Still, she offered up a prayer for Sadie.

"Hey," he called to her softly. "You were great in there."

She released a half laugh and a half sob of exhaustion.

"Annalise, are you sure you're okay?" he asked.

"I will be once Sadie is home," she replied drowsily.

"We'll get her," he murmured.

Almost immediately sleep claimed her. She slept hard and without dreams. She awakened to early-morning daylight drifting in through the parted curtains, and the scent of fresh coffee.

She bolted upright and her first thought was of Sadie. Evan sat at the table, his eyes red-rimmed and lines of exhaustion cut down the sides of his handsome face. "There's fresh coffee in the pot."

"Thanks. I guess you haven't heard anything?"

He shook his head, frowning. "Nothing. It's like they drove away from the school and disappeared off the face of the earth."

She raked her fingers through her hair and then got out of bed. She poured herself a cup of the hotel coffee and joined him at the table.

"Feel better?" he asked, although his gaze shot to someplace just over her head.

"Much better," she replied. "I certainly didn't mean to sleep as long as I did."

"I'm sure you needed it," he replied.

Evan looked tired. He wore a white shirt with sleeves rolled up to his elbows and dark pants. His hair was slightly mussed and his beard was growing out, but that did nothing to detract from how appealing he was.

She sipped her coffee as the silence grew between them. The parted curtains gave her a view of a swimming pool outside. She peeked out and then stared down into her coffee cup. She wasn't sure what to say, and she had a feeling he felt the same way about her.

Finally she gazed at him once again. "Evan, you look positively exhausted," she said. "I know you spent all your time on the bullhorn and working the scene, so maybe it's way past time you take a shower and get a little bit of sleep. I can watch the computer screen and let you know if anything happens."

He leaned back in the chair and took a drink of his

coffee. "Yeah, I guess that might be a good idea. I'm definitely reaching the end of my energy."

"Evan, you won't be good for anything if you don't stop and take care of yourself," she chided.

"Maybe you could ring me in an hour or two so I don't sleep too long," he suggested.

"I'll have to use the house phone. Jacob destroyed my cell phone when he found it on me."

He looked at her for a long moment, his eyes narrowed. "What else did he do?"

She ran her tongue over her lower lip where the swelling was barely noticeable. "I don't want to talk about…"

"I'm sorry, Annalise. I'm sorry you had to endure that kind of abuse."

"It's over now. Isn't it time for you to get some sleep?"

He took another drink of his coffee and then stood. "If you're sure you've got this, then I'll head back to my room and take a short nap. My room is next door on the right, room 108."

"I've got this. Go get some rest."

"Close and lock the door behind me," he said.

When he left the room, she locked the door then resumed her seat at the table. "Sadie, where are you?" she whispered to herself as she stared at the computer screen.

If Jacob and Gretchen hadn't put her in front of a computer yet, maybe it was because they were still traveling and looking for a safe place to land. They had to know they couldn't go back to their compound, so it was anyone's guess where they might be going.

She sipped her coffee and her mind filled with the thought of Evan showering. A bit of tension coiled in her stomach, a tension that had nothing to do with Sadie or what was going on with the crimes.

She shook her head to dispel the memories. It had been nearly three years since they had been together as a couple. That amount of time changed people. She didn't really know him now.

She had no idea what he had done or who he might have loved since they'd been a couple. It was possible he had a meaningful other right now.

She didn't know what life experiences he'd had in the time they'd been apart. There were things they hadn't shared. They were really virtual strangers now.

Still, there was no question being with him again had stirred some confusing emotions inside her, but she told herself all she wanted from him—all she really needed—was for him to bring Sadie home. Then they could both get back to their separate lives.

"MARIA," EVAN YELLED to his little sister, who had just run into the alleyway chasing a butterfly. Reluctantly he got up from the stoop where he had been sitting with some of his buddies.

"Maria," he shouted once again. Sometimes watching his little sister could be a real pain.

He entered the alleyway, the smell of the overflowing garbage cans beneath the heat of the day pungent and nearly overpowering. He narrowed his eyes as he advanced deeper into the darker narrow passageway.

He suddenly froze. A man, wearing a dirty blue bandana to hide the lower half of his face, held Maria against his body with a knife to her throat. A terror he'd never known before ripped through Evan.

"Go on, get out of here, boy," the man said gruffly.

Maria's big brown eyes pleaded with Evan to do something, anything to save her.

On trembling legs he took two steps forward. "Let her go." Sweat trickled down the center of his back. Nausea rose in Evan's throat, and his entire body flushed in horror. This was like something out of the scariest movie he'd ever seen. He had to do something to save his little sister.

"I told you to get out of here unless you want me to slit her throat," the man growled.

"No, please don't hurt her!" Evan exclaimed.

The man lunged forward and swiped the knife toward Evan's face. Evan leaped backward as the blade slashed perilously close to his cheek. "Please...let her go. She's my sister."

"You aren't in control here, kid. She's mine now." The man suddenly picked up Maria, then turned and ran. "Evan," the little girl cried.

"Maria!" Evan screamed.

EVAN BOLTED UPRIGHT, his heart racing and his body bathed in a light sheen of sweat. For just a moment, he was a frightened eight-year-old again and in that foul-smelling alley, confronting a man with a knife who had his little sister.

He wiped a hand down his face and then realized it hadn't been the nightmare that had ultimately awakened him, but rather Hendrick on a video call.

He scrambled out of bed and hurried to the desk where his computer was set up. "Hendrick, you have something for me?"

"The van."

Evan straightened, now wide awake. "What about it?"

"I found it."

"Where?"

"Believe it or not, in the parking lot of a grocery store five miles from the school," Hendrick replied. "I ran security tape in the lot, and it looked like Jacob, Gretchen and Sadie left the van and then walked out of camera range. Unfortunately, I haven't been able to pick them up on any other cameras in the area."

Evan cursed. "So, we don't have any idea what kind of vehicle they might be in now or where they might have gone."

"That's about the sum of it," Hendrick replied grimly.

"Is it possible they're on foot right now?"

Hendrick shook his head. "I don't believe so. They got out of that van with a sense of purpose. They didn't look around, but rather started walking quickly. I think they knew there was another ride waiting for them."

"Give me the exact location of the van," Evan said.

He took down the pertinent information and then disconnected. He grabbed his holster and gun from the nightstand and then left his room. He knocked on Annalise's door.

She opened the door. "Evan... I thought you were sleeping."

"I just got a call from Hendrick. He found the black van in a parking lot about five miles from here, so I'm calling some of the men to meet me there."

"I'm coming with you," she said. "Maybe Sadie somehow left some kind of clue for us in the van. Just let me grab my room key card."

Evan had hoped after a couple hours of sleep he would be able to better focus on finding Sadie. Although he felt physically refreshed from the almost two hours of sleep he had gotten, mentally he still felt half-exhausted with the weight of the case on his shoulders and trying to deal with his unexpected emotions where Annalise was concerned.

Minutes later, with her seated next to him in the rental car, he had an overwhelming need to reach out and touch her.

He gripped the steering wheel more tightly. He had to stay focused on the crime that had brought them together in the first place and not on anything else. He still had a little girl to find, and he was desperate to get that right.

While he drove he called Nick and Davis and told them where the van was parked and instructed them to meet him there. He then called Hendrick to see if there had been any stolen car reports from the area in and around the parking lot.

"Already done," Hendrick replied, and so far there were no stolen car reports. "And I think it's safe to say that if they had stolen a car, it would have been reported by now. According to the time stamp on the security tape, they had to have driven directly from the school to that parking lot."

"It's possible Jacob arranged for somebody at the compound to meet him with a car. See if you can get in touch with whoever is in charge of the traffic in and out of the compound. Maybe they'll have a record of a car that went out sometime last night and then never came back."

"On it. I'll get back to you as soon as I have something."

Evan hung up his phone and glanced at his passenger. She looked as tense as he felt as he pulled into the grocery store's large parking lot. "The van is parked in section D," he said, slowing to find the right aisle.

"Over there," she said, and pointed to their left.

He turned and slowed down even more. He saw the vehicle right before Annalise pointed it out. There was an empty space next to it, and Evan pulled in and parked.

He and Annalise both jumped out of the car at the same time. He headed for the driver's side door and she went to the back door. The side of the van had a couple of bullet holes, and he was vaguely surprised to find it unlocked.

If the police officers who were tasked to keep the van from leaving the school had done their job right, then there would have been bullet holes in the front of the vehicle. The fact that they were on the sides told the whole story of incompetence that Evan had suspected, and it infuriated him.

He'd only just begun to search it when Nick and Davis arrived. He got out of the van and instructed Annalise to do the same. "I want you two to go over this with a fine-tooth comb. As you know, we're looking for anything that might indicate where they were going from here and what kind of vehicle they might be driving now."

As the two agents got busy checking out the van, Evan got back on his phone to check in with some of the others, including Chief Cummings. Everyone had a job to do, and it was Evan's job to coordinate all the efforts to find the fugitives.

Unfortunately, the fact that Annalise believed so strongly that Sadie would contact her by using some sort of code made her an important piece of this whole puzzle. She was especially important right now since they had absolutely no leads on where the three had gone or how they might be traveling.

Before he'd fallen asleep, he'd contacted Rowan to

get Annalise a cell phone she could use for the time being. Annalise got on the phone and checked the secret page, then then shook her head. Apparently Sadie still hadn't made contact.

"Hey, I've got something here," Nick said from the backseat of the van. "It looks like something has been scratched into the back of the front seat."

Evan looked to where Nick pointed. Sure enough, it looked like a fingernail or something had been used to scratch letters, numbers and symbols that made no sense.

"Annalise, take a look at this and see what you think," he said. He backed out and gave her room to look.

She leaned in. "It's…it's from Sadie." Her voice was thick with emotion as she straightened. "It's in our secret language. It says 'Sadie was here.'" Her eyes filled with tears as she gazed at him. "She wanted me…she wanted everyone to know that she was here." She began to cry.

There was something particularly heartbreaking about a kidnapped little girl wanting her teacher and law enforcement to know that she was in the van, that she was still alive.

As Evan saw the emotion ripping through Annalise, he couldn't just stand by and watch. He pulled her into his arms and held her.

"I'm sorry," she said as she swiped her cheeks in obvious embarrassment. "I don't seem to have much control over my emotions right now."

"It's okay," he replied. "I'm sure you're still functioning on a lack of sleep and your worry about Sadie. At least we know now why they want her and they aren't going to harm her. If they were going to dump her somewhere, this would have been the perfect place. Apparently, they still need her and won't hurt her."

"Unless she can't do what they want her to, or she accomplishes what they want and then what are they going to do with her?" Annalise's tense question hung in the air.

Evan didn't have an answer to give her, but the possibilities of what might happen tortured him. He knew Jacob and his wife had no respect for human life. The man had already proven that. It was absolutely vital they find Sadie before Jacob and Gretchen decided the little girl was nothing more than a liability to them.

"I've got something," Davis said from the very back of the van. He pulled on something and then held up a license plate. "It was hidden in a slit in the carpeting."

"Good work, man." Evan took the license plate from the fellow agent. "Maybe this is the break we needed. Maybe finding out the registered owner of the van will give us more information."

Evan immediately got on the phone to Hendrick. He told the tech agent that the plate was a North Carolina plate, and he read out the numbers and letters.

"Arrange for the van to be taken into custody," he told his two men as he waited for a call back from Hendrick. He and Annalise got back into the rental car.

"We'll drive through someplace and grab some breakfast on our way back to the hotel." He shot her a quick glance. "Are you okay?"

She nodded. "I'm okay, but that message from Sadie really gutted me."

"At least it tells us she's still okay," he replied.

He swung through a drive-through, and they both ordered breakfast sandwiches. He'd just paid and received their order when Hendrick called back.

"The plates come back as belonging to an eight-seat black passenger van registered to Sandhurst School."

For just a moment Evan was speechless. He'd expected the name of a person, but this was definitely a shock. "I made a few calls and found out that the school owns three of these vans," Hendrick continued. "They are kept in a garage at a nearby vehicle rental lot, and I spoke to the owner who told me one of the vans went missing."

"There's no sign that the van has been hot-wired. Is the garage secure?" Evan asked.

"According to the owner, the vans are under lock and key. Only somebody with a key to the garage and the van could have driven one off. He hadn't even noticed that one of the vans was missing. He said he gave out four garage keys to the Sandhurst School."

"I'll make sure somebody goes to the garage and checks out the employees there," Evan said. "I know you've been busy doing other things for me, but I need the background reports on anyone who works at the school as soon as possible."

"I'll email what I already have for you and will keep digging."

"Thanks." Evan hung up.

"What does this mean?" Annalise asked.

"It's definitely an inside job," Evan said grimly. "I can tell you that the garage and van keys were always kept on a hook in the school office for when a teacher wanted to plan a field trip."

Evan digested this information and tightened his hands on the steering wheel. Now he was not only determined to find Jacob and Gretchen and save Sadie, but also he wanted the rat that might have been responsible for setting all this in motion in the first place. He definitely wanted the insider.

Chapter Eight

They took their breakfast sandwiches to Evan's room and sat at the table to eat. She felt overwhelmed with everything that was happening.

If she looked deep inside herself, she knew she'd recognize that her vulnerable state wasn't only because of the heartrending message from Sadie, it was also because of Evan.

In the past three years she'd thought she'd moved on. She'd believed she'd gotten over him. But the truth of the matter was, she was surprised to realize she wasn't over him. He still owned a large piece of her heart and she didn't know what to do about it.

Right now they were both on a mission to save Sadie, and this wasn't the time or the place to explore those feelings. She didn't want to get in the way of Evan doing his job.

"I can't believe somebody at the school might be behind all this," she said as they ate. "That possibility absolutely blows my mind."

"Hopefully we'll know more when I get all the backgrounds from Hendrick." He looked at her for a long moment. "So, what happened with you and the college in Missouri? I thought teaching there was something you really wanted to do."

"You know when I was working in the public school system I was constantly battling for better and newer equipment for the students," she replied.

"I remember how frustrated you were by the constant lack of funding."

"When I got the offer from the college, it came with the assurance that my classes would be well-funded and the students would all have state-of-the-art equipment," she replied.

"So, that wasn't the case?"

She shook her head no. "As a teacher I had the absolute best equipment I could have asked for. It was a dream job as far as that was concerned."

"Then, why aren't you still working there?" he asked.

She frowned and stared down at her breakfast sandwich. "It didn't take me long to realize the students didn't care. They really didn't care about learning. Getting a degree from that particular college was a status symbol and nothing more. If the students didn't do well enough, then pressure was placed on the teachers to make sure they passed anyway. They were spoiled, rich kids with parents who indulged them far too much."

"I'm sure giving a student a grade they hadn't earned didn't sit well with you," he replied.

"Not even," she replied adamantly. "I hated it. I stayed there for almost two years but started putting my résumé out there again. Then last year I was offered a one-year contract with the school here. It really has been a dream position. Not only do I have whatever I need as an educator, but the students are like sponges who love to learn."

Once again tears blurred her vision as she thought of Sadie. She stared down, feeling foolish for her uncontrollable emotions. What was wrong with her? Maybe

Evan was right; she was still functioning on too little sleep and her concerns for the little girl.

To her stunned surprise, he reached across the table and covered one of her hands with his. "We're going to find her, Annalise," he said with grim determination vibrating through his body and voice.

She turned her hand over and laced her fingers with his, surprised when he didn't immediately pull away. He had big, capable hands, and his larger hand nearly engulfed her smaller one. For a long moment they remained that way. She was the one to finally pull away.

Annalise released a deep sigh. "The two things that give me some bit of comfort is that Sadie is so smart and she's a survivor. Most of her life she endured being beaten and abused by her mother, and her father was never in her life. She was the one who helped me make the phone calls to you by serving as a lookout. She tried to protect me from Gretchen. She also interacted several times with Jacob, and I now wonder if she intentionally made herself the target to save the other girls who she knew weren't as strong as she was."

"Hopefully she's smart enough to know that we need help in locating her," he replied.

"She is," Annalise replied firmly. She had to believe that. She desperately needed to believe that when this was all over, Sadie would be saved.

As they finished eating, she continued to tell him more about working at Sandhurst School. "Regina Sandhurst has been a great boss." She frowned thoughtfully. "You know, now that I think about it, for the last couple of months Susan DeKalb has been worried about her finances, although I can't imagine how she or anyone else at the school would have come in contact with the likes of Jacob or Gretchen."

"Hopefully Hendrick can come up with some answers for us."

"My contract is up in December, and I'm not sure I'll sign another one."

He looked at her in surprise. "But it sounds like this was your dream job…great equipment and children who love to learn." He raised one of his dark eyebrows quizzically. "Would you not want to return because of what has happened?"

"No, something like this would never deter me from coming back to work. The real reason I'm probably going to return to Knoxville is because my father has been struggling with heart disease, and I think both my parents need me there."

It felt strange, sharing these things with him. It felt strange to be sharing anything with him. She'd never dreamed they'd ever see or talk to each other again.

"I'm assuming you're a rock star at TCD," she said. "I can't imagine you doing anything else."

He smiled. "You should know it's all in my blood, the pressure…the danger…and the desire to save people who find themselves in horrible situations. I'll work there as long as they'll have me."

"I'm sure they consider you a terrific asset," she replied.

He released a small, dry laugh. "You were always good at flattery."

"It's not empty flattery," she protested. "It's the truth. Look at the situation you just got us out of."

His smile faded and his eyes darkened. "Jacob and Gretchen got away with one of the hostages. Right now I consider this whole operation an epic fail."

"From what I've heard, the fail wasn't yours but rather that of local officials. You couldn't know that those officers would run and hide at the first gun shots outside the van window," she protested. She'd overheard just enough conversations to know what had happened.

"Yeah, but I should have made sure there were enough men in the back of the school to keep that van from leaving. I should have recognized the weakness, especially after working with Chief Cummings for any length of time."

"You can't control everything all the time, Evan. You're being way too hard on yourself," she said softly. "You did everything humanly possible. You need to cut yourself some slack."

He merely sighed and they fell into a silence. It wasn't a comfortable silence, rather it was charged with tension.

"Surely they've had enough time by now to find someplace to land," she said in frustration.

"We won't know that unless Hendrick comes up with something or Sadie gets access to a computer." He rubbed the back of his neck, a sign of his own frustration.

A knock fell on his door. He got up from the table. "Maybe that's one of my men with some new information."

He opened the door and over his shoulder Annalise saw a tall, brown-haired stranger. He offered Evan a tentative smile. "Are you Special Agent Duran?"

"I am," Evan replied.

"Uh… I have some news for you."

"And you are?" Evan asked.

The man shifted from one foot to the other, and his gaze shot from Evan to Annalise. "My name is Phil Sanders. I have some information about Jacob Noble. Uh…can I come in?"

"Why don't you just give me the information you have for me?" Evan replied.

He froze and Annalise gasped as Phil reached behind him and pulled a gun. There was a charged long minute of silence. Her heart raced, and every muscle in her body tensed with a fight or flight adrenaline rush.

"What do you want, Phil?" Evan asked calmly.

"The first thing I want is for you to toss your gun onto the bed, and if you make a wrong move, I'll kill you both."

Annalise gasped. Who was this man? What did he want? There were FBI and local authorities throughout the hotel. How had he managed to just walk up to Evan's door?

"That's not happening, so just tell me what you want," Evan replied, his voice still cool and calm.

The man looked frustrated. "I need you to get rid of your weapon."

"And I told you that isn't happening, so tell me what you want and why you're here or shoot me right now."

The man gestured with his gun for Evan to back up. He did so, and Phil stepped into the room and closed the door behind him. "I'm with the Brotherhood of Jacob, and I want you to call off the search for Jacob and Gretchen."

"And if I don't?"

Phil's blue eyes narrowed. "If you don't call off the search right now, then I'm going to kill you."

Annalise's heart banged hard against her ribs, making her half-breathless as she stared at the gunman.

His hand shook as he held the weapon pointed at Evan's chest. "Stop the search for Jacob and Gretchen right now."

"Annalise, I want you to go into the bathroom and close and lock the door," Evan said.

"Don't move," Phil half shouted at her. He aimed the gun at her and then jerked it back to point at Evan.

"Go ahead, Annalise..." Evan said calmly.

"I'm not leaving you," she replied despite her fear. There was no way she was just going to run and hide in the bathroom and leave Evan to face this threat alone.

"Listen to me, Annalise," Evan said, his voice still calm and steady. "Focus on me. I need you to go to the bathroom and lock the door."

Annalise stood and held her position next to the table. "Don't move...don't move," Phil yelled at her. Sweat worked down the sides of his reddened face.

There was no way, no matter how many times Evan told her to go into the bathroom, she was leaving him. With both of them in the room, the man would be more apt to get distracted. If he did, then Evan would be able to take control of the situation.

"Phil, you need to calm down," Evan said.

"My job is to protect Jacob, so you need to stop the search for him right now. He's our leader, and he's doing good things for the world," Phil replied.

"Phil, I don't have the power to stop anything," Evan replied. "I couldn't stop this search right now if I wanted to. It's all out of my hands. So, you have two choices right now—either kill me or put the gun down and let's talk."

"You have the power," Phil screamed. "Stop the damned search. Jacob has to be protected."

Annalise took two steps forward and then paused. Her fear was all-consuming. Phil looked half-deranged as he faced them. How had this happened? How had the man even found out where they were staying?

"Nobody can protect Jacob anymore," Evan said softly. "Jacob and Gretchen have made some really bad mistakes. Now why don't you put your gun down, and you can tell me about the good work the members of the Brotherhood do."

The gun in Phil's hand began to shake as he looked from Evan to Annalise. She took another step forward, and Phil's eyes widened in panic.

"Look at me, Phil," Evan said. "Give me your gun, Phil." Evan's voice was almost hypnotic, and she knew his use of Phil's name was to let the man know Evan really saw him and wanted to interact with him.

It was one of his strengths as a hostage negotiator... making people feel comfortable...making people want to talk to him. While it hadn't worked with Jacob, it appeared to be working on Phil, who looked far less sure of himself than he had when he'd initially confronted Evan.

"Come on, Phil. I know you're a good man who wants to do the right thing," Evan continued. "I'm sure you didn't know what Jacob and the rest of the men were planning. People died, Phil. When they went into the school they killed good people who were just going about their daily lives and doing their jobs."

"None of us back at the compound had any idea they were going to bust into a school," Phil admitted.

Evan took a step toward him and then reached out and took hold of the barrel of the gun. Phil began to weep as he finally relinquished the weapon.

Evan led him to the edge of the bed and grabbed his cell phone. As Phil continued to cry, Evan made a quick call to Davis. Annalise sank back down at the table as a sigh of relief escaped her.

"You don't understand," Phil said as Evan hung up.

"Jacob and Gretchen control everything. They tell us all what to do and we do it. They've always told us how to live our daily lives. We...we...none of us know how to survive without them."

"Phil, I'm sure you're all smart and resourceful people. Everyone will have to find a way without them," Evan replied smoothly.

"I don't even know why he went to that school in the first place." Phil swiped at his tears. "He didn't tell all of us exactly what his plans were. If I hadn't seen it on the news, I wouldn't have known they were all in that school."

"It's going to be okay, Phil. You're going to be just fine," Evan replied with assurance.

Annalise's admiration for Evan soared off the charts. Moments before, Phil had held Evan at gunpoint and threatened to kill him. Now he was talking to that same man in a calm and respectful and compassionate way.

Phil explained to Evan he'd hidden out in a storage closet until the halls were quiet, and then he'd come to the room. He'd also told them there were others at the compound who knew not only the hotel where FBI agents were staying, but also Evan's room number.

She remained silent at the table and listened to the two men talk. Finally Davis appeared at the door with Nick, and the two men left with Phil in their custody.

Evan walked back to the bed, sank down and then looked at her. "Are you okay?"

"My heart is still beating faster than it should, but I'm fine."

"Why didn't you do what I asked of you? You should have gone into the bathroom."

"I thought it was better for me not to remove myself from the room," she countered. "I figured two of us would be more of a distraction to him. As it is, it all worked out okay."

"Until we neutralize this situation, I need you to listen to me." He offered her a faint smile. "You know how I like to control my crime scenes."

"I do. Would it be possible for you to work this scene from my house instead of this hotel? I'd love to go home. I have all the office equipment we would need... We can set up a command center in my living room. I also have three bedrooms. That way we wouldn't be spending all our time in these hotel rooms. Think about it, Evan. My place is only five minutes from here."

He frowned thoughtfully. "I don't like the fact that members of this group now know where we are staying. I don't want to have to use additional resources to make sure this doesn't happen again."

"What I worry about is that the next person from the compound who shows up here will shoot first instead of talk. They might all blame you for everything because you were the main man on the scene," she replied.

He frowned, obviously thinking it through.

"Evan, let's just pack up and go. It makes sense." She wasn't sure why, but she suddenly realized she needed to be back in her own home.

She wanted her familiar things surrounding her. It felt like it had been months and months since she'd been home. Right now her emotions were all over the place. She was frightened for Sadie, and her feelings where Evan was concerned were so unsettled.

The confines of a hotel room felt far too intimate, and at least if they were working from her house she could feel like she had a little distance from Evan... distance that might help her sort out her crazy emotions about him.

This wasn't over yet. She had no idea how long it might be before it was over. Hopefully it would end with Sadie's rescue and clarity for her where Evan was concerned.

She got up from the table and sank down on the bed next to him. "I just want you to know that I was impressed with how you handled Phil."

"I had a pretty good idea that he wasn't going to shoot anyone," he replied.

"But how did you know that?"

He smiled at her. "Annalise, I'm trained to know that. I look for certain tells. More than anything I could see his fear. He held the weapon without any real confidence, and he was far too emotional. Besides, he didn't have a killer's eyes."

She returned his smile. "I always told you that you're the best hostage negotiator in the whole wide world."

His dark gaze softened. "And I always said that you were the most beautiful woman in the whole wide world."

He was too close to her. Her breath suddenly felt a bit labored as the moment between them lingered. His thigh pressed against hers, his warm body intimately near, and as the residual fear she'd felt earlier completely drained away from her another emotion surfaced.

Desire.

It rocked through her and flushed her entire body with a sweet warmth. He felt it, too. She saw it in the sudden burn of his eyes as he gazed at her.

She leaned closer and parted her lips in invitation. Her heart stuttered to a near halt as she waited to see what he was going to do. And then his lips were on hers. At first it was a hesitant, tender kiss, but then it became more insistent, far more demanding as his tongue swirled with hers.

His hands tangled in her hair, and she turned to grip his shoulders. Oh, she'd missed this…she'd so missed him. His mouth felt so familiar and yet at the same time so exciting and new to her.

The kiss spoke to a place deep inside her that had been dormant since the day they had parted ways, a place that now felt alive and as necessary as the very air she breathed.

"Annalise," he moaned as his mouth left hers and found the spot just behind her ear that often drove her wild with desire. He then blazed a trail of nipping kisses down the side of her neck.

How on earth had she ever walked away from this man? His simplest touch electrified her, and his kisses made her feel more alive than any man she had ever dated before or would probably ever date in the future.

Slowly his hands untangled from her hair and moved down her back. He pressed her tightly against him as once again his mouth found hers for another soul-stirring kiss.

She wanted him. She leaned back, pulling him with her so they both were lying on the bed. She could feel his heart beating rapidly against her own, letting her know he wanted her as much as she wanted him.

One of his hands began to caress her stomach, each stroke bringing him closer and closer to her breasts. She wanted his touch. Oh, dear heaven, she wanted them both naked and moving together beneath the sheets.

"Evan." She breathed his name as his mouth once again left hers. As he kissed down the side of her cheek, his beard created an additional pleasant sensation.

Finally his hand covered one of her breasts. Even

though she wore a T-shirt and a bra, her nipples hardened as if eager for a more intimate touch.

She pushed against him and raised up just enough to pull the T-shirt over her head and toss it to the other side of the bed.

He unbuttoned and took his shirt off as well, and once again they came together. Her skin remembered the warmth and pleasure of his. As they kissed, their tongues once again swirled together in a wild dance of half-breathless passion. His fingers moved to her bra hooks…

At that moment a knock fell on the door.

Evan jumped up, half-dazed with his desire for her. He grabbed his shirt and quickly buttoned it while Annalise grabbed her T-shirt and ran for the bathroom.

He drew in a deep breath, grabbed his gun from the nightstand and then opened the door to see Davis. "I just wanted to let you know that Phil is now a guest in Chief Cummings's jail."

"Thanks, man. I'm now wondering if all the members of that group are as rabid as Phil."

"Whatever they call themselves, they are definitely a cult," Davis replied. "According to Phil, a bunch of them are planning to set up a protest of some kind later this evening outside the hotel. I have a feeling it's going to be a circus."

That made up Evan's mind. The last thing he wanted was to try to stay focused and concentrate while a bunch of crazy cult members set up camp outside the hotel. Davis nodded to Annalise as she returned to the room.

"Annalise has offered the use of her house to me… and I'm going to take her up on it."

He had to admit that what had happened just before Davis had knocked on the door had shocked him. His desire for her had caught him off guard, and he didn't want that to happen again. Surely a house would be less intimate than the hotel rooms, and it really didn't matter where he did his work.

"My place is only minutes from here," she said to Davis.

"Sounds like a perfect way to avoid the circus that might go on here," Davis replied. "It's going to be difficult to completely secure the hotel now, and that's going to take manpower. Instead of being out looking for the fugitives, a bunch of officers will now have to be here. When are you planning on making the move?"

"As soon as we can," Evan said. He could see no downside to moving to her house.

"Then I'll get out of here," Davis replied.

"I'll text you and the others as soon as we're settled at Annalise's place," Evan said.

Once Davis was gone, he turned to Annalise. "You need to get packed up."

She stared at him for a long moment. "Shouldn't we talk about what just happened between us?"

"There isn't much to talk about," he replied. "Adrenaline was running high. We'd just been through a tense situation with Phil, and what happened between us was a mistake and we need to make sure it doesn't happen again. I've got a missing child and two dangerous fugitives on the run, and I need to be completely focused on that."

"And I want you to be completely focused on getting Sadie back, but I will tell you it didn't feel like a mistake to me. It felt wonderful, and now I'll go pack up my things."

When she left the room, Evan drew in a deep breath. Yes, it had been wonderful to have her in his arms again, but he wasn't here to explore a relationship with her. He had a job to do.

Thirty minutes later they were in the rental car and heading to Annalise's home. The ride was silent other than her giving him directions. He was grateful for the silence and he used it to recenter himself.

Annalise's rental ranch house was located in a quiet neighborhood with lots of mature trees. The first thing he did when they arrived was a quick walk around the house to orient himself to his new surroundings. Then she guided him into a pleasant living room decorated in browns and golds.

"You can use this bedroom," she said as she showed him to one of the guest rooms.

He scarcely noticed the bedroom, instead intent on getting his work area ready. The dining room table was large, and on a desk nearby was her computer with a large monitor. He set up his computer on the table and immediately checked in with Davis, Nick and Daniel back at the hotel.

While he was talking to his men, Annalise powered up her computer at the desk. He checked his watch, shocked to realize it was only a little after two in the afternoon.

He definitely wanted to have Sadie back before nightfall and right now he racked his brain to see what else he could do to make that happen.

HENDRICK AWOKE WITH a start. He sat up, raised a hand, raced it through his hair and tried to shrug off the last of his sleep.

When Director Pembrook had insisted he needed to get some rest, he'd finally gone to a break room where there were several cots for the agents to use. He'd fallen asleep almost as soon as his head had touched the pillow.

He checked his watch, thankful that he'd only been out for about two hours. What was going on with the case? What had he missed while he'd slept? He hoped it was all over, that Sadie had been found and Jacob and his creepy wife were behind bars.

He got up and headed to the locker room for a quick shower. Once the shower was done, he changed into a clean pair of jeans and a T-shirt from his locker.

Immediately after that he headed to the nearest coffee machine. He filled up a disposable cup with the dark brew and then hurried to the tech office where Agent Curt Corkland was seated in front of the computers.

"Hey, man, anything happening?" he asked.

"You weren't down for very long," Curt said. "I didn't expect you back so soon."

"I feel pretty refreshed. I've never required too much sleep. So, tell me what's going on?"

"I've just been working on gathering the backgrounds on some of the school faculty members. So far nothing is bringing up any red flags. There are still a few to check out."

Hendrick frowned. "Evan seems certain that Jacob and Gretchen had inside information when they entered the school, and the van belonging to the school seems to confirm that. I just want to catch that rat."

"Well, there are a few more people I haven't gotten to yet. Maybe you'll find your rat among them," Curt said.

"Heard anything from Evan?"

Curt shook his head. "No, nothing from anyone."

Hendrick took a drink of his coffee and motioned Curt up and out of the seat. "I'm good now. Thanks for manning the post."

"No prob," Curt replied. He showed him the list of faculty and staff that he'd managed to get through so far, and then he left the room.

Hendrick settled in his chair and began the background search on the next person on the list. He'd been dividing the background checks, not only checking out the staff at the school, but also the members from the Brotherhood of Jacob. He was trying to discover if any of them had any property anywhere, any place where Jacob and Gretchen might be able to go into hiding.

He clicked over to the page where Annalise hoped Sadie would make contact. So far…nothing. He took another drink of his coffee and fought against a level of frustration he'd rarely felt since leaving the cult behind.

Before going down for his brief rest, he'd also been in touch with the men at the compound who were sending him the tag numbers of the cars coming and going. Hendrick had been pulling up DMV records to identify the owners.

His biggest fear was that the vehicle Jacob was now using was one that had left the compound before the police presence there had been established. It was also possible somebody connected to the school had provided Jacob with another ride. Who in the hell was the insider who had helped organize the evil that had taken place at the school?

Another night would soon approach, and the more time that passed the less the odds were of finding Sadie alive. God, he wanted to help rescue this kid. He needed her to be okay.

Despite the fact he knew it wasn't true, he felt somehow if they didn't manage to save little Sadie, then it would mean he'd never really escaped the bonds of the cult that had nearly destroyed him.

Chapter Nine

It felt odd being in her house, among her things. She made them sandwiches, and then they settled side by side at the table to eat.

After two years with Annalise, Evan knew what was important to her and what was not. Almost three years had passed since they'd been in each other's lives, but he didn't really want to know anything more about her than he already knew. He didn't want to open any doors that had already been closed.

Yeah, it had been great to hold her, to kiss her once again, but he told himself their brief intimacy had been the result of adrenaline from facing Phil and the frustration from where things stood in the investigation. He told himself it had really meant nothing to him.

They ate quickly and without much conversation. When they finished, she settled at her computer at the desk and he got on the phone to check the status of all the arms of the investigation.

When Annalise's doorbell rang, he jumped up from the table and pulled his gun. He wasn't about to get caught unaware again. Annalise got up as well and followed him to answer the door.

He opened it to see Rowan. "Hey, Rowan," he said,

and immediately holstered his gun and gestured her into the house. "What's going on?"

"I just wanted to check in with you before I head back to headquarters," she said.

"You're leaving me here all alone with that waste of a police chief?" he asked.

Rowan grinned. "Afraid so. Director Pembrook called me back to Knoxville. Besides, your interaction with Chief Cummings should be fairly minimal at this point. I have confidence that you can handle it."

"Well, that makes one of us," he replied dryly.

"Evan, just don't kill him. It would make a mess of paperwork for everyone," she replied with a small laugh.

"Rowan, I want to thank you for the personal items you got for me," Annalise said. "I really appreciate it."

"No problem," she replied.

Annalise reached into her pocket and pulled out the cell phone. "I'm assuming you need this back now."

"That's okay. Keep it until Evan leaves and then you can give it to him," Rowan said, and then gazed back at Evan. "It's actually good that you two relocated here. When I left the hotel, there were about a dozen people from the compound already there for some sort of protest against law enforcement and the FBI. They have big signs declaring police abuse and all kinds of crazy things."

Evan grimaced. "Sounds like the police are going to have their hands full there." He smiled once again at Rowan. "Thanks, Rowan, as always, for everything you did to support the team."

Her eyes twinkled with humor. "I have to admit there were a couple of times when I wanted to hog-tie Chief Cummings and toss him in a barn far, far away."

Evan laughed. "There were definitely times I would have helped you with that."

"Okay, then I'm off," Rowan replied. She smiled at Annalise and then looked back at him. "I know you, Evan, and I hope you aren't beating yourself up about how this has turned out so far. I know you'll get these SOBs."

"Thanks, Rowan."

Evan walked her to the door, and once she was gone he had just sat back at the dining room table when Annalise's computer dinged with a notification. Hope speared through him as he jumped up and Annalise raced across the room to the desk. A nonsensical sentence had appeared on the special page.

He couldn't help the excitement that roared through him. Was this it? Was this finally what they had been waiting for? A note from Sadie letting them know where she was being held?

"It's not from Sadie," she said flatly. "It's from Emily."

Evan's heart plummeted. "What does it say?"

"It says, 'Sadie, I know you're missing. Where are you? We're all worried about you.'"

"You need to get on there and ask the other girls not to post anything to the page until Sadie is found," he said.

Annalise nodded and sat at the desk. She typed what looked like an equally nonsensical message and then hit enter. "Now, let's hope the next person who posts here is Sadie," he said.

He sank back down in his chair and released a deep sigh. "When I heard that notification go off, I was sure it was her."

"I feel like this is some form of terrible torture...

waiting for her to make contact with us," she said. "What happens if she doesn't? What happens if I'm wrong about this or she doesn't get any opportunity to get on the page?"

"Right now Jacob and Gretchen are on every wanted list in the nation. Law enforcement agencies all over the area will be on the lookout for them. Sooner or later they will make a mistake, and we'll find them."

She held his gaze for a long moment and then with a nod she went into the kitchen. With disappointment weighing heavily in his heart, his thoughts turned to the woman who had just disappeared from the room.

What was wrong with him? He could face an armed gunman locked in a building with his wife and kids as hostages without breaking a sweat, but being in the same space as Annalise was...difficult.

He was haunted by the ghosts of their past, tormented by how badly he'd misread her at the time and the love he'd thought they had shared.

He had to stay focused on the fact that she was an important piece of the puzzle of a missing child and nothing more. However, it did bother him that after almost three years apart he still had such strong emotions where she was concerned. It had been far easier to ignore these emotions when he had been in Knoxville and believed she had been in Missouri.

Now he was in her home and still desperate to find a little girl who was missing and in extreme danger. He drew a weary sigh and recognized his thoughts were flying all over the place. It was probably the lack of sleep. All he needed was to fuel himself with some caffeine.

When Annalise came back into the room, he asked her about coffee. "I'll get you a cup," she offered. "But while you're here, I want you to feel free to use whatever you need in the kitchen or anywhere else."

"Thanks," he replied.

Minutes later they were back at their computers. He was grateful when Hendrick called. "Hey, I think I might have a couple of live ones for you. In doing background on the school staff, some red flags have come up."

"Who?" Evan sat up straighter in his chair, all thoughts of weariness gone.

"An English teacher named Susan DeKalb and a janitor named Earl Winslow."

"Teacher first," Evan said. He was aware of Annalise listening intently to the conversation.

"Susan DeKalb is sixty-three years old and according to the financials I have, she's completely broke. Six months ago she pulled out her retirement funds and put her life savings into a restaurant her son owned, and it's now gone belly-up. She's looking at retirement with only a very small pension and a social security check."

Evan frowned thoughtfully. "So, it's possible she's helping Jacob out for a financial benefit."

"That was my thought. Unfortunately, I haven't found a connection between her and the Brotherhood of Jacob and any of its members. I'm still digging into that aspect."

"And what about this Earl Winslow?" Evan asked.

"Also financially struggling. He was hired less than a year ago as a janitor after not having worked for several years. Also a search of his name pulled up a three-month-old newspaper picture of him attending a sort of open house at the Brotherhood of Jacob compound."

Evan's blood quickened. Had one of these people sold out their coworkers and the students for a deal with the devil? There was no question he believed the motive for all of this was money.

He got off the phone with Hendrick and immediately called Chief Cummings and arranged for the police to pick up the teacher and the janitor for interviews inside the police station.

"I'm heading out," he said to Annalise. "I'm not sure when I'll be back here. Text me if Sadie writes you?"

"Of course," Annalise replied. "I'll keep you posted."

"Make sure you lock the door after me and don't open it to anyone you don't know," he said.

"Trust me, I won't," she replied. Annalise reached into a vase that stood on a stand next to her front door. "Here's the spare key."

"Thanks." He quickly attached it to his key ring.

"I hope you find some information that will help."

"So do I."

Maybe they didn't need Sadie to make contact to break the case wide open, he thought as he flew out of Annalise's front door. Maybe, just maybe the rat was at this very moment being rounded up by the local police.

THE MOMENT EVAN was gone, Annalise sat down at her computer with a thoughtful frown. Susan and Earl? Was it really possible that one of them was working with Jacob and Gretchen? Was it really possible that one of those trusted people had put fellow teachers and students at risk for their very lives? Had one of them participated in a scheme that had seen three people killed?

It was so hard to believe that anyone she knew could be a part of this, and yet somebody in the day-to-day life at the school had to be involved. Both Susan and Earl would have access to the van and garage keys that hung in the office. Both would know that on a Tues-

day afternoon Annalise would be in the school building after hours with her smartest students.

Although she knew nothing about Earl's finances,
she did know that Susan had been terribly concerned
about her future after her son's restaurant had failed.
Susan had divorced years ago and so had no one to
share the financial burdens. She also knew that Sadie
was terrific on the computer.

If one of them was behind this, she knew without
a doubt Evan would ferret out the guilty and surely
that person would know where Jacob and Gretchen had
taken Sadie.

In the meantime she tapped her fingernails on her
mouse pad. "Come on, Sadie. Talk to me."

Tears blurred her vision. Had she not heard anything
from the little girl yet because it was already too late?
Was it possible that Sadie had been unable to do what
they'd asked and she was now dead?

There were plenty of heavily wooded and moun-
tainous areas where a dumped body might take years
to find, if ever. "Please, please, don't let Sadie be lost
forever," she whispered aloud.

Annalise didn't know how long she sat watching the
page before a deep weariness overtook her. She got up
and stepped out on her back porch where woods encroached on her backyard.

She stared for several long minutes at the tall trees
and brush, which normally brought her a sense of peace.
This evening they only brought her more dreadful
thoughts about Sadie.

She stood out there for only a few minutes and then
returned to the house. After grabbing an afghan from
the hall closet, she went to sit on the sofa and pulled

the blanket around her shoulders. Her thoughts of Sadie and deep, dark woods had created a chill inside her.

Annalise glanced over at the computer and a new weariness struck her. She had her notifications turned up loud enough that if she did doze off the sound would awaken her.

With all the stress of the crime and worry about Sadie, she'd scarcely had time to process her feelings toward Evan. There was no doubt there was still something there. She didn't want to distract him from doing his job, but she hoped when this was all over, when the bad guys were behind bars and Sadie was back safely, she could have a real discussion with Evan about them.

When she'd been in the school, he'd said he'd had regrets, but the conversation had been interrupted before he could explain. She wanted to hear about his regrets, and she wanted to tell him about her own.

Yes, she hoped to have a conversation with him about what had gone wrong and the possibility of a second chance to get it right.

But first and more important, they had to find Sadie.

CHIEF CUMMINGS MET Evan at the front door of the police station. "I've got Susan DeKalb in a conference room, and an officer is on his way with Earl Winslow in tow. You want to tell me what's going on?"

"A few red flags have come up in their backgrounds that warrant a closer look at them," Evan replied.

"How do you want to approach this? Good cop, bad cop?" Cummings puffed out his chest. "I can definitely work the bad cop role."

"I don't think that will be necessary." Evan couldn't think of anything more ridiculous that Walter playing the role of bad cop. "I can handle this," Evan replied.

The chief frowned. "I will be sitting in on these interviews. I need to know what's going on."

"Of course." Evan just hoped Chief Cummings didn't do anything to interfere with the interviews. All Evan wanted to do was ferret out the guilty.

As he followed the chief down a short hallway to the conference room, he carried with him transcripts of the initial interviews that had been conducted on scene with the two employees by Nick and what Hendrick had discovered about the pair.

Evan hadn't met Earl yet, but he remembered Susan DeKalb and how desperate she had been for answers when she'd talked to him. Now he was the one needing answers.

She stood when the two men entered the room. "What's happening? Why am I here?" she asked with obvious nervousness.

"Please, sit down," Evan said. "I just have a few things we want to clear up with you." He offered her a smile, hoping to put her at ease. People who were more comfortable and at ease often talked too much.

"Would you like something to drink before we get started?" Evan asked as she sank back down at the table. "Maybe some coffee or a soda?"

"No, thank you. I just want to understand why I'm here," she replied.

Evan sat across from her, and Chief Cummings sat next to him. "You should know that we've been checking out the backgrounds of everyone who works at the school. We believe the hostage takers had somebody on the inside who gave them information, and in checking into your background, a few things came to our attention."

Susan's eyes widened and her lower lip trembled.

"You believe somebody at the school was working with those horrible people? That I was...that I am somehow involved?"

She looked at Chief Cummings and then back at Evan as her eyes filled with tears. "I would never... I could never be a part of something like this. What would make you believe that I might be?"

"We believe the person involved in this was hoping for a big monetary gain," Evan said.

"Is this about me losing money in my son's restaurant?" she asked. "I understood the risk when I gave it to him, but that doesn't mean I would invite monsters into the school."

As they continued to talk, Evan watched her body language carefully, seeking tells of deception. By the time the interview was over, Evan was certain Susan wasn't the rat he sought. For what it was worth, Chief Cummings agreed with his assessment.

Earl Winslow was a thin, wiry fifty-two-year-old with an attitude. When led into the room, he slammed himself into the chair and gazed defiantly at the two law officers.

"I really got better things to do than hanging out here," he said. "So, what's up?"

"Be nice, Earl. Special Agent Duran has some questions for you," Chief Cummings said.

"I just had some follow-up questions concerning what happened at the school," Evan said. "I understand you haven't been working there that long."

"About six months or so," Earl replied.

"And your last job before being hired on at the school?" Evan asked.

Earl frowned. "I worked as a house painter."

"But according to my records that was three years

ago. I imagine financially things have been pretty tight for you," Evan said. Once again he watched Earl carefully, seeking any sign of deception.

"I'm not going to lie to you. There's been some lean times, but I lead a fairly simple life. What does my financial state have to do with what happened at the school?" Earl changed positions in the chair and looked at Chief Cummings. "Come on, Walter…what the hell is this really about?"

"It's about your involvement with what happened at the school," the chief replied.

"My involvement?" Earl sat up straighter in the chair. "What in the hell are you talking about? I didn't have any involvement with anything."

"How long have you known Jacob Noble?" Evan asked.

Earl's eyes narrowed almost imperceptibly. His chin shot up just a notch. "Jacob Noble? I don't know the man at all."

"I have evidence to the contrary," Evan replied.

Earl stared at him for a long moment and then nodded and averted his gaze to someplace over Evan's head. "Okay, I met him a couple of months ago when they held a rally. I went to the compound to see what it was about. I'd heard it was kind of like a commune where they grew their own vegetables and all lived together in peace. I was only there for about fifteen minutes before I realized Jacob and his wife were crazy."

"Is that the only contact you had with the Brotherhood of Jacob?" Evan asked.

"Definitely. I left there and that was the end of it."

"I'm sure you have had a chance to interact with the students at the school." Evan thumbed through his notes, as if seeking more information.

"Not really. I see them in the hallways and I nod and smile, but that's about it," Earl replied, looking more and more uncomfortable with the conversation. "Look, I had nothing to do with this. I'd never do anything that might hurt those kids."

"Do you have a cell phone?" Evan already knew the answer because he could see the device in Earl's breast pocket.

"Yeah…why?" Earl's dark eyes narrowed once again.

"Do you mind if I see it?" Evan asked.

"Yeah, I do mind. I think you need a warrant for that." He got up from the table. "Walter, you've known me for years. You should know I'd never be involved with anything like the slaughter that happened in the school. Sure, I met Jacob one time because I was curious about life in the compound. I never talked to him again. I never planned anything with him. You got the wrong guy and now I'm done here. If you aren't going to arrest me, then you'd better arrange a ride for me to go home."

"He's our man," Chief Cummings said the moment Earl left the small conference room. "I feel it in my gut, and my gut is never wrong. He's definitely guilty. Why didn't you arrest him?"

"Because we don't have the evidence to arrest him right now," Evan replied curtly. "Put a couple of tails on him. If he is our man, maybe he'll lead us to where Jacob and Gretchen are holed up."

"Consider it done. But I've got to tell you, I definitely feel like we got our inside man." Chief Cummings appeared positively jubilant. Evan wasn't so sure.

He'd have Hendrick work with the cell phone company to get Earl's texts and a log of incoming and outgoing calls. Of course it was always possible that if Earl really was involved, he might be smart enough to own a burner phone that would be less easy to trace.

"Earl has always been a strange duck. He's never married and is a loner. He lives in a little house his parents owned before they died, but I heard he owes some back taxes on it and is about to lose it. I'm telling you, he's our man, Agent Duran."

Evan got up from the table. "Put the tails on him and let me know if anything breaks. I'll touch base with you sometime tomorrow."

Minutes later Evan stepped outside the police station, surprised that night was approaching and with it a deep exhaustion he couldn't deny. It had been a wild day, from Phil accosting them with a gun, the move to Annalise's home and finally a potential piece of the puzzle.

But, he was functioning on two hours of sleep, and at the moment he was so exhausted his thoughts were muddled. As he drove back to Annalise's place, he thought about the interview with Earl. While the fact that the man had met Jacob a month before was suspicious, it was also possible it was one of those odd coincidences that life sometimes sets up. The last thing he wanted was a rush to justice that might see an innocent man behind bars and the guilty still free.

He let himself in with the spare key Annalise had given him. He walked into the living room to find her talking about code on a video chat with Hendrick. For a moment he merely stood there and listened.

She was brilliant. That was part of what had drawn him to her in the first place. The fact that she could hold her own with one of the FBI's top techs was remarkable.

She must have sensed his presence for she looked over her shoulder and smiled, then turned back to the computer. "Evan just walked in," she said to the tech agent.

"Evan. Anything new come out of the interviews?" Hendrick asked.

Evan stepped into camera view and caught Hendrick up with what he'd learned from Susan and Earl. "Chief Cummings is convinced Earl is our man, and he was ready to make an arrest immediately."

"And what did you think?" Hendrick asked.

"I think we need a lot more information than what I have," Evan replied. The two men talked for another few minutes, and when they finished Hendrick said goodbye to Annalise and then he disconnected.

"Are you okay?" Annalise asked.

Evan sank down on the edge of the sofa. "To be honest, I'm completely exhausted. I assume you still haven't heard from Sadie?"

"You assume right, and you probably need to crash for the night. I have to confess I napped almost the whole time you were gone. So I'm good to man the computers while you get some sleep."

He rubbed the back of his neck. "Maybe I'll just stretch out right here on the sofa for an hour."

"Are you sure you don't want to go back to a bed?" she asked.

"Nah, I'll be fine right here."

"I'll go get you a pillow to make you more comfortable," she replied.

As she left the room, Evan's thoughts went wild. The whole plot had been for Jacob to grab Sadie to break into the banking system. Sooner or later if their plan was still the same, Sadie would be put in front of a computer. Whether or not she would get an opportunity to type on Annalise's page was another thing altogether. If the little girl was as smart as Annalise said she was, then one way or another she'd figure out a way to make contact.

He seriously doubted that Sadie would make any contact tonight. If they'd spent the day still on the run, then Jacob and Gretchen had to be exhausted, as well.

They would need to crash someplace and sleep. Or, it was possible they'd already landed somewhere and had spent the day catching up on sleep. And then there was Earl Winslow. Was he the insider who had told them which girl to grab and had provided the keys to the van and garage so they could drive in a Sandhurst vehicle? If the van was found, would it only lead the authorities around in circles?

God, his thoughts were going around and around in his head and making him half-crazy. Had he overlooked anything? Was everything possible being done to find the fugitives?

He wished he didn't need sleep. There were times he hated that he was only human and required rest. But he knew by the way his mind was working he definitely needed a little sleep.

Annalise returned with a pillow. "Are you sure you don't want to go back in the bedroom?" she asked one more time.

"I'll be fine here…unless I'll bother you." He took the pillow from her.

"You won't bother me. I'll just sit tight here at my desk and watch for any sign from Sadie." She turned off the overhead light, leaving the room illuminated only by a desk lamp.

Evan stretched out with a deep sigh. He didn't want to think about the fact that he was oddly comforted that Annalise was so nearby, that they were both fighting side by side to save a little girl.

He definitely didn't want to think about what would happen to him…to her…to them if in the end, Sadie wasn't saved.

Chapter Ten

Annalise jerked awake, surprised to realize she'd nodded off in her desk chair. The clock said it was just after midnight, and with a quick glance around she immediately knew what had awakened her.

Evan was having one of his nightmares. He'd had them occasionally when they had been together, although he'd never shared with her what they were about. He tossed and turned, his features twisted as he breathed rapidly...harshly.

Her first instinct was to wake him, to get him out of wherever he was in his sleep landscape. But she paused and hoped the nightmare would pass and he'd continue to get some more much-needed sleep.

His thrashing grew more intense, and Annalise half rose from her chair, afraid that he would end up falling off the sofa. "Maria!" The name exploded out of him and he bolted upright. He swiped his hands down the sides of his face and released a deep breath.

"Evan, are you okay?" Annalise asked softly. "You were having one of your nightmares."

"Yeah, I'm fine." He swung his legs off the sofa and sat up. "What time is it?"

"Just a little after midnight. Evan, who is Maria?"

She was sorry she'd asked him the question the minute it left her mouth and she saw his reaction. His face paled as he sat up straighter. "How do you know anything about Maria?" he asked.

"I don't know anything about her. You just called out her name and now I'm curious."

He held her gaze for a long moment and reached a hand up to rub the back of his neck. He broke eye contact with her and stared down at the coffee table, but before he did so she saw what appeared to be stark grief sweep over his features.

He released an audible sigh. "Maria is...was my younger sister."

She looked at him in stunned surprise. She'd met his mother on a trip they had taken to New York, but in the two years they had dated Evan had never mentioned he had a sister. She'd always thought it was just he and his mother.

"You never told me about her," she said.

"There's not much to tell. I don't know if she's dead or alive. She disappeared when she was five years old."

Annalise gasped. "Disappeared? What do you mean? What exactly happened?" She got up from the desk and sank down next to him on the sofa.

He immediately stood and began to pace back and forth in front of her. The grief she'd seen momentarily before now captured his features once again, along with something else...some emotion she couldn't quite identify. "Tell me, Evan," she said softly.

"It was an early evening on a Tuesday. My mom had worked all day cleaning a couple of really nasty apartments for our landlord. She was hot and exhausted by the time she got home. All she asked was that I take Maria outside for about an hour or so to let her take a quick shower and catch a nap."

Annalise could feel the tension that wafted from him as he continued to pace back and forth. "How old were you at the time?" she asked.

"Eight. I was eight years old and she was five. I loved my little sister so much." His voice cracked slightly. "Even though I was older than her, she was like my best friend. She could be a pest, but I loved her anyway."

He paused and drew in a deep breath, then released it on a shuddering sigh. "So, I took Maria outside. I remember it was a hot summer evening. Maria had a piece of sidewalk chalk. It was purple, and she sat on the stoop and was drawing pictures of me while I made goofy poses."

His dark eyes grew distant, and for just a moment a faint smile curved his lips. "I'd act goofy all the time just to make her laugh. She had such a wonderful giggle."

The smile faded and his eyes grew darker. "We were outside for probably half an hour or so when some of my buddies came walking up the sidewalk. I went to talk to them, and at the same time Maria chased a butterfly into the alley."

He stopped pacing and stood in front of her. A deep, raw pain emanated from his eyes. "I greeted my friends and then I went to get Maria. I went into the alley… and…and a man was there. He had Maria and he had a big knife."

He drew in another deep breath. "I wanted to save her. I needed to save her, but I didn't. The man ran away with her and…and we never saw her again."

She couldn't stand to see his anguish any longer. She got up from the sofa and took his hand in hers, then pulled him down to sit next to her.

She held his hand tightly. "My God, Evan. Why have you never told me about this before?"

His dark gaze held hers and then looked away. "Why would I have told you that I was responsible for the kidnapping of my little sister? Why would I share that with the woman I loved?"

"Evan, you were just a little boy. You should have never had that kind of responsibility on you in the first place."

"But I took on the responsibility and I screwed up," he replied. "I should have never stopped to say hi to my friends. I should have never taken my attention off her. I definitely should have never allowed Maria to chase a damned butterfly into the alley."

"What did the police do?" She continued to hold his hand as she watched the emotions playing on his handsome features. Loss…grief…guilt, they were all there.

He released a deep bitter laugh. "They found nothing in the alley, no evidence, no leads to find her. All they had was my description of the man, and all I could tell them was that the kidnapper was a tall, white man with shaggy brown hair."

"So, they never caught him?"

He shook his head. "Even though my mother called the police station every day, if felt like nobody really cared. My mother thought they didn't do a real investigation because we were poor and Latino."

"I certainly hope that wasn't true," she replied, appalled by the mere notion.

"The idea that it might be was what drove me into the law enforcement field." He released a deep sigh. "I've never stopped looking for Maria. I check the internet to this day hoping to find her out there somewhere."

"I'm sorry, Evan. I'm so sorry for your loss," she replied softly. She knew her words were inadequate, but she meant them to the depths of her soul.

She couldn't believe he'd had something so catastrophic happen to him when he'd been so young and impressionable, and during the two years they'd dated he'd never told her anything about it.

She gazed at him and he looked at her at the same time. His face was so near to hers. His lips were achingly close. He leaned forward and her breath caught in her throat as she anticipated a kiss.

His lips almost grazed hers, and then he jerked upright and off the sofa. "I need to check in with some people."

The night hours passed slowly. Evan was on his phone a lot, and when he wasn't, he was quiet and closed off. Annalise suspected the memories he'd shared with her still had him by the throat.

The tragic event in his life explained a lot…like his affinity for saving children in dangerous hostage situations. It also explained his occasional moodiness when they had been together as a couple.

She wanted to wrap her arms around Evan and somehow comfort him from the bad memories she'd stirred by asking him about Maria. She wanted to somehow take away the guilt she now knew he carried about that tragic loss in his life.

Still, she knew he didn't need her right now. What he really needed was for this case to come to a satisfactory conclusion. He desperately needed to be a hero.

EVAN LEANED BACK in the dining room chair and stretched with his arms overhead. It was just a few minutes after six. He glanced at Annalise, who was sleeping on the sofa.

Telling her about Maria had been one of the most difficult things he'd ever done. He'd spent most of his life trying not to access those painful memories. It had not only been a shameful secret he'd carried, but one that still had the capacity to bring him to his knees.

It had been an event that had forever changed who he was at the very core. It had stolen his belief that the world was a safe place and had created a self-hatred inside him that had never really gone away.

He'd only told one person about Maria, and that had been Hendrick. He and Hendrick had shared a few too many beers one evening at Evan's house. Hendrick confessed to Evan about being raised in a cult, and Evan had shared his heartache of Maria.

But he needed to put those memories away now. He hated himself for showing Annalise his vulnerability. And in that vulnerable state he'd almost kissed her again.

There was no question there was still something between them, a chemistry…a desire that was difficult to ignore. But he couldn't forget that she'd walked out on him before.

He got up and went into the kitchen to refill his coffee cup. He made a fresh pot of coffee and then poured himself a cup. He took a sip and leaned against the counter. Where was Sadie right now? Had they given her something to eat? Was she sleeping in a car parked on some mountain road? Or was she dead? He shook his head to dispel that particular thought.

Talking about, remembering what had happened to Maria had only made him more desperate than ever to find Sadie. One child at a time, he thought. All he could do was try to save one child at a time.

Part of what had made him a hostage negotiator as

an officer of the law before he'd been asked to join TCD was the number of domestic disputes that turned ugly.

Far too often a man locked himself inside a house or apartment with a gun and his children. Most of the time those situations ended with the children being safely released, but occasionally those kinds of hostage situations ended in tragedy.

If Evan could save a child, then it assuaged a tiny piece of the guilt that would forever haunt him, the guilt that he'd been unable to save Maria.

He stretched once again and then grabbed one of the homemade cinnamon rolls that Chief Cummings had given him before he'd left the station after the interviews. It was delicious. At least the chief was correct that his wife definitely knew how to bake.

When he went back into the living room, Annalise was awake. "There's fresh coffee," he said.

"Thanks." She got up and disappeared into the kitchen and returned a moment later with her cup of coffee and one of the cinnamon rolls on a saucer. She sat down next to him at the table.

As they drank their coffee, they talked about the elements of the crime they knew so far. He'd always liked bouncing things off her. Many a night when they were together they'd talk about his work and various crime scenarios.

They talked about his interview with Earl and other potential people at the school who might be involved. They tried to brainstorm where on earth the fugitives might have gone. He talked out all the various investigations that were taking place as she listened and commented.

It was just after eight when a ding sounded from her computer. They both jumped up from the table and hurried to the desk. The page now held another non-sensical sentence.

"It's her," Annalise said, her voice filled with excitement. "It's from Sadie."

"What does it say?"

"It says, 'Miss Annalise, I'm okay.'"

Evan pulled out the desk chair. "Ask her where she is."

Annalise sat and quickly typed out the question.

A moment later Sadie responded. "Cabin," Annalise said. "She says she's in a cabin."

"A cabin where? Is there a name of the place that she can give us? Where is it located?" Evan asked urgently. This was what they'd been waiting for. Thank God the little girl was still alive. Hopefully she could tell them where she was so Evan's team could move in and get her out of there and away from the couple who held her.

He and Annalise stared at the computer screen, waiting for a reply. A minute went by, then another and another. "She must have had to get off the page," Annalise finally said. "I'm just grateful she's still alive."

Hendrick called on Evan's computer. Evan hurried over and answered. "She said she's in a cabin," he told him.

"A cabin? There must be hundreds of cabins in those mountains," Hendrick said. "I can't do a search without more details. At this moment we don't even know what state they might be in."

"Have you managed to get anything on Winslow's phone yet?"

"Damn, Evan, you know these things take time and a lot of red tape. You've got to have a little patience."

"I'm running out of patience," Evan replied. "If

they've put Sadie in front of a computer, then time is running out for her."

"Then let's hope she can get you something more to narrow down a search area," Hendrick replied.

"I'm so scared for her, Evan," Annalise said once the two men had hung up.

He hesitated a moment and then pulled her into his embrace and stroked her hair. The last thing he wanted to do was let her know that he was scared, too.

"QUIT SCREWING AROUND and go to the page I told you to get on," Gretchen said to Sadie.

The girl quickly clicked off the secret page and did as Gretchen asked. The woman scared her. She'd already slapped Sadie twice, once the night before for complaining she was cold and then again this morning for dawdling over breakfast.

The slaps had been hard and when Sadie had cried, Gretchen had threatened to hit her as many times as it took for the girl to stop crying. Sadie had stopped crying on the outside, but she'd cried on the inside for a long time.

Jacob was a little bit nicer; he'd at least given her a pillow to use when she'd gone to bed on the little sofa in the room.

They had driven around on back roads for hours the day before. She'd been so scared, and she was still really scared. Jacob might be nice to her right now, but that didn't mean anything. Gretchen wasn't nice, and she seemed to be the boss. All she'd done since they got to the cabin was yell about how bad things had gone.

She knew they wanted her for a reason, and now she knew why. She understood what they wanted her to do was illegal, and she wasn't even sure she could do it.

Miss Annalise had never taught them how to break into places on the internet. Sadie knew if she couldn't do it, then things were going to get bad…really, really bad.

She'd had bad things happen to her before. When she was living in an apartment with her mother before she'd come to the school, there had been many times when Sadie had believed she was going to die.

Sometimes her mother forgot to buy food, and Sadie thought she might starve to death. Other times her mother would beat her until Sadie almost wished she would die. But since being at the school, Sadie didn't want to die. She wanted to go back to the school with her friends and the grown-ups who loved her.

The last thing she'd seen on the private page was Miss Annalise asking where she was and what the name of the cabin was, but she didn't have the answers.

When they had left the school, they had driven to a place where they had gotten into another car and then they had driven around for a while. They had parked on a road in the middle of nowhere, and then the two grown-ups had taken naps.

She'd stayed awake, worried that a bear might come out of the woods or some other wild animal might attack the car. After they woke up, they started driving again.

Sadie had been asleep when they'd carried her into the small cabin. The curtains were drawn at all the windows, so she hadn't even had a chance to look out.

The only way Miss Annalise and her friend would be able to come and save her was if she could somehow tell them something about the cabin.

What she was scared about was that she wouldn't be able to get Miss Annalise the information before Jacob and Gretchen realized she might not be able to do what they wanted her to do. And once that happened...she truly believed she would be dead.

WHILE THEY WAITED for Sadie to get them more information, Evan was on the phone and checking in on all the progression of the investigation.

Nick was still conducting interviews of the kitchen and housekeeping staff from the school, and Davis and a few other men were at the compound interviewing the members of the Brotherhood of Jacob in an effort to glean more information.

He then contacted Chief Cummings to find out if the tails on Earl had reported anything during the night. So far they had nothing to report. Earl had driven straight home from the police station and hadn't left his house since.

By the time he was finished with all the check-ins, Annalise had made them breakfast. They ate quickly, as if fighting against a ticking time bomb.

Evan had felt the tension before, but Sadie's contact had definitely made him feel like everything was going to explode quickly.

"I still find it hard to believe that Earl is the inside person," Annalise said as they cleared their dishes.

"Right now he's the only one who looks halfway good. Why don't you think he's the one?" Evan asked.

"He is a little reserved, but to be honest," she replied, "I don't want to sound unkind, but I just don't think he's smart enough to put this all together."

"I'm not sure it took a lot of brains to implement this plan. Somebody from the inside told Jacob and Gretchen when would be the best time to break into the school, and that same somebody lifted a key for the garage and one to steal the van."

"I just think the insider is somebody else, somebody we're missing altogether," she replied. "Have you checked out Regina?"

"So far Hendrick hasn't given me anything on her, but we're checking everything," he said.

"I know that." She put their dishes in the dishwasher. "That wasn't me being critical. I know you're in control of everything."

He realized he'd been curt. "Sorry, I didn't mean to snap at you."

She smiled. "I think we're both tense."

He pulled her into his arms and hugged her. "I'm glad you're here with me," he said.

"Me, too," she replied.

For several long moments they simply held each other, and he finally released her. Once again he realized she stirred all kinds of emotions inside him, but there was no way he wanted to examine exactly what they were as long as he was in the middle of this investigation. Right now Sadie needed and deserved all his attention and energy. He returned to his computer, and Annalise sank down at the desk in front of hers.

"Do you really believe Sadie could break into a banking system?" he asked Annalise.

She frowned. "I really don't know. She's brilliant, but I haven't really taught the girls how to do anything like that. She's never been challenged to get through all the security and firewalls that would entail."

"Now that we know she's working a computer, I've got Hendrick watching the banking systems for a breech."

"I just want her to get back to us with more information about where she's being held," Annalise replied. "If she can't do it for them, then she'll be of no use, and that's what scares me for her. She needs to help us find her."

As if her wish was granted, her notification sounded. It was Sadie again.

"She says when she looks out the window, in the distance she sees a big, wooden owl. She believes the name of the cabins has *owl* in it," Annalise told him.

"Does she have any idea where they are located?" Evan asked.

Annalise typed in the question. "She says she doesn't know. She just knows it must be owl something. She also says she doesn't think they had plans to be there."

"So, the odds are good that wherever they are, it isn't a private cabin," Evan said.

They waited several more minutes, but Sadie didn't type anything more. Evan got on a call to Hendrick and told him what Sadie had said.

"I'll start a search right now," Hendrick stated. "Later."

"We're going to get her, aren't we?" Annalise asked, her green eyes shining with a new hope.

"Yeah, I think we're going to get her," he replied. He just hoped they got to her in time. Once again he felt the ticking time bomb inside his veins.

Ticktock.

Chapter Eleven

Two hours later Hendrick called. "Man, I had no idea there were so many cabin resorts around with owl in the name. Owl's Nest, Sleepy Owl, Twin Owls…we're galvanizing local officials to make contact with each one of them to see if Jacob and Gretchen are guests."

"Why would any of them rent to these people who have been splashed across the news for the past twenty-four hours?" Annalise asked.

"Some of these cabins are completely off the grid. The owners or managers might not even know they're harboring fugitives," Hendrick replied. "We've told law enforcement to approach the cabins in unmarked vehicles so we won't spook the fugitives with any police presence."

"So, now it's just a waiting game," Evan replied.

"It's coming to an end. Thank God Sadie got us enough information to narrow the search. I wouldn't be surprised if something pops within the next hour or two."

"Let's hope so. I'm ready to put this one behind me with a happy ending," Evan replied.

"Fingers crossed, it won't be too long now," Hendrick said, and then hung up.

"I should call Chief Cummings and let him know what's going on," Evan said, more to himself than to Annalise.

"Why would you consider not calling him?" she asked.

Evan released a deep sigh. "I don't know. I just fear that if he gets involved in the ultimate takedown, things will somehow get all muddled and screwed up."

"We definitely don't need a screwup at this point," Annalise replied.

"I've got three highly trained men with me. Between the four of us we should be able to take control of a small cabin and two adults who have no warning that we're coming."

"That's got to be your call," she replied.

"I appreciate that. I haven't forgotten that Jacob and Gretchen got away from the school due to Chief Cummings's men and his decision to remove a lot of his men. The last thing I want is for Jacob and Gretchen to somehow escape the cabin, which will result in a manhunt through the mounains. I'm taking a wait and see attitude before I decide to involve Chief Cummings."

And so they waited.

As the minutes and then hours passed, Evan stayed on the phone checking in with the ongoing investigation and Annalise remained at her computer, hoping and praying for a successful end for Sadie.

The tension inside her grew with each minute that ticked by. She wanted to scream, she wanted to cry, she wanted to be in Evan's arms once again.

Spending this time with him had made her realize she wanted to try to rekindle their relationship again. She wanted to reclaim the magic that they once had. But she had no idea if he would ever want to try again with her. She wasn't even sure he'd understood why she had left him in the first place.

She shook her head, aware that she was getting too deep into her emotions about Evan because thoughts of Sadie were too frightening to entertain. Every moment that passed without additional contact with the child made Annalise wonder if she was still alive.

It was just after three when Hendrick called Evan. "We've got them," he said.

"Where?" Evan asked. Annalise got up from the desk and moved to stand just behind him.

"Owl's Nest cabins on mountain road 358. It's about three hours from where you are right now. Local authorities just confirmed with the owner there that they are in cabin number 7. The owner hadn't heard the news of a manhunt. Jacob paid cash for a four-night stay, and the locals are staying on scene with the owner until you all arrive."

"Get me the name of the chief of police in that jurisdiction," Evan said.

"Already got it. It's Chief Joe McCabe," Hendrick replied. "He's expecting your call."

As Annalise listened to Evan talk to Chief McCabe, her entire body thrummed with excitement. Hopefully in the next four hours or so, Sadie would be safe and Jacob and Gretchen would be under arrest.

"Wish us luck," he said to her when he was off the phone and heading toward the front door.

"You aren't leaving here without me," she protested.

"Annalise, we don't know how this is going to go down. It could get extremely dangerous," he told her.

"I don't care. I'm coming with you whether you like it or not. If I don't ride with you, then I'll take my own car and follow you." She raised her chin in stubbornness.

"Annalise…" he started to protest once again.

She was having none of it. She was going and that was that. There was no way in hell she was staying here. "If you get Sadie out of there, she's going to need to see a familiar face. She'll need me to be there for her," she replied firmly.

He wasn't going to stop her from coming. Sadie would need her…and more than that, she needed to see Sadie. She wanted to hold her tight, to assure herself that the little girl had not only survived physically but emotionally, as well.

"I promise you that if you don't take me with you, then I'll drive on my own," she repeated firmly.

He looked at her for a long moment and then gave a quick nod. Minutes later they were on the road with Davis driving in a car behind them with Nick and Daniel as passengers.

"I'm almost glad they are out of Chief Cummings's jurisdiction," Evan said as he pressed the gas pedal to pick up speed. "I'll be glad to deliver Jacob and Gretchen to him to put in his jail so he can have all the glory, but I'm fine working with somebody else to take them down."

"I'm just so happy this is finally coming to an end," she replied. "I just want Sadie to be saved."

"I want that, and I also want whoever the insider is behind bars," he replied.

They fell silent as he focused on the road ahead, and Annalise stared out the side window. She could feel his tension in the air, and the last thing she wanted was to be a distraction.

After driving for an hour and a half, he turned onto a narrow road where the trees encroached on either side and stole all the sunshine.

The shadowed semidarkness increased her anxiety. The optimism she'd left her house with waned a bit. It was only going to get darker as evening approached, and things could go so terribly wrong.

What if a gunfight broke out? Would Sadie become collateral damage? Would Evan be hurt? Killed? Her heartbeat quickened. Would Sadie still be alive when they finally got to the cabin? A glance over at Evan let her know he was probably entertaining the same dark thoughts that she was.

His hands clenched the steering wheel, and his jaw muscles were bunched. He looked like a warrior ready to do battle. All she could do was pray that the warrior would come through on the other side unscathed and that he'd have a living, breathing little girl in his arms.

The small police station was located on a narrow mountain road next to a bar named Whisky Dan's. Evan parked next to another police car in the lot. "Stay here," he said to Annalise. "And lock the doors."

He'd been reluctant to allow her to come along with him, and the only reason he had brought her was because he had no idea how traumatized Sadie might be. He also knew that Annalise would have followed through on her threat to trail the team in her own vehicle. But he had no intention of her being part of the arrest and rescue mission.

He got out of the car and waited for his men to do the same and then the four of them went inside. Chief Joe McCabe greeted them and introduced four of his men. "These guys are as close to a SWAT team as we have," he said.

"We've taken down a lot of men holed up in all kinds of cabins in this area," Officer Larry Knox said.

"A lot of meth-cooking goes on in some of these little cabins," Officer Nash Burton explained.

"The Owl's Nest cabins are owned by Charlie Tankersly. Charlie is something of a character," Chief McCabe said. "He claims to be an artist, and spends most of his time using trash to make things nobody ever buys. But the good news is he supports law and order, and he'll do whatever we ask of him."

"So, let's talk about a plan," Evan said.

For the next forty-five minutes, Evan and Chief McCabe talked about the cabin's location, the best way to approach it and who would do what when they got there.

By the time they left the police station, dusk had fallen, casting the area in deep, purplish shadows. Adrenaline pumped through Evan as he got back into the car where Annalise waited.

"Everything okay?" she asked.

"It's all a go." He started the engine, then waited for his men and the chief's team to load up. They had specific equipment in their vehicle that would hopefully make the takedown easier.

"McCabe seems to have a good team to work with us," he said. "They all seem bright and more than capable, and they're used to taking down people in cabins in this area."

"I just can't wait until this is all over," Annalise replied.

It took twenty minutes before everyone was ready to pull out of the police station parking lot. They would coordinate again a mile from the Owl's Nest cabins.

They had no idea how much firepower the two fugitives had in the cabin. It would be imperative for the agents to use the element of surprise to their advantage.

Evan drove approximately three miles on a road that

was little more than an overgrown trail. How in the hell had the fugitives found this place? It was definitely off the beaten path. Maybe the insider had told them to come to these cabins, knowing they were isolated.

Tree limbs brushed against the side of his car, and what was left of the sunlight was being usurped by both the woods and the encroaching darkness.

Thankfully Annalise remained quiet, allowing him to concentrate on the plan. He stopped his car and the others parked just behind him.

"I don't want you leaving this car for any reason," he said to Annalise. "According to Chief McCabe, the cabin is about a mile up the road." He reached out and touched her cheek. "I need to know you're safe." He pulled his hand back.

"I'll be here waiting for you and Sadie to return," she said softly.

He nodded and then got out of the car. It was cooler here, but he scarcely felt the chill in the air as he clipped his radio to his collar and tuned to the frequency they would all be using.

Chief McCabe opened his trunk, which contained not only a battering ram, but also flash-bang grenades and additional guns and ammo. The men loaded up.

"We want to go in fast and forcefully," Evan said. "But I want everyone to remember that there's a little girl who is their hostage. Whatever we do, we need to get her out of there safe and sound."

"Once we have the fugitives under arrest, I'll make arrangements with Chief Cummings to transfer them into his custody, but first we need to get them in handcuffs," Chief McCabe said.

"And that's why we're here," Evan replied, eager to get this done and over with. The fact that within minutes this could all be over was exhilarating. The thought that within minutes it could all go terribly wrong also flashed in his head.

"Shall we coordinate our watches?" Davis asked.

Evan's blood cooled and his nerves settled down, the way they always did before going into battle. Finally they were all ready to go. They moved through the woods like silent, stealthy shadows.

Chief McCabe was not only in contact with all members of the team, but also with Charlie in the owner's cabin. Thankfully the cabins were all some distance away from each other, and Charlie assured them that he wouldn't get in their way.

When the small cabin where Jacob and Gretchen were holed up came into view, Evan halted just behind a large tree. Some of the others found similar hiding places while a few of them circled around to the back of the cabin.

A red Ford Escort was parked out front, and while Evan was eager to find out who it belonged to, his first priority was getting Gretchen and Jacob arrested and Sadie out of there.

This was it. This was the culmination of all the hard work of dozens of agents. They were either going to get it right, or they'd completely screw it up and somehow the fugitives would escape once again.

They couldn't let that happen. They had to control the scene. He had to control it. If he somehow lost control of things, then another little girl might die.

The curtains were drawn in the cabin's windows. Charlie had said the cabin the fugitives occupied consisted of a small living room—kitchenette area and a bedroom and a bath.

Evan gripped his gun more firmly. He mentally

counted down from three, and when he reached one, he whispered into his radio. "Move in, let's move in."

He watched as the two men manning the battering ram took their position at the front door. He and Davis moved to stand just behind them while the rest of the men surrounded the cabin, ready to go into the two windows on the back side.

Thankfully the front door didn't look that solid. It was old and weathered and should be breached fairly easy. The minute it was possible, Davis and Evan would sweep in and hopefully this all would go down without a single shot fired.

"On the count of three," he now said into the radio. "One…two…three."

Boom. They hit the door with tremendous force, cracking it right down the middle. Davis and Evan swept in. "Get on the floor, get down on the floor. Facedown and hands on the back of your heads," Evan yelled.

At the same time, the sound of breaking windows came from the back, and within seconds Nick and one of McCabe's men flew into the living room.

The couple cursed. They were seated at the table, but seeing they were outgunned and outmanned, they did as Evan asked and got on the floor.

"This was all his idea," Gretchen said. "He told me he'd kill me if I didn't go along with him. He's…he's so abusive. He beats me."

"You stinking traitor," Jacob yelled. "This was all her idea. She planned it all."

"Stop talking," Evan commanded as he watched the two of them being patted down for weapons by Nick. Once it was confirmed neither of them had a weapon on them, they were jerked up to their feet and handcuffed.

Evan turned to see Sadie curled up in the corner of

a nasty-looking brown sofa. Her eyes were huge as she watched everything that was happening. Thank God she was alive and appeared unharmed.

"Hi, Sadie," he said to her with a smile. He crouched in front of her. "Do you know who I am?"

"You're Miss Annalise's friend. I saw you on her phone. Are you here to take me out of this place?"

"We're here to take you out of here."

She nodded. "Good. I really didn't want to do what they wanted me to do."

"Honey, it's over now and those people are out of your life forever," Evan replied, just grateful that she appeared to be okay. "Are you ready to come outside with me? Miss Annalise has been really worried about you, and she can't wait to see you and tell you how smart and how very brave you have been."

"Did you get Miss Annalise something to eat? Last time I was with her, her tummy was really growling because she was so hungry."

Evan stared at the beautiful child with her innocent blue eyes and felt utterly humbled. After being kidnapped and brought to this seedy cabin, that her first thought would be of her teacher being hungry spoke of how very special this child was.

"Yes, Miss Annalise has been fed several times," he replied. "Come on, let's get you out of here."

She got off the sofa and placed her little hand in his with utter trust. Together they left the cabin, and he used a flashlight to guide them back toward his car.

They walked for a little ways and then, sensing that Sadie was growing weary, he pulled her up in his arms. "I hope we didn't scare you when we burst into the cabin," he said.

"I was way more scared that Gretchen was going to kill me," she replied. "She's really, really mean."

"We weren't going to let that happen. Now she and Jacob will go to jail for a very long time."

"That's good. They aren't nice people," she said, and tightened her thin arms around his neck.

They were several feet in front of the car when Annalise finally saw them. She got out of the vehicle and ran toward them.

"Sadie," she cried.

"Miss Annalise!"

Evan set the little girl on the ground and teacher and student raced to each other. When Annalise reached Sadie, she fell to her knees and opened her arms wide.

Tears poured down Annalise's face as she hugged Sadie close. As Evan watched the two of them, he couldn't help the lump of emotion that rose in his throat.

He allowed the reunion to go on for several long moments before he finally spoke again. "I've got to go back. You two get into the car, lock the doors and I'll be back here as soon as I can."

He waited until the two got into the backseat, and then he turned and hurried back toward the cabin.

Finally, it was almost over. Two bad guys were in custody and his young hostage was safe. Considering how it all could have gone wrong, the actual takedown had been surprisingly easy and rather anticlimactic, not that he was complaining. Before he reached the cabin, he pulled his phone from his pocket and connected to Hendrick.

"We got them," he said once the tech appeared.

"And Sadie?" Hendrick asked.

"Safe and in my car."

"Thank God. Then my naked dance with torches burning and the sacrifice of a corn dog worked," Hendrick said with a wicked grin.

"You've always hated corn dogs," Evan replied.

"Okay, so that was an easy sacrifice," Hendrick replied.

Evan laughed, and it felt so good to finally reach this point and be able to laugh. "I just wanted you to know that this part of the ordeal is over." His smile faded. "But we still need to identify the person who aided and abetted these criminals."

Hendrick nodded. "You don't believe Earl Winslow is your man?"

Evan hesitated. "I can't be positive, but my gut is telling me he isn't the insider. I've got to go. We've still got a lot to finish up here."

"I'll keep digging into backgrounds, and I'll talk to you later."

Evan returned to the cabin where the two fugitives were not only handcuffed but also had their ankles bound, making it impossible for them to run.

The officers had rounded up a total of three automatic long guns and two handguns. Along with the weapons was enough ammunition to ward off a small army. Thank God they had been taken down without incident.

Chief McCabe smiled at Evan. "If you want to take off, I can assure you my men will process the scene and send you all the reports and evidence we collect."

"Thanks, and I really appreciate your cooperation in working with us on this," Evan replied. "It's been a pleasure."

"Glad we could help," Chief McCabe replied, and the two men shook hands. "We'll make sure these two are transferred successfully into Chief Cummings's custody. They have far more serious charges to face in that jurisdiction than in ours."

Evan remained for another thirty minutes or so and then returned to the car where Annalise and Sadie waited. "How are you doing?" he asked when he was behind the steering wheel.

"We're good," Annalise said. "I've been telling her how smart she was in helping us find her."

"Sadie, you've been amazing," Evan said. "You asked me if Miss Annalise had eaten, but you didn't tell me if you had eaten."

"Gretchen made me some macaroni and cheese, but the macaroni was really crunchy and it wasn't very good," Sadie replied.

"How about when we see a fast-food place on the way home we stop and get you a big cheeseburger and fries," Evan said.

"That would be awesome," Sadie replied. "And maybe a chocolate shake?"

Annalise laughed. "You got it."

Once they were on the road home, the two passengers in the back fell asleep. Evan found himself glancing in his rearview mirror and gazing at Annalise.

Without the pressure of the fugitives now burning in his brain, his emotions where Annalise was concerned came to the surface.

He was still in love with her. He realized now he'd never stopped loving her. She had surprised him with her strength throughout this ordeal. He wasn't sure if she wanted another chance with him or not, but more important he wasn't sure he would ever trust her with his heart again.

Chapter Twelve

It was just after midnight when Evan finally pulled into Annalise's driveway. They had gotten Sadie a fast-food child's meal on the way home, and her resident attendant was now with her at the hospital where she would be thoroughly checked out before returning to her room at the school.

Annalise knew her time with Evan was drawing to an end. With Sadie found, Evan had no reason to stay in town. Whatever was left of the investigation could be handled in Knoxville.

"I'm so glad that Sadie seems to be okay mentally and the whole ordeal didn't break her spirit," she said once they were in her living room.

"Thank goodness. She's definitely a special girl," Evan replied.

"She is," Annalise agreed. She cast him a surreptitious gaze and wondered if he was thinking about another special little girl named Maria. "Are you tired?"

"I am, but at the moment I'm waiting for the last of my adrenaline to burn off."

"Surely you aren't planning on packing up and leaving here this late tonight," she said.

"Actually I was hoping I could avail myself of your hospitality and spend one more night here, then head out sometime tomorrow," he replied. "In fact I'm thinking about that bed in the guest room."

She smiled at him. "It's all yours. I'd say you've more than earned it."

They engaged in small talk about the case as they lounged on the sofa. "I'm sure you're ready to get back to your own life," he said.

"Almost." She would probably not have another chance to talk to him about her feelings. The time was now, before he packed up and left her house. "Evan, I'm still in love with you."

Her words hung in the air. He stared at her for a long moment and then looked down at the coffee table. "Annalise," he protested softly, "isn't it better to just leave things alone between us?"

"No, it's not." She gazed at him and her heart began to pound with every emotion from anxiety to love. "I want another chance with you, Evan. I've never stopped loving you, and having this time with you only confirms to me that you're the only man I want in my life."

He frowned and his eyes darkened. "You walked away from me easily enough three years ago. In fact, as I remember, you sent me a text to tell me goodbye… a text for God's sake."

"Walking away from you was the most difficult decision I've ever made in my life," she replied. "And I sent you a goodbye text because I knew if I tried to say goodbye to you in person, I wouldn't leave you."

She leaned toward him. "Evan, I told you that I was unhappy a million times. I told you that you were being too controlling and I was losing my sense of self. I complained that you ran our relationship like one of your hostage negotiations."

He remained silent, his eyes dark and shuttered, and

still she continued. "Evan, I didn't want to take that job so far away from you, but I'd reached the point where I wasn't even sure you would care if I left you or not. Each time I tried to talk to you, you were so emotionless and you'd withdraw from me. I didn't want Evan the calm and skillful negotiator in my life. I needed Evan the man to give me a reason to stay... Tell me to stay now, Evan. Tell me you are willing to give me another chance."

A nerve pulsed in his strong jawline. "What makes you think it would work between us now?"

The question made hope leap into her heart. "Because I know more about you now, because I understand you better and I'm a stronger person than I was three years ago. We can make it this time, Evan. Please give me...give us a second chance."

She saw a softness in his eyes, and she grabbed his hand with hers. "I've thought about you every single day that passed. I... I kept hoping you would call me."

He jerked his hand from hers and stood up. "Call you? Do you have any idea how much you wrecked me? Annalise, I believed in you...in us...and if I couldn't trust you, then who could I trust? If I was too controlling, then we should have talked about it, but you just gave up on us. I don't remember you trying too hard to tell me what you were feeling at the time."

She saw his pain in the depths of his eyes...felt it emanating from him. "I wasn't strong enough, Evan. I admit I was weak, and it was difficult for me to talk to you about these sensitive subjects, but I can't go back and do things differently." She got up from the sofa, as well. "All we have is the future, and I know we can get this right."

He raised a hand and rubbed the back of his neck as he broke eye contact with her. "I'm afraid, Annalise," he finally said softly. "I'm afraid to give you my heart again, and then if you get unsure you just send me a text and walk away. Now I'm exhausted and I really need to get some sleep."

Without saying another word, he turned and walked down the hallway toward the guest room. She watched him until he disappeared from her sight, and then she collapsed back on the sofa as tears burned at her eyes.

She'd hoped…she'd so desperately wanted… But apparently it didn't matter what she wanted because he wasn't willing to try again. She felt so much better prepared to have a relationship with him now. She had been weak before when it came to confronting him about her feelings. She'd not only been unfair to him, but also to herself by not being strong enough to talk to him about the important things in their relationship.

Maybe in the morning she'd have a chance to talk with him one more time before he left her house. Maybe once he was better rested his heart would open to her again. A tiny flicker of hope filled her heart.

They were both exhausted tonight. It had not been a good time for her to talk to him about all this. She should have waited until they both had gotten plenty of sleep and the crime situation was truly behind them.

With renewed hope still burning in her heart, she swiped the tears from her eyes and got up from the sofa. She was exhausted, as well. There had been far too little sleep in the past forty-eight hours.

She went into her bedroom and changed from her jeans and T-shirt into a black nightshirt. She hadn't realized just how exhausted she was until her familiar mattress seemed to embrace her. The minute she closed her eyes she was asleep and dreaming of being in Evan's arms once again.

As EXHAUSTED AS Evan was, he couldn't stop the thoughts that kept sleep at bay. Hearing that Annalise still loved him had filled him with a tremendous joy until old memories of hurt and loss had intruded.

Was he willing to put his heart on the line with her once again? There was no question that she wasn't the same woman she'd been when they'd been together. She was better. There was a confidence, a strength that flowed from her eyes that he found sexy as hell.

Had he been controlling in their previous relationship? Probably. He'd controlled her in an effort to keep her safe, to make sure she didn't wind up in an alley with a knife to her throat.

He frowned and blinked at that thought. It was the first time he realized how those moments in an alley when he'd been eight years old had affected him his entire life. He'd had no control when Maria had been stolen away. Was it possible he'd been trying to get that control back through his relationship with Annalise, a woman he had deeply loved?

He finally fell into a deep sleep. The ringing of a video call suddenly awakened him. He glanced at the clock on the nightstand and realized he'd been asleep for only about an hour. Why would Hendrick be calling him now? Did he have some information about the insider?

He turned on the lamp on the nightstand and grabbed his phone. "This better be good," he said with a grin at his friend.

Hendrick didn't return the smile. "Evan, Jacob has escaped from the jail in Pearson."

Shock electrified Evan, and for a moment he was sure he'd misunderstood what Hendrick had said. "What?" Evan swung his legs over the side of the bed. "When?"

"About thirty minutes ago."

"How did this happen?" Evan asked, still stunned by the news. He stood and grabbed a pair of his black slacks and pulled them on.

"The transfer of the prisoners was made successfully by two of Chief McCabe's men. Jacob was locked in a cell by himself, and thirty minutes later somehow he just walked out."

"Is there a camera in the jail?"

"Apparently there's only one camera, and it hasn't been functional for about a month or so."

"What kind of rundown facility is Chief Cummings running?" Evan yanked on a shirt. "Did anyone see where he went when he just walked out? Did he get into a waiting car or was he on foot?"

"Right now I have no more information other than he's out."

"What about Gretchen?"

"She's still behind bars," Hendrick replied.

Evan's frustration shot through the roof. Damn it, they'd all done their jobs and gotten the two behind bars. Jacob was a dangerous man, and now he was out on the streets once again and who knew what he might do.

"Does anyone have any idea where he might be headed?"

"Maybe back to his compound. As you know, the men stationed there were pulled off when you got the two into custody."

Evan cursed once again. "I'll call Chief Cummings and find out exactly what's going on and what he's doing to get Jacob back into custody."

"I know he sent out an alert. That's how I found out about it. Let me know if there's anything I can do to help from this end," Hendrick said.

"Will do." Evan disconnected the phone.

He quickly grabbed his socks and shoes. He couldn't believe this was happening. Jacob would be more dangerous than ever now, and who knew what resources he might be able to tap into now that he was out and on the run.

When he had his shoes on, he called Chief Cummings, who answered on the first ring. "You heard," he said.

"Just now," Evan replied. "I wanted to check to make sure you have somebody stationed at the compound so Jacob can't go back there."

"Already done, and there will be a full investigation into exactly what happened at the jail."

Evan wanted to rail at the man about his department and all the epic fails, but he didn't. In the end it wouldn't solve anything, and at the moment he still needed to work with these local officials to get the fugitive back into custody.

"Did anyone see him walk out of the building? Is there anyone who can tell us whether he left on foot or had a vehicle waiting for him?" he asked.

"So far we haven't found a witness. I was in the station with just a skeleton crew, but I'll be investigating the situation. He had no access to a phone while he was in custody so I'm guessing he's on foot. I have dozens of patrolmen looking for him as we speak."

"You'll keep me updated?" Evan asked.

"Of course," Chief Cummings replied.

At least Nick, Davis and Daniel hadn't left town yet. His next phone call was to Davis. "Unpack your bags, we're not out of here yet." He explained the situation and told him to update the other two agents and then wait for further instructions.

They needed to find Jacob quickly and get him off

the streets before he managed to kill somebody else. Who knew what kind of resources he could get to with a simple phone call to one of his followers? Most of them would do anything to help their leader.

He put his holster back on and then opened his bedroom door, surprised to see the living room lights on. Apparently Annalise hadn't been able to sleep.

He thought he heard a deep male voice. Was she listening to the television? He stepped into the hallway and pulled his gun, the hackles on the back of his neck standing up.

Gripping his gun firmly, he slowly walked down the hall and stepped into the living room. He swallowed a gasp. Annalise stood before him, her face radiating sheer terror. Jacob stood behind her, one arm wrapped around her waist, the other pointing a gun at her head.

"Ah, the man we were just coming to find," Jacob said with a smile. "Put your gun down."

"Why are you here, Jacob? What do you want?" Evan asked, his heart beating an unsteady rhythm. He did not obey Jacob's command. There was no way in hell he was going to put down his weapon.

In a million years he couldn't have foreseen Jacob coming here. How did the man even know where Annalise lived? How had he gotten here? He had assumed Jacob would want to get as far away from town as possible.

The utter terror shining from Annalise's eyes made a red hot rage well up inside him. He tamped it down. He had to keep his cool in this situation, and drew in several breaths in an effort to regulate his racing heartbeat.

This wasn't like facing a frightened Phil who he had assumed wasn't likely to use his gun. Jacob had already proven that he could kill in cold blood.

"Put your gun down," Jacob repeated, and yanked Annalise closer to him. She gasped, and tears began to run down her cheeks.

"I can't do that," Evan replied. "Just tell me why you're here. What is it you want from me?"

"I want you to bring me Sadie."

Evan looked at him in surprise. Did Jacob really believe he could still get the little girl to break into the banking system and steal a bunch of money? Was he so far out of touch with reality that he truly believed he could still follow through on his scheme?

"You need to let Annalise go before you and I can have a serious talk," Evan replied.

Jacob caressed her cheek with the barrel of the gun and then brought it back up to the side of her head. "I'm not letting her go until I get Sadie."

Evan wanted to rip the man's throat out for what he was doing to Annalise. "Don't you get it, man? We all know what your intentions were, and it's over. All your men are either dead or in jail."

"It's not over," Jacob screamed. "All I need is that kid, and then when she does what I want, I'll leave the country. I'll be someplace where nobody can ever touch me."

"Even if I bring Sadie here, it's still all over," Evan replied. "You'll never be able to board a plane. Officers all over the country will be looking for you."

"Money talks, and with enough money I can buy a plane and my own pilot. Now, if you don't bring me Sadie, then I'm going to shoot your girlfriend."

Evan's stomach tied itself in knots. In all the hostage negotiations he'd ever been through, his emotions had never been so out of control as at this moment. "She's not my girlfriend. She doesn't mean anything to me. If you kill her, then I'm going to kill you. She'll be dead but so will you. Now, let her go and put your gun down," Evan demanded.

As he was talking, he was seeking any kind of weakness he could exploit to either talk the man down or take him down physically.

At the moment he saw absolutely no weakness, and that scared the hell out of him.

ANNALISE'S HEART BEAT frantically and so fast it felt like it might explode right out of her chest. She'd never been so frightened in her entire life.

She'd awakened and had been unable to go back to sleep. She'd gotten up to get a drink of water, and Jacob had come up behind her in the kitchen.

The cold barrel of his gun now dug into the side of her head, and she was terrified with each moment that passed that Jacob would pull the trigger. At this point he certainly had nothing to lose.

She understood that while Evan would not want her to be killed, his ultimate goal had to be to stop Jacob here and now. If he did his job, he would never give into Jacob's demands and she might be another…she might be the last tragic victim to Jacob's madness.

The burly man smelled of rancid sweat and complete evil, and all she wanted was to get away from him. But with the gun to her head there wasn't much she could do except weep silent, helpless tears.

"Jacob, put the gun down and let her go," Evan said calmly.

"Get me that kid," Jacob bellowed, and tightened his arm around Annalise.

"That's not happening," Evan replied. "You need to

end this now, Jacob. You need to put your gun down and face the consequences of your actions."

This was a standoff that had her life in the balance. She knew Evan wasn't going to yield and put his gun down, and Jacob seemed determined not to give himself up.

She'd never felt as helpless as she did right now. Jacob was too strong to fight against, and the longer this went on the more she was certain he was going to shoot her.

Mentally she prepared herself to die. She said a silent goodbye to her parents and hoped they would be okay without her. And she said goodbye to Evan, sorry for the three years that had been wasted when they hadn't been together.

Suddenly she knew there was really only one thing she could do. It was definitely a risk. It might not work, but she had to do something to try to save herself. She gazed at Evan, the man she would always love, the last man she might ever see, and then she opened her mouth and screamed.

She screamed as loud as she could, knowing it was one of the things Jacob hated. "Stop that," the big man yelled. For a brief moment, the gun slipped from her head and his hold on her loosened. She immediately fell to her knees, and as she squeezed her eyes tightly closed, two shots nearly deafened her.

Oh God, who had been shot? When she stopped screaming, she heard Jacob cursing from someplace behind her. Then strong hands grabbed her by the shoulders and pulled her up to her feet.

She opened her eyes and saw Evan's beautiful face. "Come on, let's get you away from him."

He pointed her toward the sofa and while she sank

down, he approached Jacob, who was lying on the floor. Blood gushed from a wound in his chest, and he held both hands over it.

Evan stepped over Jacob and grabbed the gun that the man had apparently dropped when he'd been shot and had fallen backward. Evan then got on his phone and called Chief Cummings. "I need an ambulance at Annalise's house. I just shot Jacob."

"On it," the chief said.

Evan hung up and then called Nick. "I need the three of you to get to Annalise's house. I want you to escort Jacob to the hospital and stay with him until he's well enough to be put in federal lockdown. I do not want him going back into local custody."

As Evan made his arrangements, Annalise shivered on the sofa. She was utterly traumatized by what had just happened. From the moment Jacob had grabbed her in the kitchen until this time she'd been so afraid that she'd get shot or that Evan would be killed.

Now a sickness bordering nausea twisted in her stomach and she'd never been so cold in her life. She continued to shiver as the emergency vehicles arrived along with Chief Cummings and Evan's teammates.

It wasn't until the ambulance finally left and everyone else was gone that Evan walked over to her and pulled her up and into his arms.

He didn't say a word, he just held her tight. She clung to him as emotion began to choke her. "I… I just wanted a drink of water," she said through her tears. "I came into the k-kitchen and suddenly he was right on me. I… I really thought he was going to kill me…kill us."

Evan tightened his arms around her. "I've never been so terrified in my life."

She raised her head and looked at him in surprise. "Really? But you seemed so calm and in control."

"Oh, baby, I was so afraid that I was going to mess up, and I'd have never forgiven myself if anything would have happened to you." He tightened his arms around her. "It's over now. He'll never hurt you again. He's never going to hurt anyone ever again."

"Thank God," she whispered. She continued to weep for several more minutes, and then finally she released her death grip around his neck and stepped back from him. "I'm sorry," she said as she swiped at her tears. "I've just never been so frightened in my entire life."

"You were amazing under pressure." His gaze warmed her. "By screaming and then dropping to your knees, you gave me the shot I needed. Thank God his shot went wild." He pointed to a hole in the far wall.

"When we were in the school, he told us over and over again that he hated whining and screaming," she replied. "It was the only thing I could think of to do."

"It was absolutely brilliant," he replied. He led her back to the sofa where they both sat. "Chief Cummings is coming back to get our official report. Just tell him exactly what happened."

She nodded and drew several steadying breaths. "Do you think he would have killed me?"

He hesitated a long moment. "Yeah," he finally said. "I think eventually he might have, but I was looking for a shot before that happened. Thank God your scream surprised him and shook him up."

It was the longest night of her life. Chief Cummings finally returned to take their statements, and he brought with him a loaf of pumpkin spice bread his wife had baked.

Jacob had come through the patio door, and Annalise was horrified to realize when she'd stepped out on the deck earlier she didn't remember locking the door behind her. She'd given a killer easy access to her.

Finally it was all over. The terror, the official statements…everything. "Let's see if now we can get some much-needed sleep," Evan said.

Together they walked down the hallway. "Evan—" she turned to him when they reached the doorway to the guest room "—I promise I won't expect anything from you…but could you sleep with me? Could you just hold me in your arms?"

"I can do that," he said softly.

Once they reached her room, Evan kicked off his shoes and socks, took off his slacks and shirt and then crawled into bed with her and pulled her into an embrace.

It was the first time she'd felt completely safe since the school had been taken over by gunmen. "Just think, we can get up in the morning and have pumpkin spice bread with our coffee," he murmured drowsily in her ear.

"Why does he keep giving you baked goods?"

"He told me his wife loves to bake. He mentioned she'd grown up in foster care and that she loved to bake to take her mind off the terrible existence she had there."

"It's funny, his wife went through foster care and married a policeman and Gretchen went through foster care and became a criminal," she said sleepily.

And then she knew no more.

Chapter Thirteen

Evan awoke first. He was spooned around Annalise, and she was still sleeping soundly. For a moment he remained unmoving and simply reveled in the feel of her warm body.

He finally slid from the bed, grateful he hadn't awakened her. After grabbing his clothes off the floor, he went into the guest room to grab clean ones, then took a quick hot shower in the guest bathroom.

Once Evan was dressed, he went into the kitchen and put on a pot of coffee. He'd slept soundly, but had awakened with a lot of things on his mind, like who the inside man or woman might be.

Once he had a cup of coffee before him at the dining room table, he called Hendrick. He told him his thoughts, then asked the tech agent to do several things.

"Are you sure?" Hendrick asked with surprise when Evan had finished.

"I'm positive," Evan said. "Get back to me as soon as you have some information for me."

"You'll be the first person I tell," Hendrick said, and then hung up.

Evan then called Director Pembrook and explained to her what he was thinking and what he believed. She told him to gather the facts and let her know if he needed any other resources.

He sipped his coffee slowly as the thoughts whirling in his head made him half-crazy. If he was wrong, then he'd be destroying an innocent person's life. But if he was right, then the rat would be caught before Evan left town later today.

He got up and headed over to Annalise's desk. In the second drawer he found what he needed—a blank piece of white paper. He carried it and a ballpoint pen back to the table.

Sometimes he needed to write things down in order to straighten out his chaotic thoughts, and at the moment he definitely needed to write down what was in his head and then take a good, hard look at it all.

He'd been at it for about twenty minutes when Annalise came into the room. She had obviously showered and was dressed in a pair of jeans and a pink T-shirt that enhanced the green of her eyes.

She greeted him with a bright smile. "Good morning," she said and then beelined for the coffee.

"Back at you," he replied.

She got a cup of coffee and then sank into a chair across from him. "I wasn't sure if you'd be gone this morning or not."

"I'm tying up some last-minute things, but I'll get a flight out of here this evening. I hope you don't mind me hanging out here until then."

"Of course not," she replied. For a long moment she held his gaze, and he could see love shining there. There was not only unfinished business concerning the crime, but he knew now there was still more unfinished business with her.

"What are you doing?" she asked, and gestured to the piece of paper before him.

"Last night before you went to sleep, you said something that made me realize I'd overlooked something... something that should have been checked out before now."

"And what's that?"

"The fact that both Chief Cummings's wife and Gretchen were in foster care," he replied.

She looked at him with a frown. "What does that have to do with anything?"

"Maybe nothing, or maybe everything. I'm waiting for Hendrick to confirm something for me."

Annalise stared at him. "Are you telling me you think Chief Cummings's wife is our insider?"

He smiled at her grimly. "I think she's definitely a piece of the puzzle, but I now believe Chief Cummings is the mastermind."

She gasped in surprise. "Are you sure?"

"I'm looking at the factual evidence and adding my own suppositions," he replied.

"Tell me." She leaned forward with interest.

It was like old times...the good old times. She had always been one of his best sounding boards, and he knew today would be no different.

He looked down at what he'd written. "The first thing is Chief Cummings told me that Bert Epstein was one of his best friends. Being friendly with the security guard might have given Walter not only the information as to who would be in the school at a certain time, but also access to the van and garage keys."

"Okay, what else?" she asked.

"The night that Jacob and Gretchen escaped, Walter

had pulled off a lot of his men from guard duty at the back of the school."

"Keep going," Annalise said.

Funny, he knew what he'd written down was solid, but it made him feel better that she hadn't rejected anything he'd said so far.

"Walter was at the jail when Jacob walked out," he continued. "And Walter knew where you lived, and how else would Jacob know to come here? I wouldn't be surprised if Walter was the one who drove him here."

She leaned back in her chair. "My God, Evan. When it's laid out like that, he looks guilty as hell. And when the ultimate takedown occurred, it was a complete success without Walter's involvement. So what happens next?"

"I'm waiting for some additional information from Hendrick and then we're going to get an arrest warrant. I believe I have enough circumstantial evidence to take him down. And once we get his phone records, I believe they'll prove without a shadow of a doubt that he's our man. It will be my pleasure to arrest that bastard."

She reached out and covered his hand with hers. "I always knew you were the best hostage negotiator in the world, but you're also a brilliant FBI agent, as well." She squeezed his hand and then released it.

"I don't know about that. If I was that brilliant, I would have seen all of this before now. Each incident taken separately I managed to overlook, but this morning it all came together."

"So, did anyone interview Jacob? And did he say anything about Walter being behind all this, or is he even able to be interviewed?"

"Oh, he was able. The gunshot wound was not life-threatening and he was interviewed extensively last night. But he refused to cooperate in any way. He probably thinks Walter is going to somehow get him out of this again."

"Then he's really delusional," she replied. "What about Gretchen? Is she talking?"

"Not a word except to cuss anyone who asks her anything," he replied. "Although when we arrested them she insisted that she was an abused woman and was terrified of Jacob."

"Trust me, there's no way she was abused or terrified. She had no problems beating the crap out of me."

"I hate that you went through that," he said, her words generating new anger at the person he believed had helped those people get into the school in the first place.

His phone rang with an incoming video call. "Hey, man. What do you have for me?" he asked Hendrick.

"Gretchen Owens was in foster care from the age of six when her mother gave her up. She bounced around among several foster homes, but when she was fifteen she was fostered by Jackie and Damon Huck and she remained with them until she aged out," he said.

"And Chief Cummings's wife?" Evan asked.

"Rose Mayfield entered the foster care system when she was eight. Her parents were killed in a car accident, and there were no other relatives to take her in. She was with the same foster parents until she was fourteen and, due to health issues, they had to give her back to the state. She was then placed with Jackie and Damon Huck until she aged out."

"Bingo," Evan said. "Thanks, Hendrick."

"I've got your warrant ready, and I'm faxing it to you right now. You have the full approval and authority of

Director Pembrook and the support of the department behind you. Call me on the other side."

Evan got the documents he needed and then sat back down at the table.

"So, when is this all going down?" she asked.

"Soon. I'm just waiting for Davis and my other men to come and get me." He grinned at her. "It's questionable what role Chief Cummings's wife played in all this, but I have every confidence that Walter is the insider and this will finally put this case to bed."

As if on cue, Annalise's doorbell rang. Evan's backup had arrived. For the next thirty minutes, the men sat at the table and talked about their game plan, which was really quite simple. Go in, take him down and get out.

"I know he's at the station right now," Evan said. "I have no interest in embarrassing him by a takedown in front of his men. Hopefully we can take care of business in his office and then escort him out of there peacefully and without handcuffs."

"And if he doesn't go along with that plan?" Davis asked.

"Then all bets are off," Evan said firmly. He stood up from the table. "Let's all rock and roll."

The three agents left the house, then Annalise walked with Evan to the door. "I can feel your excitement," she said. "Go get your man, Evan, and be safe while you do it."

He smiled and then grabbed her in his arms and kissed her long and hard. When he released her, he immediately turned and went out of the house.

ALL OF THEM were jazzed on the drive to the Pearson police station. "I can't believe this bastard was playing us all along," Davis said from the passenger seat.

"He obviously made a deal with the devil and now there's hell to pay," Daniel said from the backseat.

They all continued to talk about the case until Evan turned into the police station parking lot. Then they fell into a sober silence.

Evan got out of the car with a sense of purpose. He knew he was right about this. Not only did his gut tell him he was right, but the circumstantial evidence all supported it. He was also certain more evidence would come to light that would prove him right.

"Well, well, if it isn't the G-men," the chief said as they entered the building. "Come to tell us goodbye before you leave town?" He stood with two of his patrolmen just behind the reporting counter.

"Just tying up some final things. Could we talk to you in your office?" Evan asked.

"Sure, come on back." He gestured for them to follow him into a small office with a desk and two chairs before it. "I'll tell one of my boys to bring in a couple more chairs," he said.

"Oh, that won't be necessary," Evan replied. "We won't be here long." He pulled the arrest warrant out of his pocket and tossed it on top of the desk.

"What's this?" Walter asked with a frown. He picked up the paperwork.

"It's a warrant for your arrest on a variety list of charges including conspiracy to commit murder and kidnapping, just to name a few," Evan replied.

"The hell you say." Walter looked at him in shock and threw the paperwork back on the desk. "Is this come kind of a joke?"

"It's no joke, Walter," Evan replied.

"You aren't taking me anywhere. This is all a big

mistake," Walter said, and then made a move toward his gun.

Davis, Nick and Daniel drew their weapons. "Whoa." Walter raised his hands above his waist. "I'm telling you this is all some kind of a terrible mistake."

"Walter, I need you to give me your weapon and your cell phone," Evan said.

"I'm telling you this is a load of crap." Walter's face flushed red. "I'm the chief of the police around here, not some damn criminal. You got this all wrong."

"You'll have a chance to defend yourself in a court of law," Davis said. He continued to tell Walter his rights under the law.

"Walter, we can escort you out of here quietly without handcuffs, or we'll do it the hard way. We don't want to cause any drama in your police station, so why don't you give me your gun and your phone and we'll escort you out of here without the cuffs," Evan said.

Walter held Evan's gaze for a long moment, and then sighed and appeared to crumple within himself. "Do you have any idea how much they pay me as a civil servant? I got tired of working my ass off to make small-town wages. Nobody was supposed to get killed."

He placed his gun and cell phone on the desk and then straightened. "I'd prefer to walk out of here without handcuffs."

They all walked out together, and Walter was placed in the backseat between Daniel and Nick. "I suppose Jacob is singing like a bird. I should have never trusted an idiot like him to begin with," Walter said. "He's the one who killed people...he and his crazy wife."

"We have agents in the area heading to your house to arrest your wife, as well," Davis said.

Walter straightened. "Please, she had absolutely

nothing to do with this. I did it all. I knew she was friendly with Gretchen, and I knew Gretchen was married to Jacob. Rose didn't do anything wrong. She was always trying to counsel Gretchen to do good things in her life, but Gretchen is a bad seed."

"Then your wife should be able to prove her innocence in a court of law," Nick said.

Walter fell silent and so did the others. Hendrick contacted Evan with a meeting point for other federal agents to take custody of Walter and take him to a facility where he would be arraigned and await trial.

Once that was done, Davis dropped Evan back at Annalise's place. He remained on the front porch for several minutes. With the crime completely cleared up, he had nothing left but his feelings for the woman who had been by his side throughout the whole ordeal.

He had one final phone call to make, and then he knocked on her door and she opened it. "Thank God you're safe and sound," she said as she gestured him inside.

"Everything went smoothly, and Walter and his wife are now in custody."

"So, your work here is done," she replied as the two of them sank down on the sofa.

"Not quite."

She looked at him quizzically. "What's left?"

He reached out and took one of her hands in his. "Annalise, you asked me if you could have a second chance, but I've been thinking and I've realized it's me who should be asking you for a second chance."

He squeezed her hand tightly. "I screwed up, Annalise. I didn't listen to you when you were telling me you were unhappy. I was too controlling because I was afraid I'd lose you. I was so afraid you'd be another person I loved with all my heart who would disappear and I'd never know what happened to you. I need you to give me a second chance to get it right. I love you. I've never stopped loving you."

"Oh, Evan." She leaned forward and he captured her lips with his. This was the woman he wanted by his side. He wanted to brainstorm crimes with her. He wanted to cheer her on no matter where she worked or what she did, and he wanted to end each day with her in his arms.

"We owe ourselves a second chance," she said when the kiss ended. "There's way too much love between us to let it go."

"I'm not letting it go. I'm not letting you go. I promise you this time around we'll get it right. I'll get it right," he promised.

"I'm going to hate telling you goodbye later this evening," she said. "But at least I'll be back in Knoxville for good in a couple of months."

"You don't have to tell me goodbye tonight. I called Director Pembrook and told her I needed a week of vacation. So, if you'll have me for the next seven days, I'll be here."

She laughed, and her eyes lit with the sparkle that he'd always loved. "Oh Evan, I'll definitely have you."

He pulled her back into his arms and kissed her once again, and in the kiss he knew he'd found his partner and his soulmate. This was one hostage situation he'd definitely gotten right for it had brought him back to the woman he loved.

* * * * *

LEFT TO DIE

RITA HERRON

To Dotty Graves for being a fan! Happy reading!

Chapter One

Keep running. One foot in front of the other. Don't stop or he'll get you.

She touched her temple, where blood matted her hair. Her head throbbed. Her memory was fuzzy.

The wind whistled, shrill and violent, through the tall pines, hemlocks and oaks. Tree branches shook and bent, cracking. Thick snowflakes blinded her as they swirled in the darkness.

Where was she? How had she gotten here? Which way should she go?

Why was he after her?

She pawed her way through a cluster of pines. Everything looked the same. Endless trees so close together you couldn't see past them. Snow. Fallen limbs. Wet leaves and brush.

She pivoted, searching for a sign as to how to get to a road.

Nothing but more trees. The mountains rising in front of her.

Footsteps crunched behind her. Twigs snapped. A limb broke off and hurled to the ground in front of her. She stumbled and tripped over it, grasping for something to break her fall. Her hands hit the rough edges of an oak and bark scraped her already bloody palms. Her knees sank into the foot-deep snow. Her clothes were damp, freezing against her skin.

She had no coat. No hat. No gloves.

Shivering, she looked around for a place to hide. Some place he couldn't find her.

"It's over!" a deep voice shouted. "You can't escape."

No...she silently screamed. She had to get away. Instincts told her he'd kill her if he caught her.

Ice clung to her hands and clothes as she shoved herself up. One foot. Another. She trudged forward. Ahead, a path wound to the left. Up a hill. Maybe it led to the road. Or at least to a shelter. A place to hide.

An animal howled in the distance. A coyote? Bobcat?

Bears also roamed these mountains.

Another foot. Another. Her boot caught in a pile of weeds. Her ankle twisted and she lost her footing. She swayed and clawed for something to hold on to. Her nails dug into the bark of a thin pine, and she hugged it, gasping for breath.

Another howl. Louder. Closer. A wolf?

Trembling, she peered through the trees. There it was. A large gray wolf perched on a boulder ahead, its nose in the air, sniffing. Beady eyes darted across the land, searching for prey.

Terror shot through her. If the man didn't get her, the wolf might.

Forcing herself to remain still so as not to invite an attack, she eased back a step. Clung to the trees. Footfalls light. Another step. Then another. No sound.

Only the shrill wind again, and the wolf pawing at the rock.

Tears clogged her throat. She had to stay calm. Breathe in and out. Keep moving. A few steps more, and she ducked behind a cluster of rocks to hide. Maybe she could wait him out.

But the echo of footsteps crunched ice and brush again. She pushed up to run, but two gloved hands grabbed her. A big body behind her. Rough clothes. The scent of a man's musky odor.

"Let me go." Determined to fight, she raised her arm and swung her elbow backward at an angle, but she missed.

"I warned you that you couldn't escape." Something sharp and hard hit the back of her head. A gunshot followed, ringing in her ears.

Pain ricocheted through her temple. Then the world went black, and she fell into the darkness.

ALL FLETCHER—FLETCH—MAVERICK wanted to do was enjoy a little bro time and then hit the sack. He'd been working double shifts the last two days. Ever since the big snowstorm had hit Whistler and the mountains, his search and rescue team had been on the clock.

Warnings had been issued. People had been advised to stay in. Cancel their plans for hiking the trails. Stock up on food.

That part the locals had listened to. The grocery stores had run out of milk, bread and bottled water. Battery pack phone chargers, generators, flashlights and batteries had flown off the shelves.

Larry's Liquor store had lines backed out the door.

Still some people refused to stay home. As if the predicted five feet of snow and windchill temperatures below zero was propaganda the meteorologists had fabricated to stir up a frenzy at the stores.

This time the weather forecasters had nailed it, though. Clouds started unleashing snow the night before, and it had been a constant downfall of white ever since.

Trouble was weather forecasters missed so often that people didn't pay attention or just blew them off. School closings for possible snow that turned into rain made the South a laughingstock in the national news.

But this one was for real and had only just begun.

Fletch sank onto a barstool at the high top across from his brothers, Jacob, Griff and Liam. He was so bone-weary he could barely muster a smile.

"You look like hell," the firefighter of the four, Griff, said.

"I feel like it, too," Fletch muttered as Liam poured him a beer from the pitcher on the table. Liam was with the FBI.

Fletch's mouth watered as his fingers gripped the mug. The beer was an IPA. His favorite.

Jacob, the oldest of the four and Whistler's sheriff, pounded Fletch's back. "Good work finding those hikers yesterday."

Fletch took a sip from his mug, then snagged a wing from the platter and bit into it. "Glad we found them when we did." He wiped his mouth with a napkin. "Man broke his leg and needed medical assistance."

He reached for his beer again, but before he could take another swig, his phone buzzed on his hip. A quick glance at the number and he cursed. "Work."

His brothers traded grim looks as Fletch answered the call. "A family has been reported missing on the trail," his boss, Captain Hanley, said. "I know you just got off duty, Fletch, but we're slammed. Had two other calls. I need you to come in."

Fletch pushed his beer away, stood and clipped his phone back onto his belt. "Be right there."

"You have to go in?" Jacob asked.

Fletch nodded. "Missing family."

Liam motioned for the waitress and asked her to bring

a to-go box and a large sweet tea. "At least take some food with you. I know how these things go."

Fletch accepted the take-out food and tea, knowing his brother was right, then headed to the door.

Thirty minutes later, he was geared up with his pack, and he and two fellow rangers, Todd and Danny, met at the beginning of the trail leading to Whistler Falls, where the family was supposed to be hiking.

"Family's named Patterson. A father, two boys, ages seven and nine," Todd said. "They're from south Georgia."

Where it was sunny and warm. They were definitely out of their element in this frigid mess.

The family's white Expedition was parked in the lot. The Appalachian Trail consisted of over two thousand miles of trails through the wilderness running from Georgia to Maine. Designated spots where hikers began their trek still required parking and hiking in. Throughout the states, lean-to shelters had been built to provide accommodations for emergencies, but were barely pieces of wood nailed together with one side open to the elements.

Experienced hikers carried packs equipped with tents, food and water, emergency supplies, compasses, maps and tarps they tacked up over the open side of the shelter to ward off the wind when temperatures turned dangerous.

Conditions were dangerous now. He hoped the Pattersons had had the good sense to come prepared.

Danny pointed to the trail map, and they scrutinized it together. The areas had been marked with names and points along the way to guide hikers in planning their route and to keep them from getting lost and walking in circles. After a few miles, the trees and rocks all blended together.

"There are two ways they could have gone to reach the falls from here," Danny said. "East—"

"Or west." Todd gestured to the dark clouds. "Let's divide up."

Fletch nodded. "You guys take the eastern section. I'll head west."

They checked to make certain their radios were working, strapped on their packs, then pulled on gloves and hats and headed in opposite directions.

The temperature was nineteen now and dropping, the precipitation from the night before freezing to ice. More snowflakes thickened the air, making visibility difficult. Protective goggles helped, but the fog of white swallowed the ridges and paths in the distance.

Fletch used his flashlight to illuminate the ground, searching for footprints or signs the family had recently walked this way. An animal print here and there caught his eye, but no human prints.

Every few feet he paused to listen for sounds of voices calling for help, and he yelled out as he climbed the hill. Wind howled from the ridges and peaks, the trees shivering as the gusts barreled through at record speed.

His flashlight lit on something red on the ground. He stooped to examine it and decided it was blood. Could be from an injured animal.

Or a person who needed help.

He aimed his flashlight ahead and noted more blood dotting the snow. Enough to suspect the animal, or human, might be in serious trouble.

Pulse pounding, he followed the blood trail up the incline and around a cluster of hemlocks. A branch lay on the ground, soaked in blood. He scanned the area, listening again. Nothing but the shrill wind whipping through the forest and off the mountaintop.

He panned the light in each direction, then spotted drag marks across the snow. Drag marks mingled with blood.

His radio buzzed. "Located the Pattersons," Todd said, his voice cracking with the static on the line.

"Status?" Fletch asked.

"Nine-year-old sprained his ankle, father has a bum knee, and the other boy is close to hypothermia. We're warming them up, then going to get them back. I've already radioed it in. Medics will be waiting. Meet us at the car."

"No can do." Fletch removed his battery-powered camera from his pack and snapped a picture of the blood trail and the indentations where the body had been dragged. "I found blood in the snow. Looks like drag marks from a human. I'm going to follow it."

"Dammit," Todd said. "I'd help, but it'll take both me and Danny to haul the family down."

"They're our priority now. Get them to safety," Fletch said. "I'll let you know if I find something and need assistance."

"Copy that." Todd hesitated. "Be careful, man."

"Always." None of them liked to leave a coworker out here alone. But sometimes it couldn't be helped.

Besides, they'd trained for it. And no way could Fletch go home without determining the source of that blood and if it was human.

FACEDOWN IN THE SNOW, she roused from unconsciousness, dazed and confused. A dull throb occupied her head, making the trees spin.

Wind knifed through her. Where was she? What was wrong with her?

She mentally rifled through her fleeting memories for how she'd ended up here. But nothing made sense. Gunshots. Running. A fight. Blood…everywhere.

Her name was… Wait, what was it?

Panic seized her. What *was* her name?

A sob caught in her throat. A foggy blur occupied the space where her memories were stored.

The sound of footsteps crunching twigs and ice echoed somewhere in the distance. Footsteps… He was coming after her again.

This time he'd kill her.

She struggled to crawl forward, but her limbs were too heavy and stiff to move.

Her teeth chattered. Her skin stung from the cold, and her chest hurt as she tried to draw a breath.

The sense that she was in imminent danger overwhelmed her as scattered memories broke through the haze. Someone chasing her. A sharp blow.

She clawed at the ground, fingers digging into the brush and icy ground. Her feet pushed at the surface but sank deeper into the frigid snow. Tears of frustration blurred her eyes, then trickled down her cheeks, freezing on her face.

She had to move. Hide.

But her body wouldn't cooperate. She tried to flex her fingers and grappled for a tree limb, something to help propel her forward. But the branch was too far away. She couldn't give up, though. The cold could be deadly.

Summoning every ounce of strength she possessed, she managed to scoot on her stomach and dragged herself a few feet.

Every muscle in her body throbbed with the effort. Even her bones hurt.

Then a gust of wind shook the trees, sending a deluge of icy snow and more limbs down onto her, and she collapsed.

She cried out for help, but her voice faded into the howling wind. Terror bled through her as she sank back into the darkness.

FLETCH TUGGED HIS hat over his ears as he tracked the bloodspots on the ground. He'd been hiking for over an hour.

Something shiny caught his eye near a tree stump, and he waved his flashlight across the area. There it was. Glittering against the white ground. It was caught in the weeds. He hiked over to it, knelt and dug the object from the fresh snow.

A wedding ring.

Questions needled him as he examined it. A woman's ring. Too small for a man. Silver. What was it doing out here in the wilderness?

Someone could have lost it while camping or hiking.

Judging from the fact that it wasn't buried yet, it couldn't have been here long.

He studied the tracks ahead. More blood. Did it belong to the woman who owned this wedding ring?

Another violent gust of wind snapped tree limbs and sent them flying to the ground. The snow was falling faster, accumulating so quickly that it obliterated the blood trail.

He needed to hurry, or he'd get trapped out here himself.

But the mantra he and his fellow rescue workers lived by reverberated in his head—*leave no one behind.*

If someone was injured and needed help, he had to find him. Or judging from the ring—her.

He jammed the wedding band in his pocket, then set out again. Another mile. Then another. Upward toward Vulture's Point, named so because several suicides had occurred at the spot, the bodies drawing the vultures to the canyon below.

What if he was tracking someone contemplating suicide? She could have dumped the ring and then hiked toward the point. But…if so, why was she bleeding? And what about the drag marks? That indicated there was more than one person…

The storm intensified, snow thickening with each mile, the wind the kind of biting cold that stung your skin and clawed at your bones.

Finally he turned the corner past the boulder marking the rise to the point, and spotted something black. A boot? No, a dark red wool scarf…

Adrenaline churning, he took off running. The thick snow sucked at his boots, but he crossed the area and picked up the scarf. More blood drops. Indentations in the snow that looked like paw prints—no, hands digging.

He was close. He could feel it.

The flashlight fought through the blurry haze, and a minute later, he spotted a body. Facedown on the ground, body half buried in the blanket of white.

A woman.

He jogged toward her and lurched to a stop when he reached her. Long dark hair dotted with snow and ice lay in a tangled mass over the woman's shoulders.

He sucked in a breath and stooped to see if she was alive.

Chapter Two

Fletch gently raked the woman's hair away from her slender throat and pressed two fingers to her neck to check for a pulse. He quickly noted her physical description. Long black hair, pale skin, oval shaped face, high cheekbones. No makeup.

She was a looker.

She wore no hat, gloves or winter coat, though. Regular boots, not snow boots.

She hadn't been prepared for the weather, suggesting she hadn't come out here to hike. Or to kill herself.

Dammit. He didn't feel a pulse.

Her body was so still he didn't think she was breathing. Even if she was alive, hypothermia had set in. Her skin was bluish and ice-cold, and frost formed tiny crystals on the exposed surfaces.

He held his breath as he moved his fingers an inch lower and pressed again. Seconds passed. His heart hammered.

Finally he felt a pulse, low and thready. She was alive. At least for now.

He had to raise her body temperature for her to survive.

That meant moving her to the shelter over the next hill.

Blood mingled with the snow on the back of her head, and he examined the area and found a bruise and a gash.

Someone had either hit her or she'd fallen and slammed her head against a sharp rock.

Anger shot through him at the sight of the bruise on her cheek and forehead. A bruise that looked as if she'd been hit. Hard.

Blood streaked her pale pink sweater and jeans, and cuts and scrapes marred her hands and arms. He moved her legs and arms gently to check for broken bones but didn't detect a break. That was something.

Breathing out the cold air, he patted her face gently to see if she'd rouse, but she remained limp, eyelids closed. He eased one eyelid up, then another to check her eyes. Her pupils were dilated. Mouth slack.

"It's going to be okay, sweetheart," he murmured.

The snow continued to pelt them, thickening and swallowing everything in sight. He gently scooped the woman into his arms and carried her toward the shelter. The wind gusts battered him as he walked, knocking him off balance, and he had to tread slowly for fear of losing his footing. If he slipped and they slid down the mountain, it would make things worse.

A few more feet, then he topped the hill and spotted the crude shelter. Anything was better than being fully exposed. Adrenaline pushed him forward, and he made it the last few feet. He eased the woman onto the wood floor in the back corner of the hut.

An angry gust hurled snow inside, and he set his pack down, retrieved the rapid response blankets he kept for emergencies and rushed to cover the woman. After he'd wrapped her in one, he yanked out the tarp and tacked it from post to post to create a wall to shield them from the worst of the elements.

The force of the wind was so strong the tarp flipped upward, but he secured it back in place. Then he raced back to check on the woman. Still unconscious.

Her shallow breathing was barely discernible. How long had she been out in the frigid temperature?

His radio beeped and he snagged it. "Fletch here, come in."

"It's Todd. Medics transporting the Pattersons to the hospital. Your status? Over."

"Found a woman on the trail, unconscious, suffering from hypothermia. Carried her to Vulture's Point shelter. Over."

"Conditions worsening," Todd responded. "Will send a team of medics your way ASAP."

"Copy that. If it clears and she regains consciousness, I'll bring her down the mountain. For now, going to warm her and treat minor injuries." He paused. "No ID. Have Jacob check missing persons reports."

"Description?"

"I'd guess her age is early thirties. Long black hair. Approximately five-three, maybe a hundred and twenty-five pounds."

"Copy that. Keep in touch."

"Will do. Over and out." He stowed the radio with his gear, then slipped from the shelter to gather limbs so he could build a fire in the built-in fire pit. Then he hurried to collect branches that had been blown to the ground in the snowstorm.

When his arms were full, he carried them back to the shelter and put them inside. He secured the tarp, then arranged twigs and two smaller limbs into the pit. Then he retrieved matches from his pack and lit the twigs. It took several minutes for the wood to catch, but finally it flickered to life. He strategically arranged two more branches on top of the flames, then hurried to check on the woman.

She still lay unmoving, face ghost white, chest barely moving up and down with each breath. He yanked off his coat, pulled the blanket off her, wrapped the coat around her, then covered her with the blanket again.

He blew on the embers to spark the flames, hoping the warmth would breathe life back into the woman. Outside, the wind howled, beating at the tarp and the frame of the thin wooden shelter.

He kept watch over her for an hour, but she was still chilled. Desperate to bring her body temperature up, he stripped her wet clothes and laid them near the fire, then removed his own wet clothing and spread it by the fire, as well.

He used the second blanket to make a bed, then positioned her on top of it, stretched out beside her and pulled the other blanket over them. Rubbing her arms with his hands, he cradled her close, praying his body heat stirred life back into her.

He nestled her cheek against his chest and held her, rubbing slow circles across her back. Exhaustion pulled at him, but he forced himself to stay awake in case she roused or needed him.

The fact that bruises covered her body disturbed him, though, during the long hours of the night. First he had to make sure she was okay.

Then he'd find out who'd hurt her and left her in the woods to die.

HER HEAD ACHED. Her body throbbed. And a tingling niggled at her toes and feet.

But warmth seeped through her, slowly alleviating the chill from her bones. She burrowed into it, desperate to escape the cold.

She struggled to open her eyes, but her eyelids were too

heavy and her limbs felt weighted down. Big arms held her against a strong solid wall of muscle, transporting her back to the safest place she'd ever known.

She was seven years old and her father was holding her in his lap. He sipped his morning coffee, the steam rising up and floating in the air. The chicory scent was strong, but her father loved his coffee, so she didn't mind, not as long as they were working the crossword puzzle together.

"Two across, another word for light outside," her father murmured.

She tapped her fingers on the folded newspaper, then bounced up and down. "Sunshine."

He made a show of mulling it over, but his eyes twinkled, and she knew she'd nailed it. A second later, he wrote the word in the boxes and tugged at her ponytail. "You're a smart girl, kiddo."

"That one was so easy." She giggled and hugged him. She loved her daddy so much. Every Sunday, they worked the crossword puzzle together. During the week they did word searches and other puzzles that he brought home. A thousand-piece jigsaw of a mountain lion was spread on their game table now.

They finished the crossword in less than half an hour— not a record, but a respectable time—and then her mom appeared with a picnic basket that they carried to the river park for the day.

She jumped in the icy water and popped up, shivering, teeth chattering. Her father wrapped a blanket around her, and they built a fire and snuggled beside it to watch the flames flicker orange, yellow and bright red.

Wood crackled and popped, the heat so soothing that she fell into a deeper sleep.

Then the warmth dissipated, and she was twelve years old, back at home with the winter wind seeping through the eaves of the old house. It was one of those nights she couldn't sleep and she'd stared at the ceiling, listening to the rain ping off the roof and wishing it was morning so she could climb up beside her daddy and do another crossword.

A sudden loud crash echoed from downstairs. Thunder? Then a scream. Her mother.

Terror shot through her and she froze, listening again. Another crash. Something breaking. Her father's shout. "Get out!"

Panic bolted through her. Someone was inside the house.

Footsteps pounded. Her mother's scream again, shrill and terrifying. Then a popping sound. A gun!

Choking back a sob, she scrambled off the bed and ran into the closet to hide. She closed the door, then made her way through the opening leading to the crawl space. It was dusty and smelly, but her parents stored their Christmas decorations inside.

Tinsel dangled from a cardboard box, and the bag of bows her mom stuck on packages sat on top. The bag had gotten ripped somehow; red, green, gold and silver bows dotted the floor like colorful candy.

Another gunshot echoed from down below. Then a clunking sound as if someone hit the floor.

Tears blurred her eyes, and she hugged her knees to her, fighting back a scream. If someone was inside, she had to be quiet or they'd find her.

Her mind raced. Dad had a gun. He kept it locked in the drawer in the kitchen. Had he shot the intruders?

Footsteps pounded again. A door slammed. A car engine rumbled outside.

Then suddenly everything went quiet.

Too terrified to move, she rocked herself back and forth, waiting for her father and mother to tell her it was safe to come out. Tears streamed down her cheeks, but she buried her sobs in her arms.

It was hours later, and still no one had come. The house echoed with a creepy quiet, making her stomach churn. Finally she gathered enough courage to tiptoe downstairs. Her foot hit something sticky and wet on the bottom step.

Then she saw the dark crimson color. Blood everywhere. Splattered on the walls, the staircase, the carpet...

A scream died in her throat. Shouldn't touch the blood. Mom and Dad...they were on the floor... Arms sprawled, legs twisted, eyes bulging wide...

Her own eyes jerked open. God... She'd been dreaming. Or had she?

The suffocating darkness gave way to a sliver of light seeping through a thin wall of wood. She was lying on a hard plank floor. A blanket over her.

Then... A man beside her. Not just a man. A naked one.

She lurched to a sitting position and scrambled backward, dragging the blanket with her.

Where in the hell was she, and what was going on?

FLETCH INSTANTLY SAT UP, pulling his coat over his lap. Dammit, he couldn't help his morning erection.

But he had kept his hands to himself during the long cold night. He'd never take advantage of a vulnerable woman and this one was about as vulnerable as he'd seen. Bruised, battered and near dead. Maybe at the hands of a man.

And if the wedding ring belonged to her, the man who'd hurt her and left her for dead might have been her husband.

Her eyes widened in horror as she looked at him, then down at herself, then anger flashed across her slender, pale face.

"Who are you?" she said, fear and bewilderment lacing her soft tone. "And what do you want?"

He raised his hands in a gesture meant to alleviate her fear and forced his voice to remain calm. "My name is Fletch. I work with Whistler's Search and Rescue in these mountains." He watched her for a reaction. "Last night my coworkers were looking for a family lost in the storm, then I saw blood."

A war raged in her eyes. Should she believe him or was he some sort of pervert who'd abducted her for evil purposes?

"I followed the blood trail and found you collapsed, facedown in the snow, unconscious. You were barely breathing. Looked like you'd been beaten up, and you'd sustained a blow to your head."

Her eyes darted to her hands, which were still stained with blood. Then she lifted her fingers to her temple and touched the cut on her forehead. "You did this?"

His jaw hardened and he shook his head. "No. Like I said, I found you and brought you here because I couldn't carry you down the mountain during the blizzard."

She clutched the blanket to her in a white-knuckled grip. "So why am I naked?"

As much as he detested the accusations in her voice, he was glad to see she had some fight in her. Probably the only way she'd survived.

"You were suffering from hypothermia. Your wet clothes made it impossible to raise your body temp." He gestured toward the fire. "After I carried you to this shelter, I built a fire and tried to warm you. Shared body heat is the fastest way to accomplish that."

He let the statement stand for a minute, then he stood to retrieve his pack. She gasped at the sight of his naked body in the firelight.

He should apologize, but it was too late. She'd seen him. He'd seen her. What the hell was the big deal?

He dug in one of the pockets of the pack and removed his ID.

When he looked back, fear darkened her eyes again as if she'd expected him to draw a weapon. He offered her his picture ID.

"See. I'm a ranger, Search and Rescue. My job is to find missing and lost people in the mountains and bring them home safely."

Her hand trembled as she examined his badge, and she glanced from his photo back to him, scrutinizing both.

"I'm sorry for frightening you," he said, then knelt and stoked the fire again. "I radioed in our location, so we'll either hike out when the snow lets up or they'll send a team in when they can."

Her breath rattled in the frigid air. "You saved me?"

He gave a humble shrug. "That's my job."

A tense silence stretched between them, and he checked their clothes to see if they were dry. Thankfully, they were, so he yanked on his jeans and shirt, then carried her clothes to her.

"All dry now."

Her gaze met his, questions still lingering, but at least she wasn't screaming or running. She motioned for him to turn around. A sly grin lit his face. He'd seen her naked, but that was different.

Besides, he wanted to win her trust. "I'll be right back." He slipped through the tarp opening, secured it, then walked into the woods to collect more kindling.

Deciding to give her privacy, he scanned the area, but the snow was still falling in thick sheets of white, now knee-deep. The wind was brutal, the windchill factor below zero.

It would be dangerous to set off down the mountain at this point. Best to let the worst pass.

He rubbed his hands together, then gathered more sticks for the fire, ducked back inside the shelter and reattached the tarp.

"Can we leave now?" the woman asked.

Firelight illuminated her milky white skin and throat. Her bruises looked more stark this morning, the dried blood on her forehead a reminder that she'd sustained a head injury.

"Not yet, snow's still coming down hard, and the wind-chill is well below zero." He dropped the sticks by the fire in a pile, then added a few more to keep it burning.

Then he pulled two bottles of water from his pack and carried one to her. "Here, drink. You need to stay hydrated."

She looked at him warily but accepted the bottle, unscrewed the cap and took a long swallow.

He pulled a granola bar from his pack and handed it to her, then took one for himself. Although he forced himself to eat only half, he let her finish hers before he spoke. Then he sat down in front of her and offered her a gentle smile.

"Better?"

"Thanks." She tugged the blanket back over her as if it offered a sense of security.

"I told you who I am," he said gruffly. "Your turn now."

She clamped her teeth over her bottom lip and glanced down at her bloody hands.

"Your name's a good start," he said. "I can radio my team and let your family know you're safe."

Her gaze rose to meet his, pain and confusion clouding the depths.

His stomach clenched as protective instincts kicked in. "Hey, it's okay." Keeping his distance, he gestured toward the bruises on her hands. "I didn't hurt you. So tell me your name and who did this, and I'll make sure the police find him and put him away."

Chapter Three

Distrust niggled at her as she studied Fletch. His ID looked genuine, and so did the concern on his face.

But she'd been running from someone and couldn't remember who or the man's face. IDs could be faked.

What if he wasn't who he claimed to be?

She clutched the blanket he'd given her, her mind racing. Although if he'd wanted to kill her, why hadn't he left her out in the elements? Why warm her and offer her food?

Another few hours outside, and she would have died. Unless he wanted something else…

"Listen to me," he said as if he realized her train of thought. "I didn't touch you last night, except to wrap you up and treat you for hypothermia. I know you're scared and that someone hurt you. Talk to me and I can help."

She rubbed her temple where her head throbbed, searching desperately for details of the past few hours. Or days. How long had she been out here?

He stood, retrieved something from his bag, then set it in front of her. A radio.

"This is how my team communicates. I'll call them and prove that you can trust me."

She wanted to trust him but said nothing. She was bruised and battered. Common sense warned her to be cautious until she figured out what was going on.

A grim look settled in his eyes, but he picked up the radio, pushed a button and spoke into it. "Ranger Maverick, Search and Rescue, unit 9. Come in."

Static rattled over the speaker.

"Come in," he repeated.

More static, then a voice, but it was garbled. "Dammit, the storm's creating too much interference," Fletch muttered.

He tried it several more times, even walked to the edge of the shelter to see if he received better reception, but nothing.

"I'm sorry," he said with a shake of his head. "We'll try later when the storm lets up. I called our location in last night, though, so my team knows where we are."

He was trying to comfort her, but her nerves raged all over the place.

With a weary sigh, he sank down by the fire and stoked it again. "If I was in your shoes, I wouldn't trust me, either," he murmured. "But I swear on my mama's grave I'm not going to hurt you." He gestured toward the bruises. "And I sure as hell didn't do that."

His tone was so convincing and protective that she relaxed slightly.

"Now," he said again, "please tell me your name."

A cry of frustration lodged in her throat, but she swallowed it back. "I… I don't remember."

FLETCH NARROWED HIS EYES. "What do you mean? You don't remember your name?"

Her tangled hair fell in a curtain over her injured temple and the bruise on her right cheek. She'd obviously suffered abuse or been attacked. Or maybe she had taken a fall.

Fear darkened her eyes. "I don't remember what happened or how I ended up in the woods." She rubbed her arms with her hands and scooted nearer the fire. "How can I not know who I am?"

Fletch gave her a sympathetic look. "You sustained a head injury. The gash on the back of your head probably caused you to lose consciousness and may be messing with your memory."

She lifted a trembling hand and traced her fingers over her head, then winced when she made contact with the knot on the back. "You're right. It's probably that." She exhaled. "But I don't recall how I was injured." Her voice trailed off, tinged with misery and fear.

Fletch inched closer to her, then took her hands in his. Her nails were broken, dirt and blood beneath the surface. Maybe there was DNA from her attacker. "It looks like you fought with someone. Do you remember an altercation? If someone attacked you?"

A frown marred her face as she examined the particles beneath her nails. "You're right. That is blood." She pushed her sleeves up, studied the bruises on her arms and the discoloration circling her wrists, and her frown deepened.

"Those bruises around your wrists look like rope burns," Fletch pointed out.

She lifted the blanket and glanced at her ankles. "My feet were tied, too."

Emotions darkened her eyes, and she dropped her head into her hands and made a low sound in her throat. "God, maybe I was kidnapped."

"That's a possibility." Which meant her kidnapper might still be in the woods, trapped in the storm. Or on the lookout to make sure she was dead.

She looked so lost and terrified that instincts whispered for Fletch to pull her into his arms and comfort her. But that would be out of line.

"Listen, you're safe now," he said calmly. "Until you remember your name, we'll call you Jane. Is that okay?"

"Like Jane Doe," she said matter-of-factly.

"Yes, unless you want to be called something else."

She massaged her temple. "No, Jane is fine."

"When the blizzard lets up, we'll call for medical help," Fletch said. "For now, let's assume the blow to your head caused some sort of temporary amnesia. Once the swelling goes down, hopefully your memory will return." He paused. "Until then, you need to rest."

"So you're a doctor now?" she asked wryly.

Fletch cleared his throat. "No, but my job requires EMT training."

She rubbed her arms more frantically. "How can I rest when I don't even know who I am?"

"Maybe talking would help jog your memories," he said. "Tell me anything you recall. Something about your childhood? A face? Your favorite food?"

She twisted her fingers around the blanket. "I was dreaming. I think it might have been a memory."

Fletch held his hands over the fire to warm them. "Go on."

"I was about seven, and I was sitting on my father's lap," she said. "It was Sunday and we were in his big comfy chair by the fire."

"Sounds like a happy time," he said. "Do you remember your father's name? What he looked like?"

She pinched the bridge of her nose as if searching her mind. "No, but we always did crossword puzzles together. That and other puzzles. We were working on a thousand-piece one of a mountain lion. I saw the pieces spread out on a table. Then my mother packed a picnic and we went to the river for the day."

"Sounds like you grew up in a loving home," Fletch said with an encouraging smile.

The worry lines bracketing her slender mouth softened. "That was a good memory. But…" Her voice broke. "But later… I had a different dream… I think my parents are dead."

Fletch sighed. "I'm sorry. What happened?"

Pain wrenched her face. "I… Someone broke into our house and shot them."

A tense second passed. "Do you think their murders are related to what happened to you now?"

She blew out a ragged breath. "I don't think so. If my dream was real, it was years ago. I was only twelve."

"That's tough for a kid." Sympathy for her filled him. "Who did you live with after you lost them?"

She murmured a sound of frustration. "I…don't know. After that, the rest is blank."

Another tense moment stretched between them. Fletch understood the pain of losing parents. He missed his every damn day. Sometimes when he was hiking, he thought he heard his father's voice telling him the names of the trees and where the best fishing spots were. Other times he could hear his laughter echoing in the wind as if he was a little boy, and his father was chasing him and his brothers in the backyard. Their black Lab, Tag, ran in circles following them.

And his mother…in the kitchen baking. Humming beneath her breath. Her hot chocolate in the winter and her insistence on family dinners. Her hugs and smiles every night as they went to bed. The notes she'd put in their lunch boxes when they were in grade school…

But today wasn't about him, so he cleared his throat.

"How about other family?" he asked. "Maybe a grandparent or sibling? Perhaps they filed a missing persons report."

Another frustrated sound escaped her. "I…don't know. Maybe."

"You didn't have any ID on you when I found you, so I asked my team to have my brother to look for missing persons reports based on your description. He's the sheriff of Whistler. I'm sure they're working on it now."

That seemed to relax her, and she leaned back against the wall.

"There's something else," Fletch said.

"What?" Her voice took on an edge. "You know something you aren't telling me?"

He removed the ring from his pocket, then held out his palm, the wedding band nestled in the center. "I found this not far from where you were lying." He searched her face. "Does it belong to you?"

JANE'S VISION BLURRED for a moment as she studied the wedding band. Simple white gold, tiny diamond chips embedded in the band.

Not fancy or expensive. No large ostentatious diamonds or other precious stones.

Exactly the type of ring she felt like she would choose.

Although what did she know about herself?

Fletch eased it into the palm of her hand. "Look at it. Maybe it will spark some kind of memory. If you're married, your husband's name, the venue or city where you held your wedding…any detail might help."

Emotions thickened her throat as she ran one finger over the smooth band. The inside of the shelter suddenly blurred, the room swaying, and she clawed at the floor to remain upright.

Then an image. A man's large hand. Rough and calloused. Short clipped nails. Olive skin. A tattoo of a wolf on the underside of his arm.

Long nimble fingers sliding the ring on her left hand. Her wiggling her fingers as she looked at it, testing its weight, measuring how it felt to be married.

She jerked her head toward Fletch, something akin to panic knifing through her. "It's mine," she whispered.

He didn't react. Simply watched her with a calm expression. He knew how to be patient. Listen.

Extract answers.

Was he really with Search and Rescue, or did he have a police background?

"Jane, what do you remember?"

"A man's hand, sliding the ring on my finger."

"So you are married?"

She fought a wail of panic. "I suppose so. But all I saw was a hand, not the man's face." She stood and paced across the small dimly lit space. "I can't believe this is happening."

"Just give it time," Fletch said gruffly. "Things will come back to you when you're ready to remember them."

"What about until then?" she cried.

"Until then you rest and regain your strength while we wait out the storm."

She folded her arms across her middle. She needed to talk about something else. Something besides herself. "All right. Tell me about you. Do you have a wife? A family?"

He chuckled. "No, not me. But my brother Jacob just got married."

Her legs still felt weak, so she sank onto the floor beside him. Firelight flickered across his strong, angular face, illuminating eyes that were a deep chocolate brown. His hair was dark, thick, shaggy, and at least two days' worth of beard stubble grazed his jaw.

For a moment, her stomach fluttered. Fletch Maverick was handsome in a rugged, alpha male way. He could be dangerous.

But he carried you to safety.

Maybe she *could* trust him…

"Do you just have the one brother?" she asked to fill the silence.

He pulled a wallet from his back pocket, then removed a photograph and showed it to her. "There are four of us. Jacob's the oldest, sheriff of Whistler. That's the closest town."

He'd mentioned him before. And Whistler? Had she been there?

He gestured toward the photograph. "That's Griff. He's a firefighter. And Liam's with the FBI."

"You're all first responders." All ruggedly handsome, dark hair, big bodies, muscles, arresting eyes. Especially Fletch's. She could swear he was probing into her soul with those dark chocolate orbs.

"Yeah." He ran a hand through his hair, spiking the jagged ends.

"Impressive," she murmured.

He shrugged, his shirt stretching across muscles that she'd felt when she'd nestled in his arms during the depths of her nightmares.

"My father was sheriff of Whistler," he said, his voice quiet as he looked into the flames. "Five years ago, a horrific fire at the local hospital tore the town apart. Dozens of people were injured, and there were casualties. My father ran in to help and didn't come out alive."

Jane barely stifled a gasp. "I'm sorry, Fletch. That must have been horrible."

"It was." Pain streaked his face. "Jacob was Dad's deputy back then and decided to fill Dad's shoes after he was gone."

A second passed, wood crackling and popping in the silence. "What started the fire?"

"Arson," Fletch said. "Bastard who set it was never caught. That drives us all. Every time I'm on the trail, I'm on the lookout for the arsonist in case he's living off the grid in these mountains."

A shudder coursed up Jane's spine. "The mountains are a perfect place to hide."

His troubled gaze met hers in the glow of the fire, tension simmering. "He destroyed a lot of lives. We won't give up until we find him and make him pay."

She wanted to reach for him, touch his hand. In the quiet of the shed, his promise and the loneliness in his voice tore at her heart. Made her feel close to him, as if they shared a bond.

But firelight flickered off the wedding band, and she knotted her hands in her lap.

The ring was hers. She remembered that. And a man had given it to her.

But a wedding…vows…the man's face…were all lost in the void that now filled her mind.

Fletch had suggested the head injury caused her amnesia. But traumatic events could cause loss of memory, too.

Keep running. One foot in front of the other. If you stop, he'll get you.

Then his voice. You can't escape.

What if the man she'd married was the one who'd been chasing her in the woods? What if she'd been trying to escape an abusive relationship, and her husband was the one who'd hurt her and left her for dead?

Chapter Four

Jane's head throbbed as she struggled to sift through the dark blankness in her mind.

If she was married, was her husband looking for her? Or had he hurt her?

Domestic cases were rampant. Abusive men could be charming. Chameleons who looked handsome in one light and changed their colors in another. Had her husband disguised himself as a good man until their wedding, then revealed a sinister side after the honeymoon was over?

She closed her eyes, desperate to see his face or hear his name, but the effort cost her and intensified her headache. Agitated, she stood and walked over to the doorway of the lean-to. She eased the edge of the tarp open and peered outside.

A sea of white filled her vision, the heavy downpour of snowflakes across the land obliterating any signs of greenery. The sky was a smoky gray and the wind howled like a sick animal, adding to the dismal feel.

Fletch was right. It was too dangerous to hike in this blizzard.

For some reason she didn't understand, she instinctively felt she could trust him. His voice was smoky, gruff, layered with concern and tenderness. And when he'd described his family, emotions tinged his eyes.

Although how could she trust a virtual stranger she'd just met when she obviously had doubts about the man she'd married?

For a brief second, a shadow filled her vision and the world slipped out of focus. Then faces drifted through the fog coated air… *A man and woman and a child. Laughter, then the man picked up the little girl and swung her around. The woman stooped, gathered snow in her gloved hands, then threw a snowball at them. The little girl laughed and giggled, then the man and girl made snowballs and laughed and shouted as they had a snowball fight.*

Jane tensed, her breathing choppy as she realized there was no one in the snow. That the image was a memory from her childhood. A sense of peace enveloped her that she had had loving parents and a happy home.

Until they'd been murdered.

The realization made her chest ache as if she'd just lost them that second. Maybe because it felt like yesterday or maybe because it was the only real memory she could hold on to.

Why could she remember a part of her childhood and not her name or her husband's or how she'd ended up out here in the storm, bloody and bruised?

A noise startled her, and a large branch broke and tumbled to the blanket of white on the ground. Then another shadow.

An animal maybe? A wolf? Mountain lion? Bear?

There it was again. The shadow. A movement…

What if it was the man who'd hurt her? Maybe he'd hung around to make sure she was dead…

FLETCH STOKED THE fire as he watched Jane at the door to the shelter. She was obviously struggling. How would it feel to wake up with no memory of your name or your life?

Although some things he wanted to forget, like the day his father died. Talking about his family reminded him of the huge hole in his heart left by his father's death. In his mind, he saw the last few minutes they'd talked. They were having coffee at the diner when the call about the fire had come in.

They were joking about the local high school football game and the quarterback who'd put Whistler High on the map with his record stats. Fletch's mother was home making her famous pot roast with the baby carrots and peas that he and his father requested once a week. Griff had asked for peach cobbler for dessert. Liam wanted her biscuits. And Jacob her sweet tea.

It had been an ordinary day. A hint of impending rain in the air, but no sign that Whistler was about to experience the worst tragedy in the history of the town.

Then the call... *His father leaped up immediately, told him about the fire. Fletch wanted to ride with him, but his father said he'd meet him later at dinner. Neither one of them had any idea how serious the situation was.*

Sirens from the fire truck raced by. Griff was on duty, so he would probably be late for dinner just like his father. He decided to keep his mother company till then.

So Fletch paid the bill while his father jumped in his car and raced to his death.

Pain and guilt squeezed at his lungs. If only he'd stuck with his dad, maybe he could have saved him...

Two hours later, just as his mother pulled the peach cobbler from the oven, Jacob called. He'd barely been coherent and said it was mass chaos. They needed more manpower to help evacuate patients from the hospital. Some might be trapped.

Fletch and Liam left their mother to keep the food warm while they drove like maniacs to the hospital. Just as Jacob said, the scene was chaos. Hospital patients in wheelchairs and on gurneys filled the parking lot. Staff members struggled to get out while tending to the needy. Firefighters raced in, geared up, to rescue victims and evacuate the building while other firefighters worked to extinguish the blaze and keep it from spreading. Screams and cries echoed from terrified staff and patients.

As soon as they parked, they hit the ground running and dove in to help. The heat from the blaze seared his skin. Flames burst into the night sky like an orange fireball. They had to hurry.

The next half hour he and his brothers helped carry the injured and sick outside.

Then Jacob emerged, shouting their names. He was pale and panting as he dragged their father out of the inferno.

Jane made a startled sound, jerking Fletch from the depths of the tragic memory. She clenched the tarp edge, her eyes wide.

Fletch hurried to her. "What is it?"

"I thought I saw someone," she whispered. "A shadow moving. Maybe a man."

Fletch urged her behind him, then peered out into the storm. Trees bent and swayed in the throes of the turbulent wind gusts, and snow swirled in a hazy sea of white.

She was right. Fletch saw the shadow. Something moved about a hundred feet away. His body tensed, senses honed as he searched the wilderness.

Wait… There it was. A movement again.

The bruises on Jane's body taunted him. If the person who'd hurt her was still out there, he might have tracked them here.

Fletch rushed to his pack and removed his pistol. Jane's eyes widened as she watched him, fear glittering in the depths. He lifted one finger to his lips in a silent gesture to keep quiet.

He carried the gun with him to the door of the shelter, braced it at the ready and waited.

For a moment when Fletch retrieved his gun, Jane froze in fear. But the protective gleam in his eyes when he urged her behind him gave her a sense of safety. At least she wasn't facing this situation alone.

"Do you see anything?" she whispered behind him.

"A movement," he murmured. "Can't tell what it is yet. Could be an animal or a hiker who got caught in the storm looking for refuge."

Which meant he would help them.

Only the tense set of Fletch's shoulders indicated he was prepared for trouble.

Tension vibrated in the small confines of the lean-to, Jane's worry rising with each passing second. If only she could remember what happened to her, she could give Fletch insight as to her attacker's identity.

And if he might still be looking for her.

The blizzard raged on, visibility worsening as the precipitation thickened. Fletch suddenly stiffened and tightened his fingers around his weapon. He'd seen something.

Jane searched the thick snowdrifts, anxiety needling her. An image of a gun in her hand suddenly flashed behind her eyes. A second later, the image disappeared as quickly as it had come, leaving her confused.

And with more questions.

Did she know how to use a gun? Did she own one?

The few things she'd remembered about her father taunted her. He hadn't been a violent man and she didn't recall him hunting, yet he'd kept a gun locked in a drawer in his study.

She closed her eyes and willed a mental picture of him to surface. His study, the big chair by the fire where they worked the crossword puzzles. Wall-to-wall bookcases held leather-bound books. She raked her gaze over the shelves, trying to decipher the titles. Had he liked novels? Mysteries? Were they nonfiction books?

She massaged her temple again, and saw the words *Law Review* on the spine of a large black book.

Was her father a lawyer?

Fletch shifted beside her, and she opened her eyes. His shoulders relaxed slightly, and he heaved a breath.

"What is it?" she whispered.

"Bear. She's moved on up the mountain." He pointed to a ridge in the distance. "Probably looking for a place to hibernate."

A chill went through Jane. "Do you think she'll come back here?"

"Could, but I doubt it. Looked like a mama. Saw a cub farther up the trail, so she went toward her baby."

Relief softened Jane's fears, and she walked back to the fire and sat down on the blanket again. Adrenaline waning, exhaustion took over.

"You okay?" Fletch asked.

He remained at the door, gun in his hand, like some kind of rugged lawman. But his eyes pierced her with worry.

"Just a headache, and I'm tired," she said softly.

"Lie down and sleep a while. I'll keep watch and wake you if the storm lets up."

His gruff voice was so comforting that she murmured thanks, then succumbed to fatigue and stretched out, wrapping the blanket around her. Firelight flickered, the kindling popping in the quiet of the shelter. Yet outside, the wind howled, brutal and deadly.

Knowing Fletch was watching over her, she closed her eyes and let sleep claim her.

But in her sleep, the nightmares came. *The blood... She was running... Death was near. She couldn't escape it...*

FLETCH KEPT WATCH by the doorway, ears alert for sounds of someone approaching.

He tried his radio again as the hours passed, aware each time Jane startled awake from a bad dream. Her sleep was restless, as if she was fighting off her demons—or her attacker all over again.

Late afternoon, Jane roused, mumbling incoherently. She shouted no, then opened her eyes, trembling as she looked around the shelter. She was still lost in the nightmare, her eyes glazed, her hands clawing at the covers as if she needed to hide beneath them.

"Shh, it's all right, you're safe now," Fletch murmured.

At the sound of his voice, Jane turned her head toward him.

"It's Fletch, Jane. You fell asleep and were dreaming."

She inhaled deeply, chest rising and falling with her labored breathing.

"I found you in the snow, collapsed. Do you remember me?"

She slowly nodded, then shoved her tangled hair from her face.

"Did you remember something else?" he asked.

For a moment, her eyes looked blank, then finally she shook her head.

"I'm going to gather more wood, and then I'll make us something to eat."

She didn't speak, so he decided to give her a few minutes to acclimate. He stowed his gun in the waistband of his pants, removed the small pot he carried in his emergency pack and stepped outside. He scanned the land as he left the shelter, then collected more sticks for the fire. He set those inside to dry, then dipped some snow into the pot.

The wind force was so strong that snow had blown across the land and formed knee-deep drifts. His face stung, the fog so thick he couldn't see three feet in front of him. A noise made him jerk to the left and reach for his weapon, but it was only a large branch breaking off in the wind.

He hurried back to the shelter, anxious to make sure Jane was okay. He sensed she'd remembered something, but she hadn't wanted to share it.

When he entered the shelter, he found her hunched beneath the blanket, watching him warily.

"I tried the radio again, but it's still down," he said softly. "Hopefully the storm will let up by morning and we can get through." He set the pot over the fire on the grate, then fastened the tarp again.

While the snow melted and the water began to boil, he retrieved two packets of dried soup mix from his bag along with two tin mugs. He dumped the soup mix into the mugs, then poured water over it and stirred. He carried Jane a mug and she reached for it, her hand shaking.

"I figured you were hungry. You need to eat to regain your strength."

She licked her lips. "You're prepared."

He shrugged. "That's what I do." While she sipped the hot soup, he sat down by the fire and did the same.

An eerie quiet settled through the shelter. The sound of their breathing mingled with the raging wind outside that beat at the lean-to.

"You want to talk?" he finally asked.

She heaved a breath and shook her head. "I'm just tired."

Concern filled him and he rose, walked over and gently touched her forehead to see if she had a fever. Her skin felt cool, though.

"Mind if I look at that gash on the back of your head? I'd like to clean the wound to prevent an infection."

She murmured permission, and he retrieved his first aid kit from his bag. She set her empty mug on the floor and turned her back to him. He gently eased her hair away from the wound and wiped the blood with alcohol wipes. She winced slightly when he touched it, but as he cleaned it, he realized it wasn't as deep as he'd first thought.

"Looks like it'll heal on its own," he said. "Not so deep you need stitches."

"That's good," she said softly.

"Yeah." The emotions in her voice made him want to squeeze her shoulder for comfort, but he stepped back. "You cried out in your dreams," he said. "What was that about?"

Her eyes widened, and she turned back to look at the fire, then tugged the blanket around her again. "I was running from a man, but I still couldn't see his face."

"Was that all?"

She nodded, then leaned her head onto her knees. Fletch studied her, his jaw tight.

Why did he have the sense she was lying to him? That she'd seen something she didn't want to tell him about?

Chapter Five

Jane paced across the shelter to avoid eye contact with Fletch. She had had crazy dreams while she slept, bits and pieces of a jumbled life and images triggered by her fears.

At this point, she didn't know what was real and what wasn't.

A corkboard hung on the wall on the far end of the small shelter, an assortment of handwritten notes and messages tacked onto it that visitors had left to mark their stay or to pass on to others hiking the trail.

She studied the board and the crude messages, listing dates and times people had sought refuge from the elements, or when they were just weary from hiking the miles and miles of wilderness. Most who planned to hike from Georgia to Maine gave up somewhere along the way.

The terrain, weather conditions, long days of isolation and the physical exertion were too difficult. Enthusiasm for adventure waned as injuries and illness occurred, bitter cold set in, and insects and rodents infested the lean-tos with dangerous bacteria. Longing for hot showers and warm food intensified as the monotony of trail mix and dried food became increasingly harder to endure.

One message caught her eye. A note with dried flowers shaped into a heart. She smiled at the thought that a couple might be leaving each other love notes along the way.

She closed her eyes, willing images of her husband to surface. If he hadn't hurt her, then maybe someone else had, and her husband was searching for her.

Hands knotted, she scanned the others and noticed another one, more cryptic. *I'LL FIND YOU.*

Her heart hammered as her attacker's words echoed in her mind, and she looked down at her hands. Blood still stained her skin and darkened her fingernails.

"Jane, are you all right?" Fletch's gruff voice broke into her thoughts.

She hated living in the dark. She wanted answers. If she wasn't trapped here, she'd go to the police. What would they do?

"We probably should take samples under my nails to give to the police when we get out of here, in case I scratched my attacker."

Fletch's brows rose. "I thought about that, but I didn't want to do so without your permission."

Her gaze met his, and for a moment doubts set in again, kidnapping cases taunting her. If Fletch had attacked her, he could have brought her here and pretended to take care of her to win her trust.

She'd heard of kidnappers keeping victims in seclusion until they developed Stockholm syndrome.

"Jane?"

She frowned, wondering why that thought had occurred to her. Logically her theory made sense, but when Fletch examined her wound, his touch had been gentle, not harsh like a man who'd ever hurt a woman. If Fletch had wanted to kill her, he could have left her in the woods to freeze to death.

The radio buzzed, a sound that startled her in the silence.

Fletch jumped to his feet and hurried toward his radio. He tapped the receiver. "Fletch here. Over."

A rattling sound. More static.

"Fletch here. Can you hear me?"

"Todd. Checking on your status."

"Holding our own at the shelter. News?"

"Blizzard supposed to pass around four a.m. Warming tomorrow."

Jane sucked in a breath. Once the snow stopped and the temperature rose, they could get off the mountain.

What would happen then?

"About the missing woman, Jacob called."

Fletch glanced up at Jane. "Go on."

"Said…" A sudden gust of wind snapped the air, the sound of tree limbs falling outside thundering as limbs crashed against the shelter.

"Todd?"

"S…" Static crackled and popped, cutting off the man's voice.

Fletch made several more attempts to reconnect but failed.

A frisson of nerves danced along Jane's spine. Jacob was Fletch's brother, the sheriff of Whistler.

Had he learned her identity?

FLETCH SILENTLY CURSED as the radio died again. Dammit. Jacob might have figured out Jane's identity or if she had family looking for her.

Knowing who she was might lead them to answers about her attacker.

He tried the radio again, but static popped and the connection failed.

Exhaling in frustration, he decided to wait a little while before making another attempt. At least his team knew their location, and for now, Jane was safe.

"You were right about your nails," he said quietly. "There might be DNA there."

She stretched her hands in front of her and studied them. "I do want to know," she said, although fear laced her voice.

He removed a small tool and a baggie from his pack, then walked over to her. Her eyes flickered with unease at the sight of the tool.

He offered it to her. "You can do it if you want."

Relief echoed in the breath she exhaled. "No. I...trust you."

Their gazes locked for a brief second, heat flaring to life in the dim confines of the shelter. The days were shorter now, and night was already setting in. He stooped down beside her, then eased her small hand in his. Her fingers were long and slim, her nails broken and jagged from the attack. Her ivory skin looked pale in contrast to his bronzed skin, her hand soft and delicate next to his calloused one. Her eyes bored into his for a second before she broke eye contact.

She was a beautiful woman. Her features were put together in a sexy kind of way, her eyes a pale startling green. At the moment, they were intense and full of pain and questions.

A hint of sexual awareness tugged inside him, heating his blood.

Dammit, not the time. He had to wrangle his libido under control.

Focusing on his task, he lifted one finger of hers, gently eased the tip of the tool beneath her nail and scraped particles of dried blood and dirt. Hopefully there were skin cells from her attacker, too.

When he finished, he handed her sanitizing wipes to clean her hands.

She thanked him, then used another wipe over her face and throat. The slender column of her neck was smooth but marred with a bruise as well, as if someone had tried to strangle her. He hadn't noticed it before, but now the discoloration was showing, handprints evident on her skin.

Son of a bitch. Only a coward would hurt a woman.

Fresh anger shot through him at the thought. Strangulation could have dangerous aftereffects not recognized at an initial examination.

She propped her back against the wooden wall of the shelter, drew her knees up and leaned her folded arms on them. "Tell me more about your family," she murmured.

"Not that much to tell." Fletch had never been a talker.

"Please," she said. "It helps distract me."

He heaved a breath, struggling for what to say.

"Do you have any leads on that arsonist you mentioned?"

"Not really. A woman named Cora Reeves gave birth to a baby girl the night of the fire. Her baby was kidnapped, so we suspected the fire was a diversion by the kidnapper to allow him time to escape."

Jane's eyes widened. "Was it?"

Fletch shook his head no. "Cora and her husband divorced, but she stayed in Whistler. She never gave up looking for her daughter."

"I don't blame her. Did she find her?"

A small smile tugged at Fletch's mouth. "Yeah, a few months ago. She thought the little girl living down the street was her child, and got my brother involved. Turns out she was right."

"So who stole Cora's baby?"

"A woman named Hilary… She was in love with Cora's husband and thought she could break up their marriage if the baby wasn't in the picture. And she was right.

Their marriage fell apart, and Cora's husband ended up marrying Hilary."

"Did he know what Hilary had done?"

"No. He was shocked when he learned the truth."

"What happened to the baby?" Jane asked.

Fletch's heart squeezed. "She was adopted. But when Cora started looking at the little girl down the street, Hilary murdered the adoptive mother and tried to kill Cora. Jacob saved Cora and the child, and now Cora has her daughter back." He rubbed his neck. "My brother Jacob married Cora and is raising the little girl."

"So there's a happy ending?" Jane said quietly.

He heard the ache in her voice. Would there be a happy ending for her?

Fletch swallowed hard. There would be if he had anything to do with it.

EAGER TO DISTRACT herself from her problems, Jane probed Fletch for more information about his family.

Although he didn't seem like the talkative type, she managed to convince him to tell her about his childhood, what it was like growing up with three brothers and about life in Whistler.

He told her about Jacob and Cora's outdoor wedding at a small private vineyard, with Cora's little girl standing beside them.

"It was informal," Fletch said. "Cora wanted flowers from her own flower garden, with picnic-style tables for the reception."

A woman's wedding was supposed to be the highlight of her life, yet Jane couldn't recall anything about hers. Remembering even the smallest detail might lead to her husband's name or where they were living. "What about music?"

Fletch shrugged. "I play the guitar a little, so Jacob asked me to play."

Something about his humble admission intensified Jane's attraction toward him.

"I'd like to hear you play sometime," she admitted.

His sexy eyes met hers, but he made no promises. How could he when her mind was a blank slate at the moment? She couldn't move forward with her life until she figured out what she was running from in her past.

"I'll keep trying the radio if you want to rest," Fletch offered. "Hopefully, in the morning we can start down."

She twisted her hands together, then snuggled beneath the blanket, curled on her side and closed her eyes. Maybe daylight would bring answers. At least she felt physically stronger now. Her limbs weren't aching as much, and her headache had dulled to a light throb.

As she drifted to sleep, the sound of Fletch's voice as he'd described his family echoed in her head. He'd painted the picture of a loving, close-knit family. He and his brothers met at least once a week for beer and bro night. Sometimes, they worked together, as well.

Her parents were dead, but what if she had a sibling? She strained to remember her childhood again, the picnic, the crossword puzzles, yet nowhere in there did she see a sister or a brother.

Sleep finally claimed her, but her dreams were confusing and scattered. Her father again… *They finished the puzzle, and she climbed down to help her mother bake cookies. Her father's phone rang and she heard his deep voice speaking low into the phone.*

"DA made a deal. Life, no parole."

Her father…was a lawyer? No…a judge.

Then another flashback to that night and the blood again. *Police officers streaming in, snapping pictures.*

Her parents' bodies sprawled on the floor. Her mother's bloody hand reaching out as if trying to clasp her father's.

Her father dead, unable to help her.

Next she was looking at more bloody bodies. *A man and woman. Not her parents. Blood spattered the floor and walls. The white comforter and carpet, the woman's hand stretched out as if reaching for her husband...*

Then another couple. *Different faces...different bedroom. A four-poster bed with a lemon yellow spread. Red dotting it and streaking the floor. The woman's eyes bulging in death...*

The images faded and she saw the man with the tattoo on his wrist. *A wolf... His fingers as he slid the wedding ring on her finger. Then his hand clutching his chest as blood spewed... His body bouncing backward, slumping against the wall.*

Her...hand shaking as she gripped the gun...

She jerked awake, lungs squeezing for air as questions pummeled her. Why was she seeing dead people in her dreams? Who were those couples? Was it real?

And the man with the wolf tattoo—her husband. Had she pulled the trigger and ended his life?

Chapter Six

Jane had remembered something. Something that had upset her.

Fletch was sure of it. Her body trembled, and her pupils were dilated as if she was locked in the terror of her nightmares. He'd seen her tossing and turning, heard her mumbling. She'd clenched the covers as if fighting off an assailant.

He'd considered waking her from the horror but had held back, hoping she was remembering details about the man who'd attacked her.

Something to help nail the bastard.

Only now she was awake and sat hunched, knees drawn up, arms wrapped around them, staring into the fire again.

He wanted to push her but sensed that would be a mistake. When the storm lifted in the morning and he reached his team again, Jacob would have some answers, he hoped.

A noise outside startled him, and he went still, listening.

Jane lifted her head. "What was that?"

Fletch mentally sorted through the various noises outside. "The wind and more limbs breaking."

Her breath rushed out in relief, then she turned and stretched out on her side, facing away from him. Fletch itched to go to her and comfort her, but she needed space.

He also wanted to make sure no one was outside.

"I'm going to gather more wood." He settled his gun in the waistband of his pants, pulled on his gloves and eased back the tarp. He scanned the area as he stepped outside. Shivering, he tugged the hood of his coat over his head as he set off to search the area. Snow and wind blasted him, the windchill dipping lower with every hour.

Night had fallen across the land, making it look desolate, as if they were entrenched in a vast wasteland of white. Icicles hung from the tree limbs like jagged knives. His boots crunched frozen snow and brush.

The snow was falling so fast it was burying everything, but about a hundred feet from the shelter he spotted an animal's paw prints. Thankfully they were leading away from the shelter, toward the north. He wove between a cluster of trees and detected more prints ahead.

They were partially destroyed by the blizzard conditions, but these appeared to be human.

From his earlier treks on the trail, he'd discovered a few loners who lived in the woods off the grid. Some he suspected were simply homeless or had mental issues and had become recluses.

One guy called himself Homeless Joe. He carried everything he owned on his back, lived off the land and had managed to survive in the hills for ten years already. He lived like a nomad, never staying in one place for long. Another was a man in his sixties who shared a lean-to with his wife of forty years. She claimed she had psychic powers and saw the dead, which made it impossible to live a mainstream life.

Others might be hiding out from the law.

Like the person who'd set the fire that had killed his father.

He kept hoping he'd find the bastard. Although, with

no evidence pointing to a specific person, it was possible he'd already encountered him without realizing it.

Fletch aimed his flashlight beam ahead and saw more prints. Too big for Homeless Joe, who was slight-framed and dragged one foot behind him. No pattern of his gait here.

He forged ahead, checking each direction, then heard a noise. Icicles snapped and cracked, breaking off and flying through the air. He dodged them, then hiked toward Crow's Point. Another noise, and he paused. Then he spotted another print. Large.

Definitely human. Judging from the indentation in the snow, boots.

A man's.

Dammit. Did they belong to someone else stranded out here, or to Jane's attacker?

JANE WOKE THE next morning to the sound of Fletch entering the shelter. He'd stayed out late last night, then come in looking troubled. When she'd questioned him, he'd claimed he was just tired, that he'd seen a shadow, but it had turned out to be a wild animal.

She shivered as he boiled water and made them some instant coffee. His beard stubble added to his rugged appearance, making him look as if he belonged to the mountain.

He was probably just as untamed and wild in bed.

Good heavens. She shouldn't be thinking about his sex appeal now.

"Sorry, coffee's not very good," he muttered.

"At least it's hot," she said, although she would kill for a latte.

He handed her a breakfast bar and she forced herself to eat it slowly. It hadn't escaped her that Fletch had been rationing them. "Thank you for everything," she said softly. "If you hadn't rescued me, I wouldn't have survived."

He shrugged as if it was no big deal. "Just doing my job." Closed inside in this tiny space with the firelight flickering off his face, she almost felt safe, as if a killer wasn't chasing her.

He ate his bar and sipped his coffee, then tried the radio again. Static popped, and his jaw tightened. But several seconds later, he managed to connect to his team.

"Weather conditions?" Fletch asked.

"Storm has definitely moved on. Winds dying down, temperature rising. Should get above freezing by noon."

Jane massaged the back of her neck, anxious to return to civilization. Even more anxious about what she might learn.

"Do you need us to send a team for you and the woman?" Fletch's teammate asked.

Fletch motioned to Jane. "No, we can manage. Will radio you if we require assistance."

"Take the trail southwest," the other man advised.

"Copy that." Fletch hesitated. "Did you hear anything else from Jacob?"

"Yeah. He's searching missing case reports across the state. He wants an update on your status."

"Tell him we're fine for now."

"For now? Is there trouble?"

"The woman was injured," Fletch replied. "Not sure if her attacker is still around, but will be on the lookout."

The men agreed to stay in touch, and Fletch turned to her. "We're probably about eight miles from the entrance point to the trail near Whistler. I know you're still weak. Do you think you can make it at least partway?"

Jane stood and stretched. "Yes, I feel stronger now." She

just had to find the courage to face the truth about who'd attacked her. And why she saw those bodies in her sleep.

Fletch encouraged her to drink some water. She did as he said while he packed up his supplies, removed the tarp and stowed it. Then he handed her a pair of gloves, a hat and his coat.

"I can't take your jacket," Jane said. "You'll freeze."

He pulled a thinner, insulated jacket from his bag. "I'm used to it. Now, if you start feeling weak or lightheaded, let me know and I'll call for reinforcements."

"I'll be fine, Fletch."

When she stepped outside, the blast of cold hit her. She zipped Fletch's coat and bounced on her heels to warm her muscles, then followed him. He cut away limbs, moved branches and alerted her when they reached rocky terrain. Her boots were slick and inappropriate for blizzard conditions, but she grabbed tree limbs and rocks to steady herself.

With each step they took, she was moving closer and closer to civilization.

And to the truth.

A foul odor wafted toward her as they wound around a patch of hemlocks. Vultures swooped down ahead, diving toward the ground.

"Must be a dead animal," Fletch said. "Let me make sure."

She stayed close behind him, holding on to his hand to keep her balance as they descended the steep hill. They reached a ledge, and Fletch threw his arm out to prevent her from stumbling forward.

A second later, she spotted the bloody animal down below.

"Dead wolf," Fletch said.

An image of a wolf perched on a boulder searching for

prey niggled at her memory. *She was falling into the snow, thought he was going to get her.*

Then a gunshot.

She startled as if she'd heard the sound that second.

"What is it?" Fletch asked.

"The man… I was running and fell," she said breathlessly. "He came up behind me and shot the wolf." Her voice cracked.

"He saved you from the wolf?" Fletch asked, confusion tingeing his voice.

"I don't know if that's what he meant to do. But he grabbed me from behind, and a second later, I heard a gunshot. Then I passed out." She lifted her fingers to the back of her head. "The gun…he hit me with his gun."

"Did you see what kind of weapon he was carrying?" Fletch asked.

She shook her head. "No, but the bullet whizzed so close to my head that for a moment, I thought he'd shot me."

She paused. "I don't understand that. If he wanted me dead, why *didn't* he just put a bullet in my head?"

FLETCH CONTEMPLATED JANE'S STATEMENT. If the man wanted her dead and he was armed, why *hadn't* he shot her? His mind ticked away different theories.

"Perhaps he didn't want to leave evidence behind. Bullets can be traced back to a specific gun. With the blizzard bearing down, he expected you'd die in the elements, then no one would suspect murder."

Emotions darkened her eyes. "That makes sense."

Although it still left questions unanswered.

"You okay to keep going?" Fletch asked.

Jane nodded, and he set off on the trail again. Although he knew the woods and stopping points along the way, it was still easy to get turned around in the midst of the sprawling miles of forest. He consulted with his map and compass to guide them.

Fletch gestured toward a path that wound straight down-hill and looked treacherous. "That's the fastest way, but too dangerous."

Jane remained silent, her face a mask of concentration as they fought through the thick brush and dodged clumps of falling snow from the trees. The wind shook limbs and more branches broke off, but the precipitation had slowed to a light snowfall, and the temperature was warming as sun peeked through the spiny branches.

In spite of the cold, Fletch began to sweat as they hiked. He paused at the end of each mile to check Jane's physical condition, and encouraged her to drink water to stay hydrated.

He led them toward the right on a slightly less steep hill, but they had to tread slowly to maintain steady footing. Jane's boots were slick on the bottom, and she slipped a couple of times, so Fletch helped her along the steeper patches.

Another half mile and they reached a lean-to at the point called Stone's Ledge. "Let's take a break and rest a minute," he told Jane.

She followed him to the shelter, although she hesitated at the opening and clutched the wall. Her face turned ashen, her breath puffing out in a hazy cloud.

"What's wrong, Jane?"

"This place," she murmured. "It seems familiar."

He retrieved his flashlight and stepped inside. He spotted a pile of rope in one corner along with a bloody rag.

She heaved a breath. "He brought me here," she said in a ragged whisper. "That rope...he tied me up and gagged me and left me."

Fletch breathed out. "What else do you recall?"

"Being dragged through the snow. I was hurt and drifting in and out of consciousness. When I came to in the cave, though, I was alone."

"So he left you in a shelter instead of outside," Fletch commented, confused again.

"I think so." She stepped inside the dank space. An odd look crossed her face as she walked over to the corner where the rope lay. "When I came to, I didn't know where I was. Just that I had to escape."

"Then what happened?"

Jane crouched down and ran her hand over the floor, then closed her eyes and rubbed at her temple. "I untied myself, then I heard something outside. He was coming back."

Various scenarios played in Fletch's mind. None of them good.

Why had her attacker brought her here? To hold her for ransom?

Her parents were dead, although she could have other family…

Fletch's stomach clenched. The other possibilities were even more sinister.

The man could be some psycho who got off on sexual assault or torture…

JANE CURSED HERSELF for not being able to remember more details about the man who'd hurt her.

"I'm going to photograph the scene, then bag the rope and rag," Fletch said. "Hopefully the lab can retrieve your attacker's DNA from them."

Jane ran her finger around her wrist where rope burns discolored her skin. In her mind, she pictured herself working the thick rope, slowly loosening the knots.

Her fingers were aching, bloody, her nails ripping as

she yanked the knot free. She had to hurry. He could come back any minute. She ripped the gag from her mouth, then tackled the rope around her ankles. The rope slipped, her nail breaking, and she cried out in frustration.

Shh, *she told herself. He might hear you.*

"Jane?"

Fletch's voice shattered the memory like glass breaking.

"Are you ready to go, or do you need to rest?"

A shudder coursed up her spine. She didn't want to stay another minute in the place where she'd been held captive. Dried blood had crusted on one of the wooden boards where a loose nail stuck out. She must have used the nail to saw the ropes and cut them.

Fletch pulled something from his pocket and tacked it on the bulletin board. An article about the Whistler Hospital fire. Then he wrote the words *I'LL FIND YOU.*

So he had left the message she'd noticed before.

His expression was grim. "I've been putting these in all of the shelters. If the arsonist is hiding along the trail, I want him to know I'm looking for him."

"I don't blame you." She tugged the cap over her ears and stepped from the lean-to. "Let's get out of here."

Fletch stowed the baggie holding the rope and rag in his pack, then joined her outside. The wind had died down slightly, and icicles were starting to melt and drip from the tree branches.

Jane forced herself to concentrate on the terrain as she followed Fletch down another steep hill. They wove between massive tree trunks and climbed over fallen limbs and branches.

Another half mile, and they reached a sharp ridge overlooking a canyon with views of the snowcapped mountains. "This is beautiful," she murmured.

Fletch's jaw tightened. "My father used to bring me and

my brothers up here camping during the summer. He's the one who first taught me wilderness survival."

"You must miss him a lot," Jane murmured.

"Every day," Fletch admitted gruffly. "All the more reason to track down the person who set that fire and make them pay."

"You'll find whoever it was," Jane said. Fletch was the kind of man who did what he said. The kind of man a woman could count on.

Had her husband been that kind of man?

They hiked around a turn past a large boulder. The sound of brush bristling came from behind them. Someone was back there.

Fletch motioned for her to take cover. She started toward the rocks, and Fletch snatched his gun from the waistband of his pants. Before he could pull it, a gunshot echoed and a bullet whizzed by her head.

Jane ducked and Fletch pushed her forward. She hit the ground on her knees just as another gunshot rent the air.

Fletch dove behind her with a grunt. A second later, she realized he'd been hit.

Chapter Seven

"You're hurt," Jane gasped as she crawled behind the boulder.

"Just my leg. Stay down." Fletch reached for his gun. He'd dropped it when he'd fallen and it had skidded into the bushes by a cluster of rocks.

Another bullet pinged off the ground near them, and Fletch yanked his hand back. Blood was pooling in the snow like a red river. He looked slightly disoriented, the color draining from his face.

Panic seized Jane. What if the bullet had struck an artery?

Jane's heart hammered. She was closer to the gun, so she rolled sideways to her stomach, dug her hand in to pull it from the weeds. Footsteps crunched the frozen ground behind her, and the man jumped her before she could snag it.

She swung her elbow backward and jabbed him in the solar plexus. He cursed, slapped her across her temple and crawled on top of her. Jane bucked and fought him, shoving with all her might until she managed to push him off her. She crawled toward the gun, but he grabbed her by the neck and dug his fingers into her throat, choking her.

She elbowed him again and used her foot to kick at his legs. Her nails dug into his hands as she struggled to pry his fingers from her throat. But he increased the pressure, and she saw stars.

She refused to let this maniac kill her. Fletch needed her...

Rage clawed at her, and she summoned all her strength and jerked the man's hands from her neck. Fletch groaned. He tried to push himself to his knees but collapsed. He was weak, but he heaved for breath, and dragged himself toward her.

Her attacker jerked her upright by the shoulders and slammed her back against the jagged rock. Pain ricocheted through her, and her head snapped forward.

The world spun, and Fletch grabbed at the man. The man loosened his hold just enough to send a swift kick to Fletch's wounded leg. Fletch bellowed in pain. Blood spewed, and he collapsed face down in the snow.

Jane had to move quickly. She rolled sideways, snatched the gun from the bushes and raised it at the ready. Her hand was trembling, the world tilting at an angle. She blinked to focus and pressed her finger on the trigger.

The shooter suddenly lunged toward her, raised his weapon and fired. But she was quicker. She rolled sideways to dodge the bullet, aimed Fletch's gun straight at the bastard and released a round. The bullet pierced the shooter between the eyes. Brain matter and crimson red spewed from his head and spattered the white snow.

His body flew backward, and he slipped over the mountain ledge and spiraled downward into the canyon below.

FLETCH STRUGGLED TO open his eyes.

He heard a strangled sound and glanced around for Jane. She'd crawled to the edge of the ridge and was looking over. Dammit, was she shot?

"Jane!" he called. Was she all right? He'd slipped in and out of consciousness while she fought the bastard.

And she *had* fought.

Questions mounted in Fletch's mind as the last few minutes replayed in his head. She not only had fought, but her maneuvers looked practiced. Trained. She also knew how to handle a gun like a pro. Had she grown up with guns? Could she have served in the military? Or was she in law enforcement?

"Jane?" Fletch called again.

His voice must have finally registered, and she looked at him with a glazed expression. She lowered the gun by her side as she walked over to him and knelt.

"Are you all right?" he asked.

She nodded, eyes wild with shock. "He's dead."

"Did you recognize him? Was he the man who hurt you?"

"I...don't know," she said in a ragged whisper.

Fletch lifted a weak hand and squeezed her arm. She was shaking from adrenaline. "You had no choice," he said in case she was starting to experience guilt. "It was self-defense."

"I know." Her breath rattled in the air. A moment later, she straightened, snapping out of the shock. "We need to take care of your injury." She reset the safety on his gun and stowed it in his pack. Then she dug inside and found a first aid kit. She removed a bandage strip and tied it around his leg to stem the bleeding.

"Let's move you to a shelter so I can take a better look at your wound," Jane said, all businesslike.

She was right. Blood might draw a wild animal. "I'll radio for help when we're inside." His strength was waning with the blood loss, but he was determined not to pass out again. At least not until they reached the shelter. She might be strong, but she couldn't move dead weight.

She helped him to stand and slid her arm around his waist. His pride smarted, but he wasn't stupid. They had to depend on each other for survival.

He leaned on her as they trudged toward the shelter. "It's about a half mile," Fletch said as he pointed the way.

"Can you make it?"

"Don't worry, I'll be fine." Fletch ground his teeth against the pain as they hiked. One foot in front of the other.

The pace was slower than before, and he kept an ear alert for another gunman.

Jane lapsed into silence, a look of fierce concentration on her face. Her tenacity and courage were probably the reason she'd survived so far.

Finally they managed to reach the shelter, and he stumbled inside. He detested being weak, and willed himself to remain alert in case the gunman had an accomplice.

Jane clamped her lips together as she retrieved his emergency medical kit. She handed him his radio while she retrieved scissors. He connected the second go around.

"Fletch. Headed down the mountain with Jane Doe. Ran into trouble. Gunman attacked. Took a bullet to the leg. Jane Doe is okay for the moment. Over."

"Damn, Fletch," Todd said over the line. "How seriously are you injured?"

"Some blood loss, but I'll make it. The bullet didn't hit a major artery. Over."

"We'll send a med team to you ASAP. Unfortunately all teams are out on calls. This blizzard wreaked havoc on the trail. A group of teens were trapped north of Pigeon's Peak, and we dispatched units there to dig them out. Small plane went down in the eastern area, so teams have been sent to rescue them. An avalanche west of Whistler caused multiple injuries and more victims are thought to be trapped."

Fletch bit the inside of his cheek. Jane was watching him with a worried expression as she cut away the leg of his jean where he'd taken the bullet. The fabric was soaked in blood, snow and dirt.

"Inform Jacob about the gunman. His body is just south of Stone's Ledge. Shot in self-defense." He didn't point out that Jane had done the shooting.

"Copy that. Keep me posted," Todd said. "If you need emergency airlift services, let me know."

"Will do." Fletch disconnected and set the radio down while Jane examined his wound.

He propped himself up on his elbows to give himself a better view. "How deep is it?"

She twisted her mouth sideways. "Not too deep. Maybe a couple of inches."

"You need to remove the bullet," Fletch said.

Jane shook her head in denial. "I'm not a doctor. At least I don't think I have medical training."

"You don't need it." Perspiration trickled down his neck. "But you heard my team. They can't get to us yet. If we leave the bullet, there's a chance of infection. Then I won't be able to walk out of here."

Or walk again. He sure as hell didn't want to lose his leg.

Jane planted her hands on her knees and inhaled sharply. "Fletch, I…don't know if I can do it."

Fletch bit back a moan of pain. "I saw the way you fought off that man," Fletch said. "You handled yourself like a pro, Jane. You also knew how to shoot a gun."

Her face blanched as if he'd said something wrong.

"It's not a criticism," he said. For God's sake, he needed

to soothe her nerves. She'd just been attacked and killed a man. Even a professional would be shaken.

"If you can do that, you sure as hell can dig a little bullet out of my leg."

Emotions glittered in her eyes, then she lifted her chin. "All right. Just tell me what to do."

Fletch patted her hand, determined to keep her calm. For now he needed her help. Later, they'd talk about how she'd learned to fight and shoot.

JANE MENTALLY BRACED herself to remove the bullet. Fletch had saved her life twice now. How could she refuse his request?

Yet the image of that man as she'd shot him haunted her. Who was he? Why had he tried to kill her?

Would her memory return, or would she be forever lost in this suffocating emptiness?

"Look in the first aid kit," Fletch instructed. "There's a knife and tweezers in there along with antiseptic wipes. There's also a vial of alcohol to sterilize the knife with. And you can heat it over the fire."

Perspiration beaded on her skin as she removed the supplies and built a fire.

"What about an anesthetic?" Jane asked.

"I don't have one." He reached underneath his flannel shirt and ripped off the tail end of his T-shirt. "I'll bite on this. Now make a small incision beside where the bullet is lodged, then use the tweezers to pull it out."

Jane wiped sweat from her forehead. He made it sound easy. And she had just killed a man. But he had been trying to kill her and Fletch. She'd acted in self-defense.

Hurting Fletch was different. She didn't want to cause him pain. He was strong, caring, protective. If he hadn't saved her, she'd be dead.

Fletch touched her hand. "Look at me, Jane."

Her breath caught at the tenderness in his eyes. "You can do this. Remember you're helping me. It'll be over in no time, then we can both rest."

The shooter's face taunted Jane. Who the hell was that man? Did she know him?

Fletch closed his eyes as if he was losing consciousness. "It's time, Jane. Let's get it over with."

He was right. No sense stalling. Besides, she wanted and needed Fletch to survive.

She quickly sterilized the knife blade and tweezers. Then she cleaned the area around the wound, allowing her a clearer picture of what she was dealing with.

"Are you ready?" she asked.

He looked pale now, his complexion pasty. "Do it, Jane. You've got this." He stuffed the T-shirt strip between his teeth and bit down.

Focusing on the task, she gripped the knife and surveyed the opening where the bullet had pierced his thigh. Deciding that acting faster was better than drawing out the pain, she quickly pierced his skin with the knife. His body stiffened, his jaw tightening. She leaned closer and quickly dug around the bullet.

He groaned, sweat beading on his skin, but she forced herself not to look at his face. *Just do it*, he'd said.

And she did. She steadied her hand, then concentrated on extracting the bullet. Blood gushed from the area, and she wiped it away with another sterile wipe, then tugged on the bullet with the tweezers until it slipped free from where it was embedded. Her hand trembled as she dropped the bullet into a plastic bag she'd found in Fletch's pack.

Wiping perspiration from her forehead with the back of her arm, she cleaned the wound again and glanced at Fletch. He'd passed out during the extraction.

She had to finish. She found thread and a needle in his bag, cleaned the wound again, then slowly stitched together his skin to close the opening. When she was finished, she dressed it with a gauze pad and wrapped it with tape to secure the bandage.

Relieved that part was over, she sank back on her heels and inhaled several deep breaths. Fletch was unconscious now and needed rest before he could attempt to hike again. Maybe his team would finish their other missions and come after them.

Until then, she'd take care of Fletch the same way he'd taken care of her.

Afternoon came and went as Fletch slept. He shivered and moaned, a fever working through him. She mopped the sweat from his forehead with a cloth she found in his bag, wetting it with melting snow to cool his skin. She shook a couple of painkillers from the bottle in his bag and gave them to him.

He slipped in and out of consciousness, occasionally whispering her name, and she stroked his arm to comfort him. "I'm here, Fletch."

"Gun," he mumbled. "My gun."

"It's in your bag."

"Keep it close," he murmured. "Case you need it."

She tensed at the reminder. Fletch had protected her with his life.

If someone else came after her, she'd protect them both.

Night was setting in, and she finally succumbed to fatigue and stretched out beside Fletch. Knowing he was next to her gave her a sense of peace and safety, yet she kept guard in case of another attack.

But then she dozed off and the nightmares came again. *The blood... A woman's face staring up at her in death.*

A man sprawled beside her, his chest gaping open with blood soaking his shirt.

She rolled over, struggling to escape the nightmare. Not her parents this time. *No...the face was a young woman, the man lying next to her with his hand stretched toward her as if together they'd found death.*

She jerked awake. Why did she keep seeing these dead people in her mind?

Her parents' murder, her husband's...the man chasing her...the man she'd shot...

Were they all connected?

Chapter Eight

Jane surveyed the woods from the shelter's door. In the aftermath of the blizzard, the wind had died down and the forest seemed eerily quiet. Shadows seemed to move and slip away, the tall trees obliterating the moonlight.

No more hiking until Fletch was better. He needed rest and time to regain his strength.

She tacked the tarp over the opening, cocooning them into the small space and shielding them once again from the elements. Her stomach growled, a reminder they hadn't eaten since morning, and she found some trail mix in his pack.

She settled by the fire and allowed herself to eat a handful, saving some for Fletch when he woke. Occasionally he called out to his father as if he was reliving the past, then he'd open his eyes and look around in a daze.

She understood that feeling. The past haunted him. It haunted her, as well. Except she'd lost most of it and she wanted it back.

Jane cradled his hand in hers. "It's night, Fletch. We're safe here until morning."

He blinked as if confused, then recognition flickered in his eyes. "How long have I been out?"

"A few hours. I removed the bullet and bandaged your

leg." She wiped his forehead with a damp cloth. "Hopefully tomorrow you'll feel better."

"Have to get you out of here." He used his elbows to prop up, but she gently coaxed him to lie back down.

"You need to rest. It's dark now."

"You have my gun?"

She patted the pocket of her jacket. "It's right here."

"Where did you learn to shoot?" he asked, his voice breaking as he fought sleep.

Jane racked her brain for the answer. "I don't know. It just came instinctively."

"Because you've had training," Fletch murmured. "And you can fight…"

Jane massaged her temple. "Maybe I took self-defense classes. Or… I think my father had a gun. He must have taught me."

Fletch's brows furrowed, and he blinked as if trying to stay awake. Then slowly his lids closed and he succumbed to the fatigue. Jane patted his shoulder, then checked outside again. Thankfully she didn't see anyone lurking around or hear sounds of an intruder.

Her head ached, so she returned to sit by the fire beside Fletch and keep vigil. If his fever spiked higher, she'd use his radio to call for help.

The night loomed long and cold and lonely, though, and eventually when he was resting peacefully, she stretched out beside him again. Her bones felt chilled from the cold, so she crawled beneath the blanket and curled close to him.

Fletch was right. Shared body heat definitely was better than going it on your own. His big muscular body radiated such warmth, strength and power that it lulled her into a sense of safety. She suddenly wanted to tell him everything.

"Fletch," Jane said softly.

"Yeah."

"I don't know if it's important, but I've been having a recurring nightmare. Maybe it's a memory. I don't really know." She rubbed his back, needing comfort. "I keep seeing dead people in my mind. Couples who've been murdered. I...don't know if it's real or not."

Different scenarios raced through her mind. Maybe those faces belonged to a story she'd seen on the news. Or...maybe she was a journalist who'd covered the murders. Or...maybe she knew one of the victims personally...

Or...what if someone wanted her dead because she'd witnessed one of the murders?

FLETCH FLOATED IN and out of reality. Haunted by his father's death and the fire that had stolen his life, for a minute he was back in Whistler. He and his brothers were breaking the news of his father's death to his mother. He felt helpless as she fell apart. Chaos in the town followed over the next few days as reality hit. Numerous people were dead. Cora's baby was missing. Shock spread as police revealed that someone had intentionally set the fire.

He jerked himself from the tragic memory, his body shaking with emotions. Behind him, a warm body touched his.

"Shh, it's okay, Fletch."

A woman's voice. Soft. Her fingers caressed his back in a soothing gesture.

He turned toward her. Wanted her closer. To feel her comforting arms.

Soft breasts pressed against his chest. Her breathing turned erratic. A leg wove between his.

His heart pounded, heat flaring inside him, and he drew her closer. Couldn't help himself. It had been a long damn time since he'd been with a woman. Since he'd allowed himself to let down his defenses.

Since he'd felt so needy.

Part of him didn't like it. Yet her breath bathed his neck, and he couldn't stop himself. He pulled her tighter against him, then lowered his head and closed his lips over hers.

Hunger seized him, and he moved his mouth across hers, seeking, tasting, savoring the sweet touch of her lips. She returned the kiss, stroking his calf with her foot as his tongue explored her hungrily. He threaded his hands through her hair and tilted her head back to taste the sensitive skin of her neck.

She made a low sound in her throat, then pressed kisses on his jaw and cheek as she tunneled her fingers through his hair. He moaned and rolled her sideways to climb above her when a pain shot through his leg.

At the same time, she flattened her hands on his chest. "Fletch, wake up," she whispered. "We can't do this."

The sound of her voice startled him back to reality and out of the depths of his dream. Only he wasn't dreaming.

He'd been kissing Jane.

Her eyes were doe-like in the dim firelight, her mouth parted, lips red and swollen from his kiss. Silently cursing, he pushed himself off her and rolled to his back a few inches away.

"Dammit, Jane, I'm sorry." He scrubbed a hand over his face, half delirious from the desire still pumping through him.

The air became charged. Heated.

"I can't believe I did that," Fletch murmured. "I…was dreaming. But…that's no excuse." Maybe on some level he'd known exactly what he was doing.

And that he was doing it with Jane.

But he'd crossed the line. Jane was a married woman with amnesia.

A woman he was supposed to keep his damn hands off and protect.

JANE TURNED AWAY from Fletch and pressed her fingers to her lips. She could still feel his sexy mouth moving over hers, feel his hands stroking her hair and back. Feel his thick length pressing against her belly.

He had been asleep.

She'd been asleep as well, lost in the throes of memories that threatened her sanity.

One moment she'd dreamt about a suburban neighborhood where she'd gathered with friends. The men were grilling burgers while the women spread side dishes and desserts across a picnic table. While the meat barbecued, she sipped wine and chatted with the ladies who were discussing the latest book club pick.

The houses were traditional, owned by thirtysomething married couples who shared common interests and a neighborhood swimming pool where the children laughed and played in the summer.

Diamond chips sparkled on her wedding band in the sunlight as she'd reached for her wine glass.

Only nowhere in the picture did she see her husband.

She certainly didn't remember climbing in bed with him at night.

Loneliness permeated her soul, and she'd felt Fletch's arms around her. She hadn't been able to resist his warmth and comfort.

But it was wrong. Kissing Fletch when she knew nothing about herself except that someone wanted her dead.

What if the couples at that neighborhood gathering were the ones murdered?

"Jane? I'm sorry," Fletch said again.

She shook her head. "You don't have to apologize, Fletch. We were both half asleep." She lifted her chin and turned to face him. "Nothing really happened, so let's forget about it."

His gaze latched with hers, questions and doubt darkening his eyes. She wished she could give him the answers he needed. The ones she craved herself.

"I'll be right back." Needing fresh air, she grabbed the tin Fletch had used to melt snow in for coffee, stepped outside and studied the desolate terrain. Thick layers of white still blanketed everything in sight. Tree limbs hung heavy and bowed beneath the weight of frozen ice. Melting snow dripped from branches and puddles had begun to form, turning the frozen ground into a slushy mess.

Early morning sunlight fought through the treetops and slanted rays across the ground and rocks. She gathered enough snow to melt for coffee and some more small twigs and branches, then carried them inside.

Fletch had managed to sit up and was digging through his pack. She made quick work of adding the twigs and sticks to the fire, then stoked it and set the tin of snow on top. They worked silently but in tandem and made coffee. While they sipped it, she warmed her hands over the fire.

"Last night, you mentioned something about couples being murdered." He studied her over his coffee. "What was that about?"

She traced her finger around the rim of the tin mug. "I was dreaming. I don't know if what I saw was real or nightmares. Everything's all jumbled in my mind."

He remained silent for a moment, the air between them filled with a sensual awareness she didn't want to feel for Fletch. One she couldn't act upon, not again.

She might as well talk it out. They'd be back to civilization again soon, and his brother, the sheriff, might be able to fill in the blanks.

"I dreamed about murders," she said. "I saw faces of women and men who'd been killed, pictures of their bodies all bloody and ghostlike as if I was there. I don't know if I saw them on the news or if there's more to it. If it was real and if it's connected to me."

Fletch's eyes darkened. "Did you recognize any of the victims?"

She massaged her temple where a headache pulsed. "No, although in another dream I saw myself at a neighborhood barbecue in the suburbs. There were couples there."

Fletch leaned forward, his expression earnest. "Was one of the victims at the neighborhood gathering?"

She closed her eyes, struggling to discern the faces, but everything was blurred, filled with scattered bits that didn't fit together like different puzzles where the pieces had been mixed up.

"I…don't know, Fletch." She raised her head and looked into his eyes, terrified of remembering.

Terrified of not.

FLETCH STRUGGLED TO shake the memory of that kiss from his mind. But it was damn hard.

Especially when he looked at Jane's vulnerable expression and wanted her again.

"It's a good sign that you're starting to remember things," he said. "Those bits and pieces may not make sense now, but eventually you'll figure out what it all means."

She bit her bottom lip, her eyes filled with doubt. "I was thinking, Fletch. What if someone showed up at that dinner party and murdered my friends?"

He narrowed his eyes. "You mean a mass shooting?"

He ran a hand through his hair. "That would certainly be traumatizing. I don't recall hearing anything about a mass shooting at a neighborhood barbecue recently, and that kind of thing makes national news. But I can ask Jacob to explore that angle. It might be a lead."

"The man I shot could have been the shooter, and he wanted to silence me because I witnessed the murders."

"That's a possibility," Fletch said. If it was a triggering event, it might give them a timeline for how long Jane had been held captive. And with the evidence he'd collected, it might lead them to a name.

Although if the man had committed multiple murders, he obviously had no conscience, so why hadn't he shot Jane and ended her life, too?

Fletch eased the bandage on his leg away from his wound to examine it. Jane had stitched up the incision like an expert. The wound was clean, no signs of infection.

There was definitely more to Jane than what was on the surface.

Jane's hair fell in a curtain over her cheek as she checked the incision. He had the insane urge to push it away from her face and draw her back to him for another mind-blowing kiss.

But that would be stupid. And unprofessional.

Suddenly anxious to get them off the mountain, he sat up. Another night with Jane alone and he might give in to his attraction toward her.

He needed to consult with his brother. If a mass murder had occurred as Jane suggested, Liam might be working the case.

Jane handed him a fresh bandage, and he applied it while she packed up the supplies and extinguished the fire. He gritted his teeth and pushed to stand, testing his weight on his leg. Surprisingly it held up.

"Are you sure you can walk?" Jane asked, her voice filled with concern. "You could call your team to send medics after you."

He damn well did not want to go down the mountain on a stretcher, not unless he had to. His team was needed elsewhere.

"I'm fine." He raised a brow. "My gun?"

She gestured toward the floor beside where they'd lain entwined. "Give it to me," he said. "We might need it on the way."

He hoped to hell not, but precautions were necessary. For all he knew, the man who'd shot him might not have been acting alone.

She handed him his weapon. She'd already set the safety, so he jammed it in the waist of his pants.

His radio beeped in, and Jane retrieved it from his pack and handed it to him. He pressed it to his ear and stepped outside, motioning for her to wait inside while he scanned the area for danger.

"Fletch, it's Todd. Jacob's here."

Fletch froze, heart hammering. "I'm here. Over."

"I heard you were shot. Are you okay, man?" Worry sharpened his brother's voice.

"Yeah, Jane Doe removed the bullet and stitched me up."

"Really?"

"Really."

"Where is she?"

"We holed up in a shelter last night, and are about to set out. She's inside waiting for me to give her the all clear." He was just about to tell Jacob about the mass murder theory but Jacob cut him off.

"Good. Let her wait a minute."

Fletch didn't like the raw edge to his brother's voice. "What's going on?"

"Fletch, a woman matching the description of your Jane Doe is wanted for murdering her husband in Asheville." Jacob paused, his breathing strained. "Be careful, man. Her name is Bianca, and, according to the report, she's dangerous."

Chapter Nine

Fletch glanced back at the doorway where Jane stood. She looked pale yet beautiful in the early morning light. Her dark hair hung in waves over her shoulders, her green eyes serious as she searched the area.

Jacob's statement echoed in his ears. *Jane matches the description of a woman wanted for murdering her husband in Asheville. Her name is Bianca, and she's dangerous.*

"Are you sure?" Fletch asked.

"I talked to an officer there myself," Jacob said. "He texted me a picture of the crime scene. It was a bloody mess. Husband, Victor Renard, was shot square between the eyes."

Just like the man Jane had shot.

She had known how to handle the gun. Had made a shot that, for a beginner, was almost impossible. But she'd killed him in self-defense.

That heated kiss taunted him.

Dammit, just when he'd started to trust her…

"There has to be more to the story," he said, angry with himself for allowing Jane to get under his skin. "When I found her, she was bruised and suffering from a head injury. After we started hiking, we came on another shelter where we found rope and a rag. Jane claims she was tied and gagged and left there."

A heartbeat of silence passed. Jacob cleared his throat. "Could she be lying?"

Jacob scrubbed a hand over his face as memories of another woman lying to him flashed back. Hannah Miller. She'd fooled him with her damsel-in-distress act.

But this was different. Wasn't it? "Her injuries are real and she was almost dead when I found her. Rope burns marked her wrists and ankles. And I saw the gash on the back of her head." He couldn't imagine the wound being self-inflicted.

"What did she tell you about what happened?"

"So far not much. She appears to have amnesia. Could be caused from the head injury or trauma."

Another moment of silence. "Do you believe her?"

"Yeah, I do. Her frustration over her memory loss seems genuine." Fletch paused. "She also mentioned having nightmares where she thinks she might have witnessed a mass murder. Something about a neighborhood barbecue."

Jacob cleared his throat. "Let me dig around some more and see what I can find out on Bianca and her husband. And I'll look into mass murders although nothing about one at a neighborhood barbecue rings a bell."

"Thanks. We're heading out to hike down the mountain now."

Jacob's breath rattled over the line. "Be careful, little brother. And watch your back. If Jane Doe is Bianca Renard and she's on the run from the law, she could turn on you at any minute."

Fletch assured him he'd stay alert for trouble. Although he'd given Jane his gun the night before and she'd done nothing except take care of him.

Which meant her amnesia was real or she was a damn good liar.

Either way, he'd watch her every second.

JANE SENSED SOMETHING different with Fletch as they started down the mountain. Ever since that radio transmission, he'd been quiet and suspicion laced his eyes as if he was scrutinizing her every move.

Finally, a mile down the mountain, she leaned against a tree to catch her breath and confronted him. "What's wrong, Fletch? Do you have information about me?"

Fletch rubbed at his thigh. It was obviously hurting him, but he hadn't complained or allowed it to slow him down. "First, you tell me—have you remembered who you are?"

Jane's pulse hammered at the distrust in his voice. "No, why? Do you know who I am?"

Fletch shrugged. "Jacob received a missing persons report on a woman matching your description."

Jane's breath stalled in her chest. She sensed she wasn't going to like what Fletch had to tell her. "What is my name?"

"He's not a hundred percent sure it's you," Fletch warned. "I couldn't send him pics because there's no phone reception here on this part of the mountain."

Anxiety needled Jane. "Just tell me what he said, Fletch."

Fletch released a weary sigh. "The woman's name is Bianca Renard."

Jane shifted, mentally repeating the name in her head. Bianca… That didn't seem right.

In fact, Jane felt more like her name than Bianca.

Fletch remained silent, studying her with hawklike eyes. "Does the name sound familiar?"

She slowly shook her head. "Not really. What else did he say about this woman?"

Fletch pulled a hand down his chin, drawing her gaze back to his beard-stubbled jaw and those lips that had kissed her. For a moment during the kiss, she'd forgotten she was in danger. She'd felt safe.

She didn't feel safe anymore.

"She was married to a man named Victor."

"Victor?" She tossed that name around just as she had the name Bianca. "You said she was married as in she isn't anymore?"

Fletch gave a small nod. "Victor was murdered, shot to death."

Jane barely stifled a gasp as the image of the man with the tattoo on his arm surfaced. His body flying backward. Blood spewing.

Her hand shaking as she gripped the gun…

She had to swallow twice to make her voice work. "Do they know who killed him?"

Silence stretched long and thick, filled with the threat of an accusation.

"At this point, Bianca is wanted for his murder."

Oh, God.

Jane sank down onto the ground and dropped her head into her hands. She didn't remember a wedding or vows or sleeping with this man she'd married.

But she had seen his murder in her mind. Worse, she'd been holding the gun.

FLETCH STUDIED JANE'S reaction for signs she was staging it, but she seemed truly distraught.

"Does any of this sound familiar?" he asked.

She blinked as if needing to focus as she looked up at him. "I had a brief flashback where I saw the man who'd given me the wedding ring being shot," she admitted. "But I'm not sure who shot him."

The old adage "innocent until proven guilty" reverberated in Fletch's head. "Jacob didn't know details, but he's going to dig around and find out more about Bianca and her husband. When we get back to Whistler, hopefully he'll have answers."

Jane nodded, although wariness mixed with worry in her eyes.

"God, Fletch. If I killed my husband," she said, "the man who shot at us might have been a cop."

Fletch considered her theory. "If he was a cop, he would have identified himself as one instead of opening fire and attacking you."

Jane tugged her hat over her ears as a gust of wind blew through. "True."

Fletch searched for an alternative explanation. "If you witnessed a crime, that might explain the reason a hit man would come after you. Someone doesn't want you to talk."

A troubled expression creased her face.

He extended his hand to help her up. "Ready?"

She clasped his hand, their gazes locking. Jacob's warning taunted Fletch. But the woman looking back at him did not look like a cold-blooded killer.

Don't be a fool, another voice inside his head whispered. *Just because she's pretty and in trouble, it doesn't mean you can let down your guard.*

"I appreciate your honesty, Fletch. Thanks for not instantly believing I'm a murderer," Jane said softly.

"Just don't lie to me, Jane. Tell me when you remember something," he said gruffly.

Another gust of wind blew through, and Jane shivered, then released his hand. She brushed snow and debris from the seat of her pants, then took off down the trail.

He was a half mile down when he realized she hadn't responded to his request.

JANE LATCHED ON TO Fletch's theory, mentally trying to fit together the pieces in her mind to create a picture of what had happened.

But there were still too many holes.

As they hiked over brush and along jagged ridges, her boots skidded, and she clawed at tree branches to maintain her balance. Twice she slipped, but Fletch caught her, the tension between them palpable.

Although the theory that she was in danger because she'd witnessed a murder made sense, uncertainty plagued his eyes.

How could she blame him? Doubts filled her at every turn.

Fletch suddenly threw up a hand for her to wait. The sun was warming the frozen ground, slush slowing them as their shoes sank deep into the icy water and mud. A noise from the left startled her, and she realized the sound was the reason Fletch had halted.

A limb snapped off and flew downward, and she ducked sideways to avoid being hit in the head. Fletch clutched his weapon as he surveyed the area surrounding them.

More noise. Brush rustling. Twigs snapping.

A movement ahead. Then another.

Jane dug her fingernails into her palms as she waited.

Fletch motioned for her to stay where she was, and she flattened herself against the trunk of a tall pine. Snow fluttered from the shivering trees, raining down in a white shower.

Suddenly more movement ahead. She caught sight of reddish brown fur. Two of them.

Wolves.

Fletch motioned for her to be very still, and she was, waiting. At one time red wolves faced extinction, so she didn't condone killing them unless it was for self-preservation. No need to provoke them now.

She and Fletch remained immobile, giving the wolves time to create some distance between them. Finally she released the breath she'd been holding, and she inched up beside Fletch. He rubbed his leg again, and she touched his arm. "Let me check the bandage. It looks like you're bleeding again."

"I'm fine," Fletch said.

"Don't be silly," Jane said. "We need to stop the bleeding and change your dressing."

He made a low sound of frustration, then limped over to a big rock and sat down. He dropped the pack on the ground, and Jane retrieved the first aid kit. She gently removed the bloody bandage and cleaned the wound. Fletch winced, sweat beading on his forehead. He was obviously hurting but was too proud to ask for help.

"You should have called your team to come for you," Jane admonished while she pressed a blood stopper to the wound.

"In my job, we have to prioritize. Right now other people need help more than I do."

Jane fought a smile at his stubborn independence. "Right." She applied pressure to the wound. Cold air swirled around her as she waited to stop the bleeding.

"You did a nice job stitching me up," he said in a gruff tone.

Jane shrugged. "My first time. At least, I think it was." The empty void in her mind threatened to choke her with despair again.

Fletch squeezed her shoulder. "It'll be all right. We'll uncover the truth about you."

"I hope so." She bit down on her bottom lip. "At the moment, I'm worried about you hiking on that leg."

Fletch shrugged, a twinkle in his eyes. "Don't worry about me. I'm a tough guy."

Tough and sexy. And a real true-life hero.

Tears blurred her vision, but she blinked them away and made quick work of applying another bandage.

"Thanks," he said as she stowed the emergency kit again.

"You're welcome." She stood and brushed snow from her clothing.

Fletch jammed his gun back in the waistband of his pants and gestured he was ready to proceed. Jane followed his lead, winding down a trail so narrow that she felt as if they were going to slide off the mountain.

They reached another thicket of trees, then stepped through an opening flanked by a cluster of rocks.

Fletch came to a halt again, his hand pressing her behind him. Jane glanced over his shoulder, then gasped.

A man lay in the snow between the boulders, his clothing torn and bloody, his arms and legs bent at odd angles, his eyes staring wide open in death.

Chapter Ten

The sight of the dead man twisted at Fletch's gut. He lay stomach down on the rocks, with his face angled slightly to one side.

On first thought, he wondered if he'd fallen and hit his head. But in light of the fact that someone had tried to kill Jane, suspicions kicked in.

Fletch touched her shoulder. "Stay here. Let me take a look."

Jane's complexion turned pasty white. The man in him wanted to comfort her, but the professional ordered him to do his job.

Take pictures. Report the body. Let the evidence speak for itself.

Considering the circumstances, he had to ask, "Do you recognize this man?"

Jane wrinkled her forehead in thought. "No."

"Let me photograph the scene. Sit down and take a deep breath," he instructed. "I'll be right back."

Fletch retrieved his camera from his pack and captured different angles of the man's body and the surrounding area. Talon marks and his torn clothing indicated he'd been mauled by birds of prey, probably postmortem.

Fletch inched forward, senses honed for trouble as he approached the body. The man had been dressed for the elements, insulated pants, snow boots, flannel shirt, winter coat, gloves and hat, although the hat had come off and lay in the snow.

Definitely a significant amount of blood had pooled beneath the man's face.

Fletch snapped photographs of his clothing, the way his limbs were twisted and distorted, then eased close enough to examine him further.

Wiry, dirty blond hair. Blood matted on the back of his head. A scar on his face that looked old, as if he'd been in a fight with a knife at some point in his life.

Fletch pulled gloves from his pocket and slipped them on, then pushed the man's hair aside. A bullet wound had pierced the back of his skull.

He gently rolled the man's head to one side to assess the gunshot. Blood and brain matter covered the rocks and surrounding area, confirming the man had been shot from behind.

"Fletch?" Jane said in a raw whisper.

"He was murdered, gunshot wound." Fletch turned to gauge her reaction. She instinctively rubbed her fingers across the back of her own head.

"I need to call this in." He retrieved his radio from his pack and connected with the station. "Fletch here. Found a man shot to death. Looks like he's been dead a few hours at least." He gave the coordinates. "Notify Jacob. I'll look for evidence and collect what I find. Send a recovery team when possible."

Fletch ended the call, then combed the area surrounding the rocks for the bullet. A few feet away, he spotted the casing in the midst of a pile of branches. He dug it out, then bagged it and labeled it to give to Jacob for analysis.

If this bullet casing matched the one from the shooter's

gun, they could connect the two. He dug into the man's pockets in search of an ID.

A pack of non-menthol cigarettes, gum, mints, a Swiss army knife and a lighter. No ID.

The clean shot to the head suggested the killer was a professional. He'd probably taken the ID.

If this scar-faced man had been killed by a professional, and the professional was the same man who'd shot at Jane, was he a hired hit man?

Which raised another question—why would a professional killer target Jane?

JANE CURLED HER hands into fists. Fletch wanted to protect her by shielding her from the man's body, but she needed to see his face. To see if he triggered a memory.

To know if he was connected to her amnesia.

According to Fletch's brother, she was wanted for murder. What if there was a bounty on her head? This man and the bearded shooter could have been tracking her down to bring her in.

Even so, who killed this man?

She inched closer, scrutinizing his body size. "Let me see his face," she said quietly.

Fletch angled the man's head to the side. Jane swallowed hard as she studied his features. Shaggy, dirty blond hair. A narrow face, long nose, a jagged scar running from his temple down the left side of his cheek.

Her pulse hammered. Something about the man *was* familiar.

"Jane?"

His name teetered on the edge of her tongue.

Fletch hissed between his teeth. "Maybe Jacob or Liam can ID him, then we determine if his death is connected to you."

His calm acceptance helped soothe her anxiety. "Everything just seems random," she said. "I don't understand the timing, much less if the bits and pieces tell the story."

"Close your eyes and try to relax," Fletch murmured. "Take your time and concentrate. Maybe he had something to do with Victor Renard?"

A brief image of her husband's face flashed behind her eyes. Then she was holding a gun. Then…nothing. A big black hole.

She knotted her hands in frustration.

Fletch squeezed her shoulder. "Listen to me. You're making progress. You just need more time."

Maybe so. But everything she remembered became even more disturbing and was filled with death and violence.

FLETCH WAS DAMN tired of playing the guessing game. He couldn't imagine Jane's agitation.

His past was filled with happy memories of family camping trips, holidays, boisterous family dinners and game nights. He held on to those precious memories, to the sound of his father's voice, to the mouthwatering scent of his mother's homemade peach cobbler, to the joy of their laughter as he and his brothers chased each other through the woods.

One trip stood out—it was hot as hell and buggy. After dinner everyone dove into the swimming hole to escape the heat and mosquitos.

Then they'd huddled around the fire and roasted marshmallows.

The holidays were always special, too. Liam loved scary stories, especially at Halloween. Their mother had decorated the house and yard with spiders and ghosts and goblins, while his father made up a spooky story about the house down the street being inhabited by pirate ghosts.

He couldn't imagine losing those memories or living with an empty void in his mind.

Or not having a family.

Yet he'd been so focused on hunting down the arsonist who'd taken his father from them that he hadn't considered having a family of his own. Not until he'd seen Jacob with Cora and her daughter.

The love between his brother and his new wife sparked his own desire to have someone special in his life.

He glanced at Jane's pale face and grimaced. That kiss had been hot.

But she was embroiled in something deep. If Jacob's report was right, she might have murdered her husband. Of course, there could be a plausible reason.

Abuse topped the list. Or self-defense... Perhaps she'd learned something about her husband he didn't want exposed. Perhaps she'd witnessed her husband commit a murder, and he'd wanted to keep her quiet.

Or...perhaps he was grasping because he *wanted* Jane to be innocent.

His radio crackled, and he connected. "Fletch here. Over."

"It's Jacob. Todd sent a message saying you found a body. Do you have a name?"

"No, no ID on him." Fletch explained about the bullet wound to the back of the man's head. "I took pictures and gathered what might be evidence to bring back. I've also requested a recovery team."

"Copy that. I'll make sure the ME and my deputy accompany them."

"Do you want me to stay here and secure the scene until the team arrives?" Fletch asked.

A hesitation on Jacob's part. "No. I want you down here for medical treatment."

"I'm fine," Fletch said. "Jane did a good job of patching me up."

Another heartbeat of silence. "Speaking of Jane, did you ask her about Bianca and Victor Renard?"

Fletch angled himself away from Jane so she couldn't hear his conversation.

She kept looking at the dead man as if he held the secrets to her past.

"Yes, but the names don't ring a bell. Did you find out more about the Renards?"

"According to my source, Bianca worked as an interior designer with her real estate husband. He owned his own company that was worth a few million. Bianca staged new homes for him as well as handling her own client list.

"The couple just moved to Asheville. So far, I haven't located any family or friends to verify this information, but I'm working on it."

"Financial trouble?" Fletch asked.

"I'm just getting started. I'll have one of our analysts dig into their financials to see if there's anything fishy."

"Something worth murdering for."

"Yeah. I'll keep you posted." Jacob paused. "And Fletch?"

"Yeah?"

"Be careful, man. Looks can be deceiving. This woman might be serious trouble."

Hannah had certainly deceived him. She'd pretended to love him, but in the end, she'd wanted money and nice things, not a mountain man who lived his days in the woods.

Fletch ended the connection and walked back over to Jane. She looked at him expectantly. "That was Jacob."

Her sharp intake of breath punctuated the air between them. "What did he say?"

Fletch shrugged. For some reason, he couldn't reconcile the information Jacob had shared with Jane's behavior.

"Tell me what you know, Fletch."

The need in her voice roused his protective instincts again. But sharing might trigger her lost memories to resurface.

So he relayed Jacob's statement. "Does any of that ring a bell?"

Jane pursed her lips. "He said I'm an interior designer?"

He nodded. "Your husband Victor was a big wheel in real estate, worth millions."

She furrowed her brows. "In my dreams, I was at a neighborhood cookout. It was in the suburbs somewhere. And it seemed…normal." She worried her bottom lip with her teeth. "If I decorated houses, why can't I recall that? And for some reason, I can't imagine I had money like that."

"You may be repressing the memories because someone you loved hurt you. Have you considered the fact that it was your husband?"

"I HAVE." SHE'D OBVIOUSLY seen something that had been so horrible she didn't want to remember it.

But she couldn't move on with her future until she did.

The wind picked up again, howling off the mountain. Snow was starting to melt quickly, tree limbs cracking and breaking off.

She glanced back at the dead man, willing him to talk to her.

"We'd better get going," Fletch said. "I'd like for us to make it down the mountain before dark tonight."

Jane's stomach churned as they left the body lying on the rocks and began to hike again. Fletch adjusted his pack to alleviate extra weight on his injured leg, then led her down another path.

After two more miles, everything looked the same to her. Endless miles of forest, trees so thick they practically hugged each other and let in very little light. A gray fog covered the sky, adding to the dismal feel.

She was grateful for Fletch's experience on the trail or she would have been lost. The frozen ground became slushy and slippery, her boots sinking into freezing water that went all the way through to her socked feet. The trees swayed in the wind, and melting snow began running downhill like a river.

Another mile, and suddenly a loud noise sounded. Fletch went still, and cocked his head to listen. A shudder coursed through Jane as a rumbling noise boomeranged off the mountain. Fletch pivoted, and eyes widening, grabbed her hand.

"Avalanche," he shouted. "Hurry. Let's go."

Jane spotted the mounds of snow beginning to barrel down the mountain toward them.

She and Fletch tried to outrun it, but the landslide was so fast and sudden that the force of it nearly knocked her down. Fletch clutched her hand to steady her and pulled her to the right.

"Cave. Inside," he shouted.

She ducked her head as he yanked her into the opening. Snow and debris rained down in a thunderous roar, rocks and ice tumbling.

A second later, the avalanche dumped mounds of snow and ice in front of the door, blocking their exit.

Jane's lungs squeezed for air. They were trapped.

Chapter Eleven

Dammit to hell and back. How much more could go wrong on this trek?

Fletch had undertaken countless missions, some involving major emergencies, some where they recovered bodies instead of rescuing individuals.

But never one where he was ambushed by a shooter and then found a man murdered. And now, on top of the blizzard, a freak avalanche.

"Jane, are you hurt?" He quickly glanced at her as he urged her away from the cave entrance.

"I'm okay," she said. "But what caused that?"

Fletch sank back on his heels, his eyes adjusting to the dimly lit interior of the cave. Stone walls, dirt floor and wooden braces indicated it had once been an active mine. "Happens sometimes after a big snowstorm when the weather changes abruptly."

Jane fingered her tangled hair from her cheek. "It sounded like an explosion, like dynamite exploding."

He'd thought the same thing.

Which meant the avalanche might not have been caused by nature, but it could have been intentional.

Someone else after Jane? Or Bianca, if that was her name? He still couldn't reconcile the name Bianca or her job as an interior designer with the skilled fighter and shooter he'd witnessed.

Although it was possible she'd taken a self-defense class as she'd suggested. God knows, women needed to these days. There were too many damn predators on the streets.

"Fletch, do you think someone set off dynamite?"

Fletch chewed the inside of his cheek. He didn't want to alarm her when he had no answer, just suspicions. "I don't know. We can't jump to conclusions, Jane. Sometimes the sound of ice breaking and the force of the wind sound like an explosion. Remember my teammate said they were rescuing people from another avalanche."

Jane propped herself against the wall of the cave, eyes flickering with fear as she glanced at the doorway. "What do we do now?"

"Don't panic." Fletch removed his radio from his pack and tried to connect, but static rattled in the air. Dammit. "I gave Jacob the coordinates for the dead man we found on the rocks. It's not far from here. When a team comes to recover his body, they'll find us."

"But they don't even know we're missing."

Fletch pasted on an encouraging smile. "My brother was expecting us to be down the mountain in a couple of hours. When we don't show, he'll try to make contact. If he can't get through, he'll organize a search party to look for us."

Jane released a wary sigh. "How can you be so confident?"

"I trust my brothers," he said. "They'll look for us. And Jacob is logical. He knows the path I'd travel from those rocks, and he'll follow it. It's only a matter of time."

A frown puckered the skin between Jane's eyes. "It must be nice to be so close to your family, to know that your brothers are there for you no matter what."

A wealth of sadness weighted her words, and Fletch

tilted her chin up with his thumb and looked into her eyes. "You're going to remember, Jane, and whatever happened, you'll get through it. You might even have someone in your life looking for you. Another family member. A friend. Someone who loves you."

Emotions clouded her eyes. "I don't know, Fletch. I… feel like I'm alone, that I have been for a long time. That I don't have anybody."

Jacob's warning echoed in Fletch's mind. But he had to trust his gut instincts instead. And they were screaming at him that Jane was an innocent victim who needed understanding and protection.

Unable to resist, he raked debris from the avalanche from her hair, then drew her to him and kissed her.

THE AFFECTION IN Fletch's voice when he'd spoken about his family made Jane long for that kind of closeness with someone.

Made her want a family that she could count on, someone to love.

Fletch's lips closed over hers, moving gently with a mixture of erotic teasing and tenderness. The sincerity in his eyes just before he'd kissed her moved something deep inside her.

She lifted one hand and pressed it against his jaw, her senses heightened by the intimacy of the dark, cold interior. The fear and panic that had nearly immobilized her earlier dissipated as he deepened the kiss and threaded his fingers through her hair.

He angled his head, drew closer and teased her lips apart with his tongue. Desire surged through her.

Heart hammering, she met his tongue thrust for thrust. He trailed one hand down her shoulder to pull her against him. Her breasts tingled at the feel of his hard, muscular chest.

Craving more, Jane stroked his back and made a low sound of need in her throat. Fletch tore his lips from hers, his breathing erratic. Passion glazed his dark chocolate eyes, hunger flaring between them.

He was asking for permission.

She obliged and pulled him back to her, then unbuttoned the top button of his flannel shirt. His breath rushed out, and he lowered his head and dropped kisses along her throat then lower to the sensitive skin between her breasts. With a low groan, he peeled back her shirt and tasted her skin.

A frenzy of hunger seized them, and their movements became more frantic. He kissed her again, deep and long and greedily, then suckled at her neck until she unfastened the buttons on his shirt and pushed the fabric off his broad shoulders. He tossed the garment aside, then tugged his T-shirt over his head, exposing bare flesh, corded muscles and a dark sprinkling of hair that trailed from his chest down to the waistband of his pants.

Warmth pooled in her body, and an ache built, which made her run her hands over his bare skin. Heat tingled through her at his sharp intake of breath.

"Jane?"

"Yes," she said in a ragged whisper. Passion and need overcame reason, and she leaned forward and pressed kisses along his chest.

Fletch groaned, then pushed her onto her back and dove in for another long, sensual kiss. His hard length pressed into the V of her thighs, stroking her through her pants, and she lifted her hips as erotic sensations pummeled her.

Fletch dipped his head and nibbled at the sensitive skin between her breasts, then suckled her through the thin lace of her bra. Jane whispered his name and clung to him, welcoming the cool brush of air as he unfastened the front clasp of her bra, exposing her breasts. Her nipples stiffened to peaks, begging for his touch.

He tugged one into his mouth and suckled her, driving her mad with desire. She raked her nails over his back, urging him on, and parted her legs in invitation.

He moved to her other breast, giving it the same loving attention, and she tugged at his belt. He moved lower, pulling at her pants, and she lifted her hips to give him access.

He gazed at her with such hunger that her body tingled with need. He paused, eyes flaring with lust as he traced a finger along the edge of her black lace panties.

Hungry for more, for all of him, she freed his belt then tossed it aside. Then she pushed at his pants. But the sight of his bandage made her pause.

"Fletch?"

His body braced on his elbows, he looked down into her face. "Jane…we shouldn't."

Hurt battled with the realization that he was right.

"I'm sorry." He moved off her and handed her clothing to her, then snatched his and turned his back to her.

She stared at the beautiful hard planes of his back and longed to draw him back to her and finish what they'd begun.

But the stiff set of his shoulders and his apology felt like a rejection. She wouldn't beg him to make love to her.

But he *had* seemed to want her.

Why had he suddenly changed his mind?

FLETCH QUICKLY BUTTONED his shirt, silently berating himself for allowing things to go so far.

He knew damn well better than to get personally involved with Jane. She had amnesia and was vulnerable. What the hell was wrong with him?

He'd never had trouble keeping it in his pants before.

But he'd never felt so drawn to anyone the way he felt drawn to Jane.

The fear and loneliness in her eyes completely shredded his common sense and willpower.

But if she was an interior designer and came from money, she might want to return to that world. Just as Hannah had.

That life was the polar opposite of his. One he would never fit into.

Needing to regain his composure, he forced himself not to look at her. Instead he tried the radio, but once again, only static crackled off the rocky mine walls. Deciding to hunt for another way out, he told Jane to stay put and he carried his flashlight to look around.

Damp moss clung to the stone walls, the ground solid dirt. He found an area where he could stand, then noticed there was an opening leading to another area, so he followed it. He had to crouch low to keep from hitting his head in several places. Water trickled down the sides of the interior, and he rounded a curve. He wove through a few other turns and followed the tunnel hoping to find an exit, but the tunnel ended with a hard wall.

Damn.

Irritated, he turned and started back toward Jane.

Breathing out, he shined the light around, his pulse clamoring when he spotted another clearing to the right. He inched through the narrow path to it, and found an old glove on the ground.

There were also bits of wrappers from dried food packs and boot prints. He knelt to examine them and determined they were large, probably a man's. From his vantage, he noticed a small spiral notepad on the ground wedged between some rocks.

With gloved hands, he tugged it free and opened it to examine the pages. A crudely drawn map of the trail. He flipped a page and paused, his heart hammering.

An article about the Whistler Hospital fire was folded and pressed between the pages.

The newspaper clipping could mean nothing. But for five years, he'd wondered if the person who'd set that fire was hiding out in these woods. What if he was right?

What if that man had been staying in this cave?

Adrenaline spiked his blood, and he ran back through the cave to retrieve his camera and bags for the evidence he'd discovered. Jane was sitting with her knees up, arms around them, staring at the doorway, her expression a mask of worry.

"I found some things in the back of the cave," he said. "I need to collect them to give to Jacob."

Jane glanced at him. "Do you think they belong to the dead man we found on the rocks?"

Fletch shrugged. "It's possible." Although he'd rather believe they belonged to the arsonist. Then he might catch a break and give Jacob and Liam a lead.

"I'll be right back."

He didn't wait for her to comment. He hurried through the tunnels and collected the glove and notebook.

Excited at the prospect of finally catching the bastard who killed his father, he carried the evidence back to where Jane waited and stowed it in his pack.

He was anxious to give them to Jacob for processing.

Jane looked ashen-faced in the dim light, and he fought the urge to return to her and comfort her. If he touched her again, he might not be able to stop himself from making love to her.

Instead he retrieved a tool from his pack and began to chisel at the fallen snow and ice trapping them inside.

JANE SENSED AN urgency about Fletch's rush to dig them an escape hole. "What did you find in the cave?"

Fletch sat back on his haunches. "A glove and a notebook indicating someone had been staying here. An article about the fire was tucked inside the book."

Hope tinged his voice. "Maybe the crime lab can lift prints from the items," Fletch said. "If they belong to the person who set the fire, we can identify him. If not, maybe they belong to someone with helpful information."

She admired his determination. Fletch was obviously not the kind of man who gave up on a cause.

"If he is the person who cost all those lives, he should pay," Jane said and meant it.

His gaze locked with hers, his dark eyes probing. The fact that she was wanted for murder taunted her.

The air suddenly became harder to breathe. She had to look away from Fletch for fear he'd see the self-doubts plaguing her.

Desperate for the truth, she crawled over to him. "If you have another tool, I'll help."

"I've got it," he said.

She rolled her eyes at his macho tone. "I may have amnesia but I'm not helpless, Fletch." She scanned the interior of the cave and found a jagged rock on the ground, so she snatched it.

Then she began to hack away at the top edge of the opening. Fletch didn't comment. He chiseled away alongside her.

"Tell me more about your family," Jane urged as they worked.

Fletch sighed. "My mother was a great cook," he said.

"She took pride in feeding her boys. She made the best pot roast in the state, and her peach cobbler was to die for. She loved big Sunday dinners and would have really enjoyed having grandkids." A smile tugged at the corners of his mouth. "She volunteered with a children's charity and devoted her free time to help provide underprivileged children with meals at school and during summer break."

"She sounds like a great lady," Jane said.

"She was. We lost her not long after we lost Dad. I think she died of heartbreak." Sadness filled his voice. "What do you recall about your mother?"

Jane bit down on her lip. She and her father shared the crosswords. But her mother... "Not that much," she said. "I think she was social and liked to entertain." And she sensed she was the opposite. Not a girlie girl as her mother wanted. "In one of my dreams, I saw law books on my father's desk. I think he might have been a lawyer. Maybe a judge."

Fletch jabbed the tool in the ice again. "Do you think their murder had something to do with his job? That it wasn't a random home invasion?"

Jane paused in her chiseling. "I...don't remember, but I suppose it's possible."

Fletch rubbed her shoulder. "Things are starting to come back to you, Jane. When we get home, maybe everything will come back."

All the more reason to keep chiseling.

Jane turned back to work, and so did Fletch. They chipped away ice and snow, digging to create an opening, but after an hour they'd barely made a dent. Fletch refused to give up, though. He continued until a sliver of light and air appeared.

But a noise outside rumbled, then suddenly rocks and

dirt inside the cave began to tumble down. Jane screamed. The ceiling was caving in!

Fletch grabbed her hand. "Come on, get away from that side!"

They crawled toward the tunnel leading to the back, then another thunderous noise and rocks and dirt started raining down.

Fletch threw himself on top of her and covered her with his body to protect her as the deluge pummeled them.

Chapter Twelve

Rocks thundered to the ground, the crashing sound reverberating off the cave walls. Jane coughed as dust flew into her face, but she lay still, praying the entire cave didn't crumble on top of them.

She didn't want to die here buried in rubble without clearing her name. Or even knowing who she was.

Slowly, the downfall slowed, the ping of stones and debris lessening. Fletch slowly lifted himself off her. "Are you okay, Jane?"

She nodded, brushing dirt from her mouth as she raised her head and peered toward the cave entrance. The opening was completely blocked with inches of dirt and rocks. "I am. Are you?"

"Yeah." He swore beneath his breath as he surveyed the damage.

Panic clawed at Jane. "We're really trapped now, Fletch."

Fletch clasped her hand and squeezed it. "For now, maybe. But my team will find us."

She wished she had his confidence. But she was unable to hide her fear. She might not know much about herself, but she didn't like small spaces.

He gently brushed dirt from her cheek. "Remember what I said before. My brothers will look for me and so will my team. The cave is near where we found that man's body. Once they see the avalanche, they'll launch a search."

Jane desperately wanted to believe him. The thought of suffocating in the darkness terrified her.

"Come on," Fletch said softly. "Let's move away from the mess. The air will be better back there."

She clutched his hand. "But what if someone comes? We won't be able to hear them."

Fletch released a breath. "We won't go far, just far enough to breathe better."

She relented and realized he was right. The air felt cooler, clearer, her breathing more steady as they crawled to a wider section of the cave. Fletch leaned against the wall beside her, his expression calm, although worry shadowed his eyes.

FLETCH REINED IN his mounting anxiety. He wanted to start digging them out again, but the explosion had damaged the structural foundation of the cave, and he didn't trust that the whole damn place wouldn't collapse on top of them.

"What if the man who tried to kill me set off that explosion to make sure we didn't survive?"

Compassion for Jane replaced his need to keep his distance. "It's possible, I suppose. But you shot him when he ambushed us."

"He could have had an accomplice who's still out there."

"Then who is the dead man on the rocks?"

Jane pinched the bridge of her nose. "I wish I knew."

Fletch mentally sorted through the possibilities. "At this point, we can only speculate. Let's go over what we know so far."

Jane nodded. "I remember being attacked by a man, tied and gagged in that cave. I tried to escape and he found

me and knocked me unconscious and left me in the blizzard to die."

"Man number one—attacker."

"I also remember a man with a wolf tattoo on his arm.
He put the wedding ring on my finger."

"Man number two is the husband."

Jane shrugged. "Then there was the bearded man who
shot at us. The one I killed."

"In self-defense," Fletch reminded her. "So the bearded
shooter was man number three."

"And now the dead man with the scar on his face, who
we found on the rocks," Jane added. "That makes four."

"Which means the bearded shooter and the scar-faced
dead man may or may not have been your attacker. It's
possible they're connected, that one or more of them were
being paid to find you."

Jane dropped her head in her hands and groaned. "And
there's the question—why do they want me dead?"

Fletch rubbed the back of her neck. "I know it's discon-
certing, Jane. But we will solve this mystery."

Jane looked up at him with such helplessness that he
forgot his reservations. He pulled her into his arms and
stroked her back. "Just hang in there."

She tilted her head to search his face. "But what if I'm
guilty of killing my husband like your brother suggested?"

"If you did, then there must have been a good reason,"
Fletch assured her.

PANIC NEEDLED JANE, and she and Fletch fell into an awkward silence. She prayed he was right about her. She didn't
want to escape this cave only to be locked in a cell the
rest of her life.

As the hours dragged by, the interior of the cave grew
smaller and darker. Her anxiety intensified with every

passing minute. She didn't know if the air was harder to breathe because it was running out, or if the fear squeezing at her lungs was making her paranoid.

Eventually fatigue claimed her, and she curled against Fletch. He wrapped his arm around her, stroked her back again, and she drifted to sleep. Occasionally when she stirred, she heard the soft sound of Fletch's breathing.

Comforted by his presence, she closed her eyes and sleep claimed her again. But even in sleep, the nightmares returned to haunt her.

The blood...her parents' faces...her husband's tattoo, his body flying backward, the gun clenched in her hand...

Then she was running for her life. Someone was behind her. She felt his breath, heard his hiss as he closed in on her. Then his hands snatching her, a blow to the head... and she was spinning and falling into the darkness.

Then gunfire. She gasped for breath. She was trapped in a cave. The air was gone. She was dying...

She jerked awake at the same time Fletch did. A noise somewhere. Fletch released her and crawled nearer the cave exit. Jane joined him, perched on her knees, listening.

There it was again. A low noise… Voices.

Hope bloomed in her chest. Fletch snatched his radio and attempted to make contact again, but failed. Voices echoed again.

"Hello?" he shouted. "We're in here!"

She and Fletch both began to yell, shouting over and over until she heard a chipping sound. Then a man's voice alerting them they were there to help.

Someone was out there! They were going to be rescued!

Tears of relief blurred her vision. Several seconds passed. A hacking sound. A ping. Voices again.

Seconds bled into agonizing minutes. Finally the debris and snow and ice began to melt away with the rescue workers' efforts. A small hole appeared, enough to allow light and air to flow in.

Jane almost sobbed with relief.

"Fletch?"

This time the voice was loud, distinguishable.

Fletch raised his voice, "Todd, we're in here!"

"We'll have you out soon. Back away from the opening."

"Copy that."

Fletch clutched Jane's hand, and they crawled away from the exit and leaned against the back wall. Dust floated through the air, making it difficult to breathe again, and Jane covered her mouth with her hand to keep from inhaling it.

She thought the workers would never break through, but finally they cleared a hole large enough for them to slip through.

"You go first," Fletch told Jane. "I'll follow."

Jane sucked in a breath, then straightened her arms and dove through the clearing as if she was diving into a swimming pool. Two men grabbed her arms and helped pull her to the other side where she collapsed, coughing and fighting for breath.

FLETCH WAS NEVER so happy to see his buddies in all his life. Not that he'd lied to Jane. He trusted them with his life.

But they'd survived one shooter and if that explosion had been meant to trap or kill them, he needed backup.

Todd had brought a medical team, and they rushed toward Jane. Todd and Jacob approached him.

"You okay, Fletch?" Todd asked.

He nodded. "Thanks," Fletch said. "I knew my team would find us."

Todd rubbed a hand down his chin. "You helped by giving Jacob your coordinates for that body on the rocks."

"I sent my deputy with a team to recover the corpse, and another team has gone out to collect the body of the man who shot you," Jacob interjected. "Now you need to go to the hospital."

Fletch offered Jacob an encouraging look to reassure him he was okay. Knowing the trauma he and his brothers had suffered when they lost their parents, he hated scaring them.

Jacob gestured for the medics to examine him anyway.

"I'm fine," Fletch protested. "Jane needs medical attention. She sustained a head injury and is still suffering from amnesia."

"You have a damn gunshot wound, brother," Jacob said. "You're going to the hospital, too."

"That's ridiculous." Fletch pushed up to stand, but his leg buckled slightly.

"See?" Jacob said with enough emotion that Fletch relented.

"All right, I'll ride with Jane in the ambulance and we'll both get checked out."

"Fletch," Jacob said in a gruff voice. "What the hell happened between you two?"

A lot. "Nothing," Fletch muttered. "But she seriously needs medical attention. Someone who can help her recover her memory."

"We'll see she gets it," Jacob assured him. "But don't forget—if she's Bianca Renard, she's wanted for murder."

Fletch glared at Jacob. "So you told me. But nothing I've seen about Jane suggests she's a cold-blooded killer."

A gust of wind picked up, scattering snow and debris and sending melting ice from the trees down in a shower.

"You seem defensive of her," Jacob muttered, his voice distressed.

"Because I think she's a victim," Fletch said.

"Thanks, Fletch, but I can stand up for myself." Jane's voice echoed from behind him, and he realized she'd broken away from the medic.

Fletch stepped closer to Jane, his protective instincts surging to life. "Jane, this is my brother Jacob, the sheriff of Whistler."

Jane swayed slightly. "I haven't lied to your brother, Sheriff."

Anger, subtle but real, flickered in Jacob's eyes.

"Listen to me," Jacob said to Jane. "You and Fletch are both going to the hospital for tests and exams. Then you have to answer some questions."

Jane lifted her chin in a show of defiance, or bravado. Fletch wasn't sure which. "I can't tell you what I don't know. But I'll be interested to see what you've uncovered about me."

Jacob and Jane locked horns in a stare down that would have made some men weak in the knees. But Jane stood her ground as if she had her feet back, as if she intended to tackle her problems head-on.

Fletch admired her courage.

He just hoped to hell she got the answers she wanted.

Jacob addressed the medics. "I want her carried down on a stretcher and secured in the ambulance. I'll ride with her and my brother to the hospital."

Jane's mouth twisted with irritation, but she lifted her chin again. "Does that mean I'm under arrest, Sheriff?"

Chapter Thirteen

Fletch studied his brother's body language, but as always Jacob remained calm and cool. Professional.

"Not at the moment, but you are a person of interest. First we verify your identity, then we'll go from there."

Jacob turned to Fletch. "You have evidence for me?"

Fletch jammed his hands in his jacket pocket. "In my pack. I labeled each item and where I found it. There are pictures on my camera, too."

Jacob patted Fletch's back. "Thanks, man. You did good work out there."

A rescue worker helped Jane onto a stretcher, and Fletch angled his head toward Jacob. "I really don't think she remembers, Jacob. And for what it's worth, nothing about her fits with your description of Bianca."

"Liam is digging for more information," Jacob said. "Let the doctor examine her, and I'll send the evidence you found to the lab."

"Good. There's something else. I think the avalanche that caused us to be trapped may have been set intentionally. We were close to digging our way out when there was another explosion. It sounded like dynamite."

"Damn." Jacob lifted a hand to shield his eyes from the blinding morning sun flickering off the white snowy hills.

"I'll send a crime team to search for explosives." He

scanned the ridges above them. "Did you see anyone suspicious before the avalanche started?"

"Not really," Fletch said. "Maybe a shadow in the woods."

"Fletch," Jacob said in a low voice. "Be honest. Do you have any idea what's really going on here?"

Fletch's first instinct was to deny that Jane might be complicit in a crime.

But he had to know the truth.

"I have a couple of theories, but they're only that." A gust of wind sent another deluge of snow and ice on them. "Can we discuss it once we get down from the mountain?"

Jacob studied him for a minute. "Sure." He planted a hand on Fletch's chest. "But you are going to the hospital and having that leg looked at. Now get on the stretcher, too."

Fletch shook his head. "No way. I hiked in. I'm hiking out."

Jacob's eyes darkened. "You don't have to prove you're macho, brother."

Fletch laughed. "I'm not. But I refuse to make my men carry a perfectly healthy, strong man down the mountain."

Jacob muttered a sarcastic remark, and Fletch chuckled.

Seconds later the team geared up, and they began the trek down. Jane looked worried as they descended the mountain. Fletch gave her an encouraging look, but he kept his senses peeled for trouble in case another shooter was hiding along the way, waiting to ambush them.

JANE GRITTED HER teeth as the rescue team carried her down the mountain. She might not remember her name or the details of her past, but she instinctively knew she wasn't helpless.

She took care of herself and had been doing so for a long time.

As much as she'd been afraid of dying in that cave, she missed the intimacy she'd shared with Fletch. Being alone with him gave her a sense of safety.

Now she felt his brother's eyes scrutinizing her as if he feared she had sinister intentions toward Fletch.

By the time they reached the bottom of the mountain, she'd worn herself out with questions and doubt. How could she blame Fletch for pulling away when her life was a mystery? Worse, when she was wanted for murdering her own husband?

And his brother… Jacob probably thought she was some kind of Black Widow.

The medics loaded her into the back of an ambulance. Fletch stood with them while Jacob and the rescue team spoke in hushed tones, their heads bunched in conversation. The wind drowned out the sound of their voices, leaving her in the dark.

One of the medics radioed the hospital to report her condition, then Fletch joined her in the back of the ambulance.

His brother Jacob shot her a disapproving look as if he suspected she'd seduced his brother into believing her lies. "I'll be right behind the ambulance."

She reined in her temper and said nothing. If she reacted like a hothead or defended herself, she'd only appear more guilty.

At least he hadn't handcuffed her. But she sensed that was coming. Unless she remembered something in her defense.

The ride to the hospital was steeped in silence, the icy sludge on the ground creating a hazard on the road and slowing the ambulance. When they arrived at the emergency entrance, she and Fletch were wheeled into different exam rooms.

The staff immediately checked her vitals and drew blood for lab work, then encouraged her to submit to a rape exam, although she insisted she hadn't been sexually violated. Still, she understood tests were necessary, and as humiliating as it was, she did want to know who'd hurt her. If she'd had sex before she'd been abandoned in the woods, she wanted to know with whom. And if it was consensual.

A CAT scan came next and then an MRI, after which she was moved to a room. There they hooked her up with an IV to hydrate her, and brought her some warm broth.

It seemed like hours later when the doctor finally appeared. He asked her dozens of questions about herself that she couldn't answer. She struggled to tap into that empty well where her past lay, but failed. No, she didn't remember her birthday or where she'd been born. Or if she had a dog or a cat. Or what her favorite color or song was.

Or how long she'd been married…

"The CAT scan was relatively normal," he reported. "There is some slight swelling around your brain, caused from head trauma. That could account for the amnesia you're experiencing."

"And if it's not the swelling?"

"Physical and/or emotional trauma can cause memory loss. Sometimes we repress memories as a way to protect ourselves."

Except not knowing the truth was putting her in more danger.

"Most likely, with rest and time to heal, your memories will return on their own."

"And if they don't?" Jane asked.

"If you want to speak to a therapist, we can arrange

that. There are also alternative treatments, more extensive kinds of psychotherapy, hypnosis, etcetera," he said. "But I don't think we need to go there quite yet."

Of course he didn't. But he wasn't accused of murder.

IMPATIENCE NAGGED AT Fletch as the doctor examined his bullet wound.

"It actually looks good," the doctor said. "You said the woman they brought in removed the bullet and stitched you up?"

"That's right," Fletch replied. And he was anxious to see her again.

"She probably saved you from infection by acting so quickly," the doctor said. "We'll clean your incision and redress it, then you're good to go."

"Thanks." A nurse stepped in and changed the dressing, then Jacob entered the room.

"I'm done," Fletch said as he slid from the exam table. "How's Jane?"

"The doctor wants to keep her overnight for observation. She was dehydrated. He thinks rest may help with the swelling in her brain and the amnesia."

"Did you question her?" Fletch asked.

Jacob grimaced. "Not yet. But I want someone watching her room tonight in case she tries to escape."

Irritation thrummed through Fletch. "No need. I'll stand watch."

Jacob raised his brows. "You were shot, little brother. You need to rest yourself. You probably haven't had a decent meal since you left the bar the other night."

"I'm fine," Fletch insisted. "Besides, Jane trusts me. So if she's going to talk, she might open up to me."

Jacob looked as if he wanted to argue, but finally gave a small nod. "True. But the doc gave her something to help her sleep. She's out for the night now, so I'll stay awhile. Go home, shower and sleep, eat something, then come back in the morning when she wakes up."

Fletch hesitated. But his brother was right. He'd be more clearheaded if he caught some z's. And he needed a shower badly. "All right. But if she wakes, call me."

"Will do. Meanwhile, I need to take Jane's prints and plug them into the system. That will tell us who she is."

Fletch understood Jacob had a job to do. He just hoped to hell that learning Jane's identity would save her, not land her in jail.

THE NEXT MORNING Jane was more rested and less achy. The nurse gave her toiletries for a shower, which made her feel like a new woman.

Jacob's wife sent clean clothes, jeans and a soft blue sweater that were comfortable and warm. A hot breakfast also improved her mood.

Although the grim look in Fletch's eyes when he entered the room with his brother brought reality back fast.

Fletch's gaze skated over her, and for just a moment, she sensed the strong connection they'd shared in the wilderness. A sensual awareness that tempted her to hide in his arms where she'd be safe forever.

This morning he looked sexy in jeans and a denim shirt that accentuated his tanned skin. He'd shaved and she missed the rugged stubble. But the heat in his eyes simmered like the embers of a fire. For a brief second, she wished they'd made love so she could have that memory to keep with her forever.

Then his gaze turned hooded, and an awkwardness settled in the room. "How do you feel this morning?" Fletch asked.

Jane shrugged. "Better. At least clean and fed."

He gave a small smile. "Yeah, me, too."

Jacob cleared his throat. "Has the doctor seen you this morning?"

Jane lifted her chin. "He said I'm clear to go. I'm waiting on the nurse to bring discharge papers."

"What was his opinion regarding the amnesia?" Fletch asked.

Jane pulled a card from the pocket of the jeans. "He gave me a referral to a therapist who might help. She specializes in memory recovery."

"That sounds promising," Fletch said.

Jane exhaled. "I'm supposed to call and set up an appointment." She glanced at Jacob. "That is, if I'm free to do that."

Jacob gave her a flat look. "Last night Officer Clemmens contacted me again. He's the officer who contacted me with the initial report about you. He sent a photograph and confirmation of your identity." Jacob shifted. "Bianca Renard, you are under arrest for the murder of Victor Renard. You have the right to remain silent…"

Knots curled in Jane's gut as he Mirandized her. She'd known this moment might arrive, but being treated like a criminal was humiliating.

"I'm sorry, Jane," Fletch said.

Jane lifted her chin. "I guess it's time I face the truth." Even if she didn't like what she learned about herself.

The nurse poked her head inside, and Jane waved her in. She signed the discharge papers, and was forced to ride to the exit in a wheelchair where the sheriff's car waited.

At least he didn't handcuff her. But the moment the police car door shut, she felt trapped again. She had fought for her life in the woods.

Now she had to fight again.

FLETCH FOLLOWED JACOB to the police station in Whistler, battling anger at the fact that his brother had just arrested Jane. Why he should care so much about a woman he'd known such a short time, and one he knew virtually nothing about, he didn't know.

But he did care, dammit. And he didn't want to see her locked away.

What if she is a murderer?

No…if she *had* killed her husband, there was a reason. A damn good one. He felt it in his soul.

Although he'd been wrong about another woman once. Hannah. She was beautiful and blonde and had the face and voice of an angel.

Too bad she'd possessed the soul of the devil.

Jane sat stone-still as Jacob drove. Fletch admired her steely determination to maintain her composure.

He understood Jacob had to do his job, and couldn't ignore the fact that Jane was wanted in another jurisdiction for murder. If he let her go, the people of Whistler would never trust him to protect them.

Still, Fletch didn't like it one damn bit.

He arrived at the station behind Jacob, his pulse hammering as Jacob opened the back door to his car and helped Jane out.

The hair on the back of his neck prickled. Someone had tried to kill Jane in the woods.

Maybe they still wanted her dead.

As she climbed from the car, he searched the alley by the station and the parking lot for a shooter waiting to ambush.

Chapter Fourteen

A new layer of humiliation washed over Jane as Sheriff Maverick—she couldn't call him Jacob when he was arresting her—fingerprinted her and swabbed her mouth for DNA. A mug shot photo came next.

He escorted her to a small room off the hallway behind the front office. Interrogation Room 1. She was surprised the small town needed more than one, and would have expected crime to be minimal in Whistler.

Then again, the town was so close to the Appalachian Trail that it might attract criminals who wanted to hide out from the law.

She sank into the hard metal chair in front of a wooden table that was bolted to the floor. The sheriff's boots clicked on the wood slats as he crossed to the other side, claimed a seat and placed a manila envelope on the table.

He and Fletch looked like brothers, although their eyes were different and Fletch's hair was longer and shaggy-looking. Fletch also possessed a sexy rawness that made her stomach flutter where Jacob seemed closed off.

Part of his job. He was here to question her, wrangle a confession from her, send her to prison for murder. Not be her friend.

The stain from the fingerprint ink mocked her, and déjà vu struck her. Something about the room, the table, the situation seemed familiar, as if she'd sat at a table like this before. Had she been arrested in the past?

The sheriff pushed a bottle of water in front of her. "The doctor said to stay hydrated."

A sarcastic chuckle rumbled from her. "You're concerned about my health?"

The man's eyes turned stony. "Listen, Jane or Bianca, whatever your name is. I'm aware my brother thinks you're innocent, and I'm not here to railroad you into jail for a crime you didn't commit. But we have to talk."

Jane bit her lip. He was right.

"Let's start with what happened to you. How you ended up on the trail where Fletch found you."

Jane inhaled a deep breath and relayed what little she remembered.

The sheriff studied her, his expression neutral. "So you remember seeing the man you believe to be your husband fall to his death. Then the next thing you remember is running from a man in the woods?"

Jane nodded, straining to recall more details, but the effort was futile and made her head throb.

"What do you remember about the man chasing you? Body size? Height? Color of hair?"

She pinched the bridge of her nose. "He was tall, I think, taller than me. He approached me from behind, so I didn't see his face." She traced her fingers over the back of her head. "He hit me and knocked me out."

Jacob continued, "Then he tied you up and left you in a cave?"

Jane pursed her lips. "I think so, although I just vaguely recall being dragged through the snow there, then I passed out. When I came to, I untied myself and was escaping when he caught me again."

The sheriff folded his arms. "Do you think he was the man you shot?"

Jane released a weary breath. "I honestly don't know. Have you identified him?"

"Not yet. The rescue team recovered his body, and he's on the way to the morgue. So is the other dead man you guys found on those rocks."

She shifted. "I have no idea who he was, either. Although something about him seemed familiar."

"Interesting." He worked his mouth from side to side. "What about the name Bianca? And Victor Renard?"

She fisted her hands on the table in frustration. "Not really… Bianca doesn't feel right."

His mouth quirked up. "Well, we should know soon enough. We're running the DNA and your prints ASAP. Meanwhile, Officer Clemmens faxed me photographs of your husband's murder."

His look darkened as he opened the envelope and spread several photographs on the table.

Jane's pulse hammered at the sight of the man's bloody body. This man was supposed to be Victor, her husband.

She leaned closer and peered at his twisted arm and hand. The tattoo…it was there. The wolf…

Lone wolf… He'd given himself the nickname because he considered himself a loner.

But he'd definitely slipped the wedding ring on her finger. If he was a lone wolf, why had he decided to marry her?

The sheriff pointed to another photograph. This one of a .38. "This is the gun that killed Victor Renard," he said. "We're running the prints on the weapon and will compare to yours. The crime report from the scene revealed a hair strand was found, one that matches your color and length."

Of course they did, Jane thought. Everything, even the snippet of her memory, pointed to her as the killer.

He set a sheet of paper on the table. "This is a printout showing financial reports from Victor and Bianca Renard's account. It appears there are large sums of money that disappeared, payouts to an offshore account in the name of Sonja Simmons. Does that name sound familiar?"

"No," Jane said flatly.

"The policeman I spoke with believes she was Victor's lover, and that they were planning to disappear together." He produced another sheet with a photograph that resembled her. "He also discovered that you had another alias. Geneva Armstrong."

Jane didn't know what to make of the alias or any of this. "Let me guess," Jane said. "They think I killed Victor because he was leaving me for another woman."

Jacob lifted his shoulders in a small shrug. "It's a motive."

Jane kept her mouth shut. Somehow she didn't picture herself as a jealous woman. Or one who cared about money.

But it was difficult to argue with cold, hard evidence.

WATCHING HIS BROTHER interrogate Jane gnawed at Fletch's nerves. It had taken a half hour to convince Jacob to let him watch the interview, but he'd finally persuaded his brother he could read the nuances of Jane's expressions.

Jacob had stipulated that Fletch remain in the viewing room and not interfere.

It was getting more difficult every second to keep that promise.

Especially when Jacob was presenting such strong evidence against Jane. Evidence that made Fletch question whether he really knew her.

Jacob gestured toward one of the crime photos. "Do you recognize Victor Renard?"

Jane's face looked ashen. "Yes. And no."

"What does that mean?" Jacob asked bluntly.

Jane sighed and ran a hand through her hair. "I don't really remember him, but I had a nightmare about him. It was just a quick flash, but I saw his body bouncing backward as the bullet struck him."

Fletch swallowed hard. For the first time since Jacob had met them outside that cave, he realized Jane probably needed a lawyer.

"Did you see the murder weapon?" Jacob asked.

Jane cut her eyes toward the camera in the corner. Fletch shifted restlessly. Did she know he was watching?

Jacob leaned across the table, hands folded. "Did you see the gun, Jane?"

"I saw the gun dropping to the floor, but I don't remember seeing the shooter's face."

Jacob drummed his fingers on the table. "Victor was a real estate broker. He and Bianca worked together," Jacob paused. "Apparently they made millions in Florida and recently moved to North Carolina."

Jane sat unmoving, her shoulders squared.

Jacob removed another photo from the envelope and pushed it toward her. The photograph was an advertisement for Renard's Real Estate and Brokerage Company with a picture of her and Victor smiling side by side in front of a large Colonial house.

Her stomach fluttered as she examined it. "I… This can't be real."

Jacob crossed his arms. "What do you mean, it can't be real?"

Jane stared at him blankly, then a knock sounded on the

door, and Jacob stood and went to answer it. Jacob's receptionist appeared at the door and spoke in a hushed tone.

He frowned, then turned, and walked back to the table. Anger hardened his voice as he began to shove the pictures back in the envelope. "I guess this interview is over. Apparently your lawyer has arrived."

Jane's brows shot up as if she hadn't expected the lawyer's appearance. "My lawyer?"

"That's what he said," Jacob replied. "I'll show him in."

Jane looked baffled as Jacob left the room, and Fletch hurried to talk to him.

He cornered him in the hallway before he reached the front. "What's going on? Did Jane call a lawyer?"

"No," Jacob said. "But one showed up."

"Who is he?"

"I don't know. I'm going to meet him now."

As they stepped into the front reception area, a tall man with short dark hair stood by the receptionist's desk. He was slender and polished, his expensive suit and manicured nails screaming old money.

He buttoned the top button of his charcoal gray jacket, then extended his hand to Jacob. "Sheriff, my name is Woodruff Halls. I'm here about Bianca Renard."

As Jacob shook the man's hand, Fletch couldn't help but compare the two. Like Fletch's own hands, Jacob's were calloused and rough from doing hard work. This man's skin looked so smooth he'd probably never done a minute of physical labor in his life.

Jacob cleared his throat. "How did you know Jane Doe, the woman you call Bianca Renard, was here?"

Halls tapped his finger on his phone. "I spoke with Officer Clemmens." He adjusted his tie. "I also happen to know Mrs. Renard personally. She and her husband and I were friends. I understand Bianca is accused of murdering Victor, but I believe wholeheartedly in her innocence. That's the reason I rushed here. I don't intend to allow her to be tried and convicted for a crime she didn't commit. Or…to be assigned some legal aid attorney who has too many cases to investigate and represent her properly."

Fletch jammed his hands in the pockets of his jeans but kept his eyes trained on Halls. The man spoke with conviction, as if he strongly believed in Jane's innocence.

But Fletch still couldn't reconcile what he'd learned about Victor and Bianca to Jane. She didn't strike him as the type to care about money or fancy houses, or to hang around with men like Halls.

Of course he'd only known her for a few days, and in that time they'd been fighting to survive the blizzard and a hired gunman.

Jacob cleared his throat. "May I see your ID please?"

"Of course." Halls removed a business card from the top pocket of his jacket and handed it to Jacob. "Now I'd like to see my client, please."

Jacob gestured for Halls to follow him. He shot Fletch a look warning him to stay put. But Fletch didn't intend to stand by and let this guy take over without seeing Jane's reaction to him.

He waited until Jacob and the lawyer entered the interrogation room, then he hurried down the hall into the viewing room.

Jane's jaw worked as she swallowed, and when she raised her head to look at the lawyer, every muscle in her body stiffened. She went so still that for a moment, Fletch wondered if she was even breathing.

"Jane," Jacob said. "This man is Woodruff Halls. He claims he's representing you."

She folded her arms and offered the man a cool look.

Halls's tone turned curt. "I'd like to speak to my client

in private." He gestured toward the small camera in the top corner of the room. "And shut that thing off."

Jacob held his arms by his sides, but Fletch recognized anger in the slight tensing of his body. "Jane?"

Her eyes turned to ice chips as she stared at Halls. Then she lifted her hand in a tiny motion signifying it was okay for Jacob to leave her alone with the man.

Fletch didn't like what was happening, but he felt helpless to stop it.

A second later, the TV screen blurred into snowy static, and he was left in the dark as to what was happening in that room.

JANE FELT AS if she was shutting down. She had no idea who this man who claimed to be her lawyer was.

But something about him sent chills up her spine.

"Bianca, or should I call you Jane?" the slickly dressed man asked.

"Jane for now," she said. *Bianca* still didn't feel right. Maybe she was in denial because she didn't want to believe that she was a cold-blooded killer.

"All right, Jane, I have to warn you that as of this moment, you talk to no one but me. Don't answer any more questions. Don't make any calls. Don't give in to the sheriff's pressure tactics and confess to something you may or may not have done."

Jane swallowed. "You think I killed this man Victor?"

Halls ran long, slender fingers through his gelled hair. "That's not what I said. But I'm advising you against a confession. Not until we exhaust all possibilities."

Anger simmered deep inside her, but she forced herself to be calm. "What do you know about Victor and his death?"

He pressed his lips into a thin line. "Just what the police

have told me. But I understand you have amnesia, and we can use that to bargain for time. I've requested an emergency bail hearing for this afternoon so I can arrange for your release. Then we can explore your defense strategy."

He reached out and covered her hand with his.

A shudder coursed through Jane. Every bone in her body screamed that something was wrong here.

That this man wasn't who he claimed.

Chapter Fifteen

Fletch's stomach knotted as he watched Jane and her lawyer file into the courtroom. Due to Jane's amnesia, Halls had managed to finagle an emergency hearing with the local judge that afternoon.

He was relieved Jane wouldn't have to spend the night in jail, but the thought of her being released with nowhere to go disturbed him.

Jacob addressed the judge and read the charges. Halls stood and suggested bail be set and Jane be released into his custody.

"At this point, all evidence against my client is circumstantial and this woman is ill and does not appear to be a flight risk. I will personally assure the court that she will not flee the country and will be available for questioning when necessary. Meanwhile my client has agreed to enter a therapy program to help her regain her memory of the night in question."

The judge's hand shot up. "We are not here to try the case, Mr. Halls. But considering the extenuating circumstances, I agree the best course for obtaining justice is for Jane Doe to enter counseling. Bail is set at one hundred thousand dollars."

Halls smiled and adjusted his tie. "Thank you, Your Honor."

The judge pounded his gavel and dismissed the court.

Jacob stood and Fletch moved up beside him. He silently willed Jane to look at him, but she didn't. She seemed stoic and resigned.

Halls escorted her to the court clerk to settle bail. "I don't like him," Fletch said in a low growl.

"Any specific reason?" Jacob asked.

Fletch scrunched his nose in thought. "I can't put my finger on it."

"Maybe you're just too close to the situation," Jacob said. "Too close to Jane."

Fletch made a low sound in his throat. "I guess since I found her, I feel protective of her," he admitted. "Part of my job. Now it's hard to walk away."

Jacob gave him a half-cocked smile. "You sure it was just the job?"

No, he wasn't. But he wasn't about to confess that he'd almost made love to Jane. That he still wanted to. That he'd fantasized about clearing her name and taking her to his house and spending all night giving her pleasure.

"Just check that lawyer out," Fletch said, avoiding the question. "Make sure he's who he says he is."

"I plan to. And I'm still waiting on fingerprint and DNA results on Jane, as well as the evidence you brought in."

"Where do we stand on the bodies recovered from the trail?"

"Both men are at the morgue. Waiting on autopsies."

"Identifying them might tell us more about what happened," Fletch said.

While Halls posted bail, Fletch crossed the room into the hallway and called Jane's name.

She'd looked calm and composed in the courtroom, but he detected fear beneath that calm facade.

"Jane, do you recognize this lawyer?"

She shook her head. "He says he knows where I live,

that he's driving me to my house." She gave a small shrug. "Going home might trigger my memories."

True. "I can go with you," Fletch offered.

Halls stepped over to join them. "That's not a good idea," Halls said. "Bianca, this man is the sheriff's brother. He could be fishing for information to share with the sheriff, information to use against you."

Jane's eyes flickered with unease as if she hadn't considered that possibility. Fletch gritted his teeth. Didn't she know him any better than that?

Halls took Jane's arm. "Come on, let's get you out of here. Being in your own environment might prompt a breakthrough with your memory loss."

Fletch rushed to catch up with them as Halls herded her out the door. Fletch slipped his business card into the pocket of her jacket. "He's wrong about me," he murmured close to her ear. "Call me if you need me."

Halls glared at him. "I thought I made myself clear, Mr. Maverick. Leave my client alone. She is to talk to no one but me."

Then he hustled Jane out the door toward a black Cadillac. A minute later, Halls drove away, carrying Jane with him.

JANE HAD DREADED spending the night in jail, but leaving with this virtual stranger intensified her feelings of trepidation.

When he'd addressed the judge, she had a sudden flashback. Halls was standing in the room with her when her husband had been shot.

But that didn't make sense. Was her mind playing tricks on her?

If Halls had been at the scene, did he know who'd killed

her husband? If so, why hadn't he pointed the police in the direction of the real killer?

He steered his Cadillac out of town and veered onto the highway. "Where are we going?" Jane asked.

His cool gray eyes skated over her, then back to the road. "To your weekend house," he said. "Like I told the judge, being home might help trigger your memory of that night."

Jane twisted her hands together in her lap. "Is that where my husband was shot?"

He breathed out, low and steady. "Yes. You guys own a beautiful mountain cabin outside of Asheville."

"And I was an interior decorator?"

"That's right. You and Victor worked together."

Jane studied him. "What kind of law do you practice?"

He kept his eyes on the road as he sped around a curve. "Currently I handle divorce cases, but I litigated criminal cases early in my career."

But now he specialized in divorce? "How did you know me and Victor?" Jane asked. "Were we filing for a divorce?"

He tapped the steering wheel as he turned off the main highway onto the road leading toward Asheville. "No. Victor sold me my house, and you decorated it. You were such a power couple that I recommended your services to some of my acquaintances, then we became friends."

Jane worried her bottom lip with her teeth. "You said you believe that I'm innocent. What about the evidence the sheriff had against me?"

"All circumstantial." He loosened his tie.

She latched on to that fact. "Tell me more about my relationship with Victor."

"You were madly in love with Victor, and he felt the

same about you. Your marriage was stable. No infidelity on either part. In fact, you were planning a family."

They were? Jane mentally chastised herself. If they were so in love and planning a family, why couldn't she remember him or their wedding?

Because his death was too traumatic? Because she'd witnessed it?

"Nothing feels right," Jane said. "One of the few memories I have is the moment his body flew backward when the bullet pierced his chest."

Halls's breath punctuated the air. "So you witnessed the shooting?"

Jane shook her head. "I think so, but I don't remember the shooter's face, although..."

The car slowed as he maneuvered a turn, and he cut a sideways look at her. "Although what?"

Jane decided on the direct approach. "I thought you were there. I...saw you."

A vein throbbed in his neck. "You're obviously confused, Bianca. I have been to your house, but I was definitely not there the night Victor died."

His gray eyes skated over as if to say that was the end of the subject.

"Why don't you close your eyes and rest? It'll take about an hour to reach the house."

Jane's heart hammered. She didn't trust Halls. But hopefully when she revisited the place where Victor was killed, the past would come back to her.

"SOMETHING ABOUT THAT lawyer seems off to me," Fletch told Jacob.

Jacob chuckled. "Maybe you don't like the fact that Jane is with him and not you."

His brother had hit the nail on the head. Not that Jane

was with him… "Can you run a background check on him?" Fletch asked. "Verify he's not some fake?"

"I'm on it as soon as we get back to the station," Jacob said. "I called Liam for help, too. He has resources that I don't."

Fletch thanked him, then they both climbed in their cars and drove back to the police station. He spoke to Jacob's deputy, Martin Rowan, and grabbed a cup of coffee on his way to Jacob's office. Jacob did the same, then sank in his desk chair and turned to his computer.

Jacob entered the name Woodruff Halls and ran a search. Fletch pulled a chair up to the desk and stared over Jacob's shoulder as information spilled onto the screen.

"He has no record, no arrests," Jacob said. "Here's his website. Halls Attorney at Law." The photograph of the lawyer was even more polished than the real man who'd appeared in court. Photoshop could do wonders these days.

Jacob maneuvered the site, and Fletch skimmed several reviews from clients, all glowing and praising his professionalism. Male clients seemed to be especially vocal about their settlements. Two had raved about how he'd stuck it to their cheating spouses.

Another section detailed criminal cases Halls had tried when he'd first graduated from law school. Nothing major, mostly petty crimes.

"He probably realized divorce cases were more profitable and switched specialties," Jacob muttered in disdain.

Fletch grimaced. On paper, the man was exactly who he claimed to be.

A knock sounded at the door and Liam poked his head in. "Hey, guys."

Jacob waved him inside, and Liam glanced at the computer screen.

"Just checked out the lawyer representing Jane Doe," Jacob said.

Liam gave them a grim look. "That's what I wanted to talk to you about."

Fletch's pulse jumped. His brother had answers. Hopefully to help clear Jane, not to prove her guilt. "Tell us what you learned."

Liam leaned one hip on the desk. "That's just it. I didn't find anything on Bianca and Victor Renard."

"What do you mean?" Jacob asked. "No record of arrests on their part? Their business was legit, with no complaints?"

Liam rested his arm on his leg. "I mean I didn't find *anything*, as in no record that Bianca or Victor Renard even exist."

Fletch's response died in his throat.

"How is that possible?" Jacob pushed away from his computer. "The report I received about the missing person matching Jane Doe's description came from a police officer. So did copies of the prints and crime scene report."

Liam made a clicking sound with his teeth. "I don't know what's going on, Jacob. But I looked into that officer and he's been suspended for accepting bribes. He could have intercepted your inquiry about the missing persons, and responded with a fake report."

Fletch's mind raced.

A second later, panic seized him. "If Bianca and Victor Renard don't exist, why the hell did Halls show up to defend Jane? Why did he claim he knew them personally and that Jane was innocent?"

"Good question," Liam said.

Jacob coughed into his hand. "If Jane is not Bianca, who is she?"

Fletch stood, fear hacking away at his calm. He'd started

to believe that Jane had lied to him. That she was making a fool out of him as Hannah had done.

But this was different. Very, very different. Something was wrong.

Jane was in danger.

JANE STARTLED AS the car jerked to a stop. She was dazed and confused. She'd been dreaming about Fletch, not the shooting or her dead parents or other dead bodies and blood.

Halls veered onto a side road that led into deep woods. The hair on the back of her neck prickled.

"I thought we lived in a subdivision," Jane said, drawing on the fleeting pieces of memories she'd recovered.

Halls rolled his shoulders. "You own a house in a subdivision, but this was your second home, your private getaway."

Jane gripped the edge of the seat. Something about these woods seemed familiar. Yet strangely odd.

Ominous. Deserted.

"I'm not ready for this," she said, her voice cracking. "I…think I should go to a hotel for the night or at least to the house in the subdivision."

His voice grew icy. "I thought you wanted to remember what happened so you could clear your name."

Perspiration beaded on Jane's neck. "I do, but the doctor warned me not to push it, that I would remember when I'm mentally ready."

The car bounced over ruts in the road, the woods swallowing them into the darkness as he drove down a narrow graveled road.

"Really, Mr. Halls—"

"It's Woodruff, Bianca." He covered her hand with his. His skin felt clammy, cold, and his reassuring squeeze made her skin crawl. "Remember, we're friends. And I'm here to help."

"Then please take me back," she said firmly. "I told you I'm not ready to do this."

He kept driving. "It may be difficult to face what happened, but once you remember who shot Victor, you'll thank me."

She doubted it. But it seemed futile to argue. He was barreling ahead, oblivious to her rising panic.

They drove deeper into the woods. A few cabins dotted the hills here and there. The towering trees and sharp ridges reminded her of when she'd been lost on the trail, running for her life.

Finally they reached a clearing where a small log cabin sat. The mountains rose in the background, tall and ominous-looking, as if the cabin had been built in the center of the ridges to offer privacy. Yet it was so secluded, it also seemed...dangerous.

Her skin prickled again. She didn't want to be isolated right now. She ached to be back with Fletch, with people surrounding her, people she could trust.

"Here we are." The lawyer parked and slid from the vehicle, then walked around to the passenger side and opened the door.

Jane sat frozen in the seat, her chest aching with the effort to breathe.

"Come on, Jane, let's go inside."

Fear choked her. Halls reached for her hand, and she stared at the long, manicured fingers. That black signet ring with the gold *H* on it. Those fingers wrapped around a...gun...

Suddenly the world blurred...

A gunshot sounded, then a shout, and she saw her husband falling, blood spraying.

She screamed, turned and picked up the gun on the floor. But someone jumped her and threw her to the ground. The gun went off again, then she was clawing at the man on top of her, fighting him off.

"Bianca?"

A man's voice jarred her from the images, but when she looked up at the lawyer, she knew he had lied.

Halls had been there. His hands…that signet ring…

She had to get away from him.

She shoved her feet upward and kicked him, knocking him to the ground. Then she jumped over the console, started the engine again and peeled down the driveway.

Whoever Halls was, he wasn't her friend.

Chapter Sixteen

Jane pressed the accelerator and flew down the narrow road, gravel spewing from the lawyer's car.

Maybe she was making a mistake. Maybe she'd simply had an anxiety attack at the prospect of revisiting the scene of her husband's murder. Maybe Halls hadn't been at the scene of the shooting.

But the moment he'd walked into the interrogation room at the jail, an eerie sense that he was dangerous had overwhelmed her.

And that signet ring. She wasn't paranoid. He *was* there. He had lied.

She glanced over her shoulder to see if he was following. Thankfully she hadn't seen another car at the cabin, so he couldn't be behind her.

Relief rushed through her, and she maneuvered the turns through the woods until she connected to the main highway. She didn't know where she was going, only that she had to escape Halls.

She didn't trust him.

Without knowing who she was, she couldn't trust anyone.

Except... Fletch.

Halls's words about Fletch feeding information to his brother taunted her. He could be right.

Except she'd felt a connection between her and Fletch. A trust that she certainly hadn't felt with the lawyer.

She pressed the accelerator and checked over her shoulder again. He might have called the police on her. Traffic on the main highway buzzed by.

A siren wailed and she froze, body rigid as she glanced up and saw a police car zooming closer behind her.

Dear God, he had called the cops on her. Told them she was skipping bail. That she'd stolen his car.

She held her breath, slowed and pulled over into the right lane. A second later, the police car raced by.

Thank God.

Her hands felt clammy as she clenched the steering wheel. She had no idea where to go or what to do now.

Mentally, she tossed around different ideas as she drove toward Whistler. She could find a place and hide out. No. Running like a criminal would only make things worse. She wanted the truth, to know who she was.

And why someone wanted her dead.

Traffic thickened, and she fell into one lane, maintaining a steady speed so as not to attract attention.

She had to get rid of Halls's car. If he had reported it stolen, the police would be looking for it. Worse, they'd add auto theft to her murder charge.

Heart racing, she drove another thirty miles until she ventured into the farmland and countryside between Asheville and Whistler. Mountains rose, the snowcapped ridges gleaming in the light, a reminder that she'd almost died on the trail.

She would have if not for Fletch.

Making a snap decision, she scanned the exit signs for a place to get off. Then she could ditch this car and figure out what to do.

She steered Halls's Cadillac onto a dirt road not far

from the next little town. Fear pulsed through her along with guilt.

She wasn't a criminal...she felt that in her bones. But she had to do what she had to do. Halls was dangerous. She just needed to prove it.

Desperate for answers, she rummaged through his car. Except for an overcoat and gloves, the back seat was empty. She searched his console and found some loose change and cash. Next she looked inside the dashboard.

Insurance, registration. A pack of cigarettes and a lighter. Mints. A photograph. She pulled it out and looked at it. Halls's face stared back, but he wasn't alone. He was posed with a brunette about his age, his arm around her shoulders. The woman was attractive but looked stiff in the picture, as if she was unhappy about something.

Hmm. Must be his wife. She flipped the photograph and searched for a name. If she could talk to the wife, maybe she'd tell her if Halls was legit.

Or maybe she'd turn you in.

Hoping to find something helpful, she tugged her jacket around her and slid from the vehicle, then unlocked the trunk. She held her breath, half expecting to find a dead body inside. Maybe she'd watched too many horror movies.

No body, but she found a briefcase. She jimmied the lock and peered inside it. A couple of file folders containing papers and notes about divorce cases he was working on. Business cards.

She stuffed one of his cards in her pocket. Then she checked the side compartment and found another photo.

A picture of her and the man with the wolf tattoo on his arm. Her husband...

The world blurred, her legs buckling as emotions swirled inside her. Nausea rose to her throat, and she leaned against the car and bowed her head to stem the sick feeling. The ground seemed to open, and she felt as if she was falling into it, sliding deeper and deeper into a dark hole.

She pounded the car. Dammit, she wanted to see what was in that dark void.

Forcing air through her mouth, she fought through the nausea until the world finally righted again. Angry at her loss of control but more determined than ever to unearth her memories, she stuck the photograph in her jacket pocket, then shoved the briefcase back into the trunk and closed it.

Traffic noises from the highway echoed in the distance. She slipped past several boulders and walked along the shoulder of the narrow side road to the little town, ducking behind rocks and bushes as cars passed.

A sign for a coffee and pastry shop named The Bean caught her eye as she entered the town, and she walked up to the gas station beside it and asked if they had a pay phone.

An older man in overalls gestured toward an ancient-looking landline on the counter. "Long as it's not long distance, you're welcome to use it."

She thanked him then removed Halls's business card from her pocket and punched the number.

A minute later, a receptionist answered. "Andrea Horton, Halls Attorney at Law. How may I help you?"

"I'm trying to reach Mr. Halls's wife—"

"I'm sorry, but Mr. and Mrs. Halls are divorced. I couldn't divulge her personal contact information even if they were together."

Jane wondered exactly what had happened between them, but she didn't have a chance to ask. The line went dead in her hands.

FLETCH PACED JACOB'S OFFICE. "If Halls lied about Jane being Bianca Renard, what else did he lie about?"

Jacob pulled a hand down his chin. "Good question."

Liam phoned the lab and asked them to put a rush on Jane's fingerprints and DNA. "Do you have some results?" A pause, then Liam switched the caller to speakerphone.

"Yeah," Chad, the FBI analyst, said, "some info on the body of the man found on the rocks at Crow's Point."

"Go on."

"His name was Neil Akryn. PI out of a small town near Asheville."

Fletch, Jacob and Liam exchanged looks. "Did he work alone?" Liam asked.

"No, had a partner named Wiley Farmer. I put in a call to him but haven't heard back."

Liam's expression turned dark. "Have an officer check his office and home. See if they can locate him ASAP."

Fletch gritted his teeth as he waited.

"Ballistics from the bullet we removed from Akryn match the gun from your other dead man," Chad continued.

Liam made a clicking sound with his teeth. "So the man our Jane Doe shot killed Akryn?"

"Appears to be that way," Chad answered.

"Who is the man our Jane Doe shot?" Liam asked.

"Still working on his ID."

Liam snapped his fingers. "Officer Clemmens fabricated the evidence against Jane. But she recalls seeing a man she believes was her husband shot. Check morgues in and around Asheville and neighboring cities. See if any bodies turn up under the name of Victor Renard. And alert me as soon as the results of Jane Doe's prints and DNA are in."

"Will do."

Jacob furrowed his brows as Liam ended the call. "So what was a PI doing out on the trail? Looking for Jane Doe?"

Fletch shrugged. "Or Bianca? But we know Jane isn't Bianca." Fletch ran a hand through his hair. "And what's happening with Clemmens?"

"He disappeared, but our people are looking for him." Liam pinched the bridge of his nose. "Fletch, I need to know everything Jane told you while you were in those woods. Even the smallest detail might help solve this case."

Fletch sighed. "Let me grab some more coffee."

His brothers followed him for refills, and they carried their mugs back to Jacob's office.

Fletch sighed. "Before I found Jane, I saw blood in the snow. I followed it, then spotted a wedding ring in some bushes, then I found her. After I carried Jane to the shelter, it took her a while to regain consciousness. When she did, we finally talked. She recognized the ring, said she had a flashback of a man putting it on her finger, but she didn't remember a wedding or her husband's name." He touched the underside of his arm. "The husband had a tattoo of a wolf on his underarm near his wrist."

"Good detail. I'll have someone research that type of tattoo," Liam said. "What else?"

"When Jane was sleeping, she had nightmares about her parents' murder," Fletch said. "She was in her bedroom when she heard a noise. It sounded like someone breaking in. Then she heard gunshots. She hid in her closet for hours after the noise stopped and found her parents' bodies the next morning." He paused, disturbed by the image of a little girl discovering her parents' bloody corpses. "She was only twelve."

Jacob cursed. "That must have been traumatizing."

"A home invasion," Liam commented. "The question is was it random or was the couple targeted for a reason?"

Fletch cleared his throat. "She didn't remember, but she did say she thought her father was either a lawyer or a judge."

Liam worked his mouth from side to side. "Was the killer caught?"

Fletch shook his head. "That's all she told me about them."

"So we can't totally discount a connection to Jane's current situation?" Jacob muttered.

Liam folded his hands. "What would you estimate Jane's age to be now?"

"Early thirties. Maybe thirty-two, thirty-three?"

"That murder was bound to make the news. It's a long shot that it's related to Jane's current problems, but it will help narrow down her ID. I'll get someone on it right away."

"What else did she remember?" Jacob asked.

Fletch debated on how much to say. But they couldn't find the truth if he wasn't honest. His brothers were here to help. "She remembered seeing her husband's body flying backward and blood spewing, but she insists she didn't see the shooter's face."

A strained silence for a minute, then Liam shifted. "Tell us about the shooting with the bearded gunman. How exactly did Jane obtain your gun?"

Fletch hardened his jaw. "We were hiking and came upon the shelter at Stone's Ledge. I saw rope inside, and Jane recalled being tied and gagged and left there. She managed to untie herself and escape, but her attacker caught her. That's when he knocked her over the head and left her out in the storm to die."

"What a bastard," Jacob said.

Fletch gritted his teeth. "I collected the rope and bagged it, then we set off on the trail again. A little while later, we were ambushed. I grabbed Jane and we darted toward a boulder to take cover, but I took a bullet to the leg. As I fell, my gun slipped from my hand."

"Dammit, Fletch," Liam said. "You could have been killed."

"But I wasn't," Fletch said. "Then the man jumped Jane. She fought him off, grabbed my gun and shot him."

"She fought him off?" Jacob asked.

Fletch nodded. "I know it's hard to believe, but she had serious skills. Maybe from self-defense classes."

"And the shooting?" Liam asked. "She shot the man right between the eyes."

Fletch wiped sweat from the back of his neck. "It was impressive."

"She had experience, Fletch," Liam said. "Coupled with her fighting skills and marksmanship, it sounds like she had training in the military or…law enforcement."

Liam clenched his phone. "Let me text Chad and have him check military and police databases. If she had training either place, her prints will be in the system."

Fletch's phone buzzed on his hip, and he checked the number. Unknown. "I need to take this call. Work."

Fletch stepped from the room and quickly connected the call. "Hello."

"Fletch…" Jane's voice sounded breathless. "I'm in trouble. Please help me."

His blood turned to ice. "Where are you?"

She gave him an address somewhere between Whistler and Asheville. "Is Halls still with you?"

"No," Jane rasped. "He's not who he says he is. I…took his car and ran."

Relief momentarily filled him. "Good. Stay put. I'll be right there."

He didn't bother to tell his brothers where he was going, for fear they'd try to stop him. Instead he rushed past Jacob's receptionist and through the door. Outside, he jogged to his car, jumped in and peeled away.

He had to find Jane before Halls did.

JANE SAT HOLED up in the back of the tiny coffee shop, every nerve cell in her body on edge. She'd used the money in the console of Halls's car and bought one of the souvenir ball caps sporting the name of the town to wear as a disguise.

The waitress, a sweet young girl named Trish, approached, a pencil and order pad in her hand. Trish's smile was big and wide, her lipstick a little too pink, with matching blush on her cheeks. Jane ordered plain coffee.

Trish insisted The Bean also served the best apple pie in the state. "Add a scoop of homemade vanilla ice cream on it and you'll think you died and went to heaven, honey."

Jane thanked her but politely declined. Her stomach was rolling too much to think about food.

Instead she noted the decor on the walls. Local artists' paintings depicted beautiful mountain scenes, fishing camps, hiking trails, white water rafting excursions, animals and the natural wonders of the forest.

A mixture of country and gospel music wafted through the room, and CDs by a local singer/songwriter was displayed by the cash register for sale. Trish and the owner, an older woman with wiry pink hair and a flour-dusted apron, greeted everyone who entered by name.

Except for her. She was the stranger. Alone. Trish had asked her what she was doing in Beaver Ridge, and she relayed the story she'd fabricated as a cover. She and her boyfriend were meeting for a romantic getaway at some cabins three miles north of Beaver Ridge. She'd noted the sign advertising the rental units on her way into town.

She'd left Halls's Cadillac parked a couple of miles outside of the city limits on what appeared to be a deserted graveled road, and walked the rest of the way in.

Trish brought her a refill, and she was grateful she'd ordered decaf. Any more caffeine and her hands would be shaking like a leaf in the wind.

The wooden door opened, and two men in police uniforms loped in, both brawny and ominous-looking. Jane held her breath as one of them glanced around the café, then they scooted onto the barstools at the coffee counter.

Jane tugged the ball cap lower on her head and angled herself so she could watch them without looking conspicuous. They ordered coffee and, no surprise, the pie with ice cream, then chatted with Trish while they waited on their orders.

Jane felt like a criminal on the run. She didn't like it, but she had to lay low until she could prove her innocence.

While she sipped her coffee, she jotted down the details she knew so far about herself on a napkin. Bianca and Victor Renard's name went next, then Woodruff Halls. She wished she had a computer so she could do some digging on her own.

A loud static sound cut through the silence, and she realized the officer was receiving a call. The taller one snagged his piece and responded.

Jane strained to overhear the conversation.

"Stolen vehicle belonging to Attorney Woodruff Halls, 2019 Black Cadillac, License LW2FU, found on Old Salter Road outside of Beaver Ridge. Party responsible thought to be wanted…"

The words faded and the officer glanced across the room again. Fear seizing her, Jane left a ten on the table, then slid from the booth, hunched low and darted toward the rear exit.

Voices echoed behind her, but she didn't look back. She dashed around the corner of the building into the alley and started to run.

Chapter Seventeen

Fletch's pulse pounded as he rolled into Beaver Ridge. He immediately spotted The Bean, where Jane was supposed to be waiting on him, and exhaled in relief.

Although relief vanished when he noticed the police car parked in front. Damn, had Halls reported that Jane had jumped bail? If the man was involved in the crime Jane was accused of committing, why would he tip off the police?

Halls had also met Jacob at his station and appeared in front of a judge.

Pretty audacious to put his face in front of law enforcement if he was trying to hurt Jane.

Praying the cops hadn't found Jane and arrested her, he cruised into the parking lot and swerved into a spot. He quickly surveyed the area. Several cars were in the lot, patrons coming and going.

No Jane.

Willing himself to remain calm, he remembered the cover story Jane had invented and climbed from his vehicle. He kept his senses honed as he crossed the parking lot to the entrance.

By the time he reached it, two cops loped outside, one on his radio, the other jangling his keys.

"We'll canvass the area," the officer informed Dispatch.

They both jumped in the squad car, and the driver

started the engine and backed from their parking spot. Fletch pretended he was deep in conversation on his phone as he passed them.

Before he went inside the café, though, he once again surveyed the parking lot. No Halls. No Jane, either.

The scent of cinnamon, apple pie and strong coffee engulfed him as he entered. The coffee shop was full of mountain charm, a testament to the local artists and an invitation to visitors to explore the area.

People gathered in booths with red checked tablecloths; a seating area near the front boasted a couch and several lounging chairs, and the bar provided seating for individuals and takeout orders.

He scanned the room for Jane but didn't see her at a table or booth. A young waitress sauntered over and smiled up at him. "Hi, I'm Trish. You can sit anywhere, sir. I'll take your order when you're ready."

"Actually I was supposed to meet a young woman here," Fletch said, returning the girl's friendly manner.

Trish's eyes brightened. "Your girlfriend?"

Either she was fishing or she'd spoken with Jane. "That's right. A pretty brunette. We're planning a romantic getaway in the mountains—"

"In those cabins," the girl finished with a grin. "She told me about it. How nice."

Fletch shifted and looked across the room again. "I guess I might be too early?"

"No. She was right back here." Trish walked toward the rear of the shop and paused at the last booth where a half-full coffee mug still sat. "Well, darn, this was her booth."

Fletch pressed his hand over his phone, willing Jane to call. "Would you mind checking the ladies' room for me?"

"Of course not." Trish turned at the end of the hall and ducked inside the ladies'. A second later, she came out, her brows furrowed. "No, not in there. Maybe she stepped out for some fresh air or to grab some souvenirs."

"Probably. I'll give her a call." He squeezed her arm. "Thanks, Trish."

Fletch noticed the back exit. If Jane saw the police officers inside, she might have gotten nervous and left out the back.

He waited until Trish moved to the next booth to take an order, then he hurried through the exit and began to search the alley.

JANE DARTED DOWN several alleys, staying in the shadows, keeping low and out of sight as traffic crawled through the sleepy little town. But even as she ran from the police, she knew she couldn't run forever.

She might not remember her name, but she wasn't a coward. She had to face this situation head-on.

Still, she wasn't ready to go back to jail. Although Fletch might turn her in to his brother, it was a chance she was willing to take.

The police car that had been parked at the café suddenly zoomed by. She released a breath, trying to ignore the acrid odor of garbage, rotting food and stale beer permeating the alleyway.

Knowing Fletch was supposed to meet her at the coffee shop, she turned back toward The Bean.

The rear door of one of the shops opened, and two employees stepped outside and lit up cigarettes. The scent of smoke mingled with the foul garbage odors, and she hurried away. She wove between two other stores until she had a vantage point to the coffee shop parking lot.

Fletch's Wrangler was parked toward the back of the lot beneath a live oak. Jane's breath quickened, and she scanned the area for signs someone was watching. More police could be looking out.

Or Halls. He'd had enough connections to get her bail hearing moved up. What if he had other connections with the law?

She wished like hell she had his cell phone. But he'd had it clipped to his belt and in her haste to escape, she hadn't thought about grabbing it.

She rubbed her temple to regroup.

Seconds ticked by. The feeling that she needed to escape Halls didn't dissipate. The feeling that she wanted to see Fletch didn't, either.

She opened her eyes and glanced across the parking lot again. Two young women and their babies strolled into The Bean. No cops. No one lingering in the parking lot, looking suspicious.

Deciding it was now or never, she ducked low, slinking between a place called the Burger and Brew and Carlos's Cantina. She gripped the edge of the concrete wall and watched. Waited. The coast was clear.

Just as she lunged forward to break into Fletch's Jeep Wrangler, to hide and wait for him, someone grabbed her from behind.

She started to fight, but a hand covered her mouth and a firm muscled arm gripped her around the waist, pressing her so tightly against the man's body that she could barely breathe.

God help her. Had Halls found her?

"Be still, it's all right," Fletch said in a low whisper. "It's me."

Jane froze, her body trembling.

"I'm going to release you," he said into her ear. "Trust me, okay?"

She gave a little nod, and he moved his hand from her mouth and loosened his hold. Her body sagged in relief against him, and she turned in his arms and shoved at him.

Her eyes were wide, dark with anger. "You scared me to death."

"I'm sorry," he said and meant it. "I didn't mean to."

Her chest rose and fell on a labored breath, and she planted her hands on her hips. "There were cops here. Did you call them?"

Fletch felt as if he'd been slapped. "No, Jane. I told you that you could trust me."

"They're looking for me, for Halls's Cadillac," she said, her breathing unsteady.

Fletch scanned the alley, then the parking lot. "Come on, let's get in my Jeep. Then we can talk."

Jane's lower lip quivered. "You're not carrying me back to Jacob, to jail?"

"No," Fletch said earnestly. "But we do need to talk."

Jane's gaze shot to his Jeep as if gauging the distance. Anxious, she started to run, but Fletch caught her and curved his arm around her shoulders. "Hold on. Remember we're a couple on a romantic getaway. We don't want to draw attention."

Jane's eyes brightened. "You're right." She slid her arm around his waist and leaned into him. "Thank you for coming."

Fletch offered her a smile, but his heart was pounding. He wanted the romance to be real. For them to be a couple. For her to be safe and this mess tied up so they could figure out if there was really something between them.

Together they sauntered toward his Jeep, hugging and taking their time so as not to arouse suspicion. When they reached the Jeep, Fletch unlocked the door and Jane slid inside. Just for show, or at least that was what he told himself, he leaned over and gave her a kiss.

Jane's breath caught when he pulled away, a seed of longing sprouting. Or maybe it was surprise. Either way, he closed the door and smiled to himself as he walked around to the driver's side.

A few seconds later, they were buckled up, and he guided his Jeep back onto the highway.

Jane twisted her hands together and stared out the window as if she might find answers somewhere in the ridges and forests. "Where are we going?" she finally asked.

Fletch gritted his teeth. He should call Jacob and Liam. And he would. Just not yet.

"My place," Fletch said. "No one will look for you there."

Except his brothers. And he'd handle them if he had to.

JANE PRESSED HER fingers to her lips. Fletch's kiss taunted her with what-ifs. What if she wasn't mired in a murder investigation? What if someone wasn't trying to kill her?

What if she and Fletch could run away together, for forever?

He hit a pothole, and she winced. *Get a grip. Running isn't the answer.*

But it sure as hell was tempting right now.

Fletch remained silent as he drove, his jaw firmly set. She closed her eyes and forced herself to analyze the shooting and Halls's behavior.

None of it made sense, especially the fact that she kept dreaming of her parents' murder as if it had something to do with the mystery riddling the present.

Her parents had been killed around twenty years ago. She was almost certain the killer had been caught and locked away.

The strain of the day took its toll, and she must have fallen asleep because sometime later, she woke with a start. Fletch's Wrangler bounced over ruts in the road, spewing gravel as he drove down a narrow road into the woods.

For a moment, fear prickled at her. The place looked isolated, far away from the town.

She swallowed hard. God help her, she *was* paranoid. Fletch had saved her life and been nothing but good to her. They'd depended on each other in the wilderness. She had to trust him now.

He parked in front of an A-frame log cabin with a picture window that occupied the entire front of the house. A chimney and the rustic features gave it an inviting feel. Trees, bare of leaves, snaked across the back, climbing into the snow-capped mountains.

"It's beautiful," she murmured.

"I like it," Fletch said, a hint of pride in his tone. "Let's go inside and talk."

Jane opened her car door and climbed out. Mounds of snow and melting slush covered the ground. The sound of river water rippling over rocks echoed from behind Fletch's cabin. He led the way up to his front porch, unlocked the door and stepped inside, flipping on lights as he entered.

Jane followed, awed by the stacked-stone fireplace running from floor to ceiling. A black leather sectional and a blue-and-green braided rug made the room look masculine, but homey and warm. Paintings of the wilderness adorned the wall, and an acoustic guitar leaned against the big club chair by the fireplace.

She imagined Fletch strumming a country song with the firelight flickering off his chiseled jaw, and her body hummed with need.

He walked straight to a wet bar situated in the built-ins flanking the fireplace. "Wine or scotch?" he offered.

"Scotch," Jane said. She wasn't sure she liked it, but the answer came so quickly that she must.

He poured them both two fingers into a tumbler, lit the gas logs, then gestured for her to sit on the sofa. She did and he joined her, then handed her the drink. Jane's hand trembled.

He took a swallow of his scotch, then pinned her with his dark chocolate eyes. "What happened with Halls?" he asked in a tone tinged with barely suppressed anger.

"He lied to me, to you," she said. "He's not who he says he is. And I don't think we were friends."

Fletch heaved a wary breath. "Go on."

"Like I said before, I saw an image of the man with the tattoo, my husband, being shot, his body bouncing backward." She licked her dry lips. "Then the gun. It was in my hand, but I don't remember shooting it."

She hadn't mentioned that detail before.

"Halls was there," Jane said. "In the room when Victor was shot."

Fletch's fingers curled around the arm of the sofa. "You're sure?"

Jane nodded. "Yes, I'm certain of it."

"Did he admit this?" Fletch asked.

Jane ran her finger around the rim of her glass. "No, that's just it. He completely denied it, claimed he'd been in the house visiting before, but that he wasn't there when Victor died. He insisted I was confused." Her nerves pinged just thinking about being in the car with him. "I know I've been confused, but I'm not confused about this, Fletch. I saw his face. And every instinct in my body screamed that he's dangerous."

"What else happened?"

"He drove me to a remote cabin that he claimed belonged to me and Victor. I...don't think that was true, either. When we passed this cluster of rocks shaped like a cactus, I got chills. None of it feels right, Fletch."

She rubbed her arms with her hands. "When he parked and got out, I had a flash of him shooting Victor. I panicked. Then I shoved him, took his car and drove away as fast as I could. When I reached that town, I called you."

Fletch's silence unnerved her even more. Did he believe her?

"He probably reported his car stolen," she said. "That's why the police were looking for me at the coffee shop."

Fletch tossed back the rest of his drink, then set his tumbler on the coffee table and gripped her arms. "You were right not to trust him," Fletch said. "His story about Bianca and Victor Renard doesn't pan out."

Jane's breath quickened. "What do you mean?"

"My brother Liam, with the FBI, investigated the Renards. Jane, there is no Bianca or Victor Renard."

Jane's head swirled with confusion. "Then I'm—"

"I don't know who you are, but your name is not Bianca," Fletch said.

Jane's pulse clamored. "I didn't think that name felt right."

"If Halls lied about your identity, he may have lied about everything else."

"But I do remember a ring and a man being shot," Jane said. "And Halls was there."

"Then it's possible Halls *is* the one who shot the man. You witnessed it, and he's framing you."

"If that's true, who was the bearded man I shot? And why was he trying to kill me?"

"Still waiting on information on him," Fletch said. "But the dead man with the scarred face was a PI. He may have been hired by Halls."

"What motive would Halls have to kill my husband?"

"That's what we're going to find out. Liam is putting a rush on your prints and DNA. Soon, we should know who you really are."

"I still don't understand, though. Your brother had all that evidence against me."

"Liam discovered Officer Clemmens faked that information. He could be in cahoots with Halls somehow and fabricated it to make you look guilty."

A sick feeling slithered through Jane. "Then Halls came to my rescue and bailed me out so he could silence me."

"Elaborate but feasible." Disgust laced his tone. "I guess he thought Whistler had some country bumpkin cop who wouldn't check things out. His mistake."

Jane threw back the rest of her drink. Questions lingered, the future uncertain. She held all those answers inside her head, obliterated as if they'd been erased like words on a whiteboard.

"Jane?"

She offered him a tentative smile. "Thank you for helping me, Fletch. I...didn't know where else to turn."

His dark gaze raked over her, sending a tingle of awareness through her. Then he angled his head and tilted her chin up with his thumb. "I'm glad you trusted me."

Tears threatened, but she blinked them away. He moved closer, his mouth only inches from hers. Jane wanted him so badly she ached.

"Fletch, we shouldn't...not until we know who I am."

He grunted, a small sound of frustration underscored with need and desire. "I don't care what your name is. I know who you are, and you're not a murderer."

An image of her hand holding that gun haunted her. But then Fletch's lips touched hers, and she blocked out the image as hunger overcame her, and she pressed her lips to his.

Chapter Eighteen

Fletch lost all rational sense when Jane's lips melded with his. When they learned her identity, there might be a dozen reasons she wouldn't, or couldn't, be with him.

Another man. A child.

But he banished those possibilities for the moment.

When he'd watched Halls drive away with her, it had done something to him. Scared him because he didn't know the man or what would happen with Jane.

Scared him because he wanted her with him.

He'd never felt this way about a woman before.

He didn't like this desperate need, but he couldn't deny his feelings for her, either. Was this how Jacob had felt when he'd fallen for Cora? She'd seemed unstable to some folks, but Jacob had recognized she was suffering, and love made them both feel whole again.

Cora kept a magnet on their fridge that boasted the phrase *Live in the Moment*.

That was exactly what he wanted to do now.

Jane murmured a low sound of desire, and he deepened the kiss, tasting her sweetness and passion as he thrust his tongue inside her mouth. She raked her hands through his hair and drew him closer, and he pulled her up against him. Her soft breasts pressed against his chest, heightening his hunger.

He tore his mouth from hers and trailed wicked tongue lashes along her throat and around her ear. She moaned and clawed at the buttons on his shirt until she opened one, then the other. Her hands dove between the folds of the fabric, then she raked her nails over his bare skin.

Enflamed with passion, he nibbled at her neck, then tugged at her sweater. She lifted it over her head and tossed it onto the chair, then reached for him. But he held her arms by her sides so he could look at her.

She was beautiful. The bruises were fading on her creamy skin and her breasts swelled over the lacy bra. He wanted her breasts in his hands.

He wanted everything off so nothing separated them. Bare skin to bare skin.

Heat flared in her eyes, and she lowered her head and flicked her tongue against his nipple. He'd never realized how sensitive they were until she ran her tongue over each one then tugged one between her teeth and sucked it just as he wanted to do her.

"Hell, woman," he moaned.

She trailed her fingers lower to the waistband of his jeans and unsnapped them. He moaned and captured her hand in his. If he didn't slow down, he was going to explode before he was inside her.

He stood, his voice commanding, raw hunger pulsing through him. "Come on." Afraid his leg would give way if he tried to carry her, he tugged her hand and coaxed her to his room.

He paused in the doorway and lifted her chin to study her, to make sure this wasn't one-sided.

"I want you, Jane."

"I want you, too, Fletch." Desire flickered in her eyes, the same kind of desperate hunger mounting inside him. His body was wound tight with sexual tension. His sex throbbed.

He kissed her again, deep and hard, then walked her back toward the bed. She pulled off his shirt and reached for his jeans.

He shucked them, and in seconds had her naked in his bed, just as he wanted.

EVERY NERVE CELL in Jane's body was on sensory overload. Hunger and need built inside her as Fletch trailed his fingers over her breasts and belly.

His lips came next, painting a sensual trail over her bare body. Her nipples stiffened to peaks, and he teased them with his tongue then drew one into his mouth, firing liquid heat all the way to her womb.

She raked her nails over his back, feeling his corded muscles tighten as he crawled above her. He sucked one turgid peak, then the other, a throbbing ache consuming her.

She wanted him. Naked. Hard. Inside her.

He'd already done away with her panties, and she parted her legs, begging for his body to join with hers. Instead, he trailed his tongue down her belly to her heat. Then he nudged her legs further apart and pressed his lips to her slick, wet center.

She moaned and gripped his shoulders as he dipped his tongue inside her and teased her unmercifully. A flick of his tongue to her sweet spot, then another and another, and she lifted her hips and urged him to come inside her.

But he had his own agenda, and he tormented her with his mouth and fingers until pleasure shivered through her.

Finally Fletch climbed above her, reached into his nightstand, removed a condom and ripped open the package. Seconds later, she helped him roll it on.

He kissed her again and stroked her hot spot with his thick length. She parted her legs, aching for him to make love to her. He entered her in one quick thrust, filling her completely, then pulling out and thrusting into her body again.

Time after time, he teased her opening with his shaft, then plunged his erection inside her until they built a frenetic rhythm. Slick, hot skin against slick, hot skin.

Teasing. Filling. Big. Hard. Her body quivered with sensations that mounted and made her ache for more.

She clawed at his firm backside, driving him deeper, then wrapped her legs around his waist. He suckled at her neck, and another orgasm teetered on the surface.

Fast. Hard. Deep. Over and over again until she spun into a world of pleasure. His big body went tense, still for a moment, then a guttural groan sounded as if it was ripped from his gut.

A minute later, his body shook as his own pleasure overcame him.

Jane clenched his hips as he pushed deeper into her and colors exploded behind her eyes.

Fletch's ragged breathing mingled with hers in the aftermath of their lovemaking, their bodies slick with perspiration and heat.

She stroked his back, savoring his strong body on top of her.

"Ahh, Jane," he said on a rough whisper. "I don't know who you are or what you do to me, but I can't stop myself from wanting you."

A smile formed on her lips, and she kissed him hungrily. She didn't know what had come over either of them, but she wanted their lovemaking to go on forever.

Although reality threatened to intercede and brought guilt. Had she felt this strongly about the man who'd put that wedding ring on her finger?

Should she be planning his funeral and honoring him instead of crawling into bed with another man?

FLETCH SENSED JANE's tension but cradled her in his arms and soothed her by whispering nonsensical words. His body still zinged with passion in the aftermath of their lovemaking.

He didn't want to release her. Not yet. Maybe never.

"Are you going to tell your brothers I'm here?" Jane whispered.

Fletch angled his head to study her. "Do you want me to?"

Jane traced her finger over his bare chest. "I suppose it's not fair to ask you to hide me."

Fletch chuckled. "None of this is fair." He touched her bruised wrists. "It wasn't fair that someone tied you up and tried to kill you."

Jane nodded against him. "Tonight, can we just stay here alone?"

Fletch wanted time as much as she did. "Yeah. Jacob and Liam are working on your case. Liam put a rush on your prints and DNA at the lab so hopefully tomorrow you'll know some answers."

Relief and anxiety reverberated in Jane's slow exhale. "Then we figure out everything else," she said softly.

"That's right." He only hoped the truth didn't send her back to jail.

She nestled against him, and he wrapped his arms around her, and she fell asleep in his arms, safe for the night.

The idea of seeing Jane locked away for the rest of her life made his stomach coil. He'd definitely crossed the line and let his emotions get the better of him with Jane.

But he had to believe that things would work out.

Nothing that felt this good could be wrong, could it?

Finally exhaustion sucked him into a restless slumber. He startled awake a few hours later with early morning sunlight streaming through the window. Jane looked so peaceful and sexy in his bed that he dropped a kiss on her forehead and memorized her features, afraid today might take her away from him.

Another possible theory occurred to him as he slipped from bed and brewed a pot of coffee. What if there wasn't any information on Victor and Bianca Renard because they were in WITSEC? That might explain the reason Jane had an assumed name. It might also explain the images she'd mentioned of those dead people.

She might have witnessed a crime, entered witness protection, then killed this man Victor because he turned on her. The same with the two guys in the woods.

But how did the lawyer play into it? Had he killed her husband, or had he represented her to the Federal Marshals and helped arrange her new identity?

JANE WOKE TO the heavenly scent of coffee brewing. At first, she was disoriented, but she rolled over and saw sunlight streaming through the window. The bed beside her was empty.

Fletch.

She was in his house, in his bed. They'd made love last night. And it had been wonderful.

But what would happen today?

She rose and slipped on one of his shirts lying on the chair, buttoned it up, then tiptoed to the bathroom and washed her face. She ran her fingers through her tangled hair, loosening the knots as she examined her image in the mirror.

The bruises were fading, but she still had some discoloration on her forehead. Her eyes looked brighter and more rested, although her forehead wrinkled into a frown. For all she knew about herself, she might as well be looking at a stranger's face in the mirror.

"Who are you, Jane?" she whispered. "And who was this woman Bianca?"

The sound of Fletch's footsteps brought her from the bathroom, and she walked through the bedroom and yanked on socks, then stepped into the living room. The strong scent of coffee wafted toward her, luring her into the kitchen.

Fletch stood on his back deck, facing the beautiful mountains, a mug in his hand. An extra one sat on the counter, so she filled it and carried her cup out to the deck.

Her breath caught at the sight of the snowy ridges, then the rippling river water below. The sight of Fletch's handsome chiseled body sent a hot flame of desire through her.

"Morning." Fletch tilted his head to look at her, his sexy eyes meeting hers as if searching for regrets.

She had none, at least not about sleeping with him. "Morning." She warmed her hands by cradling the hot coffee. "Thanks. I may not remember my name, but I think I'm a coffee addict."

A sly grin tugged at his mouth. "Me, too."

For a moment they stood still, sipping their coffee and simply enjoying the scenery.

"This place is breathtaking," she murmured.

"Thanks. I had it built," Fletch said. "Once Mom and Dad died, the four of us decided to build our own places. Too many memories at the old homestead."

"And I have hardly any," she said.

"Sorry, that was insensitive."

"No, you were being honest. And I have to recover my

past in order to clear my name and have a future," she said earnestly.

"You will." Fletch leaned against the deck rail, almost pensive. "I was thinking about possible theories this morning, trying to fit the random clues together. The fake name Bianca, your memory of seeing dead bodies, the men trying to kill you. We talked before about you possibly witnessing a crime. What if that is the case, and you entered WITSEC until you could testify?"

Jane massaged her temple. WITSEC would explain her name change, and could mean she wasn't a killer.

"I texted Liam and asked him to consult with the Federal Marshals."

A knock sounded on Fletch's front door. Jane jerked her gaze to Fletch. "Did you tell anyone I was here?"

He shook his head. "No. Go into the bedroom and stay while I see who it is."

Nerves pinged inside Jane as she hurried into Fletch's bedroom. She closed the door and locked it, then pressed her ear to the flat surface to listen to the conversation. Through the slit in the doorjamb, she watched two of his brothers storm in.

"What in the hell is going on, Fletch?" Jacob barked.

Fletch ran his hands through his hair. "What do you mean?"

Jacob strode through the room, looking around as if he was searching for something. "That damn lawyer called me. He said Jane assaulted him and stole his car."

Fletch crossed his arms. "If she did, she must have had a good reason." He turned toward Liam. "What about the WITSEC angle?" Fletch said, dodging his brother's question.

A chill went through Jane, and she snatched her clothes and quickly dressed.

"I've got calls into the Federal Marshals and am waiting to hear back," Liam said. "But they don't share information easily, even to the FBI."

"Listen to me, little brother," Jacob continued. "At this point, Jane is considered a fugitive. She jumped bail, assaulted a man and stole his car. If you're hiding her, then you can be charged with aiding and abetting a felon," Jacob bellowed. "Perhaps even as an accomplice to murder."

Oh, God. Jane couldn't let Fletch get in trouble because of her.

She couldn't find the truth if she was locked in a cell, either. And it sounded as if Jacob had already convicted her in his mind.

Panic and reason warred inside her. She had to return to that cabin and see if being there triggered her memories. But going back would be dangerous.

She rushed to Fletch's pack and removed his weapon. She grabbed an extra magazine and put it in her pocket with the gun.

Tiptoeing, she ducked out the sliders leading to the back deck, then jogged down the steps into the woods.

She'd find a ride somehow, then she'd face her demons. The memory of Fletch making love to her taunted her.

She had to protect him. And that meant going alone.

Chapter Nineteen

Fletch inhaled a deep breath. "I thought you suspected Halls was lying."

Jacob and Liam exchanged looks. "Your theory about WITSEC made me start thinking," Liam said. "Halls could have worked with Jane to enter her into the program."

Fletch jammed his hands in his pockets. "I considered that possibility, but if so, why didn't he tell us that?"

Liam cleared his throat. "Part of the reason WITSEC works is the safety and security it provides for the witness. That means extremely limited access to information regarding the person, their new identity and their location. All communication between family, friends or former co-workers is completely cut off."

"I understand that," Fletch said. "But Jacob is law enforcement."

"One leak, even unintentional, can endanger the person in the program," Liam said.

Fletch scratched his head. "We need to talk to Halls. Force him to tell us what's going on. If he arranged for Jane to enter WITSEC, then he has information about the crime she witnessed and who's after her."

"I'll contact him and ask him to meet us," Jacob offered.

Liam leaned against the kitchen island. "Did Jane tell you anything else, Fletch?"

Fletch considered confiding that Jane thought Halls had been at the murder scene, but he wasn't ready to reveal she was hiding in his bedroom.

She trusted him and he wanted to keep it that way.

So he opted for focusing on the couples she'd seen in her nightmares. "She also had dreams where she saw the faces of men and women who'd been murdered. Married couples."

Liam went very still. "Couples?"

Fletch nodded. "A man and woman lying together, dead. She said it was just flashes of images, that it could have been photographs from the news."

Liam drummed his fingers on the bar. "The FBI is investigating a case involving married couples being murdered. What if Jane witnessed one of them?"

Fletch crossed his arms. "That sounds feasible."

Jacob shifted. "But how does her husband play into it?"

"Maybe he was the killer," Fletch said. "She could have found out what he did or saw him kill one of the couples and confronted him. He came after her to silence her, then she killed him in self-defense."

"All possibilities," Liam admitted. "Although just theories at this point." He snapped his fingers. "Let me see what I can find out." He removed his phone from his belt and stepped onto the deck to make a phone call.

Jacob tapped his phone. "I'll call Halls and see if I can convince him to come in."

Fletch nodded as Jacob made the call. He placed it on speaker, but Halls's voice mail picked up, so Jacob left a message saying it was urgent he return his call.

Fletch watched Liam pace the deck as he talked. He paused by the table and stared at the coffee mugs on the table.

Two of them.

Dammit.

A second later, Liam strode in, jaw set, eyes flaring with suspicion. "She's here, isn't she, Fletch? You've been hiding her and lying to us ever since we arrived."

GUILT NAGGED AT JANE as she darted through the woods. She hated leaving Fletch in the lurch, but she cared too much about him to cause him trouble with his family. He'd suffered enough anguish with his parents' deaths.

Her memory loss, the past, the shooting—they were her problems.

She dealt with her problems on her own. She had to. She had no one to rely on.

She halted for a moment, the realization that she was truly alone clear in her mind. She had never been married.

So who was the man who'd put the ring on her finger?

Shaken, but hoping for another breakthrough, she followed the river east toward the outskirts of Whistler to the road leading out of town. Logic warred with panic. She needed transportation.

A car whizzed by and her stomach somersaulted. Not knowing who was after her made her hesitant to climb in a vehicle with a stranger.

Another car rumbled behind her, and she dove behind some bushes to hide until it passed. As soon as it sped by her, she began walking again, ears peeled for other cars approaching as she followed the road.

Two-foot snowdrifts still stood along the side of the road. Melted snow and ice clogged the shoulder, forcing her to tread more slowly than she wanted. Finally she spotted a farm complete with a barn and a couple of horses and cows in the pasture.

The house was set back down a mile-long drive, but an

old truck sat abandoned near the road with a For Sale sign tacked on the windshield.

She scanned the drive and road but didn't see anyone watching so she opened the driver's door and slid in. The seats were worn, the truck battered. She just prayed it would start.

No keys in the ignition. Instinctively, she checked the vehicle but found nothing, so she hotwired the engine. It purred softly, bringing a relieved smile to her face. On the heels of relief came the question—how had she known how to hotwire a car?

She didn't have time to dwell on that question, though. The owner could appear any minute.

She shifted into Drive, pressed the accelerator and veered onto the road. An old farm hat lay on the seat, so she picked it up and jammed it on her head as a disguise.

Knowing Fletch and his brothers might be looking for her, and the truck owner might report his truck stolen, she maintained a steady speed limit so as not to draw attention.

The country road was practically deserted, with only an occasional car and a couple of eighteen-wheelers passing by. A few more miles, and a truck carrying crates of live chickens zoomed past, heading in the opposite direction.

She wasn't sure she remembered how to find the cabin where Halls took her, but as she drove, she searched for landmarks she'd noticed on the drive. A horse farm. Sign advertising strawberry picking, although that was out of season. Signs for apple orchards a little farther north.

A siren suddenly blared, and she glanced in her rearview mirror, dread curling in her belly. She searched for a side road to turn onto, but there was nothing.

The wailing grew louder. She maintained her speed, praying the police weren't after her.

Blue lights twirled in the sky, the siren taunting her as the police car grew closer and closer.

"WHAT THE HELL?" Liam snapped. "We're helping you and you're lying to us."

"Look, I was going to tell you," Fletch said. "But I wanted to know if you had information first."

Jacob glared at him. "Where is she?"

Fletch hurried to block the way as Jacob barreled toward the bedroom.

"Don't tell me you slept with her," Liam said darkly.

Fletch held up a hand to prevent them from storming in. "Let me explain. She came here last night. She was scared, said when Halls drove her to the house she and her husband supposedly lived in, she knew something was wrong. That he was lying. She was afraid of him, and didn't want to go inside with him, so she took his car and drove to a coffee shop to meet me."

His brothers frowned in disapproval.

"Why was she afraid of him? Did he say something? Try to hurt her?" Liam asked.

Fletch gritted his teeth. "She remembered seeing him at the house when her husband was shot. She thought he killed her husband and framed her."

Jacob heaved a breath. "Or maybe he showed up to consult with her after the shooting and tried to help her enter WITSEC like we discussed."

"Tell her to come out here," Liam ordered. "We have to talk."

Fletch wanted to protect Jane. But the only way to do that was to uncover the truth. So he knocked on the bedroom door, then eased it open.

The sight of the sliders open with the wind blowing through indicated she was already gone.

Jacob burst in behind him, and Liam followed, searching the room and master bath.

Fletch hurried onto the deck and scanned the woods. But he didn't see Jane.

"Where the hell did she go?" Jacob asked from behind him.

Fletch shook his head. "She must have panicked when she heard you guys."

"Or she's been lying and using you," Jacob suggested.

No…he couldn't have been a fool. Not again.

Liam shook his head. "Running doesn't look good for her case, Fletch."

His brother didn't have to tell him that. He'd trusted Jane. And he thought she'd trusted him.

He stepped back inside and he checked his pack.

Dammit to hell, she'd stolen his gun.

As the police car raced up behind Jane, déjà vu struck her. Another time when she'd been chased. Another siren.

No…that didn't seem right…

The car suddenly veered around her. She pressed the brake, preparing to pull over. She was armed, but she didn't intend to shoot a cop.

Instead, though, the officer sped up and shot past her at lightning speed, disappearing around the curve ahead.

Relief whooshed through her chest. She'd lucked out twice now. Her luck wouldn't last forever.

She couldn't keep running, either. But before she saw Fletch again or turned herself in, she wanted to be able to tell him the truth. Everything.

After he'd protected her and saved her life, he deserved it.

Anxious to get this over with, she sped up slightly, maneuvering the curvy road. She passed the cactus rock formation with a shiver.

Why had Halls had that photograph of her and her husband in his briefcase where he kept his files on divorce cases?

The old truck bounced over ruts in the road as she veered down the dirt road to the cabin. The shadows in the trees looked ominous as she drove beneath the canopy of oaks with moss dripping down like dead snakes hanging from the branches. The truck's tires churned through the soggy, snowy ground, sucking at the wet mud and rocks.

Hopefully Halls was long gone, and she'd have time to explore the inside of the cabin alone. A tree branch snapped off under the weight of the melting snow and struck her windshield, and she startled and swerved off the road.

The truck's front rammed into the ditch, and the tires churned at the soggy ground. She flew forward, hands clenching the steering wheel in a white-knuckled grip to brace herself. The steering wheel snapped tight, nearly choking her as the truck lurched to a dead stop.

She pounded the steering wheel, then shifted the truck into Reverse to back up. But mud and gravel spewed as the truck ground itself deeper into the muddy mess.

Realizing she was only making matters worse, Jane cut the engine and leaned her head against the steering wheel to calm herself. She wasn't that far from the cabin.

She'd walk the rest of the way. God knows, she'd hiked her share the past few days. What was another mile or two?

Resigned, she snagged Fletch's gun, tucked it into her jacket pocket, then slid from the pickup. Her boots sucked at the slush, but she climbed back onto the dirt road and began to walk. Sunshine tried to steal its way through the spiny branches of the trees and failed, adding a chill to the air.

Limbs cracked and twigs snapped from the tree branches as she wove around the narrow, winding road. Somewhere in the distance, an animal howled, and a dog barked. Squirrels scampered up the trees and dug in the snow for food. A deer darted past in the woods, startling her, and she automatically put her hand in her pocket to access the gun.

A mile through the forest, and she was almost there. She saw the house on the hill. She froze as she neared, scanning the property for a car in case Halls was there.

The driveway was empty. So was the area to the side of the house.

Breathing easier, she rounded the last curve into the clearing where the house sat. She studied it, hoping for something in her mind to click. The cabin seemed familiar.

Except the house she remembered being at with the man with the tattoo was in a neighborhood. She'd seen other couples, the grill firing up, wine floating…

She had not lived here. That realization was so strong that she forged ahead. If she hadn't shared this house with her husband, why had Halls brought her here and told her she had?

Because something bad had happened here.

Bracing herself for whatever might happen, she took a deep breath and walked up the hill toward the cabin. The house had a chimney. In her mind, she saw a fire burning inside the fireplace.

It seemed cozy. No, not cozy. All wrong.

Heart racing, she passed a wooden wagon that must have been used to house a flower bed, because weeds had overtaken it.

She'd done this before. Walked up to this cabin, knowing something was wrong.

A face appeared in the shadows of her mind. A man's. The man with the tattoo.

Then a voice behind them. "I've been expecting you."

Jane froze as something hard jabbed her lower back.

The voice in her mind. It was the same one speaking now. "I knew you'd come back here. I've just been waiting until you showed."

Images of being shoved in the house at gunpoint blended with reality as the man pushed her up the steps to the porch door.

Chapter Twenty

"She ran, didn't she?" Jacob asked.

Fletch wanted to defend Jane, but the answer to his brother's question was obvious. "She went searching for the truth. I told you she saved my life."

"By shooting a man," Jacob interjected.

Fletch shrugged. "In self-defense."

"She can't get very far on foot," Jacob said. "Which means she may be looking for a car to steal." He snatched his phone. "I'll see if there have been any reports in the last hour." Jacob stepped into the den, then outside on the back deck.

Liam scowled at Fletch. "You mentioned those couples in Jane's nightmare. I want to check something. Your laptop in the den?"

Fletch nodded and motioned for Liam to follow him. He'd left his computer on the small desk in the corner. He retrieved it and carried it to the breakfast bar. While Liam connected to the FBI's database, Fletch brewed another pot of coffee and handed his brother a mug.

Jacob joined them a minute later with a grim look. "Nothing so far. But Deputy Rowan said he'd let me know if anything comes in."

Fletch watched as several pictures appeared on the computer screen. Three different couples, dead, blood pooling around their lifeless bodies.

"This first couple, Deidre and Arnie Richter lived outside Asheville," Liam said. "At first, police thought it was a murder suicide. Wife's throat was slit. Husband died of a gunshot wound to the chest. From interviewing neighbors, we learned the couple was having marital problems. Wife cheated on husband. We suspected he killed her and then turned the weapon on himself."

"Is that what happened?" Fletch asked.

"I'll get to that. But one point that stuck out was that the letter *C* was carved in the palm of the woman's hand. Police speculated *C* for cheater." Liam sighed. "There's more." He scrolled to another set of crime photos. A red-headed woman sprawled on the bed with blood sprayed across the white comforter. A dark-haired man slumped in the chair beside the bed, his body limp, blood soaking his shirt from a gunshot wound to the chest.

"This is Renee and William Purdue," Liam said. "Similar story. Marriage in trouble. Woman was seeing the husband's best friend on the side." Liam zeroed in on a close-up shot of the woman's hand. "The letter *C* on her hand exactly like the first female victim." Liam looked up at them. "This is when we realized there might be a pattern, that the murder/suicide theory on couple number one might be off base."

"Or the second murders could have been a copycat of the first," Jacob suggested.

"We considered that." Liam scrolled to a third couple. "But meet Bailey and Jim Hearst."

"The same MO," Jacob said.

Liam clicked his mouth. "Exactly. Which suggests that—"

"There's a serial killer murdering couples," Fletch finished.

"That's our theory now," Liam said. "So far the press hasn't gotten hold of this, but we've dubbed him the CK, couples killer."

"Do you think Jane witnessed one of these murders?" Fletch asked. "Or that she knows who the CK is?"

"Considering what you told me about the images of dead couples she remembered, that's a possibility. Or—" he hesitated "—perhaps she and her husband were having marital problems and the CK tried to kill them, but Jane escaped."

Fletch couldn't imagine Jane as the type of woman to cheat on her husband. "If that's true, why didn't he slit her throat the way he did the other women, when he carried her into the woods?"

"Good point." Liam's phone buzzed. "The lab." He connected the call and stepped to the deck again.

Jacob was studying him with a pensive expression. "You really like this woman, don't you?"

Fletch shifted. "I just don't want to see her get hurt."

"Be careful, bro. She may not be the person you think she is."

"So you've told me." Fletch tightened his jaw. How could he argue when there were so many unknowns?

Liam's boots pounded on the floor as he strode back inside. "Talked to the Federal Marshals."

Jacob folded his arms. "And?"

"Jane's not in WITSEC. In fact, it looks like we were wrong about everything about her."

Fletch's stomach knotted. So who was Jane?

JANE TENSED, grinding her teeth as Halls shoved her up the steps. Her right hand slid to her pocket to retrieve Fletch's gun, but Halls's sardonic laugh sliced through the air.

"Not going to happen." Instead he jerked her arm out of the way, reached inside and withdrew the weapon.

She silently cursed herself for walking into an ambush. He pushed her forward so hard she had to grab the door-jamb to keep from hitting the floor on her knees.

"I thought your amnesia was a blessing and decided I might just let you live, but then you hooked up with that damn cop's brother, and I knew it was only a matter of time before you figured out the truth."

Only she hadn't.

She scanned the property as she stumbled toward the front door. The area was surrounded by thick, tall trees. Shadows clung to the walls of the dark interior as she entered. She stumbled, the room swaying as the scent of blood and death assaulted her.

Foul odors wafted from the hallway to the right. She rounded the corner and saw the fireplace.

But her vision blurred and she saw blood spatter dotting the stone.

Then blood spatter on the floor and walls, on her hands and clothes.

She slowly pivoted to stare at him. "You killed him."

"Yes, Jade, I had to. The two of you were getting too close to the truth."

Jade, not Jane? Reality hacked at the frayed edges of her mind. Jade…that was her name.

Jade Jenkins.

Her husband's face looked back at her, ghostlike and eerie.

She saw him sliding the wedding ring on her finger, their heads bent in hushed whispers as they made plans.

They were in an office with a whiteboard on the wall. A whiteboard full of pictures of dead people. Three differ-

ent married couples, the women's throats brutally slashed, pale skin bloody, eyes wide open in the shock of death.

Then the men, their husbands. In close proximity to the women's bodies, as if they'd been staged. A female hand reaching for help from her loved one. Or vice versa.

But their hands couldn't touch. The letter C was carved on the women's palms. Symbolic.

A gaping hole in the men's chests, blood-soaked shirts shredded by the impact of the bullet.

Three murders with the same MO. A serial killer was targeting couples. They'd dubbed him the CK, couples killer.

He had to be stopped before he took more lives.

She and Louie hadn't been married. She was a detective and Louie was her partner. They'd gone undercover as husband and wife to sniff out the killer.

The cookout in the neighborhood, the wine and her interior design business—all part of the undercover story. She'd chosen that career because her mother was a designer and she knew enough about the business and lingo to fake it.

The neighborhood had been in the targeted area. She and Louie infiltrated the close-knit group because they suspected the CK was friends with at least one of the couples.

That they'd met him when seeking a divorce attorney.

She and Louie were onto him. And when he'd invited them to his house to discuss their proposed divorce, they'd come. Prepared. At least they thought they were.

But Halls had made them for cops. They'd barely walked through the door when he slammed the butt of his gun against her temple. She'd swayed and stars danced behind her eyes as she grappled for control.

Low, muffled voices echoed through the fog...Louie's. Halls's.

Halls had slashed the women's throats while the husbands watched as a form of punishment.

Jade struggled to reach her weapon, but Louie opened fire on Halls. Halls ducked aside and fired, shooting Louie in the heart. Blood gushed from his chest, and his body bounced backward. His gun hit the floor. She scrambled on her hands and knees to reach it. She picked it up to shoot Halls, but he grabbed her hair and jerked her head backward. Then the knife...the sharp blade coming toward her.

She threw her arm up to deflect the blade, but Halls bellowed, jammed the knife in his pocket and used the gun instead. This time the blow was so hard and swift and violent that the world tilted and went dark.

Sometime later, she came to and found herself in a dark cave. She was tied and gagged. It was pitch-dark, and snow was falling. Then she heard footsteps. She struggled to untie herself. Had to hurry. Finally the knot slipped free. She lurched up to run, had to get away from him.

He hadn't slit her throat and left her with Louie because he didn't want their deaths to be labeled CK kills. But he was going to kill her. Out here in the middle of nowhere, where the animals could ravage her body and destroy any evidence he might have left.

SHE BLINKED BACK into focus. Woodruff Halls, attorney at law.

"You are the CK," she said. "My partner and I figured it out."

Halls was a chameleon. His handsome, polished smile could be charming at times. But he morphed into a demented monster in a flash. His skin looked sallow and his eyes bulged, creating deep, dark ugly pockets.

"Yes," he said in a menacing tone, "and this time you're going to die, and no one will ever find you."

FLETCH SHIFTED ONTO the balls of his feet. "Don't drag it out, Liam. Who is she?"

"Detective Jade Jenkins," Liam said.

"Jane is a police officer?" Fletch's mind raced. Her ability to fight, shoot…it made sense.

"That's right," Liam replied. "She and her partner Detective Louie Germaine were working the couples killer case. I spoke to her commander myself. According to him, Detective Jenkins and Detective Germaine went undercover as a married couple named Bianca and Victor Renard to trap the CK."

"That's the reason they didn't show up in WITSEC," Jacob said.

"And the reason for the fake identities and story about the real estate agency," Fletch added.

Liam nodded. "Acting as a real estate agency with interior design services allowed them access to people's homes where they could meet the neighbors and couples in the community."

Liam's news echoed in Fletch's ears. Jane and her partner went undercover. She was never married. *Never* married…

"Her partner was killed?" Fletch asked.

"Yes, shot in the chest like the other male victims of the CK. My guess is Jade and Germaine determined the killer's identity, and he realized they were onto him, so he had to shut them up."

"So he shoots the male partner and takes Jade into the woods to kill her," Jacob filled in. "Leaving her with her partner and using the same MO would have pointed to the CK."

"Instead, he planned to frame Jane, I mean Jade, for her partner's death," Fletch said.

Jacob crossed his arms. "Then he used Officer Clemmens to plant evidence and lead us astray."

"Dammit, and I let her leave with Halls that day," Jacob muttered.

"Don't beat yourself up," Liam said. "Halls looked legit. But one of our techs dug deeper into the lawyer. He and his wife divorced about six weeks ago."

Jacob's brows shot up. "About the same time as the CK started?"

"Exactly," Liam said. "We're obtaining search warrants for his home and office."

"You think Halls is the CK?" Fletch asked, piecing everything together.

"Everything's pointing that way." Liam jangled his keys. "I'm going to his home to search." He gave Jacob a pointed look. "It'll be faster if we divide up. You take his office."

"Will do."

"Damn, Halls might already have Jade, and he's hell bent on silencing her." Fletch stepped forward to follow Liam.

"Then stay here in case she calls you or comes back," Jacob said.

Fletch scrubbed his hand over his face, panic threatening. "I can't lose her," he muttered before he even realized what he'd said.

"Then let us do our jobs," Liam said quietly. "We'll find her, Fletch."

He hoped to hell Liam was right. "At least leave the files open about the case. I'll search through them and see if anything sticks out. Maybe another property Halls owns, some place he might take Jade."

He ushered his brothers out the door. They had to hurry.

Chapter Twenty-One

Fletch pulled up everything he could find on Detective
Jade Jenkins from the databases Liam had accessed on
his computer.

Jade was thirty-two years old, had studied criminology and behavioral science before attending the police
academy. She worked as a beat cop in Asheville for four
years before becoming a detective, first in the robbery
unit, then homicide.

The photograph of her receiving a commendation for
saving a child from a cold-blooded killer, aka the child's
father, stirred his admiration.

He had been right about her. Jade wasn't a killer. She
risked her life to save others on a daily basis.

He searched deeper and found information about her
family. Born to Mildred and Herman Jenkins, she was an
only child whose father was a judge. Her mother was an
interior decorator. Probably the reason she'd used a design
career as her cover story.

A reporter named Lynn Wellman had covered the couple's murder and included family photographs of the couple together with Jade as a child. One picture showed her
sitting on her father's lap, doing the Sunday crossword
puzzle just as she'd described.

He skimmed for details of their murder. According to

the investigating officer, Detective Roger Stint, the couple had been killed in what first appeared to be a home invasion. The fact that the wife's expensive jewelry and silver hadn't been stolen, though, indicated robbery wasn't the motive. The judge's safe had been opened, yet cash left inside.

The judge's secretary stated that Judge Jenkins often carried photocopies of important documents and files home to review, and that he kept those in a home safe. The fact that he'd sentenced numerous convicted felons to prison opened up a wide suspect pool.

Persons of interest in the case included a gang member who'd been sentenced to life. However, police couldn't prove gang involvement. Another suspect was the father of a convicted rapist who insisted the girl got what she deserved.

Scumbag.

But the father had a rock-solid alibi for the time of the double homicide.

Later, the crime team matched a partial fingerprint lifted from the back door to a man named Otis Rigley, who was then being tried for his wife's murder. Rigley had a list of arrests a mile long. He'd killed the Jenkins couple so the judge's death would cause a mistrial. While awaiting a new trial, Rigley was out on bond. Then he'd suddenly disappeared.

Finally, the following June, he was stopped on a routine traffic violation. The officer ran his name and realized he'd skipped bail. So Rigley was arrested and this time convicted.

After serving twenty years of his life sentence, he had been paroled just a month ago.

Fletch tensed. Rigley was the man Jade had shot. The man who'd shot him.

Fletch drummed his fingers on the counter. As a lawyer, Halls had connections to police officers, parole officers, PIs, and inmates and ex-cons.

What if Halls had arranged for early parole for Rigley, then hired him to kill Jane?

Jane's—Jade's—face flashed in Fletch's mind. Jade as the little girl whose parents had been brutally killed in her own home. Jade hearing the gunshots and her mother's screams.

Jade discovering their bodies and calling 911 the next morning.

She'd been sent to live with her grandmother, but lost her at age nineteen.

Then she'd been truly alone.

A hollow ache dug at his gut.

Now she was alone out there again. Looking for the truth. Justice. Battling a ruthless killer who wanted her dead.

Her job as a cop explained her toughness. And her instincts that Halls couldn't be trusted.

But she was still vulnerable, and a serial killer was after her. A serial killer who looked normal. One who no one would suspect if they saw him with Jade.

FEAR TWISTED JADE'S gut inside out, but she fought its vile clutches. She would not give in to fear. And she would not die at this madman's hands.

He had killed Louie. Her partner. Her friend.

Along with six other people so far.

Seven if the vile smell emanating from the house was what she suspected.

"So," she said, determined to get him to spill his guts before he did hers. "You discovered your wife was cheating on you and that made you angry." She offered him a sardonic smile. "What happened? Did your long hours get to her? Didn't you give her enough attention? Or was she just a whore who became bored and liked to sleep around?"

Rage flared in his eyes and he drew back his hand and slapped her across the cheek. The sting smarted, but she clenched her teeth to keep from crying out.

The last time they'd fought, he'd won. Today the outcome was going to be different. It had to be.

"I did not neglect that woman," Halls said bitterly. "I gave her everything. A beautiful home, fancy clothes, expensive jewelry and elaborate vacations. But she didn't appreciate my hard work."

"No, she didn't," Jade said, playing along. She had to stall. "She took you for granted, enjoyed the nice things you gave her. Then she was selfish and wanted more, didn't she?"

"Exactly," he snarled as he waved his gun in front of her face. "Just like those other bitches. Their stupid, pathetic husbands were like me. They sacrificed their time and worked hard to provide, but their wives were spoiled and demanded more and more."

"After a while, nothing you did was enough," Jade guessed. "The country club dinners and wine and parties weren't exciting anymore. So your wife went looking for fun on the side."

Halls began to pace, his features lined with agitation, his movements jerky. "She did. After all I sacrificed to make her happy, she was an ungrateful bitch." He paused and stared at her, anger oozing from his pores. "I even gave up criminal work and accepted divorce cases to have more time for her. And then she lied to me, just like all women lie." He waved the gun toward her. "That's one thing my job taught me. You can't trust anyone in a skirt."

Jade resisted the urge to snap at him for his sexist remark. "I'm not a liar," she said. "If I was married, I would never cheat on my husband."

"Hell, you're the worst kind," Halls shouted. "You lied about being married! I watched you play the part in front of all those other couples." He gripped her arm, fingers digging into her skin painfully. "You're so good at it, you fooled them all. Because that's what you do. You lie to get what you want. You entrap people with your lies. You lie to suspects and even to the victims when you tell them everything will be okay." He shook her. "But nothing is okay when you're lied to."

Jade forced her voice to remain calm as she mentally struggled to formulate a plan. She was a detective, she knew how to do that.

And she and Louie had narrowed the suspects down to focus on Halls.

What else did she know about him?

He dragged her toward the back of the house down the hallway. The stench of death grew stronger, nauseating, permeating the air.

"You don't have to do this," she said. "You've punished your wife. She paid for her sins."

"And you're going to pay for yours."

FLETCH HAD BEEN pacing for over an hour, but still no word from his brothers or Jade.

Dammit, he was about to lose his mind.

He snatched his keys to start hunting but realized that would be foolish. He had no idea where she'd gone.

Or where to find Halls.

His phone buzzed, and he lurched toward the bar to answer it. Jacob.

Please, dear God. Let it be good news. Please let his

brother be calling to say they'd found Halls and arrested him. And that Jade was alive.

His pulse hammered as he connected the call. "Jacob?"

"Yeah. You're on speaker with me and Liam."

Fletch released a ragged breath. "What did you find?"

"Sorry, we haven't found her yet," Liam said. "But we may be getting closer."

Fletch stepped onto the back deck and stared into the thick pockets of woods. He'd met Jade in a blizzard and they'd both nearly died. But they had survived.

She had to survive this time.

"Go on," he said through clenched teeth.

Jacob spoke first. "A report just came in. Stolen pickup truck a few miles from your cabin. Gray, rusted out, nineteen eighty model." He recited the license plate.

"Did the owner see who stole it?" Fletch asked.

"No, it was parked by his barn near the road. A BOLO has been issued. Truck was spotted due north about a half hour ago."

Fletch racked his brain. He knew the area. Countryside. Farms. Roads weaving past small towns as they snaked up the mountains.

"Could be teenagers," Jacob said.

Fletch ran a hand through his hair. He had a feeling. "It's her."

"Where the hell is she going?" Liam asked.

Fear clawed at Fletch as the truth dawned. "Back to that cabin where Halls took her. She wants answers and is going after them herself."

Alone. With no backup.

Dammit, he had to find her. "I've looked for other properties Halls owns but had no luck. Did you find something?"

"A crime team is going over his house from top to bottom. So far, nothing about another property or anything pointing to him as the CK."

Jacob cut in, "Halls's secretary has been helpful. Said Halls used to be calm, orderly, good with clients, meticulous with the details of his cases. But when he discovered his wife was cheating on him, he started acting differently." Jacob paused. "He became enraged for his clients, sympathized with husbands claiming infidelity on their wives' parts."

"Fits with the CK's MO, the *C* carved on the women's palms," Liam said.

"Right." Jacob heaved a breath. "I did find a link to the PI. Odd thing is that he didn't work for Halls. He was working for the daughter of one of Halls's victims. He was on Halls's scent. So Halls either killed him or had him killed."

Fletch filled them in on what he'd learned about the Jenkins's double murder. "Rigley was sent to finish Jade. He probably killed the PI as well, because he was getting too close to the truth."

"That fits. I'm alerting all law enforcement agencies to look for Halls," Liam said. "As of today, he's on our Most Wanted list."

Jacob cleared his throat. "Now we just have to figure out where he's going."

Fletch worked Search and Rescue. He knew the mountains. The trail.

"Let me know if you find an address for a second property."

"Copy that. I'll look into the wife and her family. Property might be under her name." Jacob disconnected, and Fletch walked over to the corkboard above his desk and studied the map on the wall.

He inserted a pushpin at his location, then another at

the address where the truck was stolen, and analyzed the roads in the area.

Halls might take Jade to a second home if he had one. Or…in desperation, he might kill her and dump her on the side of the road or off the mountain. Somewhere no one would ever find her.

God… He pinched the bridge of his nose. He couldn't let that happen.

Chapter Twenty-Two

Fletch's keys jangled in his hand as he scribbled a note to Jade telling her he was looking for her, that if she showed up, to hide in his house and call him.

But he couldn't just sit around and do nothing. He wanted to be nearer where that truck was last spotted, in case Jacob or Liam learned a location for a second property or Jade was seen by the police.

He spread his map on the console. He knew these mountains better than anyone and had a good idea where that truck was heading. At least the general direction. There were hundreds of cabins tucked away to the northeast of Whistler, where skiing and whitewater rafting were popular.

That cactus-shaped formation of rocks seemed familiar.

He relied on his built-in GPS to showcase the roads as he drove. Impatience nagged at him as he encountered traffic, and he maneuvered around a minivan and a pickup carrying farm supplies. Two teens on motor scooters sped down the shoulder of the road, weaving in and out of traffic, on a joyride.

Once upon a time, he and his brothers had been daredevils, too. Truthfully, he still was, to a degree.

But losing both parents so quickly had taught him how

precious life could be. That a loved one could be swiped from you in a second.

Jane's face flashed behind his eyes. Jade—not Jane.

Jade…a loved one?

Hell, he knew he cared about her. And the idea of losing her terrified him.

JADE SWALLOWED BACK bile at the strong odor of blood and death permeating the walls of the cabin.

Her ears were ringing where Halls had slammed her head against the hard wall.

"She's here, isn't she?" Jade rasped.

A maniacal laugh punctuated the air. "Who?"

"Your wife," Jade said, memories beginning to slip through her foggy mind as her vision cleared. "She cheated on you, so you killed her."

"She deserved it, the ungrateful bitch. I took her to Tahiti!"

He was escalating. Jade had to keep him talking, buy some more time. "That sounds romantic," she said. "You planned a special trip for her."

Another sarcastic bark of a laugh. "She used me to pay for spa treatments and massages, and then, while we were on a midnight cruise, I found texts on her phone from another man. Not just texts," he said shrilly. "Naughty texts. She suggested kinky stuff she never wanted to do with me."

Ah, his ego was bruised. "That was a terrible way to learn she was unfaithful," Jade said.

His eyes flared with rage. "When I asked her about it, she didn't even bother to deny it. She had the gall to tell me about him, how I didn't satisfy her anymore, that she needed a young stud."

"I'm sorry that happened to you." Jade scanned the

room for something to use as a weapon. He'd set her gun on the end table in front of the fireplace, out of reach.

"I'm sure you suggested couples counseling, didn't you?" Jade asked. "Told her you wanted to save your marriage."

The whites of his eyes bulged as he glowered at her. "Hell, no, I didn't offer to see a damn shrink. She was the one with the problem, not me!"

"So you decided to get revenge," Jade said quietly.

"I decided she had to pay and she had to suffer," he bellowed. "And she did. I held her down and sliced her neck and laughed as the blood spewed and ran down her pale white throat."

He was mentally ill. Jade remembered now. At one of the dinner parties with the neighbors, she'd seen this strange look in his eyes when he'd watched the women. It had been her first inkling that she and Louie were on the right track. After that, they'd started digging deeper into Woodruff Halls.

Louie… Her heart gave a pang of regret and sadness. They'd been partners for two years, had been friends. He'd taught her how to read people, study body language and identify the little nuances that were some people's tells.

Woodruff had one. When he lied, his right eye twitched slightly. Subtle, but once she'd noticed it and tested him, it had been evident.

That and his temper and underlying bitterness toward women.

He'd passed out his business cards to the neighborhood men like candy to children. More than once she'd overheard him regaling a sordid tale about a cheating spouse.

"I understand why you killed your wife," Jade said calmly. "She hurt you and deserved to be punished."

"She did." His voice cracked.

"But I don't understand why you killed the other couples. They did nothing to you."

He tunneled his fingers through his hair, spiking it until it stood on end. Sweat trickled down the side of his face. "Do you know what it was like listening to my clients blather on and on about their cheating spouses? It was like mine was carving the knife deep in my gut and twisting it."

"That's the reason you carved the letter *C* in your victims' hands."

"You got that right."

"Maybe those women lied to their husbands, but you don't know what went on behind closed doors."

"You think betraying their vows is justified!" He lunged at her, and she pressed a hand to his chest.

"That's not what I mean. But those women weren't totally bad," Jade said. "Deidre Richter had a three-year-old child. She loved her little boy. I saw pictures of them at the park. She volunteered at his preschool. Now that sweet little boy will grow up without a mother." She paused. "And a father. Because you stole his parents from him." She summoned her strength, had to find a way to get that gun from him or reach her own. "That's where I'm confused, Woodruff. I can call you by your first name, can't I?"

Rule number one in negotiation—get personal with the perp. Make them see you as human, and humanize them.

She needed to defuse the situation. Give herself time to retrieve her weapon.

"I...guess so," he stammered, although he looked confused by the request.

"Good, your name is so distinguished." She slowly pushed herself up from the floor. He shot her a warning look and stepped forward, the gun wavering in his trembling hand.

"I just needed to stand up for a minute," she said. "For us to talk face-to-face."

A sneer twisted his mouth. "I watched you with your so-called husband, and I knew you were just like all the others. I could tell you didn't really love him, that it was an act."

Because they hadn't been married. They'd been working undercover.

"Why did you kill the husbands?" she asked. "Can you explain that to me?"

He began to pace again, gun hand flinging out in a wide arc. "Because those idiots came to me whining. Whining and wanting revenge against their wives for being so sorry. But then they started wimping out and begging the stupid whoring women to take them back." His boots clicked on the wood floor, the old boards squeaking. "That bitch Renee slept with her husband's best friend, and William actually wanted to forgive them. Can you believe that?"

"Maybe he didn't want anger to destroy his life."

"He wasn't a real man. None of them were!"

"So you shot them in the heart because their wives broke their hearts, then you killed them because they—"

"Because they should have punished their wives like I did mine!" He turned and aimed the gun at her chest, his lips twisting again. "Just like I'm going to take care of you."

FLETCH FELT LIKE a crazy man as he headed farther up the mountain. The images of what could be happening to Jade taunted him.

Halls had proven he was not only violent, but that he was sadistic. Carving the letter *C* into the women's palms was meant to inflict pain and to mark them like the letter *S* had in *The Scarlet Letter*. Slitting their throats had signified personal rage. And the fact that he'd killed multiple victims meant the murders were not only premeditated, but that he enjoyed the thrill of the kill.

Fletch's phone buzzed as he rounded a curve. Liam. He quickly connected.

"Fletch, any word from Jade?"

"No. Do you have information?"

"One of our analysts dug deep into Woodruff Halls. Apparently his wife divorced him. We tried to reach her, but no one has seen or heard from her in weeks."

Knots of tension coiled inside Fletch's stomach. "Do you think he killed her?"

"That would be my guess. According to a friend of hers, she had an affair. When Halls found out, he went ballistic. She moved to get away from him, but he may have found her."

"She was his trigger, his first kill," Fletch said. "Then he got a taste of blood and decided other cheating wives should suffer."

"That theory fits," Liam said. "As a divorce attorney, he was privy to his clients' personal information. The question is—what did he do with his wife's body?"

An icy chill raced through Fletch's veins. "He could have buried her or hidden her in the mountains."

"Hang on, a text is coming through." A pause, then Liam returned on the line. "Okay, we may have something. Halls's wife's family owned a cabin in a remote section of the mountain. It's possible he killed his wife there."

Fletch's pulse thundered. "That's where he took Jade."

"I'm a half hour away," Liam said.

"Text me the coordinates," Fletch said. "I'm closer."

Liam cursed. "Fletch, this guy is dangerous. He's already killed several people."

"Exactly the reason we can't waste time," Fletch said. "Send me the damn coordinates."

A heartbeat of silence. "All right. But Jacob should be there around the time you arrive. If she's at the cabin or if Halls is, hang back until Jacob arrives."

Fletch mumbled that he would, although he had no intention of waiting.

If Jade was with this maniac, he'd do whatever necessary to save her.

JADE LIFTED HER chin in a show of courage. She was a trained detective. She wouldn't go down without a fight. "Killing me won't serve any purpose," she said. "The police know who you are. They'll find you and you'll go to prison anyway."

"Then I have nothing to lose by adding another body to the count."

"Killing a cop will definitely earn you life without parole. Besides, I don't fit the profile of your other victims. The reason you started killing in the first place."

"Ah, but you've given me another reason," he said with a sinister smile.

His hand trembled. He was rattled, off his game. He'd obviously caught the other couples off guard. Planned the murders and how best to execute them. Details of the crime reports registered in her head. There had been evidence of alcohol in the victims' systems.

She was a loose end he needed to take care of. "Because I'm exposing you as the monster you are." It was now or never. She lunged toward him and he swung the gun toward her and fired.

She dodged the bullet, moved her arm upward and knocked the gun from his hand. It skittered across the floor, and she threw him to the ground. He raised his fist and punched her in the jaw.

Pain knifed through her cheek, and her head spun. Determined not to let him win this fight, she shoved her fist into his belly. He grunted, caught her hair and yanked her head backward. She ground her teeth and tried to jab him in the eyes with her fingers but missed. They traded blows, and she connected with his nose. Blood spurted, and he pressed his hands to his face with a howl.

She took advantage of the moment and scrambled toward his gun.

He bellowed like a crazed animal, then grabbed her leg and yanked her so hard she collapsed onto her stomach. Before she could recover, he kicked her in the lower back sending sharp mind-numbing pain through her extremities. Then he climbed on her back and she suddenly felt the sharp point of a knife at her throat.

"Move, and it's over," he growled.

Jade went still, breath puffing out, anger searing her veins. He climbed off her, snagged the gun and dragged her to her feet. The barrel of the weapon dug into her back.

"Come on, since you've been so chatty, I'm going to satisfy your curiosity before I kill you."

She channeled her anger into a lethal calm. But he pressed the gun to her head and pushed her down the steps. She grasped the stair rail to keep from tumbling into the darkness, and he clenched her arm and hauled her over the steps and across a concrete floor.

The odor grew stronger, sickening decay at its worst.

Then he shoved her up against an old freezer, opened it and forced her to look inside.

"See, that's where you're going now."

She clawed at the edge of the freezer edge to escape. This man was much more disturbed than she'd imagined.

He'd enjoyed killing his wife so much he hadn't disposed of her body. Instead he'd kept it as a trophy and watched it rot.

"I used to think she was beautiful," he said in a sick voice, as if he was far away, lost in a memory. "But cheating made her ugly. And now look at her."

A sinister laugh echoed off the walls in the cold dank basement, then he lifted the lid of the second freezer.

Terror swept through Jade.

She threw her elbow back and slammed it into his chest, then swung around to fight. But he was too fast.

He whacked the butt of the gun against her temple, and the world spun out of control. She struggled and clawed at him, at the freezer edge to keep from falling inside.

But he hit her again with such force that she tumbled into the darkness.

Chapter Twenty-Three

Jade roused from unconsciousness to a cloying odor. The air felt stale and she couldn't breathe. She tried to move, but her hand made contact with a wall.

The freezer! Oh, God, he'd locked her in the freezer and left her to suffocate to death.

No air. And it was hot. She wouldn't freeze to death, but unless she found a way out, she would die.

No…she couldn't die. She'd just finally remembered who she was, how her partner had died. The reason she'd jumped at the assignment to go undercover and capture the CK. Her parents had been victims. Not related cases, but seeing a wife and husband lying dead together had triggered the trauma of her past. Because of that, she'd volunteered for the undercover assignment to catch the CK.

And the man in the woods who'd come after her…the one she'd shot…she suddenly remembered why he seemed familiar. He'd been serving time in prison for her parents' murder. Woodruff Halls had taken advantage of that fact. Hired him to come after her. Probably told the man that she remembered him.

Knew that seeing him would add to her trauma.

No wonder she'd repressed her memories.

She inhaled shallow breaths to conserve air as she clawed at the top of the freezer. She pushed and shoved, then raked her fingers along the inside, searching for a release latch.

Finally she found one, but when she twisted at the latch, nothing happened. She struggled with it again, and the heavy lid slipped slightly, but refused to budge. A clanging sound echoed from above.

Dear God, the maniac had locked the freezer shut with a chain lock.

Tears pooled in her eyes as terror gripped her. How had she let him get the drop on her?

She blinked back tears, her chest aching with regret. If she didn't find a way out of here, she would die.

Fletch and his brothers might eventually figure out the truth about Halls and find her body.

But Fletch would never know how she felt about him.

For years, she'd been driven by the need to obtain justice for others who'd suffered the loss of a family member as she had. She'd been so focused on the job she'd avoided getting close to anyone.

It hurt too much to lose someone. It was better not to care. Not to dream about love or marriage or children.

But now in what might be the final moments of her life, that was all she could think about.

A life with love. Maybe a wedding and babies. A family that she hadn't had in a really long time.

A family with Fletch that she might never have.

FLETCH RACED AROUND a curve, brakes squealing as he sped up the graveled road to the address Liam had sent.

Sludge left from the snowstorm spewed from his tires, mud and ice spraying. He accelerated and bounced over the ruts, then spotted the small cabin set off the road with the mountains rising behind it.

He searched for Halls's Cadillac, but he didn't see it.

He didn't see the truck Jane had stolen, either. Although Halls could have hidden a vehicle or the truck in the woods nearby.

Adrenaline pumped through him. Jacob was close, but he couldn't sit and wait. If Halls was holding Jade here, there was no telling what he might be doing to her.

Jade was strong, experienced, could fight and shoot. But Halls could have ambushed her and she might be at his mercy right now.

It took only seconds to kill someone. The bastard had slit the other women's throats.

Fear choked him as a dark image filled his mind. No... he couldn't let Jade die like that. He hadn't even told her he loved her.

And he did love her, dammit.

He swung his vehicle to the side of the road a few hundred feet from the clearing, wishing he had his gun. No time to waste, though. Jade's life depended on his quick action.

He slid from his Jeep, eased the door closed, then slowly wove behind the trees flanking the drive toward the cabin.

He scanned the front yard and surrounding property for signs of Halls or Jade. The place seemed eerily quiet, though. Dark inside. No movement. No noise. No signs anyone was here.

Heart hammering, he crossed the distance, ducking and keeping low until he reached the house. He peeked inside the side window at the living room. Empty.

He kept low and moved around the back of the cabin, then peered through another door. Laundry room. Dark. No one inside.

He continued to scope out the property as he inched around to the rear of the cabin. A small deck backed up to what appeared to be a sunroom. All glass along the back. No one visible.

He walked around the far corner and came to another window. This time when he looked inside, he saw a shadow. His breath stalled in his chest as he eased a fraction of an inch closer for a better view of the room in its entirety.

He didn't see Jade. But Halls sat at a desk flipping through a photo album. The hair on the back of his neck bristled at the sinister leer on the man's face. Fletch gritted his teeth and stood on tiptoe to see what he was looking at.

He choked back revulsion when he saw the macabre snapshots. Photos of Halls's victims.

The wind picked up suddenly, rattling the windowpane, and Halls jerked his gaze toward the window. Fletch ducked. But dammit, Halls had seen him.

Hoping the man wasn't armed, Fletch circled to the back deck, then started to climb the stairs. Before he reached the door, it swung open and a gunshot blasted the air.

Fletch dodged the bullet and jumped behind the railing for cover just as Halls barreled down the steps and opened fire. Then Halls darted to the right and ran around the side of the cabin. Fletch chased him, but Halls shot at him again, and he had to seek cover behind a tree.

The man raced down the hill, and Fletch spotted a compact sedan parked beneath a cluster of trees, hidden by the gnarled branches.

Halls jumped inside the vehicle and started the engine. Fletch dashed toward the car, but Halls fired at him again through the open window. Then Halls accelerated and spun around in the driveway, slinging gravel.

Mud and snowy slush spewed from the back of the car as Halls tore down the drive.

Fletch knotted his hands into fists as he started toward his Jeep. He could go after him. But he wasn't armed.

And if Jade was inside, she needed him. Every second counted.

He punched Jacob's number, his chest heaving for breath as he ran back to the cabin.

"I'm almost there," Jacob said.

"Halls was here. Fired at me and just escaped in a compact dark green sedan." He recited the man's license plate.

"On it."

"I'm going inside to search for Jade."

"Copy that."

Jacob's siren wailed. He *was* near. Maybe he could catch the bastard.

Fear drove him into the house, and he combed the living room. "Jade? Are you here?"

No sound except for his boots pounding the rustic wooden floor. "Jade, where are you?"

He continued to shout her name as he strode through each room, searching closets and cabinets and beneath the beds. No Jade. Dammit, where was she? Was she even here?

He finished searching the kitchen, then the pantry, then walked through the house again, flipping on lights this time. A terrible stench hit him. Blood? Death?

He followed the source and found a doorway in the hall. He'd missed it in his haste to search the rooms.

He turned the knob, but it was locked. Palms sweating, he jiggled it over and over, but the door refused to budge. He shined his pin light on the lock and realized it was the old-fashioned kind that required a key.

Halls probably had the damn thing with him. He checked the kitchen drawers and cabinets and the desk in the bedroom. The photo album of Halls's victims mocked him. Dear God, he didn't want to see Jade's picture among those faces.

He searched the top of the desk, the shelf above it, then the drawer. No key.

Cursing, he raced outside to his car and retrieved the lock-picking tool set he kept in the trunk. He hurried back into the house with it and darted straight to the door. Dropping to his knees, he jammed the small tool into the keyhole opening and wiggled it until the lock clicked free.

Nerves crawled along his spine as he jerked the door open. Darkness bathed the basement. That horrible, acrid odor assaulted him. Worse down there.

Please, God, no… "Jade!" Nothing.

He raced down the wooden steps. The stench grew stronger, vile in its intensity. Someone had died here.

Jade?

Nausea threatened, but he swallowed it down and scanned the dank interior. A couple of garbage bags in the corner. Two compact freezers.

He darted over to the garbage bags first. Holding his breath, he untied the bags and looked inside. Relief came momentarily. Just trash.

But the freezers… The odor was coming from there.

"Jade!" He shouted her name over and over as he crossed the room to the first one. Both were locked with padlock chains.

Dread curled through every cell in his body. No time to waste. He scanned the basement until he located a storage closet. He ran to it, ripped open the door and found bolt cutters inside.

Shaking with fear, he hurried back and opened the first freezer. The raunchy smell of decay assaulted him the moment he lifted the lid. Then horror. A dead woman inside.

Her body in serious stages of decomposition. Eyes blank, inside deep hollow sockets where skin and bone had rotted.

He shoved the door shut, leaned back and exhaled, forcing himself to focus. He couldn't vomit now. Had to find Jade.

Cold terror gripped him as he cut the chain on the other freezer. "Jade!"

Praying she was still alive, he lifted the lid.

God help him… Jade lay curled inside, unconscious.

Chapter Twenty-Four

Fletch called Jade's name again, but she didn't move. Fear pulsed through him, and he leaned over the freezer and lifted her from the inside. She was limp, her face bruised.

But thank God, Halls hadn't slit her throat.

Still, what had he done to her?

He carried her up the steps into the den and laid her on the couch, then checked for a pulse. Barely discernible.

But she was alive.

"Jade, I'm here. Help is on the way." He quickly checked her body for visible injuries. Cut marks from a knife—no. Bruises—yes. Another blow to the head—yes.

He punched 911 on his phone, gave the operator the address and described Jade's condition. "Hurry," he finished. "Please hurry!"

Footsteps sounded outside, and he jumped up and checked the window. Relief hit him.

Liam.

He yanked open the front door. "I found Jade," Fletch stammered. "And called an ambulance."

Liam grimaced. "The smell?"

"A body downstairs."

"Probably Halls's wife," Liam said. "No one has seen her in weeks. I'll get the ME and a CSI team out here ASAP. Jacob issued a full-scale hunt for Halls."

Fletch wanted to hear that the man was caught. Or dead. Not that he was still on the loose. Still a threat to Jade.

"We'll catch him," Liam assured him.

Fletch darted back to Jade while Liam made the call for the evidence recovery team and ME. She still lay unconscious, breath shallow, complexion pasty white. He dropped onto the sofa beside her and cradled her hand in his. "Jade, an ambulance is on the way." She didn't respond, intensifying his anxiety. He gestured toward the hallway as Liam ended the call.

"There's evidence in the bedroom, too," Fletch said. "Halls kept a photo album with pictures of his victims."

"His souvenirs. Sick bastard," Liam muttered.

"Yeah, and he has to pay." Fletch gently brushed a strand of hair from Jade's face. "Hang on," Fletch whispered. "Just hang on, darlin'."

JADE STIRRED FROM unconsciousness and gasped. A male voice, gruff and concerned, floated to her through the darkness.

The last thing she remembered was being knocked over the head and shoved into a freezer. She gasped again. She was suffocating. Lost in the darkness. She was going to die.

"Jade, it's okay, you're in the hospital now."

The voice, gruff, worried, tender… Fletch.

She opened her eyes and couldn't believe she was looking at him. "Fletch?"

A smile flickered onto his face. "Yeah, I'm here."

Confusion muddled her mind, then a shiver rippled through her as she relived the horror of seeing Halls's dead wife in that freezer.

"He killed his wife," she said in a low whisper.

Fletch stroked her hair from her forehead. "I know, I

found her body just before I found you." He lowered his head and laid it against her chest for a moment, then lifted it again. "God, Jade, I was afraid I'd find you the same way."

It was her turn to smile. She threaded her fingers in his hair, so grateful to see him that her chest ached. "No, not me. You know I'm tough."

He chuckled. "Still, you had me worried. You shouldn't have gone off alone."

She licked her dry lips. "I didn't want to cause problems between you and your brothers. I know how much they mean to you."

His breath rattled out, then he kissed her hand. "You mean a lot to me, too, Jade."

Her eyes flickered with surprise. "You know my name?"

He nodded. She longed to tell him that she loved him. But that wouldn't be fair, not when he didn't know the real Jade. "I remember now. I know what happened."

He kissed her hand again. "I know who you are, about your undercover work."

Her heart fluttered. "You do?"

He nodded, eyes searching hers. "Tell me what you remember."

"Everything," she said. "When Halls took me into that house, it all came rushing back. He was the couples killer. My partner, Louie, and I were undercover in that neighborhood to catch him."

"And Halls made you two as detectives," Fletch said.

She nodded. "Louie… He took a bullet to save me."

Fletch gripped her hand. "Were you two…involved?"

Tears threatened. "No, just good friends and partners. He taught me a lot about detective work."

Fletch nodded. "What do you remember about your personal life? Do you have someone special waiting for you?"

"You mean, do I have a boyfriend?" she said softly.

Fletch shrugged, but before she could answer, his brothers Liam and Jacob rapped on the door and stuck their heads in.

Jade clenched the sheets. "Did you catch Halls?"

FLETCH WANTED THE answer to his question to Jade. But first, he needed to know if Halls was in custody.

"Our agents caught up with him at the airport," Liam said. "He was about to fly to South America."

"So he's in custody?" Fletch asked.

"Yes," Liam said. "Thanks to you, Jade, and you, Fletch, for the evidence you collected, that bastard is going away for a long time."

Jacob offered Jade a sheepish smile. "I'm sorry I had to arrest you."

Jade's mouth quirked. "You were just doing your job. I don't understand where that evidence against me came from, though."

"Officer Clemmens, the one who contacted me, was on suspension for accepting bribes, but apparently he'd hacked back into the station's system so he intercepted the missing persons inquiry. Halls paid him to fabricate the evidence to frame you. When he was arrested, he spilled everything."

"And the man on the trail, the bearded man I shot," Jade said. "I remember him. His name was Otis Rigley. He was the man who killed my parents."

"Right," Jacob said. "Halls helped him make parole and offered him money to finish you off."

"The man with the scar on his face," Fletch interjected, "was a private investigator."

"I think I met him before. Was he working for Halls?" Jade asked.

"No, it turns out the daughter of one of Halls's victims hired him. He was onto Halls. Rigley killed him to get him off Halls's scent."

Jade ran a hand through her hair. "So it's really over, then?"

Liam and Jacob nodded, and Fletch squeezed her hand. "It's really over."

"One more thing," Jacob said. "Your commanding officer called. You're getting a commendation."

Jade shook her head. "I don't want a commendation. I'm just glad Halls can't hurt anyone else."

"He said to tell you to take some time off," Jacob added. "To come back when you're ready."

Fletch gritted his teeth. Jade was safe now. But her job was in Asheville. Would she return there now the case was solved?

JADE WAS SO relieved Halls was in jail she felt like sobbing. He had killed her partner and all those couples. And that private investigator. And his own wife...

"Are you okay?" Fletch asked gruffly.

She blinked back tears. "Just grateful Halls will pay for what he did."

"Me, too." Fletch looked down at his hands, then back at her, his expression more closed than it was before his brothers had come in.

"Fletch," Liam said. "There's more. That notebook and map you gave me. We got a hit on fingerprints."

"Yeah, whose were they?" Fletch asked.

"Guy named Barry Inman," Liam replied. "He was suing Whistler Hospital claiming negligence. According to the lawyer handling the claim for the hospital, Inman became unhinged after his wife's death. Lawsuit was thrown out the day before the hospital fire."

"Apparently Inman threatened revenge," Jacob said. "We have a BOLO out for him now to bring him in for questioning."

Hope flared in Fletch's eyes. They finally had a possible lead on his father's killer.

"Will keep you posted," Liam said. Then he and Jacob left the room.

Jade tugged the sheet over her. "That's good news."

Fletch shrugged. "It's a start."

A heartbeat of silence fell between them. Fletch's earlier question about her relationships taunted her.

He cleared his throat. "Congratulations on the commendation. I guess you're anxious to return to your job."

Jade twisted the sheet between her fingers. She'd thought they were on the verge of some kind of revelation about their feelings. But he seemed to be shutting down.

Was he ready for her to leave town so he could go on with his life?

"I think I'll accept my boss's offer to take some time off. It's been a long few weeks."

"That's understandable. You've been through a lot." He stood. "I guess I should let you rest."

Jade watched him walk to the door with her heart in her throat. Was it really over between them?

Keep running, Jade. One foot in front of the other. You have to escape him.

That's what she'd told herself over and over when Halls and his hired gunman had been after her.

But she wasn't running from them any longer.

She'd had the courage to face her attacker. She had to have the courage to run toward what she wanted now.

And she didn't want her relationship with Fletch to end.

He opened the door and started to walk out, and she called his name. When he turned and looked at her, longing burned in his eyes.

"You asked me a question before your brothers came in," she said softly.

He released the doorknob and closed the door. "I did. But you didn't answer."

"Do you still want to know?"

A tiny smile flickered in his eyes. "Yeah, I do."

Her heart fluttered. "I have feelings for a man," she said quietly.

His eyes twinkled, although uncertainty flickered there, as well. "You do?"

"Yes, but I'm not sure he feels the same way."

He walked back over to the bed and looked down at her. "Tell me about him."

She tugged his hand in hers. "He's brave and courageous. He rescues people in trouble," she said. "He rescued me."

Fletch sank into the chair beside her bed again, then leaned toward her, his lips inches from hers. "Actually, it's the other way around. You rescued him."

Hope overrode her insecurities. Maybe she wasn't making a fool out of herself. "From what?"

"From living a life without love."

Another heartbeat of silence stretched between them. "You have my love if you want it," she said in a raw whisper.

Fletch brushed his lips over hers. "I want it, Jade. I want you." He kissed her tenderly, then placed his hand over his chest. "I love you with all my heart."

Hers burst with happiness. In the midst of a terrible blizzard, she and Fletch had found each other. They'd survived the elements and a murderer together.

No more uncertainty or holes in the past.

Now they could build a future based on the truth and on their love.

And maybe…she'd use her skills to help him track down his father's killer.

* * * * *

COMING SOON!

We really hope you enjoyed reading this book. If you're looking for more romance, be sure to head to the shops when new books are available on

Thursday 2nd April

To see which titles are coming soon, please visit

millsandboon.co.uk/nextmonth

MILLS & BOON

LET'S TALK
Romance

For exclusive extracts, competitions
and special offers, find us online:

f facebook.com/millsandboon

🐦 @MillsandBoon

📷 @MillsandBoonUK

Get in touch on 01413 063232

For all the latest titles coming soon, visit
millsandboon.co.uk/nextmonth

MILLS & BOON
A ROMANCE FOR EVERY READER

- **FREE** delivery direct to your door

- **EXCLUSIVE** offers every month

- **SAVE** up to 25% on pre-paid subscriptions

SUBSCRIBE AND SAVE

millsandboon.co.uk/Subscribe

WANT EVEN MORE
ROMANCE?
SUBSCRIBE AND SAVE TODAY!

'Mills & Boon books, the perfect way to escape for an hour or so.'

MISS W. DYER

'Excellent service, promptly delivered and very good subscription choices.'

MISS A. PEARSON

'You get fantastic special offers and the chance to get books before they hit the shops.'

MRS V. HALL

Visit millsandboon.co.uk/Subscribe
and save on brand new books.

MILLS & BOON

THE HEART OF ROMANCE

A ROMANCE FOR EVERY KIND OF READER

MODERN

Prepare to be swept off your feet by sophisticated, sexy and seductive heroes, in some of the world's most glamourous and romantic locations, where power and passion collide.
8 stories per month.

HISTORICAL

Escape with historical heroes from time gone by. Whether you passion is for wicked Regency Rakes, muscled Vikings or rugg Highlanders, awaken the romance of the past.
6 stories per month.

MEDICAL

Set your pulse racing with dedicated, delectable doctors in the high-pressure world of medicine, where emotions run high ar passion, comfort and love are the best medicine.
6 stories per month.

True Love

Celebrate true love with tender stories of heartfelt romance, f the rush of falling in love to the joy a new baby can bring, and focus on the emotional heart of a relationship.
8 stories per month.

Desire

Indulge in secrets and scandal, intense drama and plenty of si hot action with powerful and passionate heroes who have it all wealth, status, good looks…everything but the right woman.
6 stories per month.

HEROES

Experience all the excitement of a gripping thriller, with an in romance at its heart. Resourceful, true-to-life women and stro fearless men face danger and desire - a killer combination!
8 stories per month.

DARE

Sensual love stories featuring smart, sassy heroines you'd want best friend, and compelling intense heroes who are worthy of
4 stories per month.

To see which titles are coming soon, please visit

millsandboon.co.uk/nextmonth

JOIN US ON SOCIAL MEDIA!

Stay up to date with our latest releases, author news and gossip, special offers and discounts, and all the behind-the-scenes action from Mills & Boon...

 millsandboon

 millsandboonuk

 millsandboon

It might just be true love...

GET YOUR ROMANCE FIX!

MILLS & BOON
— *blog* —

Get the latest romance news, exclusive author interviews, story extracts and much more!

blog.millsandboon.co.uk

MILLS & BOON
HISTORICAL

Awaken the romance of the past

Escape with historical heroes from time gone by. Whether your passion is for wicked Regency Rakes, muscled Viking warriors or rugged Highlanders, indulge your fantasies and awaken the romance of the past.

ix Historical stories published every month, find them all at:

millsandboon.co.uk/Historical

MILLS & BOON
MEDICAL
Pulse-Racing Passion

Set your pulse racing with dedicated, delectable doctors in the high-pressure world of medicine, where emotions run high and passion, comfort and love are the best medicine.

Eight Medical stories published every month, find them all a

millsandboon.co.uk

JOIN THE
MILLS & BOON
BOOKCLUB

* **FREE** delivery direct to your door

* **EXCLUSIVE** offers every month

* **EXCITING** rewards programme

50% OFF
YOUR FIRST
PARCEL

Join today at
Millsandboon.co.uk/Bookclub